PRAISE FOR *THE BALLAD OF TOM DOOLEY*

"Ms. McCrumb may have written the Americana historical thriller of the year."
—*Midwest Book Review*

"Sharyn McCrumb uses historical records and masterful storytelling to put a fresh spin on the infamous North Carolina crime."
—*The Charlotte Observer*

"In a story with parallels to *Wuthering Heights*, McCrumb makes a strong case for a sociopathic servant as the catalyst for the deadly events that ensue. True to the language and culture of its time and place, this latest entry in the Ballad series could be headed for bestsellerdom."
—*Library Journal*

"McCrumb's tale is impeccably researched. . . . McCrumb's novel casts light on the often bleak context surrounding characters who have become legend."
—*Publishers Weekly*

PRAISE FOR *THE DEVIL AMONGST THE LAWYERS*

"The old families who live in proud seclusion up in these hills produce a number of wise souls whose voices are pure poetry."
—*The New York Times Book Review*

"This is storytelling as those Celtic bards meant it to be: lyrical, haunting, and truly unforgettable."
—Cathie Pelletier, author of *Running the Bulls*

"Flat-out brilliant and transcendent, a book that gets everything exactly right. Simply put, novels don't come any better than this."
—Martin Clark, author of *The Legal Limit*

"A superb novel that, once started, is so well written and so expertly researched that readers will find it impossible to put down."

—Ron Rash, author of *Serena*

"Being a McCrumb novel, *The Devil Amongst the Lawyers* brims with compelling characters who are passionate, flawed, and unforgettable."

—*Rapid River Magazine*

PRAISE FOR *THE ROSEWOOD CASKET*

"McCrumb's love for the mystical beauty of modern Appalachia . . . and her fascination with the history of the region add depth and charm to a story that's warm without being sentimental. A best-seller in the making!"

—*Booklist*

"The lyric writing pulls the reader from page to page. There also are the colors of the South that McCrumb stitches so masterfully into this hauntingly beautiful quilt. This book should be on everyone's summer reading list."

—*Richmond Times-Dispatch*

"What a voice this writer has. . . . She is superb at telling tales as sweet as wild honey and as special as the changing colors of the leaves."

—*The Washington Times*

"Grave, poignant, and altogether magical."

—*Kirkus Reviews*

"Sharyn McCrumb deftly manipulates reality and fantasy here by fusing fact with the rich lore of rural mysticism. She crystallizes Appalachian vernacular around a fascinating plot."

—*Southern Living*

"This mystical book is a must-read for anyone who believes that the spirit of the pioneer should not disappear from the land—a wonderful book."

—*The Courier-Journal* (Louisville, Kentucky)

"Suspenseful . . . spellbinding." —*The Washington Post*

"What a rich and hearty Appalachian stew McCrumb has cooked up this time—and how satisfying to body and soul, especially for those of us who love these hallowed hills of which she writes."
—Jerry Bledsoe, author of *Before She Wakes*

PRAISE FOR *THE BALLAD OF FRANKIE SILVER*

"A dense and lovely but very dark design that illustrates the social hypocrisy of the legal system as much as the harshness of mountain justice—then and now." —*The New York Times Book Review*

"Some stories wait more than a hundred years for the right teller to come along. . . . McCrumb shifts easily back and forth in time, combining police procedural with an old-fashioned historical narrative worthy of Dickens or Jane Austen." —*Asheville Citizen-News*

"From snippets of rural life, scraps of memories, and fragments of tragedy, [McCrumb] has stitched together a vivid American heirloom."
—*Newsday*

"A novel of mesmerizing beauty and power."
—*Richmond Times-Dispatch*

"One of our most gifted authors . . . She has never been better in this masterful blend of fact and fiction, in which men and women—some real, some imaginary, all convincing—play out their lives in ways both tragic and inspiring against the ghost-haunted backdrops of the Appalachians." —*The San Diego Union-Tribune*

Also by Sharyn McCrumb

THE BALLAD NOVELS

If Ever I Return, Pretty Peggy-O

The Hangman's Beautiful Daughter

She Walks These Hills

The Ballad of Frankie Silver

The Songcatcher

Ghost Riders

The Devil Amongst the Lawyers

The Ballad of Tom Dooley

King's Mountain

THE NASCAR NOVELS

St. Dale

Once Around the Track

Faster Pastor (with Adam Edwards)

EARLY WORKS

The Elizabeth MacPherson Novels

Sick of Shadows

Lovely in Her Bones

Highland Laddie Gone

Paying the Piper

The Windsor Knot

Missing Susan

MacPherson's Lament

If I'd Killed Him When I Met Him

The PMS Outlaws

The Jay Omega Novels

Bimbos of the Death Sun

Zombies of the Gene Pool

SHORT STORY COLLECTION

Foggy Mountain Breakdown

The ROSEWOOD CASKET

A BALLAD NOVEL

SHARYN McCRUMB

THOMAS DUNNE BOOKS

ST. MARTIN'S GRIFFIN

NEW YORK

This is a work of fiction. All of the characters, organizations, and events portrayed in this novel are either products of the author's imagination or are used fictitiously.

THOMAS DUNNE BOOKS.
An imprint of St. Martin's Press.

www.thomasdunnebooks.com
www.stmartins.com

Grateful acknowledgment is made for permission to reprint from the following:

"Small Farms Disappearing in Tennessee" by Jim Wayne Miller, from *Brier, His Book*, published by Gnomon Press. Used by permission.

All chapter-opening epigraphs, excluding chapters 1, 3, and 13, are from *Daniel Boone: The Life and Legend of an American Pioneer* by John Mack Faragher, published by Henry Holt and Company.

Library of Congress Cataloging-in-Publication Data

McCrumb, Sharyn, 1948–
The rosewood casket : a Ballad Novel / Sharyn McCrumb.
p. cm.
ISBN 978-0-312-38886-7 (trade paperback)
ISBN 978-1-250-02269-1 (e-book)
1. Farm life—Fiction. 2. Women—Appalachian Region, Southern—Fiction. 3. Appalachian Region, Southern—Fiction. 4. Mountain life—Fiction. 5. Domestic fiction. I. Title.
PS3563.C3527R67 2013
813'.54—dc23

2013014561

First published in the United States by Dutton, an imprint of Dutton Signet, a division of Penguin Books USA Inc.

St. Martin's Griffin books may be purchased for educational, business, or promotional use. For information on bulk purchases, please contact Macmillan Corporate and Premium Sales Department at 1-800-221-7945 extension 5442 or write specialmarkets@macmillan.com.

10 9 8 7 6 5 4 3 2

For my fellow Appalachian writers
Garry Barker, David Hunter, and Clyde Kessler—
sons of the pioneers

SMALL FARMS DISAPPEARING IN TENNESSEE

Sometimes a whole farm family comes awake
in a close dark place over a motor's hum
to find their farm's been rolled up like a rug
with them inside it. They will be shaken onto
the streets of Cincinnati, Dayton, or Detroit.

It's a ring, a syndicate dismantling farms
on dark nights, filing their serial numbers
smooth, smuggling them north like stolen cars,
disposing of them part by stolen part.

Parts of farms turn up in unlikely places:
weathered gray boards from a Tennessee burley tobacco
barn are up against the wall of an Ohio
office building, lending a rustic effect.
A Tennessee country church suddenly appeared
disguised as a storefront in downtown Chicago.
Traces of Tennessee farms are found on the slopes
of songs written in Bakersfield, California.
One missing farm was found intact at the head
of a falling creek in a recently published short story.
One farm that disappeared without a clue
has turned up in the colorful folk expressions
of a state university building and grounds custodian.
A whole farm was found in the face of Miss Hattie Johnson,
lodged in a Michigan convalescent home.

Soil samples taken from the fingernails
of Ford plant workers in a subdivision
near Nashville match those of several farms
which recently disappeared in the eastern end of the state.
A seventy-acre farm that came to light
in the dream of a graduate student taking part
in a Chicago-based dream research project
has been put on a micro-card for safekeeping.

Divers searching for a stolen car
on the floor of an Army Corps of Engineers
impoundment, discovered a roadbed, a silo, a watering
trough, and the foundations of a dairy barn.
Efforts to raise the farm proved unsuccessful.
A number of small Tennessee farms were traced
to a land-developer's safe deposit box
in a mid-state bank after a bank official
entered the vault to investigate roosters
crowing and cows bawling inside the box.

The Agriculture Agency of the state
recently procured a helicopter to aid
in the disappearing farm phenomenon.
"People come in here every week," the agency head,
Claude Bullock, reports, "whole farm families on tractors,
claiming their small farm has disappeared."

Running the Small Farms arms of the agency
is not just a job for Bullock, born and brought up
on a small Tennessee farm himself. "We're doing
the best we can," says Bullock, a softspoken man
with a brow that furrows like a well-plowed field
over blue eyes looking at you like farm ponds.
"But nowadays," he adds, "you can load a farm,
especially these small ones, onto a floppy disk.
Some of these will hold half a dozen farms. You just store
them away.
So they're hard to locate with a helicopter."

Bullock's own small farm, a thirty-acre
remnant of the "old home place," disappeared
fourteen months ago, shortly before
he joined the Small Farms arm of the agency.

—Jim Wayne Miller
Kentucky Poet Laureate

The ROSEWOOD CASKET

PROLOGUE

I believe the future is simply the past, entered through another gate.

—PINERO

On the mountain a child was crying.

Nora Bonesteel sat in the rocking chair by her fireplace, piecing together the squares of a Jerusalem quilt, half listening to her visitor's recital of the week's events: a toddler's birthday party, a potluck supper at the rescue squad, an ailing neighbor. Nora liked to hear about the doings in the valley, even though age and inclination kept her close to home.

It had become a ritual now that every Sunday night, after evening church service, Jane Arrowood would drive her home, and the two of them would sit together, sewing and talking, a widow and a lifelong spinster, passing the long hours of Sunday evening together.

Nora's coarse-veined hands were steady in the dim light, feeling their way along the even stitches of the quilt. She barely looked at the scraps of colored cotton as she sewed, and she spoke no more than usual, but every time Jane ran out of things to say, Nora would get her talking again, asking more questions about flowers or recipes to fill the silence. This was so unlike her that several times Jane nearly asked her if anything was the matter, but she told herself that the old woman was lonely, and that she missed the sound of a human voice.

Outside, a night wind rattled the shutters and set oak branches tapping against the tin roof. Puffed clouds scudded across the moon and back, patterning the landscape alternately light and dark.

Jane Arrowood finished telling about the early crocuses in her garden, and held her sewing up to the light of the table lamp to examine her stitches. "Listen to that gale out there," she said, nodding toward the curtained windows. "You'd never know it was spring."

Nora Bonesteel closed her eyes and listened for a moment. "It's early days yet," she said. "We might be in for another snowfall before the weather breaks." Then noting the stricken look on her visitor's face, she added, "But not tonight, Jane. It's just a wind tonight. Nothing to hinder you getting home. I'll get us some tea."

"Oh, don't trouble yourself. I'll have to go soon. It's nearly ten o'clock now, and Spencer always calls to make sure I've gotten home all right." Jane Arrowood stood up and stretched. She could not call her son, the sheriff, to tell him she'd be late. There were no telephone lines strung up Ashe Mountain. Nora Bonesteel was its only resident. Her house was warm and comfortable, and from its picture windows you could see ridge after ridge of cloud-streaked mountains, stretching away in the distance, ranging from green to blue and finally to purple on the horizon, where it was hard to tell mountains from clouds. If you looked out that window when the trees were bare, you could see a black line that had once been the Wilderness Road, that great route westward, where more than two centuries ago, pioneers had taken their wagons through the Carolina mountains to the fertile Tennessee valleys beyond. Tonight, though, the windows were slabs of black shrouded in heavy curtains. Jane Arrowood could see nothing beyond them. But Nora Bonesteel still could.

"Don't worry about the sheriff," she said, ambling toward the kitchen. "He'll be late. He has enough on his mind tonight, I expect."

Her visitor sat back down. She did not question the old woman's statement. Nora Bonesteel knew things. Even when the mountain was dark, even with the radio off and no telephone for miles, Nora

Bonesteel knew. "I will have that tea, after all," said Jane. After a moment she added, "Spencer's all right, isn't he?"

She heard the sound of a kettle being filled, and the clatter of crockery. "Other people's troubles!" Nora called out from the kitchen. "He's doing his job, I expect. Somebody with car trouble, likely as not, and won't they be glad to see that patrol car pull up behind them. Your Spencer is an angel unawares."

Jane Arrowood smiled at this biblical phrase, picturing the sheriff's reaction to it. "A dark angel," he would no doubt reply, thinking of all the sorrow he had to bring into people's lives, with warrants and subpoenas and news about loved ones who weren't coming home. It would please him tonight if he could balance out the troubles with an act of kindness. Jane did not doubt that when she spoke to him later that night, he would tell her a story of a driver stranded somewhere on a country road near Hamelin, and she would listen without letting on that she already knew, because Nora Bonesteel's gift of the Sight made Spencer uneasy, as it did most folks in the valley. It wasn't something Nora talked about if she could help it, but Jane had known Nora all her life, which was more than sixty years, and there was an easiness between them that allowed for an occasional unguarded remark, provided that it was of no consequence. Jane didn't talk to her son about Nora's visions, though. Spencer was determined not to believe in such things, and any evidence to the contrary only annoyed him.

Jane picked up her embroidery again, but a sound outside made her drop the cloth and hold her breath, as she strained to hear above the wind. "Miz Bonesteel, what's that noise outside?" she called out.

"I hear the wind," said Nora Bonesteel.

"No. Listen hard." She waited, motionless, until the sound came again. "Did you hear that? It sounds like crying, doesn't it? Almost like a child."

"There's a painter somewhere over the ridge," said Nora. She stood in the doorway, watching Jane. "Hunters see a glimpse of him now and again. Maybe he's out tonight."

Jane Arrowood shook her head. "I know the scream of a mountain lion. It can freeze your stomach to your backbone, but it doesn't sound like that. What I'm hearing now is a low keening sound, the way a child cries when it's cold or hungry. Don't you hear it?"

"No." The old woman turned and went back into the kitchen.

"It was probably the wind," said Jane as the silence stretched on. "Sometimes, when I'm alone upstairs and the wind whips around the trees and the tin roof, I could swear I hear voices out there. It sounds like a choir singing in Latin, and I can hear it so plain I can even hum the tune. Just the wind, though."

She went back to her needlework, an embroidered pillowcase to be offered at the women's club craft fair in June. The wind had died down, and now she could hear the whistling of the kettle, the click of the stove being shut off, and the plop of boiling water into the rose-patterned teapot that had belonged to Nora's grandmother. Jane listened for the swish of Nora's slippers on the pine floor, but for a moment all was quiet. Then she heard footsteps from another direction—as if someone were running across Nora's front porch, but the tread was light, like that of a small animal—or a child.

"There's somebody out there," said Jane aloud.

Nora Bonesteel stood in the doorway, holding the tea tray. "No," she said.

"But I heard it! Just now when the wind died down. It was as if something little came bounding up on the porch." Jane walked toward the door.

"Don't open it!" Nora called out. She finished quietly, "Jane, no one is there. Let's sit back down now, before the tea gets cold."

For the next hour, while the wind howled and the branches rattled against the tin roof and the crying rose to a long wail, almost indistinguishable from the storm, the two women sewed. Nora Bonesteel hummed the tune of an old hymn, and Jane kept her eyes on her needlework, willing herself not to hear the cries, the footsteps, and finally the knocking. *No one is there*, Nora had told her. Jane did not look toward the dark windows for fear that what was not there would be staring back at her.

SPRING 1824

The old woman had climbed the mountain to take one last look at spring, and to say good-bye to the beautiful world that she would lose when death came to take her. She had risen before dawn, as she had all her life, mindful of the Hunters, who waited with their arrows to take the souls of Cherokees they found sleeping after daybreak. Perhaps they watched her more carefully now that she was old, but she would disappoint them. She always wakened in darkness now, and she would greet the sunrise with a song of thanks to Selu, the Corn Mother, for the gift of another day in this green and holy place.

The mountain was called *Udawoguhda*—the bald mountain. Here the great Shawnee conjurer Groundhog's Mother had fought a magical giant lizard he had encountered in his search for the serpent monster Utkena. Treeless, and buffeted by ceaseless winds, the bald mountain still slept in winter, its yellow grass unchanged by spring. But along its slope, she had seen coltsfoot flowers and the white mist of blossoming sarvice trees. She paused at the yellow flowers of a spice tree and snapped a twig, breathing its deep, heavy perfume and remembering other springs.

Now she was atop the bald mountain, and the world spread out before her. She had passed through spring and back into the heights of winter. She could see the new life flowering in the valleys, but she was beyond it here—perhaps death was like that: being able to see the world of the living, but being lost in bleakness in some other place. Smoky mountains ringed the valleys like the sides of a serpentine bowl. The ridges were cloudy to her eyes now, even on the clearest days, but she could see with her heart. She could hear the cry of birds overhead, and she knew that the hawks and the lesser birds of the north were flying home, following their own Warriors Path—the chain of mountains marked a trail that would lead them back to their far-off nesting places, now that the earth was warm again.

She wished that she could die in winter, when the loss of the earth would not be such a great sorrow to her. Even greater was the pain she felt at the thought of losing the land—the fortress of mountains and the peaceful valleys cradled within them. She had given much for the sake of the land—a husband, the lives of her kinfolk, and at last even the respect of some of her people, who called her traitor because she would not agree that fighting was the only way to keep the land. She would miss the land, more even than her family, more than the little great-grandson who played in the grass at her feet on warm afternoons.

Perhaps even her spirit in the afterlife would be denied the sight of the mountains, because soon the land would no longer belong to her people. She could see that day coming more clearly than she could see the distant mountains before her. From the valleys beyond that first ridge, trails of chimney smoke rose to mingle with the clouds—signs of farmsteads where once there had been only field and forest, and enough elk and buffalo to feed the nations of the Cherokee, the Shawnee, and the Catawba without contention and without want. She had thought that the whites could learn their custom of sharing the land, but it was not their way, although some of them, too, had loved the land. They had wanted to own bits of the earth, a parcel for each man, and with their long rifles they had killed the great herds for their skins alone, leaving the meat to rot in the fields. She supposed that it was only a different kind of love. Her people loved the land as children love a mother, but the whites' love seemed to be the longing men felt for a beautiful and fertile woman.

She was ancient now—past eighty in a time when people were old at forty-five. Now would ordinarily have been the time that her people would honor her for her years and her wisdom by naming her the *Ghighau*—the title in Cherokee meant Beloved Woman, and it was a sign that the gods would speak through her, conveying their will to the people in the voicing of her decisions.

She smiled to think of it. She had been Ghighau now for more than sixty years.

She could hardly remember a time when she did not carry the swan's wing, the symbol of the authority of the Beloved Woman. It had been a different world then. The bestowing of the great honor had been mingled with her grief for the loss of that young husband, whose face she could not quite call to mind in her imaginings. She remembered, though, his shining hair, worn loose and waist-length, and the single braid in front of his left ear, the sign of the warrior.

For a long time she had tried not to think of him because his memory was tangled into scenes of battle. They had been at war with the Muskogeans—the whites called them Creeks—and her husband Kingfisher was a warrior whose hatred of the invaders had so inflamed her that she went with him, accompanying the war party into the territory held by the enemy. They had gone underhill on the Warriors Path to meet their foe at the Battle of Taliwa. Even the names had changed in the years since. The land her people called "underhill" was "Georgia" to the white settlers, and now she herself was called Nancy Ward. But in those distant days, when all creation seemed young to her, the warrior's bride had been called

Nanyehi, and she had been wellborn, with a child's grace and dignity, so people had thought her beautiful.

At Taliwa the fighting had been fierce. She had chewed her husband's bullets so that they would cause great, tearing wounds in the Muskogeans' flesh. When Kingfisher was shot and lay dying beside her, she hardly had time to think about courage. She thought, later, that it must have been both anger at her husband's killers and fear for her own life that made her lunge from behind the big chestnut tree, pick up Kingfisher's gun, and run screaming toward the enemy, shooting and hitting what she aimed at.

They won the battle. Perhaps the sight of a raging woman warrior charging their ranks had caused the enemy to hesitate for just a moment too long. Or perhaps both sides believed that the Spirit Warriors must be fighting alongside this girl to make her shots ring true and to keep her unharmed in the heat of battle.

The Cherokee fighters went home with high praise for the young woman who had fought well, and when the decades-old war with the Muskogeans ended soon after, the tribal council at Chota and the clan spokesman declared that young Nanyehi should become the Ghighau.

The young girl's honor had become a mature woman's burden, for the world itself had become a shapechanger these days, and the advice of the Ghighau could now mean life or death for all of the people. She sat next to the council fire, and by raising the swan's wing, she could pass judgment or overrule decisions made by the entire council. What if the gods who spoke through her were mistaken? Surely these alien white settlers were strange, even to them.

The whites had signed a treaty, promising to leave the hunting lands to the Indians. No settlers would make farms in the mountain hunting lands. They swore it in words on a piece of paper. But Nanyehi had taken one of the whites for her second husband, a trader called Bryant Ward, and Nanyehi became Nancy. People said that Ward had married her because the Cherokee refused to let a white trader stay long in their land unless he married into the tribe. Well, perhaps the Ghighau had married the Irishman in order to understand the ways of the whites. He was not a young man or as handsome as Kingfisher—and most important, he did not respect females as her people did. He had a strange idea that women should be like servants, and he thought that the Creator had wished such a thing. How Selu must have smiled at that! Bryant Ward and the Ghighau had a child, Elizabeth, but the union did not last.

Nancy Ward learned much from this husband, however. She learned that his tribe numbered as many as all the trees on all the mountains, while the Cherokee were few. The whites, with their guns and their horses, and their strange ways, would not go away some day, as the Muskogeans had done. Between the whites and the Cherokee it was not war; it was water falling upon stone. The stone is hard and ancient, yes; but the ceaseless water eventually wears it away. Nancy Ward knew that fighting the tide of settlers would only kill her people needlessly, and still the stream of whites would come. She counseled living in peace with the newcomers.

Learn their ways, she would say, each time the Red Chief argued for war. Learn to spin, to plow. She herself studied the trading practices of the white settlers. She studied farming and acquired horses and a herd of cattle. *If we become as they are, they will accept us, and we can all live in peace*, she reasoned.

The meeting at Sycamore Shoals in March of 1775 told her that she was wrong, but she did not want to believe it. More than a thousand Cherokee, led by the great chief Little Carpenter and his son Dragging Canoe had camped beside the Watauga River at Sycamore Shoals, in the heart of the white settlement area. Daniel Boone was there, speaking for those of his people who wanted to claim the lands to the west. He had explored the far country, and, speaking through mixed-breed interpreters, Boone and his men explained that they wanted to buy the land.

They brought six wagonloads of trade goods and spread them

out on blankets, inviting the Cherokee to take what they wanted in exchange for possession of that far-off place.

The younger warriors were bewitched by the woolen goods and the glass beads, and even more so by the rifles and cases of whiskey offered in the bargain. They fingered the goods, murmuring to one another, "Why not sell the western land to these men? After all, it does not belong to us. Let us sell them the sun as well, if they want it." And they laughed. What fools would give good rifles and blankets to pay for something that cannot be bought, that the Cherokee did not have to give? Why not take the white man's offerings and promise them whatever words they wished to hear in exchange? Where was the harm in words?

The older chiefs had agreed to sign the document, fearing to deny the young warriors the rifles and spirits they were determined to have. Sign or face revolt within the ranks, the chiefs had reasoned. But old Oconostota, the war chief, warned the whites that his people made no claim to the lands beyond the Cumberlands. They were giving away what was not theirs to give, he cautioned the settlers. Even so, Dragging Canoe had argued against the treaty, saying that if the whites were given the land in Kentucky, they would some day want the land in between as well—the land of the Cherokee. He stamped his foot in rage when the whites asked for a "path grant," permission to make a road through Cherokee territory so that they could reach their newly bought lands in Kentucky. "We give you from this place!" he said, pointing west.

Finally the agreement was signed, and the path grant was given, but as the two sides parted, Oconostota shook the hand of Daniel Boone, and told him, "We have given you a good land, my brother, but I believe that you will have much trouble settling it."

Dragging Canoe waited, and his anger grew.

One year later—spring of 1776—the whites were in a war with England. Knowing of the Cherokees' distrust of the settlers, the British approached them. If they and the other tribes of the federation would take the British side in the fighting, they could drive the settlers from their lands. "Your lands will be returned to you," the Englishmen promised.

The leaders gathered at Chota to discuss this plan: the Shawnee, the Delaware, the Mingo, the Iroquois, and the Mohawk. Many of the elders spoke against this plan for war.

"Do not do this," said Nancy Ward. "We are beginning to learn to live together in peace."

But Dragging Canoe scoffed at the old men who could no longer fight, and at the Ghighau, an old woman who had even married a white man once. Only he could guard the ways of his people, he said. "There is nothing left but the bloody path."

Years had passed now, and she still wondered if she had done the right thing. Was she a traitor to her people, as Dragging Canoe had called her, or did she save many lives and prevent worse tragedy?

She had meant well. She had meant to stop the slaughter of both Cherokee and whites, and yet many died. She had meant to forge a peace between the two peoples that would allow them to share the land, so that the Cherokee might stay in the mountains of their ancestors. But that would not happen. Although she would not live to see her people in exile, she knew that the day would not be long in coming. Now it was too late for war: the whites outnumbered the stars, and their armies were invincible. Had they not twice won in war against their British masters? What chance would the Cherokee have against such might? The days when Dragging Canoe could dream of victory were gone. They might yearn to go back to a time when the land was theirs, but not even the bravest young warrior believed that such a thing could be. Their sun was setting. The old woman was glad that she would not live to see the night.

Nancy Ward—Nanyehi—was old. Soon she would go to the Darkened Land, her soul traveling westward to the lands of the dead to begin its afterlife. The Cherokee nation, too, would be traveling westward soon, moving on to new lands to begin a new life as a people, as more settlers poured into the mountains needing acreage for their crops and their livestock. Gold had been discovered in the mountains underhill. The white men prized gold even more than they loved land. It would not be long now.

She must go, and her people must go. Now the new race would have the forests and the mountains beloved of Selu and Kanati. It was their time. But their time, too, would pass. She knew that someday the settlers' descendants would lose the land as well. Then they would know the sorrow of leaving a place that was part of you. She wondered what manner of people would come after them.

CHAPTER ONE

Curiosity is natural to the soul of man.

—first words of *The Adventures of Colonel Daniel Boone,*
John Filson, 1784

Dying cost nothing and could be done alone; otherwise, Randall Stargill might have lived forever. As it was he turned loose of life by inches. In a span of months he narrowed his gyre from the woods and pastures of his hunting days to the yard and garden patch surrounding the small white-frame house. Then the brisk winds of autumn confined him to the back porch and, finally, to the sofa in the square of parlor in front of the old black-and-white television. The wild tabby cats, who lived in the otherwise empty barn, subsisting on field mice and table scraps, grew tired of the meager handouts that came at irregular intervals and went elsewhere. Randall called to them a time or two after that, then forgot them.

His letters to his grown sons, scattered now between nearby Jonesborough, Tennessee, and Cincinnati, Ohio, always brief and infrequent, stopped altogether. His writing sprawled with his dimming eyesight, and he filled page after page of a pad of lined paper with his thoughts, but he sent them to no one.

Randall's journeys into town in his old pickup all but ceased, as his vision failed even in the strongest daylight. Finally he lost interest in his last companions, the undemanding friends on the television screen who stayed with him hour after hour, and whose faces he remembered even when those of his long dead mother and his late wife, Clarsie, faded from his consciousness. As winter set in, he could no longer walk up the hill to the family burying ground, and the graves went untended. His wife's new granite marker stood close to the wrought-iron gate, a few yards down the slope from the rounded tombstones of the older Stargills, and well away from the rows of upright splinters of rock that had never been carved with names or dates. No one now remembered whose graves these rough stones marked. They were already old when the century began, and Randall had never asked his elders whose bones lay beneath them.

The farm had been Stargill land since 1793, not that they cared much for family history. No Stargill had ever stood for Congress or headed an army or attained sufficient prosperity to be a pillar of the community. All they had done was to claim their mountain, farm it faithfully, and keep it in the family through two centuries and a civil war. No matter what party was in power, the Stargills hunkered down and went about their business. They'd been draft dodgers in the War Between the States, because in the Tennessee hills the wrong side was to *take* a side. They got more from their Celtic forebears than blue eyes and short stature: in their blood was the knowledge that who you are is tied to the land, no matter which government wins the election or whose flag flies over it. The land stayed the same, and the Stargills mostly had, too. When they died, they and the land became one.

The one grave that was not there was that of Randall's second son, Dwayne. He had been a wild, wilful boy, seldom in school, scarcer still when there was work to be done on the farm. At seventeen, he left home and hills for a drunken, rootless life that finally ended on a dark highway in Florida, in a wreck that killed four people—Dwayne's fault. Clarsie wanted to bring him home, but Randall said no. They sent money for cremation, and Clarsie went down and spread his ashes on the ocean. It was the only time she had ever left Tennessee. Randall did not go with her.

And Fayre. Fayre was not there, either. Of course, she wasn't a Stargill. If she had rested there, he might have found the strength to climb the hill, despite his failing health. But Fayre was not to be found in the family burying ground. There was a drawing of her in a dimestore frame tucked into one of the drawers of the walnut bureau, torn from an old newspaper, and so brittle now that the creases in the yellowed page had begun to split. The sketch showed a wraith of a child with strange, staring eyes too old for her tiny face. The newspaper artist had never seen his subject, so he had fashioned his drawing from descriptions and family resemblances, using the mother's eyes, drawn from life—the same dark blue as that of her child, but holding a weary sadness that Fayre had been spared. Even before his eyes began to fail, Randall Stargill seldom looked at that drawing. He saw her plainly enough.

In January, the plastic Christmas wreath on Clarsie's marker faded and cracked in the cold, but Randall was not there to see the desolation. His oldest son and his wife had brought the wreath when they drove in from Cincinnati for a visit on Christmas eve. The next morning Robert Lee had taken the wreath up to the burying ground himself, and he'd come back from his mother's grave red with cold, his cheeks crusty with tears. Then Robert and Lilah had sat on either side of him on the sofa, making cheerful chatter, and patting his hand, and trying to make him eat the cookies they'd brought, while he smiled faintly and wished they would go away.

Randall said over and over that he felt fine, and he thanked them patiently for the slippers and the shaving lotion, which now lay forgotten on the lamp table in the sitting room. The other boys called in on Christmas night: Garrett from overseas somewhere, and Charles Martin from a hotel in California, because he was on tour for the entire month of December, opening for the Statler Brothers.

Clayt, the youngest, had come by late that evening, and offered to take him down to the diner or to scramble some eggs in the kitchen that Lilah had just cleaned, but Randall said he was tired, not hungry. After a few more minutes of awkward conversation, Clayton wished him a merry Christmas and left. Randall was glad. He had never had much to say to the boys, except to straighten them out when they broke the rules, but when Clarsie was alive, it hadn't been so obvious. Her passing left a great silence that neither side could be bothered to fill.

Nobody called on New Year's.

As the weeks drifted by, he ate when he remembered—the contents of whatever can came to hand in the pantry, or the scraps of Lilah's stale cookies—and his body grew brittle and wasted.

When the cold blasts of early March and his own infirmity drove him to his bed, he stayed there, curled up in a snowdrift of dingy sheets and sticky pillowcases, drowsing, unmoored from his house and his life, but not yet gone.

He dreamed.

The white pillowcase became apple blossoms, and he was straddling the limb of an old tree in the high meadow. He was small—the ground seemed far beneath him, and the hands clutching the limb were the stubby, unveined hands of a child. The brown feet that dangled beneath it were bare, already toughened from a month of wandering unshod over rocky hillsides. At the base of the tree, a brown and white puppy barked up at him, but he paid it no mind. He was looking for Fayre.

He saw a movement and a flash of gold on the edge of the meadow, and she was there, waving impatiently. He swung down from the tree limb and ran toward her. She was seven years old—two years his senior—but she was reed-thin in her flour-sack pinafore, and her heart-shaped face, ringed in blond curls, seemed translucent in the morning sun.

"What are you doing playing around this old tree for?" she demanded, hands on her hips.

"I almost got to the top, Fayre."

"You did not. You were on a branch bigger than you are. And you know Mama said you wasn't to climb the apple trees. You'll break off the blossoms, and then we'll have no fruit come fall. You might break your neck, too." She sounded less concerned about this latter possibility.

"I was careful."

"Any baby can climb an old apple tree. Wouldn't you rather go exploring?"

"We're not supposed to wander off."

"Well, what if we don't go too far? If we can still hear somebody calling us, we'll be close enough. I want to go look for that tree with the writing on it." She nodded toward the dark woods. "I want to see can I read it."

Randall shifted from one foot to the other. "By ourselves?"

"You're not a-skeered, are you?" Her freckled nose wrinkled and she sneered at him. "You think a bear might get you?"

"Tree says there's bears out there. If it's real, and not just another fairy story, like the one about the beanstalk." Randall tried to sound skeptical of the whole idea, but he was peering around her at the blackness beyond the chestnut grove.

" 'Course it's real," said Fayre. "Mama told us, didn't she? And she didn't say once upon a time, like she does when it's a fairy story. She said there was a tree on *this here* mountain with words carved on it by Boone hisself. She said she seen it lots of times when she was little. I reckon it ought to be close to the creek bed. You gonna help me find it nor not, Randy?"

He ducked his head, and thrust his hands into the pockets of his overalls. "Why couldn't we ask Mama to take us there herself, then?"

Fayre gave him a scornful look. "She's too busy working around here, now that your daddy's gone. Besides, she never goes into the woods any more. I reckon girls just don't have no fun after they grow up."

The part of his mind that wasn't five years old anymore stirred, and wanted to cry out, but the little boy in the meadow nodded. With only one glance back at the shabby frame house below, he took his half-sister's hand, and walked into the forest.

It hadn't happened that way. But after more than half a century he had told that story so many times that it had taken on a kind of truth even in his imaginings.

Randall Stargill had been dreaming for two days and a half when Angie Jordan began to wonder about him. She had pulled up to the mailbox with his day's allotment of circulars and mail-order catalogues, and when she pulled down the metal flap to insert the pile of junk mail, she saw that yesterday's delivery, and the one before that, was still there. At most residences, Angie would have attributed this lapse to oversight or absence. She would have shoved the new batch into the mailbox without a moment's thought and gone on, but Randall Stargill was old and frail, and, besides, his truck was still in the driveway, exactly where it had been when she last drove by. She left the circulars, and drove on to her next delivery, but the unclaimed mail still troubled her.

When she reached the next mailbox over the ridge, J. Z. Stallard had walked down the hill from his farmhouse and was waiting for her, wanting to buy some more stamps for bill paying. She asked him about the old man, because the Stallards and the Stargills had been neighbors since their mountain was in the lost state of Franklin instead of the state of Tennessee. Besides, to Angie, who was twenty-four, the angular, silver-haired J. Z. Stallard, who was sixty-five, and scraggly old man Stargill, seventy-eight, passed for contemporaries. "Has Mr. Stargill gone visiting his sons this week?" she asked as she counted back his change.

J. Z. shook his head. "Not that I know of. He almost never leaves home since Clarsie passed on. He never was one to travel. Why do you ask?"

"I just wondered," said Angie. "He hasn't taken the mail out of his box in a couple of days. I thought he might have gone visiting, and forgot to have his mail stopped. Lots of people go off on vacation without telling the post office. You'd be surprised."

J. Z. Stallard nodded, ready for the conversation to end. "I believe he'd come and ask me to watch out for things if he did take a mind to leave," he said. "I'll look in on him directly."

As Angie's station wagon eased off down the road, Stallard fished his keys out of his pocket and walked to his truck, hoping it would start. It needed a new carburetor, but he was trying to put off the purchase until his tax refund came back.

As he drove the half mile to the Stargill place, J. Z. Stallard tried to think of all the bad things that could have possibly happened to Randall Stargill—everything from a heart attack to armed robbers breaking in and tying the old man up while they ransacked the house—because he half-believed that if you thought of a bad thing in advance, it wouldn't have happened. In his experience, bad luck was always the unexpected disaster, like the lightning striking the barn roof in October. The fire department had managed to get there in time to save the structure, but the roof was badly damaged, and there hadn't been any insurance to pay for replacing it. These days farming was supposed to be a part-time job, but it was all he had ever done, and he was too old to change now.

If he had thought about it, J. Z. Stallard might have been forced to admit that he didn't like Randall Stargill all that much. The old man kept to himself most of the time. Perhaps it was a habit that he had got into as a youth, when people still remembered the old tragedy and either steered clear of him or tried to pry into family matters. Whatever the reason, he seemed to expect people to take against him, and there was a wariness about him that made folks uneasy without knowing why, so they left him alone.

When Clarsie was alive, the Stargills went to church, and they had showed up at community get-togethers, where Clarsie talked and Randall stood around holding a plate of food and saying as little as possible, but now that he was a widower, he seldom ventured past the gate to his farm. Randall's lack of charm and neighborliness was not an issue today, though. He was a neighbor—maybe even distant kin if you checked the family pages in the Bible to way back when—and duty required J. Z. Stallard to do all he could for the man.

He pulled his truck in behind the faded Ford F-100 that had been Randall's vehicle for more than a decade. That it was still there did not rule out anything, in J. Z.'s opinion. Randall might have left the mountain in an ambulance, and robbers would not have stolen such a decrepit truck, regardless of what else they might steal. As he walked to the house, he looked for signs of broken windows or any evidence of forced entry. Maybe he should have called Sheriff Arrowood, he thought. At his age, J. Z. Stallard was in no shape to play hero against a gang of vandals. All seemed peaceful, though.

He found the back door unlocked, and after waiting a few moments while his knocking went unanswered, he let himself in. The kitchen was rank with stale food and unwashed plates, but he still didn't see any sign of intruders. The only disarray was the ordinary detritus of a solitary man who had ceased to care how things looked, or even how they smelled. He walked to the living room, to get away from the kitchen stench, and cupped his hands over his mouth, calling out for Randall, but all was silent. Illness, then, thought Stallard.

He walked from one littered room to the next, praying he wouldn't trip over his neighbor's remains in the dimness. He found Stargill in the little back bedroom, burrowed under a load of quilts and blankets, eyes closed. He was pasty-faced and gaunt, but when

Stallard pulled back the blanket he could see a faint movement of the old man's chest, and he sighed with relief that he had not come too late.

Stargill wasn't dead, but he wouldn't wake up. J. Z. Stallard went back to the kitchen, intending to call the rescue squad. He had just lifted the receiver when he noticed the white envelope atop an address book by the telephone, addressed "To Whoever It Concerns." J. Z. replaced the receiver and picked up the envelope. He reckoned that the act of intruding with good intentions made it his concern. He hoped it wasn't a suicide note, because it suddenly occurred to him that he might be the closest thing poor Randall Stargill had to a friend, and he didn't want to blame himself for his neighbor's despair. He could have visited oftener, he told himself, as he tore open the envelope. Not that Stargill ever seemed grateful for company.

For an instant, before he looked at the contents of the envelope, Stallard wondered if he would learn the end to the old tragedy. He hoped not. It was best forgotten. It had nothing to do with him, and he did not want the task of deciding what should be done with the truth.

"I DO NOT WANT TO LEAVE HOME." The words were printed in shaky block capitals on the top of a sheet of lined paper. "I WILL DIE HERE."

Below that, Stargill had written the names of his sons: Robert Lee; Dwayne (deceased); Charles Martin; Garrett; and Clayton, with a phone number listed only for the oldest and the youngest. Beside Charles Martin's name, the old man had written, "*Unlisted. Keeps changing it.*" And after Garrett's name the words "Warrant Officer" appeared in parentheses, with the notation: "*On active duty. Hard to find.*" On the succeeding pages the handwriting became more crabbed, words packed close together, filling one sheet after another with instructions. J. Z. stared at the contents of the envelope, wondering what he ought to do.

Mr. Stargill was still hanging on to life, but he remained in a coma. There was no doubt in Stallard's mind that his neighbor belonged in the hospital in Johnson City. The county ambulance could transport him there in less than an hour, but the note was adamant: he was to be left at home. That seemed clear enough, but Stallard wondered if such a document would legally absolve him from the responsibility of getting the old man more help than perhaps he wanted.

What if Stargill really was at the end of his long life? He was nearly eighty, and failing; his family was gone. Sometimes nursing homes kept you from dying without really keeping you alive. They could hook old Stargill up to purring machines that fed him and breathed for him without really bringing him back, and he could linger like that for months, tended by strangers, trapped in the concrete walls of the old folks prison.

It wasn't cheap, either. Somebody at church had mentioned an elderly aunt who'd had to go into a nursing home for long-term care, and her children had ended up selling the farm to pay for a comatose existence that may have been intolerable to her. J. Z. hoped that if he ever hovered between living and dying, with his foot caught in the trap, that his daughter Dovey would have the good sense to let the end come quickly. He didn't want to die by inches among strangers.

He looked again at the scribbled sheet of lined paper. Old man Stargill didn't want a drawn-out death, either. That was clear. But it was also clear that J. Z. couldn't turn around and walk out as if he had not found the sick man. Regardless of Stargill's wishes, J. Z. could not live with such an act of abandonment on his conscience.

He picked up the phone, hesitated a few moments longer debating the possibilities, and then dialed his own number. He let it ring a dozen times to give Dovey time to answer in case she was at the clothesline or out checking on the livestock. They had an Angus heifer that was nearly due with her first calf. Finally he heard his daughter's gasping hello, and he talked quickly while she caught her breath.

When he'd finished explaining the situation, he heard her sigh. Finally she said, "You didn't call an ambulance, did you?"

"No, Dovey. I haven't yet. He's set against it in his note. I figured the least we could do is to notify the boys, and let them make the call. But he needs somebody with him, and I'm no good at sickbeds."

The sigh again. "All right, Dad. I'm coming over now."

An hour later, Dovey Stallard came out of the bedroom, wiping her hands on a dingy towel. "I cleaned him up, and changed his sheets, anyhow," she told her father, who was sitting at the kitchen table. "His condition hasn't worsened any. Now what? Have you notified his kinfolks?"

J. Z. shook his head. "I couldn't sit still. Besides, I was trying to straighten up a little in here. I got most of the garbage bagged to take out and the floor swept, so it won't stink so much. I wouldn't want the boys to come home to that." He picked up Randall Stargill's letter. "I figured I'd call them when I finished the kitchen. Not that I think any of them will be home this early, and, to tell you the truth, I'm not looking forward to the conversation when I do get up with them. This letter is the damnedest thing, Dovey."

"What is it? A will?"

"Not in so many words. It says Stargill doesn't want to leave. Says he wants to die at home. He wants his boys to build his coffin. I believe his mind was going toward the end. But, of course, he ought to be in intensive care, because this might be a treatable illness. Maybe it's not his time yet."

"I don't think he has a chance of making it," said Dovey, glancing at the crabbed writing on the paper. "He must be nearly eighty, and he's in a coma. Suppose we take him to the hospital, and he gets better, and then he gets out and sues us for violating his instructions?"

Stallard shrugged. "He couldn't get much from me, Dovey. I can't even pay the taxes on the farm this year. What with the fire and all."

"He could sue for spite, and we can't afford to pay a lawyer. Let somebody else decide what happens to him. You've done as much as duty demands."

"We could call the county attorney," said Stallard. "See what he says."

Dovey shook her head. "You ever try to get a straight answer from a lawyer? We need to know now—not next week. Call Mr. Stargill's sons about this. You've put it off too long already."

J. Z. Stallard hesitated. He hated telephones. "Clayt still lives around here, doesn't he?"

"He tells people he lives in the state capital," Dovey sighed. When her father looked blank, she added, "You know—Jonesborough." The village had a one-block business district and a population of a few thousand at most, but in the era of history that was Clayt Stargill's passion, frontier Jonesborough had been a state capital. By 1788, when the lost state of Franklin was reabsorbed by North Carolina and Tennessee, Jonesborough's brief flicker of glory was over, and it reverted to a paintbox-pretty mountain town where Norman Rockwell would have felt at home.

Dovey Stallard turned on the hot water, and began piling stained coffee mugs and food-encrusted plates into the sink. "Might as well do these dishes while we're tidying the place up."

"What's he doing now?" He noticed that Dovey's expression had not changed when he mentioned Clayt, and he was relieved. She had been mighty taken with the Stallard boys in her young womanhood. He never could figure out which one broke her heart. Dovey wasn't much on talking about feelings.

"What's Clayt doing?" Dovey laughed. "What day of the week is it? Clayt's the same as ever. He does ten things at once, and hardly scrapes together a living out of the lot of them. White-water rafting guide. Freelance photographer. Local artist. Park service employee. I can't keep track. All that education, and not a lick of ambition in his whole body. Of course, he's the baby of the family."

"I always thought he'd make a good farmer," her father replied.

"He's got the hang of being poor," said Dovey. "But he doesn't have a lot of practical know-how. You'd think that Charles Martin Stargill would have paid to have live-in help for his father. He must be making good money. I saw him on the Nashville Network last month, singing with—somebody. Might have been Louise Mandrell."

J. Z. Stallard looked doubtful. "Charles Martin's number isn't here, and I'm sure the operator won't give it out, with him being famous and all. Besides, he might be on tour or something—hard to reach. Same thing with Garrett in the army."

"That's too bad," said Dovey. "Because Garrett is the likeliest one to take charge. He's the only one who could make decisions and stick to them. When we were kids, he was always the one who decided what we played and whose side we were on."

"I say we try Clayt first, because he's closest, and Robert in Cincinnati."

Dovey shrugged. "Fine. See if you can reach him."

Stallard dialed the Jonesborough number, and waited, moving his lips a little as he rehearsed what he had to say. After nearly a minute, he hung up. "No answer."

"Didn't think there would be. I can't see Clayt being cooped up inside on a fine afternoon. I expect he's out wandering some place, and calling it research. You call Robert Lee in Cincinnati, Dad. After I finish these dishes, I suppose I could go out and see if I can find Clayt. He's useless, but he's the closest. If he's still not home, I'll leave a note on his door and then drive around and try to find him. I still remember most of his haunts."

J. Z. Stallard glanced toward the dark hallway. "Should I stay here?"

"It would be best," said Dovey, seeing his reluctance to be left alone with the dying man.

"I'll be back with Clayt as soon as I can. And when you talk to

Robert, see if you can get the phone number for the other two. Maybe one of them will have the sense to let you call an ambulance."

In the small back bedroom, the old man slept on.

Clayt Stargill had climbed to the highest meadow because he wanted to feel spring coming. Actually, what he wanted to see, and try to experience, was the spring of 1761, and while this was as close as he was going to get to that far-off wilderness, it was still wrong by a long shot, and he knew it.

Daniel Boone, on one of his long hunts from the Yadkin settlement had watched for spring on just such a mountaintop in the Smokies, and Clayt was trying to capture the feel of the wilderness from Boone's eyes. He had grown up hearing stories about Daniel Boone, mostly from the old-timers in the community, but sometimes at school, too. The eighteenth-century pioneer was considered a favorite son by the people of the mountains; there was hardly any place he hadn't visited. Before Boone pioneered Kentucky, he had lived in the Virginia Blue Ridge, then on the Yadkin River in North Carolina. From there he had made winter expeditions into Indian country, the mountain land that was the communal hunting ground of the Cherokee, the Catawba, and the Shawnee, forbidden to settlers until the American Revolution nullified the British treaty. Each spring he would return to his family on the fringes of civilization, bringing furs that could be sold for the necessities of pioneer life.

He'd had a camp near what is now Boone, North Carolina, and he had roamed the Clinch and Holston river valleys in search of game. Legend had it that Boone had abandoned a dying horse in a meadow near Roan Mountain, only to return a few months later to find the animal restored to health by the abundance of the land, and many a county in Tennessee and southwest Virginia claimed to have once had a tree with Boone's name carved deep into the trunk.

There was such a Boone tree in the Stargill family legend, and although Clayt had never succeeded in finding it, he could not quite lose his belief that such a thing existed, somewhere on the wild mountain land beyond the Stargill fence line. *D. Boon cilled a bar on this tree—1761.* Crude words carved into the bark of an old tree, a monument to an ancient battle between a great man and an even greater wilderness. Clayt and his brothers had spent long hours on the mountain looking for that fabled tree that his father insisted lay somewhere in the woods on Stargill land, but the old man never went with them, nor did he seem to care whether they found it or not.

Clayt grew up loving the land, and wanting to know everything about the plants and animals around him, but he'd had to find it out on his own. Randall Stargill, if he knew such things, kept them to himself. It was the same with Daniel Boone. Born in Pennsylvania in a Quaker farm community, his love of the wilderness had made him almost a changeling among his village-dwelling kinfolk. The way Clayt Stargill saw it, he and Daniel were a lot alike, except that it was easier to be that way in the eighteenth century than it was in the twentieth.

Clayt was 5'8" and sturdy, dark-haired with blue gray eyes, as Boone himself had been, and when he was dressed for the part—in leather breeches and moccasins, a long coat in the eighteenth-century fashion, and a Quaker-style beaver hat—there was a passing resemblance. Clayt always had to explain the beaver fedora to schoolchildren when he visited their classrooms as a living history instructor in the part of Daniel. No coonskin cap, he would tell them. Boone never wore one. That was just television, getting it wrong as usual.

The Boone outfit would have kept him warm enough up here, except for the wind, but he was glad of his boots and his modern down parka today. It was still winter by the calendar, and the wind that whipped across the open field numbed his cheeks, and pierced his lungs when he drew breath, but the signs of the coming glory would warm him more than the central heating down in his little house in the valley. He had work to do, a grant proposal to write and letters to answer from schools interested in his living history program, but all that would have to wait. Spring days like this were all too few, and he couldn't waste them indoors. This was research, too, he told himself. He had to live the part to be convincing.

It would be cold for weeks yet here in the high country, but you could see spring coming from a long way off. On the far ridges across the valley, the maple branches were red-tipped with buds, and here and there beneath the bare hickory and oak trees, an early redbud flamed. Its deep pink, the solitary flash of color in the sepia woods, made him think of the burning bush in Exodus. Boone had named one of his sons "Israel." Had he seen himself as Moses, leading his people into the promised land of Kentucky?

Clayt lay on his back, and looked up at the blue sky, streaked only with wisps of cirrus clouds far in the distance. It was a perfect day to watch the travelers on the celestial interstate. Migrating birds used the two-thousand-mile mountain chain as a path for navigation. The hawks would ride the thermals between the peaks and valleys, and the lesser birds followed the north-south ranges as their guide from winter to summer.

A flock of shiny black starlings flew past, and Clayt scowled up at them. Starlings didn't belong here. They weren't just passing through, like the falcons and the arctic buntings. They were invaders who came to stay: noisy, dirty interlopers who swarmed into a habitat, devoured all the food, and chased away the songbirds. They would have been a nuisance even if they had been native creatures, but they weren't, and the fact that they were inflicted on the continent by a well-meaning idiot made their presence all the more galling to Clayt.

He wished he had been around just a hundred years ago: yesterday in geologic time, but in some ways an eternity ago. There were no starlings here then.

Daniel Boone had never seen a starling.

Clayt tried to picture the mountain as it would have been in 1761. First, he had to imagine being able to see for ninety miles into the distance instead of the paltry twelve miles of visibility you got in clear weather nowadays. Air pollution had shrunk the vistas as surely as clear cutting had felled the forests. Ninety miles. What could he see from those high meadows with such a range? Asheville? The Virginia Blue Ridge? He could not even imagine such wonders.

In 1761, there had been elk and buffalo in the North Carolina / Tennessee mountains, now remaining only in the place names: Banner Elk, Elk River, Buffalo Mountain. And over in Mitchell County there was a community called Pigeon Roost, named for the great flocks of passenger pigeons that were also gone forever. They had looked like large blue-tinged mourning doves darkening the sky in their flight, millions of them at once. They had been the most populous species of bird in North America. The last of them died in 1914—blasted into oblivion in less than two hundred years by hunters who slaughtered them by the ton, and then would not believe that the birds were gone forever. "They have flown away," people said. "They've gone to Australia." Now there was hardly anyone alive who had even seen one. Here and there a sad bundle of feathers gathered dust in a museum—all that was left of a mighty species.

Clayt looked out at the distant hill, silvered with the bare limbs of maple trees, and wondered how it would have looked in Boone's day. There would have been chestnut trees on the hillsides then. Until sixty years ago these sprawling giants of the forest, with trunks twenty feet around, soared up into the sky a hundred feet or more, but they, too, were gone, killed by the fungus from an imported plant. The last of the great chestnuts had died in the thirties in these mountains, but Clayt saw their remnants sometimes in the deep woods, the bodies of fallen giants rotting away into compost in the green silence. Much of the mountains was national forest land now. He wondered if the government's attempts at preservation would change anything in the overall process of destruction.

A single starling swept past Clayt Stargill, and he waved his hand to frighten it away. It spoiled the scene for him. Still, who was he to say that the bird did not belong to his Appalachia? As much as he longed for the mountains of his pioneer ancestors, he knew that the land had always been in the process of change, and that every species, past and present, was, at some point, an interloper.

He smiled at his own hypocrisy, condoning some species and excluding others, based on his whims. In fairness he had to admit to himself—and to those who went on his wildlife walks—that the Kentucky bluegrass was as much an interloper as the starlings, but it was a pleasant addition, and because it had been established a century earlier people had forgotten that it was not native to North America. Bluegrass is English timothy, used in straw form by pioneers as a packing material to protect their trade goods. When bits of seed escaped from the packs, they sprouted along the trails, and thrived in the new environment. If you banished the starlings from your perfect world, the bluegrass, too, must go.

What time would he call "real," anyhow?

The mountains looked frozen in time, so immutable were they within the span of man's lifetime, but he knew that they had changed many times over the millennia. Mountains had risen up, been ground down into dust, and rose again when the shoulder of Africa butted the Old Red Sandstone continent, making dents that were the peaks and valleys of the southern Appalachians. These mountains had once been higher and grander than the Rockies, but they were old now, headed once more toward the dust. Those young, jagged mountains were not his, though. They belonged to a tropical time, when warm fern wetlands stretched across Kentucky and West Virginia, laying down the deposits of vegetation that would turn into coal over the succeeding millennia.

Twelve thousand years ago, then. When the Ice Age had retreated back to the North, and perhaps human beings settled in the mountains for the first time. Wonderful creatures walked these hills then—the shaggy elephants called mastodons, American lions that would dwarf their modern African cousins, saber-toothed tigers, sloths bigger than pickup trucks, bears double the size of today's grizzlies, birds of prey with wingspans of twenty-five feet, musk oxen, and camels, and horses. Perhaps among this bestiary were the inspirations for the legends of monsters in Cherokee lore. What a wild and magical place it must have been in that springtime following the Ice Age.

No. He would not have known the land here as it was then, a spare, frozen place, forested by spruce and fir trees that tolerated the cold better than the oaks and hickories of this warmer time. Although the glaciers were retreating by then, twelve thousand years ago, the highest points of the southern range would have been a tundra zone, with ground that seldom thawed, and unceasing winds that withered all but the hardiest of plants. Those harsher, younger mountains did not stir his blood, despite their wonders—tigers and wooly mastodons in a kingdom of ice. He had no place in that world.

He always came back to 1761.

The land would be familiar to him in its eighteenth-century guise, but cleaner, truer to its own spirit, unspoiled by the invaders: settlers and starlings.

CHAPTER TWO

The history of my going home and returning with my family forms a series of difficulties, an account of which would swell a volume.

—DANIEL BOONE

Charles Martin Stargill clicked off his cordless phone and set it on the sofa beside him, but he didn't pick up his guitar again. He just sat there for a few minutes, gazing at a framed picture of himself and Johnny Cash without really seeing it, as if he were still listening to a disembodied conversation. He was still lost in thought when Kelley came into the room, bringing the beer he'd asked for.

"What's the matter, hon?" she said, but he just sat there, looking like a pole-axed steer, and then she saw the phone on the sofa beside him, and thought, "Uh-oh," hoping that the bad news, whatever it was, wouldn't cloud the rest of their day. Charles Martin Stargill might have a trademark smile in his publicity photos, but when he was offstage and out of the spotlight, he could be moody, and sometimes downright rude if you didn't stay out of his way.

In the few months they had been together, Kelley had grown used to the dark silences; she had even seen rages that the country music fans wouldn't have believed. Not that she would ever tell them. She never talked to the press. That was the fastest way to stop being close to a performer. No way did she want to go back to five bucks an hour and a one-room apartment with two locks on the door and walls like a paper napkin. Charles Martin's house was no Graceland, that's for sure, but he had twenty acres and a pond with a little waterfall at one end and goldfish as big as your hand swimming around in it. The first time they visited him there, Kayla had thought it was Disney World.

Kelley thought he was still more country boy than country music star, and she liked that about him. Sometimes he had an innocence that almost matched Kayla's, and sometimes he was tougher than wet leather. The first part made her like him, and the second part made him rich. She wasn't with Charles Martin just for his money, though. She hadn't even known he was somebody important when he first asked her out. He just seemed like a nice, straightforward guy who wasn't out for what he could get.

So far things were working out better than she'd expected, men being what they were. Charles Martin was moody, sometimes, sure, but Kelley knew that people in the music business are under an incredible amount of pressure, so his bad nerves were understandable. He didn't do drugs, or beat up on her, or on Kayla, who was six. He just needed his space from time to time, especially when he was writing his songs, and they had to respect that. Kelley tried to smooth his path as best she could, so he wouldn't end up the way Elvis did.

Charles Martin didn't exactly act like a daddy to Kayla, but he treated her with courtesy, and listened to her just like she was a grown-up, which was more than you could say for her real daddy, who sent a check every couple of months but never remembered her birthday. Kelley wasn't sure if things were going to work out permanently between her and Charles Martin Stargill—she never did have much luck with men—but for now she thought they were as much of a family as she could hope for.

Charles Martin was still staring off into space, so she set down the beer in front of him and tried again. "If the phone is bothering you, I could take it out of here. Are you working on a song?"

He shrugged. "I was, I guess. It's gone now. That was my brother Clayt calling from up home." He gave her that smile he wore when he lost the Country Music Award. "At first I thought he wanted to borrow money but that wasn't it. He said Daddy is in a bad way, and that I should come home."

"Oh, Charlie, I'm real sorry." Kelley was relieved but she was careful not to show it. This kind of trouble was something that they could share, not like business worries, when he would shut her out, saying she didn't understand and she had to let him weather it on his own. Family troubles were something women understood better than men. She remembered how hopeless her grandfather had been when Mamaw died, and she thought, "I can get Charles Martin through this. He'll need me," because men couldn't cry, and they seemed to have absolutely no idea what you were supposed to do as one of the bereaved. They just stood around like children waiting for food to be put in front on them, and having to be told every single thing, like what to wear to the viewing.

She wondered if he was taking it hard, or if he was just shocked by the news. He had never talked much about his folks back in east Tennessee, and there had been no calls or visits that she knew of in the months they'd been together. He had a brother at Fort Campbell, but the two weren't close, as far as she could tell.

Kelley knew little more about him than the sugared biography printed in the souvenir program for his concerts: *A true son of the pioneers, Charles Martin Stargill hails from the coves of east Tennessee, where his forefathers settled in the late seventeen hundreds. He was raised on the family farm with his four brothers, taking part in church and community singing, and he worked as a logger and a truck driver before coming to Nashville with a guitar and a dream. . . .* The article was interspersed with black-and-white snapshots of Charles Martin: a five-year-old with a grin and a beat-up ukelele; a scowling teenager, holding a chainsaw; and his first publicity photo—the one he called his Buck Owens yard sale picture—looking rawboned and awkward in a white-fringed cowboy outfit.

Kelley sat down beside him, and put her arms around him. "I'm really sorry to hear about your dad," she said. "I guess you'll want to leave tonight."

"Don't guess I got much choice. I just hope it'll be over before the tabloids get wind of it. I don't want the funeral turned into a circus."

Kelley didn't see why the media would care about the natural death of a minor celebrity's elderly father, but she knew better than to argue with a performer's ego. "Were you close to your dad?"

Charles Martin shrugged. "I believe I sent him every single article I was ever mentioned in, hoping he'd be impressed. Bought him a Rolex the Christmas I signed with MCA."

Kelley thought about his answer for a moment, and instead of what she had been thinking, she said, "It's a shame you couldn't get home more often."

"Yeah, well, we got along better at a distance. It will be strange to have us all together again. First time I've been back since Mama died."

"This will mean changing your schedule around. Do you want me to call Mr. Iselin for you?"

"No. I need to talk to Ray myself." He smiled a little and patted her thigh. "Why don't you go pack the suitcases, honey?"

She was going with him. She nodded, not smiling back, and started toward the bedroom. Charles Martin called after her, "You know what to pack, don't you?"

Kelley nodded. "Your good suit and dress shirts, silk ties, Italian loafers, and some around home jeans and stuff, right?"

He smiled again, but not like anything was funny. "Not for Wake County, darlin'," he said. "I tried that a time or two, and learned my lesson. The homefolks don't like to see the local celebrity dressed like a regular guy. They like to be able to point me out at the grocery store or have their picture taken with me on the street, and have everybody know I'm a country singer just by looking at me. Famous people are no fun if they're ordinary. Pack the buckskin shirts, the concho belt, and the stuff I wear for daytime interviews."

Kelley started to ask him another question, but he had picked up the phone and was already punching in numbers. That was it, she figured, and she was worried. Going home was going to be another performance, and she didn't know who she was supposed to be.

In Cincinnati, Robert Lee Stargill came into the kitchen after work and found his wife sifting flour, with tears rolling down her plump cheeks.

It was early evening, and Robert was still wearing the sky blue jacket and string tie that were his uniform at the car dealership where he was assistant sales manager. Lilah Rose occasionally suggested that he try a new look—a nice conservative black suit was her latest recommendation—but Robert refused to alter his appearance. "This is how people expect a car salesman to look, Lilah," he would tell her. "If they came on the lot and I was dressed like a college professor, they'd be afraid I'd look down on them when they had to ask for a five-year loan to get the payments low enough. They'd think I'd sneer at the junker they brought to trade in. They'd shy away, and buy the car from somebody else—somebody younger, most likely. I know I'm no fashion plate in this old jacket, honey, but it's the right thing to wear. It makes people feel a little bit superior to me, no matter how little they have, and that's good for business." All that was true, but so was the fact that he rather liked the sky blue jacket.

Robert Lee took a look at his wife, with her tear-stained face, at the flecks of Martha White flour on her turquoise caftan, and at the baking ingredients scattered all over the countertops, and he wondered if he ought to ask her what was wrong or if it was a woman thing that he should pretend not to notice.

"How are you, sweetheart?" he asked.

She wiped her eyes with the back of her hand. "Well, Robert, I'm fine. It's you I'm worried about."

He felt his stomach muscles tighten. He was fifty-one, still young enough to think that bad news meant money troubles rather than health problems. The furnace? The washing machine? The transmission on Lilah's car? He sat down at the kitchen table, willing his breathing to stay regular, and wondered why life had become an endless round of belittlings, ending in a great terror. Was it better in the old days when people died tragically and young? "What is it then, Lilah?" he said.

Lilah had gone back to her wooden spoon and mixing bowl, transforming the flour into a yellow batter. "I have been meditating on death," she told him. "And I'm making cupcakes. Rudy says that it is important to keep busy in times of sadness. You wouldn't think that angels would be so understanding about our reaction to death, because, of course, from their point of view it's such a small event in the course of our eternal lives, like a leaf falling on a page as we're reading. I mentioned that to Rudy when we heard the news, but do you know what he said? 'A child is no less afraid because the monster in the closet is not real.' "

"That's real good, sweetheart." Robert Lee supposed they would have to go through a few more minutes of small talk about her angel before he found out what was bothering her. Probably some movie star had died, knowing Lilah. But he was relieved. At least it wasn't money.

Humoring his wife took more patience than Robert Lee Stargill sometimes possessed, though, in truth, he hardly minded this delusion of hers, or her change-of-life game of pretend, or whatever it was. He figured an angel was less trouble than a little yappy dog, and cheaper than a collection of childlike porcelain dolls.

At first, he had debated the expense of a therapist, fearing that people might think Lilah was a little nuts, but no one in their small circle of friends had ever said so. Even the most skeptical neighbors were polite, because it seemed like everybody was seeing angels these days, and to doubt a sighting would be sacrilegious. Billy Graham even wrote a book about them. Everybody else seemed entertained by Lilah's accounts of her angel's pronouncements. At least she didn't harp endlessly on her ailments, like Mrs. Rickey, or get maudlin drunk at parties, like Alma Henson.

Robert Lee thought she was lonely.

He was grateful that Rudy wasn't a fanatical angel: they didn't have to go to church three times a week, or give their belongings to the poor. An occasional check to help starving elk in Wyoming or earthquake victims in Japan was the extent of his charitable meddling—cheaper than poodle grooming, Robert figured. He did wonder, though, why Lilah's guardian angel was black and male with a pencil-thin mustache, eagle's wings, and an Alabama accent. Lilah was born and raised in pre-integration-era Cincinnati. She was the least Southern woman Robert could think of. Why, she put carrots in her potato salad! As for her Alabama angel: the Lord works in mysterious ways, had been Lilah's—and presumably Rudy's—reply.

"Why were you fretting about death?" asked Robert.

"It's your father," said Lilah, her eyes welling again. "The poor, old man is on his deathbed."

The churning in Robert Stargill's stomach ceased. Sad news, but not, in terms of his day-to-day survival, a catastrophe. Not like being fired. "He's had a good life, Lilah." Another thought struck him. "Was it—ah—Rudy who told you this?"

"Of course not, Robert. You know he never interferes. Your father's neighbor, Mr. Stallard, called. He advised us to come right away."

"What about Clayt? He lives right there."

"They can't find him. They're still trying, though."

Robert's lip curled in irritation. "Clayt never did have a lick of sense. Dad's in the hospital, then?"

"Well, no. But he's terribly ill. It seems he left a note saying that he wanted to die at home. They think Clayt will want all of you to come back and decide what to do."

Robert Lee glanced at the calendar. It was only the middle of the month, and he was a little behind in his sales quota. "Maybe we ought to wait," he said. "We don't know how this will turn out. He could linger. You know how they are about time off down at the lot."

"But if you explained—"

He ignored her. In a sales job, you didn't explain. "And if there is a funeral, we'll have to budget time for that, and then there'll be things to see to afterward. That will take even more time." He wouldn't have said such things out loud to anyone but his wife. With outsiders, even with his brothers, he would express a willingness to go home at once, and to stay for as long as necessary, because that's what you were supposed to say and feel, but the fact was that he had a real job, and, like it or not, the amount of time that he could be away from that job was limited. Life wasn't like a soap opera, where feelings were everything, and everyone could afford to have them.

It was all right for his younger brothers to drop everything and run back home. Charlie was a country singer, and Garrett was career army, on the government payroll with all kinds of benefits and time off and free health care, paid for with taxpayers' money. Clayt, the back-to-nature dilettante, had no career to jeopardize, but he lived back there anyhow, so no sacrifice would be called for on his part. It was easy for Clayt to insist that they all come home. Only Robert Lee would be caught in the pinch of family demands—as usual.

"Rudy says we ought to go, Robert. You should make peace with the dying."

"I'm more at peace with Daddy than the rest of the family, I reckon," snapped Robert. "Is Rudy going to sell cars for me while we go gallivanting off to Tennessee?"

Lilah sighed. "You have to trust Providence, Robert."

"I have to use my vacation time," he replied bitterly. "I wish the Lord would schedule disasters for weekends."

Lilah listened to empty air again and smiled, but Robert turned away. He had no interest in the clever reply of an angel.

It was nearly midnight when Chief Warrant Officer Garrett Stargill got home, but he wasn't surprised to see the lights on in the kitchen. He knew Debba would be waiting up for him, because she always worried when he was scheduled for a night jump. He had long ago ceased to be flattered by her anxiety. He had given up explaining to her that he was too experienced to be in much danger, that he enjoyed the thrill of parachuting into a sky full of stars, and that he was probably safer in free fall than he was driving the two-lane road home from the base. Pointless to say any of this to Debba, because terror was Debba's vocation, her constant companion in life. Take her out of one obsession and she would latch on to another. Now that he had survived the parachute jump, she would go back to worrying about terrorists, or germs in the tap water. He scarcely listened anymore.

He let himself in through the kitchen door, calling out loudly, "It's me, Deb!" He had steadfastly refused to let her buy another gun, but he was always careful to make noise when he came in, telling her it was him, in case she had acquired one on her own, at some military family's yard sale, perhaps. Pistols were easy enough to come by in a neighborhood of army personnel, or in Tennessee, in general, for that matter.

She appeared in the kitchen doorway, tiny and wraithlike, wrapped in a chenille bathrobe and looking twelve years old, with her face scrubbed pink and her hair in pigtails over each ear. "Hi,

Garrett," she said with the tremulous smile that made him want to shake her. He knew that he had once found her vulnerability appealing, and her curveless body sexy, but he could not remember why.

"Everything went off without a hitch," he said. "Is there coffee?" She nodded toward the Mr. Coffee machine. He poured himself a cup, and kept talking. "The kids were nervous, but they were game. We didn't have to push anybody out of the plane. And the wind didn't pick up, so we all made it into the drop zone." He yawned. "It makes for a long day, though."

She nodded. "I watched the eleven o'clock news. I figured that if anything had gone wrong, they would have said so. I'm glad you're back." She put her arms around him, and he patted her head, as if she were an anxious child. The robe opened a little, and he saw that she was wearing his black T-shirt for a nightgown—the one his unit had made up, that said "We Rule the Night."

Then he noticed the blinking light on the answering machine.

"Were there any phone calls, Debba?"

She nodded, a flash of guilt crossed her face, and she buried her face in his shoulder. "I thought it might be the base. A wreck, maybe, or your unit being put on alert. You just got back."

"That doesn't mean I won't have to go again," he said. He pushed the button and waited for the machine to rewind. "Did you hear the message?"

"No. I turned the TV up when the phone rang."

The machine clicked on, and he heard his brother Clayton's voice. "We have to go home," he told her. She looked up, her eyes wide with panic. It would have made no difference if Debba had married an accountant instead of a chopper pilot. Her terror was a constant. He knew that Debba would find east Tennessee no less terrifying than the prospect of Haiti or Somalia.

. . .

In the darkness Clayt Stargill was pacing the flagstone walk in the backyard of his father's house, his vigil punctuated by frequent glances at the luminous dial of his watch.

"They won't be here for hours," said Dovey, who was sitting on the porch steps. "Nashville is a good five hours away, and Cincinnati is even farther. They may not be here until morning. It's not like there's anything they can do once they get here."

"I know," said Clayt. "There's nothing I can do, either. Except pace."

At sunset, when he had returned to Jonesborough from his visit to Beverly Tipton's farm, a black car was blocking his driveway, and Dovey Stallard was sitting behind the wheel, reading a paperback in the fading light. Without preamble she told him about his father's illness, and she went in with him while he telephoned Dr. Banner, who had all but retired from half a century of general practice, but he agreed to meet Clayton at the Stargill farm.

Dovey followed his truck back to Wake County and up the ridge to the old homeplace, nestled between two old maples that brushed the tin roof with their branches. They found Alton Banner already in the house, tending to his patient.

"Will he get better?" asked Clayt as he entered his father's bedroom.

"I doubt it," said Dr. Banner. "He's had a serious stroke, and his heart wasn't any great shakes to begin with. You can't leave him like this, though. If you don't get some fluids in him, he'll die of neglect."

"He doesn't want to go to a hospital." Dovey Stallard appeared in the doorway, and handed the physician a yellow legal pad. "Mr. Stargill wrote down everything he wants."

"Never mind what he wants," said Clayt. "If he has a chance, then do whatever you have to."

Alton Banner skimmed the first page of Randall Stargill's instructions. "It says he doesn't want life support. Hooked up to machines, he calls it. Well, we can give him his way on that, but just in case this is not his final hour, he is going to the hospital, so that he can at least have clean sheets, intravenous fluids, and a fighting chance to beat this thing. I'll call the rescue squad. Have you notified your brothers?"

"We got in touch with Robert in Cincinnati this afternoon," said Dovey. "Garrett and Charles Martin have unlisted numbers, so we decided to let Clayt call them."

He nodded. "Phone for the ambulance, doctor. Then I'll call them."

They said almost nothing while they waited for the ambulance. Clayt was grateful that Dovey did not feel the need to cover every silence with small talk. She had insisted on staying with him, offering to fix him coffee and sandwiches and tidying up the house while he paced the braided rug in the living room.

When the ambulance arrived, Clayt said, "I'm going with them. I have to sign him in, and see what they say. Thank you for coming for me, and for staying."

"I'll wait here, Clayt," said Dovey. "One of your brothers might have decided to hop on a plane. On your way back, you need to stop at Krogers. I checked the pantry, and you have nothing to feed a houseful of people. Here's a list."

It was past ten o'clock when Clayt returned to find Dovey curled up on the sofa asleep, with the television blaring. He set the groceries on the kitchen table, wondering if he should wake her. It was late. She needed to get home.

"How is he?" she said, yawning. "I heard you come in."

"He's stable for now. Still in a coma, though, so I didn't see any point in sitting there all night. I'll go back tomorrow when the rest of them get here. Guess you should be going."

"I'll just make that tuna salad first, in case they get here late and hungry. You'd just dump mayonnaise into the tuna and call it done."

He wondered if, despite the broken engagement all those years ago, Dovey still felt like a part of the family, but he didn't ask. Perhaps she was just being neighborly. He hadn't seen her since his mother's funeral. He got out the onions and the pickles, and watched while she chopped them, and mixed them with the tuna. "We don't need to do too much preparation," he reminded her. "Garrett and Robert Lee are bringing their wives."

Dovey gave him a look, and went back to spooning mayonnaise into the glass salad bowl.

When she finished, she put aluminum foil over the top of the bowl and set it in the refrigerator. "Now don't forget and leave it out," she told him, "Or else you'll *all* be in the hospital."

Finally they ran out of things to do in the house, so Dovey put on her coat and went outside. Clayt went with her. "I'll walk you to your car," he said. "I'm too restless to stay in that house. Maybe I'll just sit outside for a while."

"Well," said Dovey, "if anything can calm you down, it's being outside. That hasn't changed."

Clayt took a deep breath. "It isn't cold. You want to sit awhile?"

"A few minutes, I guess." The night sounds from the woods, and the sight of the stars glittering above the mountains, made her feel more peaceful than she had for a long time. She wasn't sure why she had been so determined to stay and help, but now wasn't the time to talk about it. The darkness was cold and clear, and Dovey let the silence grow between them until she became aware that the night was not still or silent at all.

A bat swooped into the spotlight at one end of the barn gulping down moths as it flew past. Far off, on the ridge, she heard the cry of a bird.

"Barn owl?" she said softly.

Clayt stood still, listening with his whole body until the cry came again. "Great horned owl," he said. "Barn owls scream or make a hissing noise. There! Hear it? A low whoo-oo—that's a great horned. He'll be after the rabbits tonight, when they go out courting."

"They say it's a sign of death—hearing an owl."

"It is if you're a field mouse," said Clayt, and for the first time that day, they smiled at each other. He stopped pacing and sat beside her on the concrete step. "It's been a long time since we talked, Dovey."

She shivered a little. "Remember when we were kids, and we used to play until way after dark on summer nights? Catching lightning bugs in a jam jar, and playing hide-and-seek when it was too dark to even see."

"I remember playing pioneer. I was always Daniel Boone—"

"You still are, Clayt!"

"Yeah—in my living history lectures, but it was more fun as a kid, when I could make it up as I went along. I remember how Dwayne and Garrett and I used to try to make you be an Indian princess in our game."

"I finally went along with it, didn't I?"

He laughed at the memory. "Sure, you did. How old were you then? Ten? You must have spent hours in the Hamelin library getting ready for that one." He mimicked her little girl's voice. "*All right, boys, I'm a Cherokee princess. I'm Nancy Ward!*

"And then you proceeded to kill all of us, and when we cried foul, you went home and got the book, and shoved it under our noses." He shook his head. "Sure enough, it told how she chewed bullets for her husband during the Cherokee's war with the Creeks, and how she took up his gun after he was killed and turned the tide of battle herself. I should have kept on reading, though. You tricked us. She never did harm any whites. Protected them, even from the wrath of the Cherokees. You didn't tell us that."

"Of course I didn't!" said Dovey. "I wanted to be a warrior, not a peacemaker. That's why I picked her. You all wanted me to be Rebecca Boone, sweeping the smokehouse while you boys went off to have adventures. *'Be careful, Dan'l,'* " she said in mocking falsetto.

In the darkness, Clayt Stargill smiled. "Nancy Ward. It was the first time I'd ever heard of her. I talk about her sometimes now in my school presentations."

"Good. Little girls ought to have somebody to relate to besides pioneer housewives and goody two-shoes Pocahontas. What do you say about Nancy Ward?"

"Well, I'm in costume as Daniel Boone, who must have met her—they were both important people in the same place and time—so I tell them that she was my friend, and a friend to all the settlers in the western mountains. She tried to keep the peace between the Cherokees and the whites. I talk about the time she warned Fort Watauga about the coming attack planned by Dragging Canoe and how she saved Mrs. Bean from being burned at the stake, stamping out the flames herself and promising the village that if they spared this captive, Mrs. Bean would teach them how to make butter and cheese. I tell them that Nancy Ward was named the Ghighau when she was still a teenager, even though that honor is usually reserved for one very old and revered. The female students are always especially pleased about that part."

"I hope you make it clear that women played an important role in Cherokee society and that she had real power and influence."

"You ought to come with me, Dovey," said Clayt. "With that dark hair of yours and a little pancake makeup to cover your Irish freckles, you'd make a great Nancy Ward. You might even be part Cherokee, who knows? I could rig you up a pioneer costume and some turkey feathers for a swan's wing—you remember, the symbol of her authority."

"No thanks, Clayt," she sighed. "Maybe men don't outgrow play-acting, but women do."

"Grandma Flossie, where are they taking the hounds?"

Nora Bonesteel was five years old, a big-eyed, solemn child, who watched more than she spoke. She was sitting on the back porch on a May morning, watching her grandmother peel potatoes to boil for dinner. In the soft wind Nora could smell the blossoms on the apple trees, as white as her pinafore against the green mountains beyond. She had been watching a mourning cloak butterfly drift among the clumps of purple irises in her mother's garden beside the smokehouse, as she listened to her grandmother sing an old hymn, joining her on the chorus: *Safely walking close to thee; Let it be, dear Lord, let it be.*

The dogs' barking drowned out the harmony of old woman and child. Nora looked up to see her father and their cousin Roy heading for the dog pen beside the barn. They pulled open the wooden door in the chicken wire fence, released the yelping hounds from the enclosure, and loaded them into the back of Sam Teague's flatbed Ford. Watching them, Nora felt afraid, and it took her a moment to sort out why. It was the silence. The men performed the tasks without speaking, expressionless. They did not laugh and talk as they usually did when they went for the hounds, nor did they wave to the womenfolk on the porch. Even though they wore boots and brush clothes, Nora decided that they weren't fixing to go hunting. It was too late in the day. She didn't see any rifles. She looked up at her grandmother, who was also watching the men in a grim silence far removed from the usual good humor she showed to the departing hunters. Something was wrong about this day. Nora knew not to ask if she might go along. "Where are they going?"

Grandma Flossie sighed. "They're hunting a child, Nora," she said. "A little girl is lost out on the mountain. They say she wandered off into the woods, and can't find her way home again, so all the menfolk are going out with the dogs to look for her."

"What little girl?"

"She was staying over at the Stargill farm. She was a little towheaded girl about as old as you, Nora. You haven't seen her, have you?" Grandma Flossie spoke slowly to the child, and Nora understood that the question was meant two ways. Had Nora seen the little girl playing in the woods, and a second meaning, the secret between them—had little Nora *seen* anything that other folks weren't likely to see? A black ribbon on a beehive, perhaps, or a mound of flowers at the church altar that didn't turn out to be there after all when she tried to touch it. Such things had happened to Nora before, as they happened to Grandma Flossie, but nobody ever talked about these occurrences, not in the family, and never, ever to strangers. Sometimes grandmother and child would talk about things they saw, but Nora understood that this gift of Sight was a thing best kept to herself. It made folks uneasy to have a little girl seeing things that weren't there—bad things, most of the time. The worst of it was that they would come to see these things, too, a few days or weeks later: a burned-out barn, a new grave, an empty cradle . . .

Did you see anything?

Nora shook her head.

"It's a sad thing to lose a child," said Grandma Flossie.

"Maybe Daddy and the dogs will bring her back safe."

"It's past two days now," said the old woman. She raised her hand for a solemn wave as the black truck seething with hounds eased its way past them. "Nights are cold out on the mountain in May."

"Are you telling the child about the lost youngun?" Nora's mother stood at the screen door, frowning at the pair of them. "Now don't go giving her nightmares! She's moony enough as it is. She might think she'll be taken off next."

"I'll stay close," Nora promised.

Grandma Flossie turned to look at her daughter-in-law. "Nora will be all right," she said.

"Well, of course, she will," said Nora's mother. "She wouldn't be fool enough to wander off in those woods. Besides, it isn't as if Nora was a stray, like that poor youngun at Stargill's, with her mother deserted by one man and dumped on his kinfolks' doorstep by the next one. If it had been me, I'd have gone north with Ashe Stargill, babies or no, instead of having to eat humble pie on the farm with that mama of his. I know they didn't take to Luray, but they had to accept her, on account of her having their grandson, and Ashe Stargill finally up and marrying her. But I can imagine how they feel about having the other one underfoot, with times as hard as they are now. I'm not casting blame, but I'll bet there were sighs of relief when that girl youngun ran off. Probably knew she wasn't wanted."

"Pray about it," said Grandma Flossie, "but don't scare this child here." She nodded toward Nora, who was twisting her pinafore, and looking as if she might cry.

When her mother was no longer a shadow in the doorway, Nora leaned over to her grandmother and whispered, "If those Stargills don't want that little girl, do you think we could find her and take her in?"

Flossie Bonesteel sighed. "I don't think your mother would take kindly to that, Nora, but she may be right about things at the Stargill place. And the Lord knows best. Perhaps the child will be happier . . . this way."

Nora heard the sorrowful tone and felt cold in the May sunshine. "Reckon what happened to her, Grandma?"

The old woman motioned for Nora to sit down beside her. She picked up another potato from the bucket and began to peel it as she talked. "I don't rightly know," she said softly. "But, I'll tell you what: the Cherokees that used to live in these hills told stories about people who got lost on the mountain. They would wander away from their villages, and never be seen again. Cherokees said that some of these mountains are hollow underneath, and that a race of little people called the Nunnehi live inside—only instead of being a dark cave underground, the rocks give way to a bright, beautiful land where it is always high summer."

"What do the little people look like?"

"I don't know that anybody has ever seen one, and come back to tell the tale, but the Indians thought they looked like little bitty Cherokees: copper-skinned, with long black hair. I always fancied that they had pointy ears, and cat-eyes, and hair like crow feathers, black and shiny. I never wanted to meet one, though. They say that if you go off with the Nunnehi, and visit their beautiful land, you will never be happy on earth again. Especially if you eat any of their food, you can never come home. But if you leave the earth to go and live with the little people, you never grow old, either."

"I'm glad you never went off with those little people," said Nora. "I'd sure miss you."

"Well, I reckon I might go one day," said her grandmother. "They are said to be kind to those that mean no harm. Someday when my rheumatism gets too bad to stand, and my eyes get to where I can't see my needle, and I get too tired to walk to meeting, I think I might just go calling on those little people, and stay awhile in that bright land of theirs. I'd like being young again in the summer of always. I reckon I'd miss you, too, Nora, but I wouldn't want you grieving to see me go. They say that those who dwell with the little people are forever glad."

"Do you think the little girl in the woods is glad?"

"Well, Nora, I think she is peaceful, and—and—that she will never be cold or hungry again. She will never grow old." Tears glistened on the old woman's cheeks. She brushed them away with the back of her hand, and went back to peeling potatoes.

Nora wondered why her grandmother was sad if the little girl was in such a beautiful and happy place with the little people. What a blessing never to be cold or hungry again. She put the thought out of her mind. Even when the men returned after dark that evening, penning up the muddy, exhausted hounds without a word or a smile, and ate a cold supper in silence, she did not wonder.

CHAPTER THREE

Were there a voice in the trees of the forest, it would call on you to chase away these ruthless invaders who are laying it to waste.

—SIMON GIRTY,
white adoptee of the Shawnee,
from *John Bradford's Historical Notes on Kentucky*

Even when he had no clients to chauffeur from one property to another, Frank Whitescarver spent a lot of time in his Jeep Cherokee, scouting the back roads of the county in search of suitable parcels of land. March was a good time for such expeditions. Dirt roads that had been rendered impassable by winter mud and ice were navigable again, and the still leafless trees provided a good view of the land and the vistas that could be seen from them. People these days seemed to care more about the land they could see from their property than they did about the property itself. In March the views were not blocked by foliage. March was not too bitterly cold for walks through the woods and along old logging trails to reach parcels without road frontage; and the snakes were not yet awake to prosecute trespassers into their domain.

Whitescarver tried to do his scouting in early March, so that when spring fever hit the prospective buyers, he could be ready with a good selection of properties to offer. Every spring, about the time the dogwoods bloomed and the Blue Ridge Parkway became clogged with cars from Charlotte, Knoxville, Roanoke, and all points in between, the upwardly-mobile gentlefolk of east Tennessee would start picking up the real estate brochures from the racks at Krogers and at local restaurants. They would look longingly at poetic ads for mountain land (Deer for neighbors in your own wilderness paradise . . . 360-degree view! Commuting distance to Johnson City, to East Tennessee State!). And they would call.

His real estate clients were mostly city people, although they would have said otherwise, and they all wanted the same thing, and would not get it, mainly because it was not available, but also because, Whitescarver knew, if he did provide them with what they asked for, they would hate it. "We want a little farm, Mr. Whitescarver," he was told by slender blondes in earth-tone cashmere sweaters. Their faces bore an earnest glow as they spoke of the noise and confinement of suburban life, of wanting room for the children to play without fear of traffic or strangers. He supposed they had been raised watching *The Waltons* and *Little House on the Prairie* in centrally heated split-levels in Greensboro or Lexington, and they dreamed of such an idyllic existence without having the least idea what it was like to live on a farm.

Their husbands, Professor This or Doctor That, would talk about land as a good investment, and mumble about wanting to do a little gardening. A subdivision did not fit their self-image: it diminished their status, lumped them into the herd of overachievers. They really wanted a fiefdom, a country estate that would proclaim their success by its very exclusiveness. Whitescarver would solemnly agree with all this piffle, and ferry them down muddy roads to a selection of brambled sites, overgrown with scrub pines because the mountain's valuable timber was always harvested for the thousands of dollars profit it would bring before the land was put up for sale. The prospective pioneers would wonder why the woods looked so meager, but they wouldn't ask the realtor, and he never told them.

As the city couple hiked through underbrush in search of the elusive view from the top—of more scrub pines—Whitescarver would affect his most genial country-boy drawl, while he advised his clients of the cost of running a paved road up the mountain so that one could get to work in winter. "Reckon you'll need a four-wheel like mine," he'd say with a chuckle. By the time he moved on to the hazards of well drilling, the expense of obtaining a power line, and the impossibility of getting cable television, the couple's L.L. Bean topsiders were caked with brown mud, and they had ceased to enthuse about the glories of country life, and they directed most of their attention to the ground, watching for the rattlesnakes Frank had casually mentioned.

Frank Whitescarver was an expert in gauging the exact psychological moment when the city couple had seen enough scrub land. Then they were ready to be taken to Boone's Mountain, an upscale subdivision of brick homes in styles ranging from Tudor to contemporary, all situated on carefully landscaped five-acre lots, with views, city water and power, paved streets, and cable—all for a mere $250,000 and up. Twenty-seven houses artfully arranged on one mountaintop—owned and developed by Frank Whitescarver himself. There were no lovely mountaintops to be had for a thousand dollars an acre, because when such land went up for sale, Frank bought it himself, carved it up into five-acre lots, selling for thirty thousand dollars apiece, and had his construction firm put up two dozen houses. For an outlay of a hundred thousand dollars, he could expect a profit of close to a million.

The would-be country gentry almost always found a house they liked at Boone's Mountain or Deer Meadow or one of his other planned communities. Here were people like themselves, who drove the right cars and played golf and had upscale careers of their own—and they weren't *too* close—five acres is a comfortable amount of living space between neighbors. By the time the husband said, "I suppose it isn't a subdivision really," it was time to produce the offer-to-purchase forms. The final deal clincher was Frank's casual remark as he handed over his ballpoint pen, "And, one thing about living here, folks, nobody's going to put a trailer up near your beautiful new home." Frank knew that *trailer park* was Yuppie-speak for leper colony. The gambit seldom failed him.

He parked his Jeep close to the ditch on an old logging trail, and got out to inspect the land. He saw a flock of Canada geese winging their way past the treetops, a sure sign of spring. The migrations had begun. Soon the subdivision people would catch a whiff of spring and begin their own migrations, and he would be ready.

He had lived in east Tennessee all his life, so he knew most of the old families: who was likely to sell, and who might be forced to sell by the death of a parent or because of financial hardship. He kept a close eye on the courthouse records, too. You never knew what might turn up. He would be needing some new land soon. It was time for the old pioneers to move on and make way for the new.

"You've never talked much about your family," said Kelley.

Charles Martin Stargill shrugged. "I wouldn't call us close," he said. He flipped off the radio, much to Kelley's relief. He always tuned it to a country station, and if they didn't play his record within a half hour, or if they played certain other people's records, Charles Martin would begin to tense up, and he'd frown, and sometimes forget to answer her when she asked him something. Sometimes, too, he drove to the tempo of the music, which terrified her, but she never complained about it, and she knew he wouldn't let her drive. The sudden silence made her unclench her fists and take a deep breath. It was better to talk.

They had decided that leaving at rush hour would have slowed them more than it was worth, and then Charles Martin got busy making phone calls, and rearranging things, so that it was past nine o'clock before he could approve Kelley's packing. By then he was tired, so they went to bed, then got up at five so that they could get through Nashville before the morning commute got in gear.

Kayla was asleep in the backseat, wrapped in an old quilt, and hugging Sally, the stuffed Steiff camel Charles Martin had brought her from a concert tour in Germany. She had fallen asleep just as they got on I-40 east in Nashville, lulled by the predawn darkness and the soft hum of the Lexus's engine. Now the ride would be a peaceful one, and Kelley didn't even want to stop for coffee for fear of waking the child.

Kelley cast about for something else to say before Charles Martin noticed the silence and turned the radio back on. "But you got the guitar from your family."

He nodded. "The rosewood prewar Martin. I swear I think I was named for it."

The guitar was in its case in the backseat, on the floor behind the driver's seat. Charles Martin always put it there, and he always warned Kayla not even to touch the case. Kelley didn't like to touch it, either. She knew that the guitar was worth thousands of dollars, and that it had been in the Stargill family for more than fifty years, but that wasn't what made her leery of the instrument. That guitar was like a part of Charles Martin, as if they were connected somehow, the way she'd heard that twins sometimes share feelings between them. He always knew where it was, and sometimes he'd take it out and rub the strings with a chamois cloth, as he was talking or watching television, stroking it as if it were a dog. She wasn't surprised that Charles Martin had brought the guitar with him, even if he had ho intention of playing a note while he was at the homeplace. If he left Nashville for more than a day, the rosewood Martin went with him. Nobody else was even allowed to touch the case.

"Was it your father's guitar?" she asked.

"My grandmother's. His mother. They say it skips a generation. People used to say that I got my musical ability from her. Daddy said that she knew all the old ballads, and that she could play just about any instrument she picked up, without ever having a music lesson, or knowing how to read a note."

"Was she a country singer, too?"

"No. The Carter family was a rarity back then. Mountain women generally didn't get careers in show business. The story is that she had a homemade guitar that sounded like two cats in heat, and my grandaddy gave her the Martin for a Christmas present one year, with money he earned on his logging job in Carter County. Or maybe he won it at poker in the logging camp. She gave it to me when I was four, because I was the only one of the younguns that could carry a tune. And she never did sing any more by then. Daddy said she quit a long time before I was born."

"You've had that guitar since you were four?" There wasn't a scratch on the gleaming rosewood, and the fretwork looked new.

"Not to play," he said. "Mommy put it up for me until I got older, for which I am eternally grateful to her, though they tell me I pitched a fit about it at the time. Thank goodness she didn't take the strings off, or put it in a trunk in the attic. She didn't even know it was worth anything, but she took care of it because it was a family treasure. Isn't it funny? I bet that guitar is worth more than Daddy's farm."

Clayt spent the night up at the farm, sleeping in his clothes on the sofa because he didn't have the energy to clean up an upstairs bedroom. It was probably knee deep in dust up there. Besides, he thought that one of his brothers would arrive any minute, and he wanted to be sure he heard their knocking so he could let them in. He half expected the hospital to call with news of his father's passing, but when he opened his eyes to the gray light of early morning, all was still quiet.

He put on a pot of coffee, hurrying to the front window every time he heard a car go by, but he ended up drinking three cups by himself, and pouring the rest down the sink. They hadn't tried to drive straight through, then. He took a shower before he remembered that he had brought no clean clothes to change into. His father's clothes were too small for him, but he took a clean pair of socks, and left his dirty ones in the hamper. He would have to go back to Jonesborough anyhow, though, because he had a school program that afternoon, and he needed his costume. He called the hospital, and was told that there was no change in Randall Stargill's condition.

"I'll be by later in the morning," Clayt told the nurse.

When Robert and Lilah reached the house at eleven, they found a note taped to the front door. "*Come on in,*" it said. "*Daddy is in the hospital, and I've gone to do a school program on Daniel Boone. Be back as soon as I can.—Clayt.*"

A semicircle of third graders looked up at the frontiersman with expressions that ranged from wariness to open delight. Hands waved in the air before he even began to speak, but their pretty young teacher shushed them and said that the visitor would answer questions when he finished.

"Hello, I'm Daniel Boone," said Clayt, leaning down to shake hands with a boy and a girl in the front row. "You're probably wondering how come I'm not wearing a coonskin cap, like you've seen in the movies. Well, the fact is, I never did wear one of those things. I considered myself a frontier gentleman. This hat I'm wearing is a Quaker-style beaver hat, like the kind folks wore when I was growing up—in Quaker Pennsylvania. This buckskin shirt and the leggings and moccasins are my frontier outfit, good clothes to hunt in. I usually carry a big knife in my belt, but Mrs. Sampson here didn't think the principal would care too much for that." He made a sad face. "She wouldn't let me bring my long rifle, either."

There was a ripple of laughter from the nine-year-olds, and he knew that they would listen now. The lesson could begin. A straight-backed wooden chair had been provided for him, but Clayt knew better than to sit down while trying to hold the attention of a room full of kids. He rested one foot on the seat of the chair and leaned forward, relaxed, as if he were telling tales at a campfire. He had to transport them back to frontier Tennessee, make them forget that they were sitting in a glass and cinder-block classroom with computers on the tables behind them.

"Bet you thought I was born in a log cabin in Kentucky, but I wasn't. I was born in a proper wooden house in eastern Pennsylvania in the year 1734. America was still a colony of Great Britain in those days, and my father had come over from England as a young man about twenty years before I was born, hoping to make his fortune in the new world. My parents were Quakers, and, like most everybody else in the community, they were farmers. I didn't want to be a farmer, though." He grinned at them. "I didn't like school too much, either. Schooling and farming interfered with my hunting. But I sure did love to read. I used to take a book with me to the woods on my long hunts. I went on my first one when I was sixteen. We left eastern Pennsylvania, which was downright civilized in 1750, and we headed for the back country, where it was wi-ild!" He roared the last word and stooped down to give his audience a mock grimace. "Where it was primitive! Where it was downright dan-ger-ous!"

He waited a moment while they shivered in anticipation.

"Where do you-uns think I went?"

Nobody ventured a guess.

"Why, right here!" he roared at them.

He let the shock sink in for five heartbeats before he continued.

"Right here in east Tennessee! I didn't get here right away, of course. Place as dangerous as this, you have to work up to it. First place the Boone clan settled was in Bedford County, Virginia, which is about the anklebone of the Blue Ridge, and then we went on to a farm near the Yadkin River in North Carolina. From there I hunted all the way into Tennessee, stayed gone months at a time. There were a lot of deer in these mountains then. And elk. And bear. And buffalo." He peered down at the pinkest blond girl. "You ever eat buffalo?"

She gaped at him for a moment, then slowly shook her head.

"Well, you ought'a try it. It's better for you than cow's meat. Lean. Yes, there was a lot of game in these mountains. It was the common hunting ground of the Cherokee, the Shawnee, and the Catawba, and they didn't take too kindly to outsiders coming in and shooting their game. I figured there was enough for everybody, though, so I camped up in the mountains, sometimes near what folks now call Boone, North Carolina, and I hunted all winter. A time or two I'd meet up with Cherokee or Shawnee, but they never hurt me. They'd just take my pelts, and let me go."

He grew solemn. "That's not to say it wasn't perilous to wander these mountains. One of the great sorrows of my life happened right near here, in the Powell Valley, close to where Tennessee, Virginia, and North Carolina all come together.

"It was 1773, after I had married Rebecca Bryan, and some of our children were most nigh grown. We were headed out to Kentucky with a group of pioneers to found a settlement, a whole caravan of loaded packhorses and livestock, and women and children—families going to Kentucky to start a new life. It wasn't a wagon train, mind you, like you see in the western movies. The trail to Kentucky was just a one-man trail over the mountains and through deep woods—we'd have to go single file a good part of the way. So we put our goods in hickory baskets slung over a packsaddle—and younguns littler than you folks would ride in one, too—and we aimed to walk all the way to Kentucky—going slow and noisy—through Indian country.

"Kentucky was a far piece away in those days—beyond the pale of civilization. We were glad to go but sad about leaving some of our loved ones behind. I saw my mother for the last time when we set off on that journey.

"But there was more sorrow to come.

"We got to about here—near what's now Gate City, Virginia, when I began to think we hadn't brought enough provisions. I sent my son James and some of his friends ahead of us to Castle's Wood to get extra supplies for the journey from Captain Russell there. They couldn't have been more than a couple of miles ahead of us, but that's a long way in a dark and savage wilderness. He was sixteen years old, that's all he was. We didn't even hear them scream."

He took a deep breath, waiting for his words to sink in, while he sized up his wide-eyed audience. They were too young for details, he decided. Horror movies were one thing, but this was a true story that had happened nearby, no matter how long ago: this was the stuff of nightmares. Clayt had them himself often enough when he first read the account of the killing of James Boone and his party.

"While they were asleep that night, a party of Delawares, and maybe some Shawnee and a Cherokee called Big Jim, ambushed them, and hurt them pretty bad." One of Captain Russell's slaves got away into the forest and was able to observe all that happened next. The young men were shot, slashed with knives, and then tortured. The nails of their fingers and toes were torn out, the agony drawn out until they begged for a quick death. James called out for his mother. Such terrible details were more than these youngsters needed to hear, two hundred and twenty-two years later, on a bright sunny morning.

"They were dead before morning. Captain Russell's men buried the bodies, putting two in each grave. The next spring I went back alone, and I dug up that grave, and buried my boy separately, and said words over him. The rest of the party lost interest in Kentucky after that tragedy. They turned around and headed back to North Carolina, but my family didn't go back. Rebecca and I stayed the winter in a little cabin on the Clinch River. We were going to Kentucky.

"You know, I was acquainted with Big Jim, the Cherokee that tortured my son. I'd met him before on one of my long hunts, and I'd meet him again, thirteen years later. I saw him killed and scalped by some of my own men, but it wasn't me that dispatched him off to the Hereafter. I never did hate the Indian people, like some of the settlers did. Even after what happened to my boy, I still respected them, and I called one or two of them friend. They were only protecting their land—land that was given to them in a treaty by the king of England—and they figured on teaching trespassers a lesson when they killed James and his friends. I might have done the same, if I was protecting what was mine. Land is a powerful thing. City people may have forgotten what it is to be one with the land, but the rest of us feel it, pulling us back like the current in that big Clinch River.

"That's why I was going to Kentucky, you know. It wasn't just to get away from big cities and fancy society. It was because all the land in the east was already taken. I wanted land. And the Shawnee and the Cherokee wanted it, too. We wanted it the same way—not like the folks back east who wanted it as an investment, but would never set foot on it. I wanted land that I could belong to, more than the other way around. I guess I had more in common with those Shawnees and Cherokees than I did with my own people. . . ."

He came to himself then, and remembered that he was talking to Mrs. Sampson's third grade class, and that this wasn't the side of Daniel Boone they needed to hear about on first acquaintance. He reserved history's complexities for high school students and adult groups. Clayt paused for a moment, and smiled at the puzzled children to ease the tension. "'Course the Indians didn't beat me all the time, neighbors. Why, one time in Kentucky, they kidnapped my daughter Jemima and two of her friends out of a boat, and it took me all afternoon to get her back!"

Robert Lee tore his brother's note off the front door of the farmhouse. "If that isn't just like Clayt!" he told Lilah. "He goes off and leaves the door unlocked with a note on the door. Why not just invite the burglars to a yard sale? Put up signs along the highway, why don't he?"

"Well, Robert, I don't suppose your poor old father had much in there that would be worth stealing," said Lilah. She didn't think Clayt had showed good sense, either, but there was no point in letting Robert get all worked up about it. Rage always made Robert Lee dyspeptic, so she tried to soothe him as best she could. No use having to drive twenty miles for Pepto Bismol.

"What we have worth stealing is not the point, Lilah. This carelessness just goes to show how hopeless Clayt is. He doesn't think. Lives in his own rosy little world. Besides, Mother had some nice dishes that Daddy got her from overseas, and her good Oneida silverplate. You want to see them sold in some pawn-shop in Johnson City?"

Lilah shook her head. "You have enough on your mind with your daddy's illness, without getting all upset about a burglary." She couldn't help adding, ". . . which didn't happen."

"We might as well go in and make ourselves at home," muttered Robert. "Knowing Clayt, he's probably left a mess of dishes and dirty laundry for you to do."

The pronoun was not lost on Lilah. She sighed. Just her luck to be the first one here, even though the other two lived hours closer to east Tennessee. Still, she supposed that the other Stargill women wouldn't be much use, anyhow. Charles Martin had him a sweet young thing that they hadn't even met yet—probably a model or some gal trying to be the next Crystal Gayle. A lot of help she'd be—all press-on nails and hair mousse. And Garrett's wife, Debba, had about as much gumption as wet Kleenex. It would be faster to do the work yourself than to follow around behind her, telling her every single thing. And Rudy had better not come out with any angelic homilies about the virtue of good works, either, because after a long drive and a lumpy motel bed, she was in no mood for it.

Robert Lee opened the door for her and went to get the bags out of the car, so Lilah went in by herself, feeling a little odd to be there alone for the first time in her life. She had never really felt comfortable in the home of Robert's parents. They were always carefully polite, but she always felt their indifference. She was as much a stranger after twenty-five years as she had been as a bride.

The Stargill homeplace was not considered fancy when it was built, but now with its high ceilings, fireplaces, hardwood floors, and solid plaster walls, it would be a showplace if anybody could be bothered to fix it up. Randall Stargill never had. Anyhow, the place was kept in decent repair, and it was big enough. They had large families a century ago when the wood frame house was built. The front hall, with oak flooring and wainscotting, contained the stairs and doorways leading left to the living room and right to a sitting room and Randall's bedroom, which had been a dining room in the days when a large farm family gathered there for hot, noisy dinners. The kitchen was a long narrow room stretching across the back of the ground floor. The big iron range had been gone nearly half a century, replaced by a small white gas stove and a refrigerator. No need anymore to store perishable food in the earthen icehouse built into the hill out back.

Upstairs there were four bedrooms, unused for a decade or more. When the Stargill boys had grown up and gone, Randall and Clarsie had closed off the unheated upstairs, turning the dining room into a bedroom, as age and infirmity shrunk their territory into three dingy rooms.

"This place feels hollow," Lilah said aloud.

Although the rooms looked just the same as always, with nothing out of place, Lilah could feel the emptiness. The house was a box with some furniture in it now; nothing more. It was not a home, not the boys' home, and not even Randall's any more. She felt that. Randall Stargill had left it not only physically, but spiritually, she thought, leaving not even a spark of feeling behind him. Perhaps the spark of feeling had not been there to begin with, and it was only now that she had the solitude to notice it.

"Well, it's not as bad as I expected," said Robert Lee as he set the bags down beside the sofa.

"We haven't been upstairs yet," Lilah reminded him.

"Lord, I can picture it." Robert shuddered. "I hope the vacuum cleaner still works. You know how my dust allergies act up. I say everybody ought to have to clean his own room. Clayt won't have done it, that's for sure."

"Clayt had quite enough to worry about with your dad taken ill," said Lilah. "He doesn't live here, either, you know."

Robert scowled. "I don't suppose there's any food in the house, either."

"I don't suppose Clayt would know what to buy," said Lilah. "People's eating habits are so peculiar these days. Clayt's a vegetarian—or he was, last we heard, and who knows what Charles Martin and his friend will be wanting? Besides, we'll be eating out mostly, won't we?"

Robert pursed his lips. "This is Wake County, hon. What restaurants there are fry everything in lard. I'm not risking my arteries on down-home cooking."

Lilah correctly interpreted this to mean that Robert did not want to bear the expense of an indefinite span of restaurant meals. She supposed she would have to draw up a grocery list for him, and she might as well put Pepto Bismol on the list, because she could see it coming. Robert always got nervous when he went home. She thought it would be different with the old man in a coma, but apparently the habit of anxiety was too ingrained for Robert to break it now. Robert was the oldest, and he felt that any success enjoyed by his younger brothers was a reproach to him for not being more successful. The old man hadn't helped matters any, either. He would listen to Robert's recital of small triumphs with an expression of polite disinterest, then say something like, "Salesman of the month, huh, Robert? That's real nice. You know, Charles Martin wrote to me the other day from Rome, Italy. He's doing a concert over there this month. Sent me a picture of himself with Loretta Lynn at the Opry—got her to sign it to me, too. You want to see it?" Or Garrett would have done something heroic in his helicopter, or Clayt caught a three-pound brook trout last week. She wondered if Randall Stargill's reaction was calculated to wound his eldest son, or if he honestly didn't realize the pain he caused. She wondered if the other boys had their egos deflated by the old man in similar hurtful exchanges. Perhaps she would ask them, if she ever got the chance.

Clayt Stargill was tired. He had finished his Daniel Boone presentation around three, and without changing out of his pioneer costume, he'd driven straight to the hospital to check on his father. There was no change. The old man slept peacefully, impervious to hospital routine—and to visitors. After twenty minutes of silence in the sterile beige room, Clayt felt that he had postponed the family reunion as long as he could, so he left.

When he got back to the Stargill homeplace at five, he saw his brothers' cars: two in the gravel driveway and one in the side yard, far enough from the road to be safe from vandals, and far enough from the other cars to be in no danger from scrapes when they backed out. That would be Charles Martin's car, of course.

It was easy to tell which car belonged to each of them. Robert Lee's was the newest make of his dealership, but not the most expensive model, and it was a fishy green color that probably didn't appeal to most of the customers. Clayt wondered if Robert had chosen the car, or it if had been foisted off on him by the dealership.

Charles Martin had a silver Lexus. Befitting his image of the successful celebrity. He probably had something a little more rugged in his garage when photo opportunities called for a down-home look, but the Lexus suited him. Charles Martin had always been very shrewd about tailoring his image. Clayt remembered reading an interview once in a country music magazine in which his brother had said, "I think the Chieftains' *Long Black Veil* album is one of the finest I've ever heard. I have that CD in every one of my cars."

Now, on the face of it, the remark was a generous compliment to fellow musicians, but Clayt thought it no accident that the reader was also left with the very clear message that Charles Martin Stargill was so successful that he owned a fleet of cars, each with its own CD player. A simple statement about someone else's album was turned into a plug for Charles Martin. The shiny silver Lexus said style, success, and affluence. Clayt wondered if it was anywhere close to being paid for.

The third vehicle, a black Blazer, belong to Chief Warrant Officer Garrett Stargill, U.S. Army, a fact attested to by the 101st Airborne bumper sticker and the Fort Campbell parking decal. Rugged and sensible: that was Garrett, all right. His wife was another matter. Clayt couldn't imagine what she would drive. It would have to be something feminine and yet utterly safe: perhaps a pink Sherman tank.

Clayt parked his '78 four-wheeler behind the Lexus. He noticed that Dovey's car was not there, but then, he didn't blame her for not wanting to be around at this stage. First the four brothers would have to talk, and then, after the dust settled, they could be neighborly.

Before Clayt was even out of the truck, Garrett came out, letting the screen door bang behind him. "We were going to the hospital," he said, leaning down, as Clayt rolled down the driver's side window.

"I just came from there," Clayt told him. "Daddy's in a coma, but holding his own. He won't know you're there."

"Maybe he will," said Garrett.

"We need to talk about some things," said Clayt. "He left instructions."

"Save it," said Garrett. "The rest of us have had long drives, and worrying about Daddy's health comes first. Then we'll have a business meeting. How about later tonight, when we get back from Johnson City. If you don't mind the late hours. You have any place to go early tomorrow morning?"

"Tomorrow? No."

Garrett Stargill grinned. "Didn't figure you would."

Nora Bonesteel didn't know what had awakened her. It hadn't been a sound. More like a feeling that something was there. She sat up in the old iron bedstead and strained her eyes looking into the shadows. The curtains were drawn, and the nightlight from the hall did not quite reach into the corners of her room. Something was there. No use to turn the light on for what had come.

She blinked herself into full wakefulness and stared in the direction from which she felt the presence. After a moment she saw Randall Stargill standing at the foot of the bed, looking lost and bewildered. He didn't seem to see her. He just stared at nothing, with round eyes and a haunted look. He stood stooped and gaunt in a hospital gown as white as his hair, looking around as if he had been sleepwalking and found himself in a strange place far from his bed. In a way, that was what had happened.

Nora leaned forward, clutching the counterpane at her throat. After a moment she said softly, "You're not dead, Randy. It's time to go back. Go on now."

He seemed to hear her words. After one imploring look, the presence faded, and Nora knew that she was alone again in her little house on Ashe Mountain. She turned on the bedside lamp, wide awake now. Randall was in a hospital somewhere, and hadn't long to live from the look of him, but her thoughts were not about the baking of a pound cake for the family, or even about her own sense of sorrow at losing one more link with her own past. Randall had been trying to tell her something.

She opened the drawer of her nightstand, and took out a well-worn Bible. She thought she knew what Randall's message to her had been, but she knew that listening to him would cause trouble and sorrow to his family, and perhaps to herself as well. "Take this cup away from me, Lord," whispered Nora, and she put her hand flat on the cover of the Bible.

Even people who call it a superstition resort to Bible cracking if they have nowhere else to turn, and Nora had never doubted that questions sincerely asked were always answered. Nora's ancestors in Britain had petitioned their god with just such a ritual, and even the medieval church had used a variant of the custom in the ordination of bishops. Ask and you shall receive.

"What shall I do?" whispered Nora. She closed her eyes, took a deep breath, opened the book, and put her finger down on a verse at random. She had to take out her reading glasses to read the fine print. Her finger rested on two verses of the seventy-ninth psalm: *Wherefore should the heathen say, Where is their God? Let him be known among the heathen in our sight by the revenging of the blood of thy servants which is shed.*

Let the sighing of the prisoner come before thee; according to the greatness of thy power preserve thou those that are appointed to die.

She laid the book aside, satisfied that she had received her answer, although it was not the one she had hoped for. She must do what Randall required of her, come morning, and if all hell broke loose in Hamelin because of it, then that must be what heaven wanted.

CHAPTER FOUR

She is by nature a quiet soul, and of few words. She told me of her trouble, and the frequent distress and fear in her heart.

—Moravian missionary George Soelle,
describing Rebecca Boone

"This is just like every other family gathering I've ever been to," said Lilah Rose, pouring herself another glass of iced tea. "Men in one room, women in the other."

"Women in the *kitchen,*" said Kelley, and they both laughed. "Of course, I wouldn't go in there anyway, not being family, but you two are, so if you want to go on in there with your husbands, please don't mind me. I need to check on Kayla soon anyhow."

"Oh, that child went to sleep as soon as her head hit the pillow," said Lilah. "Don't you worry about her. And I don't suppose we'd be too welcome in there, family or no. They'd probably send us back in here to make coffee for them."

Debba Stargill turned her pale face toward the young mother. "Aren't you afraid to leave the little thing alone up there?"

"Kayla? Oh, she can sleep through anything," said Kelley. "When she was two, there was a neon sign that used to flash on the bedroom window, and trucks went by all night on the highway, so she learned not to be fussy about where she slept. As long as she has her stuffed camel, she's all right. I just look in on her to make sure she doesn't kick the covers off."

Debba shivered. "I don't know if I can sleep in this house," she whispered. "I hope we don't have to stay long."

"It looks okay to me," said Kelley. "It could use a good cleaning, and a lick of paint here and there, but the woodwork is beautiful. I want to walk around outside tomorrow, and look at the mountains."

"I heard they released wolves into the mountains somewhere around here," said Debba.

"Oh, wolves never hurt anybody," said Lilah, who had no patience with vapory women. "They weren't timber wolves, anyhow. They're some little doggy kind of wolf that used to live up here before people trapped them all to death. I read about it in one of the park guides I found at a rest stop. It says they only released a dozen or so, and they're so shy you'd be lucky to ever catch a glimpse of one. I think they have little collars on to make sure that people don't hurt them. Sure is a far cry from olden times, isn't it? Now we have to protect the wolves from the people. The way I see it, you're a lot safer here than you would be back in Nashville."

Kelley smiled. "There sure are some wolves in Nashville, all right. I dated a few of them." She added hastily, "But Charles Martin isn't one of them!"

"Well, there are certainly wild bears out in these woods," said Debba. "And wasps, and poison ivy, and maybe moonshiners, for all I know. People do get killed in the forest these days, I don't care what century it is. Just don't let your little girl stray too far from the house."

"She'll be fine," said Lilah. "I'll ask Rudy to keep an eye on her."

"Who is Rudy?" asked Kelley, wondering if there was an extra brother Charles Martin had neglected to mention.

"Why, Rudy is my guardian angel," said Lilah. "Of course, I just call him *Sir*." She smiled modestly as the two women stared at her. People always did seem to expect an explanation when she mentioned Rudy. But this time was the exception. Debba and Kelley looked at each other, and then turned away.

"I have to go unpack," said Debba softly, and she hurried from the kitchen before anyone could reply.

Kelley stood up, but she was smiling. "And I have to go check on Kayla, but, hey, you thank your angel for me, okay? I'd be real glad to know that he's looking out for her." One thing about being an item with a country music star: she had sure gotten used to being around strange people. After a while they started to seem just like everybody else.

In the dimly lit parlor, Clayt Stargill was hunched under the circle of light of the table lamp, reading the sheaf of yellow lined paper to his older brothers. "All I can figure is, he seems to have gone all traditional in his old age," he told them.

"He's lost his reason," said Robert Lee. Even though the television was not turned on, he sat facing it squarely, as was his custom at home. "We didn't do any of this when Mother passed away. She had a proper burial in a new metal casket from Graybeal's, and there was none of this foolishness about salt and covered mirrors. It's pagan is what it is."

"I think a man is entitled to face death on his own terms," said Garrett.

"It could have been worse," said Charles Martin, smiling. He was cradling the Martin in his lap, occasionally strumming a soft chord as he listened to his brothers. "Daddy once said he wanted me to get Johnny Cash to sing 'Peace in the Valley' at his funeral. Uh, that's not in there, is it?"

Clayt grinned. "Wish it was, Charlie, but the answer is no. Guess you'll get to provide the music yourself, with Grandmaw's old guitar, there. He wants an old hymn that he calls 'Just Beyond the Eastern Gate.' Ever heard of it?"

Charles Martin shrugged. "I can ask around."

"You might try some of the old-timers around here. I've read Daddy's list of instructions three times now, and, aside from that song, he doesn't have much to say about the service itself. He picks out odd little things that he wants done, and he mentions them as he thought of them, I guess. In no particular order. Take this one here—a scripture cake. Anybody know what a scripture cake is?"

They shook their heads. "We don't cook," said Robert Lee.

"Well, maybe one of the—uh—wives will know." Clayt glanced at Charles Martin as he hesitated over the word "wives," but Charles Martin had not seemed to notice his awkwardness. "We can ask them tomorrow, I guess. I think they're all upstairs."

"What about Dovey, Clayt?" asked Garrett. "Are you two friends again? You said she made the tuna fish. Seems like she knows her way around a kitchen and is willing to put herself out for you."

Clayt reddened and looked back at the papers in his hand. "Dovey was just being neighborly, that's all. Let's get back to the instructions here. Like I said, Daddy isn't much on choreographing his own funeral, but he's most particular about the coffin. Listen to this: *I have got some seasoned rosewood laid by in the barn loft, and it would suit as the wood for a proper coffin. I want you boys to use the old woodshop in the back of the barn and work together to build me a proper casket. Do it right, boys. I want brass handles, dovetailed joins, and the best woodcraft you can manage among you. I have taught you all the craft of woodworking, and it is not a skill you lose so I expect you can do a fine job if you set your mind to it and take pains with your work. I have a mind to leave this world in a homemade coffin.*" Clayt broke off. "Well, he goes on like that for a bit more. Rambling-like."

"It would take weeks to build a hand-finished casket of rosewood!" said Robert Lee. "Where does he think we'll find the time to do that? I don't know about you boys, but I have a responsible position in Cincinnati. I can't drop everything while I sit up here on a mountain whittling."

"What kind of tools are we supposed to use?" asked Charles Martin, looking at his manicured hands. "I don't know that I want to be around band saws and such. If anything happens to these hands of mine, I lose my whole career. Can't pick a guitar with your elbow."

"I think we could do it in a week," said Garrett. "It's just a big box. Why don't we look at the wood tomorrow, and see if it's any good, and if the tools are still in usable condition. Then we can decide what to do next."

"We may not even need a coffin," said Clayt. "He's a tough old man, Daddy is. He may pull through."

His brothers frowned at him.

"Well, we will certainly pray that he recovers," said Robert Lee, "but that eventuality will only postpone the inevitable. Someday we are going to have to come to terms with Daddy's last requests, be it now or later. There's something else we have to consider, too. Clayt, what does he say about the farm?"

"What about the farm?"

"Well—who gets it? Or how is it to be divided up among us?"

"There's nothing in here about that," said Clayt, handing him the sheaf of papers. "I guess he's leaving it up to us."

"He probably didn't think it was worth much," said Garrett. "I remember Grandmommy saying once that land up here used to go for fifty dollars an acre. It's too steep to be much good for farming."

"It's worth a lot more than that now," Robert Lee said. "People don't buy land anymore. They buy views. And this farm certainly has plenty of scenic vistas. Rich people put vacation homes in high places like this. Why, Highlands, North Carolina, is a veritable nest of millionaires, living on land just as steep as this farm, and they're willing to pay a fortune for the acreage. A for-tune."

"I could ask around in Nashville," said Charles Martin. "Maybe somebody's looking for a summer place, though they mostly like to stay within driving distance of Nashville. Vince and Reba probably wouldn't be interested, being from Oklahoma. They like wide open spaces, and these woody hills might make them nervous, but I could check with Randy. This strikes me as his kind of place."

"Just hold on," said Clayt. "Daddy isn't even cold yet. It's a little too early to be divvying up the property, don't you think? Besides, you all seem to take it as a foregone conclusion that we'll sell out."

"We're not farmers, Clayt," said Garrett. "None of us is going to chuck in a promising career to come home and tend cornfields on a hardscrabble farm. Maybe you would—until you found out what hard work it is being a farmer. But the rest of us can out-vote you."

"Clayt's right, though," said Charles Martin, yawning. "Daddy is still hanging in there, so it's too early to talk about this—and too late. Must be nearly midnight. I, for one, am wore out. Let's get some sleep and squabble tomorrow."

Lilah was alone in the corner bedroom, too sleepy to read, but not yet ready to turn out the light. Robert hadn't come upstairs yet.

The room still had the musty smell of a place that had been closed and unheated for many months, but it was newly swept, and the bed linens were fraying with age, but they were clean. She felt no sense of menace about the room. Like the rest of the house it seemed quite empty of feeling. The faded roses on the wallpaper, the rag rug on the old pine floor, and the simple oak dresser and nightstand were neither cozy nor frightening to her. *Not much living has gone on here*, Lilah thought. *I wonder whose room this was*.

She and Robert were next door to Garrett and Debba. At the top of the stairs was a square hallway, and leading off from it left and right were two narrow passageways to the bedrooms. Down the right-hand passage, Charles Martin and Kelley occupied the room next to the cupboardlike bedroom that was little Kayla's. It was barely big enough for the single bed, its only furnishing. Anyone remodeling the house would convert that cubbyhole into a bathroom for the adjoining bedroom. Lilah supposed that people would talk about Charles Martin and Kelley staying together in the same room, what with them not being married and all, and Robert Lee would likely be high on the list of complainers, but she thought that everyone would ignore him. They usually did. She herself didn't plan to object, and Rudy the angel was, as ever, unconcerned with other people's doings, so that was all right. Charles Martin's sleeping arrangements were none of her business, and she figured that folks ought to know what show business people were like by now and not be shocked by a little thing like the lack of a marriage license. Besides, they all had enough to worry about with poor Daddy Stargill on his last legs, and all the business about the property to see to, without worrying about two grown people sleeping together without having the necessary paperwork.

She had been married to Robert Lee now for thirty years and then some, and she didn't honestly feel that their union was all that much more sanctified than that of Charles and his redhead. People either loved each other or they didn't, and you couldn't legislate feelings, though sometimes she surely did wish you could.

Rudy was no help on that score, either. He declined to discuss Robert Lee or to listen to Lilah's thoughts on the matter, even when she had tried, a time or two, to disguise them as prayers. Rudy once said, "What man has joined together, let no god put asunder," and that had been his final word on the subject. Rudy wasn't interested in Robert Lee, or in politics, wars, air pollution, or much of anything as far as Lilah could tell. Maybe there were other angels handling those things. Rudy's mission was Lilah, and he was never tempted to stray from that purpose. "Just don't get all depressed on me, Lilah child," he would often tell her. "Because despair is a sin. And, let me tell you, it's just as boring as ditch water to watch, too, honey."

So she stayed busy and tried to be a good person, and she made up her mind to take care of her husband, in case he didn't have an angel of his own. Robert Lee was a good man, and there had been a time when he was young that he had been happier—pleased to have a steady job in the big city, though he couldn't actually bring himself to live there. So they had settled in Batavia, not far from Hillbilly Highway, as the Cincinnatians called Rt. 32, on account of so many mountain people traveled back and forth that way, needing the work in the city, but wishing every minute that they could go home to the mountains. Robert Lee didn't go home much, especially after he met her at the church mixer and they started courting serious. He seemed to quit the mountains cold turkey, like someone hooked on a killing drug, and if he ever longed for home in the springtime, when the Tennessee hills were ablaze with white flowers while Cincinnati was still gray with asphalt and steel, he didn't let on. He had told her once that living in the mountains was living poor, and Robert Lee was flat out determined to outrun, outwork, and outlive *poor*.

He had been so proud of their first new car and their mortgaged-to-the-rain-gutters brick house with carport. He wasn't a handsome man, even at twenty-four, but he had been kind, in a hang-back sort of way, as if he just expected people to take against him right off the bat. Not used to a city full of strangers, Lilah thought back then. He'll come around. But being in car sales hadn't helped his people-shyness any. Years of contempt from suspicious customers had driven him so deep inside himself that not even Lilah could reach him any more. Now he was past fifty, the beginning of knowing that a lot of your dreams are just flat *never* coming true, and the bitterness of that, coupled with his fear that being poor would catch up with him in his old age, in spite of all his efforts to outdistance it, had just curdled any joy or sorrow he might have felt about anything. He would not be comforted. All Lilah could do was love him as best she could. For Robert, it was not enough, but it seemed to be all he could expect to receive in this world of tribulation.

She knelt on the cold oak floor beside the bed and began her nightly devotions, a ritual she kept unchanged since childhood, beginning: "Matthew, Mark, Luke and John, bless the bed I lie upon. Four posters round my bed; four angels round my head . . ." It was the rote prayer of her Baptist girlhood, but she never really felt that she was praying unless she began with those hastily spoken syllables. She would pray for guidance for Robert Lee. Rudy always said that worrying was spinning your wheels in neutral, but praying was third gear.

The others had gone to bed, but Clayt couldn't sleep. He was still sitting in the circle of light cast by the brass table lamp, rereading his father's scrawled testament, as if it would rearrange itself if he stared at it long enough. What a fool thing he was asking of them: to be cooped up together, building a coffin, for well nigh onto a week, when he knew full well the four of them hadn't done much more than pass the time of day since they were teenagers.

"Are you really Daniel Boone?" said a tiny voice from the hall doorway.

In spite of himself, Clayt nearly jumped a foot, and his heart pounded through his sweatshirt like a trip-hammer. A little girl in a long white nightgown stood in the doorway, watching him with old and solemn eyes. Her fair hair was tousled from sleep, and she was clutching a stuffed animal in her arms. Then he remembered this was the daughter of Charlie's girlfriend. He couldn't recall her name.

"What are you doing up, little one?" he asked her, keeping his voice low. "Don't you know it's past midnight?"

She came forward, not as shy as he expected a small child to be, and peered up into his face. "Are you Daniel Boone?"

"Oh, you must have heard the grown-ups talking about me this afternoon." Clayt patted the sofa cushion beside him, motioning for her to sit down. "Well, no, the truth is I am not Daniel Boone. Old Daniel has been dead since 1820—that's about a hundred and seventy-five years. I just pretend to be him sometimes, with a costume and all."

"Why?"

"Well, because he used to live around these parts, and he loved the land, same as I do. He was the most famous pioneer there ever was. And because I think children here should learn about him when they're young, so when they hear all that hillbilly nonsense about mountain people later in life, they'll have words inside themselves to fight it with." He was talking more to himself than to her. Then he smiled. "You know, you standing there with that stuffed camel in your arms puts me in mind of a Daniel Boone story right now."

She perched on the edge of the sofa, and looked up at him with solemn gray eyes, too old for her face. "Okay. Tell me."

"Now this story happened when Daniel was a young man, not yet twenty, living over in North Carolina near the forks of the Yadkin River. He was courting Miss Rebecca Bryan in those days, and one night he went out hunting in the woods with her father, Mr. Jim Bryan, who had a log cabin and a little farm there on the river. They were going out hunting painters—mountain lions, you'd probably call them."

The child nodded. "I seen pictures."

"The mountain lions were bold that year, carrying off a newborn calf or a lamb, without a by-your-leave. And they hunted at night.

"So Daniel and Mr. Jim Bryan got their long rifles and a pan of hot, glowing wood coals, and they went out hunting painters. Now the reason for the wood coals was this: a cat's eyes will glow in the dark if there's the least little bit of light to be reflected in them. So the hunters would hold up those glowing coals, and the light would shine in the mountain lion's eyes, and then the hunter would shoot—bang!—right between those two glowing circles of eyes, and he'd kill that lion.

"Well, they bagged quite a few that night, and they were headed home in the dark, with the big cats' bodies slung across the packhorse for skinning later, when they got almost back to the cabin, and here was another pair of green eyes shining up ahead of them in the trees. Before you could say 'painter,' Daniel Boone had slung that rifle up on his shoulder, and blam! He shot right straight at those glowing eyes.

"And then he heard the crying. He and Mr. Bryan went running through the thickets, following the sound of that crying, and what do you think they found?"

Kayla shook her head. She was hugging the toy camel as she listened. Clayt reached out and touched the furry head of the toy. "You holding your friend there is what reminded me of the story," he told her. "What Daniel found in the clearing was pretty, dark-haired Rebecca Bryan herself, hugging the dead body of her pet kitten, but she wasn't hurt at all, thank goodness. Daniel would have taken it hard if he'd harmed Rebecca, because he was already thinking about making her his wife. What he shot wasn't a mountain lion at all, you see. Just a little old house cat, with its eyes shining in the darkness.

"Rebecca cried all the way home, and Daniel had to do a lot of apologizing to get himself out of that mess. But I guess he got her to forgive him, because not two years later, she did marry Daniel, and the two of them had a lot of children and a lot of adventures in the fifty-seven years they were together."

"Is that long?" asked the girl.

"I bet it could seem so," said Clayt. "But I like to think they were happy." He smiled at her solemn expression. "Now, miss, I've answered a passel of your questions, and told you a bedtime story to boot, so the least you owe me is a ready answer to a question of mine. How come you to be up at this hour? Mountain lion under the bed?"

She laughed, and shook her head.

"You're not scared, are you, sleeping in a strange house?"

"Nope. I'm not particular where I sleep. Why? Is this place haunted?"

Clayt shrugged. "When we were real little, my brother Dwayne used to swear he saw a little girl walking around upstairs sometimes, but I don't think I ever believed him. Until tonight," he said, smiling. "You're not her, are you?"

"No, 'cause ghosts don't eat, and I'm hungry."

Clayt hesitated. Storytelling was the extent of his child care skills. "You want me to get your mamma for you?"

"She's asleep with Charlie, and their door is locked. I'm not supposed to wake 'em up. Can't you fix food?"

"Well—I guess I could." Clayt roused himself from the sofa, stifling a yawn and stretching. "If you're not too awful hard to please. I might even join you. What'd you say your name was, again?"

"Kayla Louise Johnson. And if you're not Daniel Boone, what do I call you?"

"Why, I reckon I'm your Uncle Clayt, Miss Johnson. Pleased to make your acquaintance."

"And that's your job? Playact being Daniel Boone?"

He escorted her to the kitchen. "Oh, I do a lot of things. I can guide a raft through the white water of the Nolichucky River, and I can tell birds from the sound they make, and I can track a deer through the woods and take his picture without him ever knowing I'm there. I guess if Daniel Boone were around these days, he'd be doing pretty much what I'm doing. Trying to keep out of a necktie and an office."

"How come y'all don't sing with Charlie?"

"Well, sometimes we do. Or we used to. Sitting around on the porch of an evening."

Kayla shook her head. "No. I mean like the Statler Brothers. I met them. They sing together for a living."

"Well, Kayla, I'll tell you: Charlie is the best guitar player in the family, but that's not all there is to it. The truth is that he's the only one who could put up with being famous. The rest of us either don't care to work that hard, or we don't have the charm to travel all the time and smile at strangers day in and day out. Not even for Charlie's money."

The kitchen was lit by a bare bulb suspended from the ceiling on a thick wire. Clayt groped for it in the darkness and switched it on. "You're not scared of the dark," he said approvingly to the child.

"No. Mama likes me to be brave about things, so I put up with them, and pretty soon they don't bother me anymore. Is there any milk?"

"I got a quart, for folks to put in coffee, but I don't suppose anybody'd object to you finishing it off." He took the carton out of the refrigerator and set it on the table in front of her. "The clean glasses are over there in the dish drainer. Get you one. Now, what would you like to go with that? Peanut butter sandwich? Cookies?"

"Cheese eggs," said Kayla, pouring the milk with intense concentration and great care.

Clayt stared at her. "Say what?"

"I guess cooking isn't one of your many jobs, Clayt." He noticed that she had omitted the word "uncle." Come to think of it, she didn't call Charlie "uncle" either. Clayt wondered if Kayla and her mother would become a permanent addition to the family or if this was just another one of Charles Martin's phases. "You take some eggs and put 'em in a frying pan with butter," Kayla was saying. "And you grate some cheese. White cheese is the best, but any old kind will work. And you stir them up together until the cheese melts and the eggs stop being runny. It's not hard. I can do the stirring, but I'm not allowed to mess with the stove."

"Butter, cheese, and eggs. Okay. What about milk?"

Kayla shook her head. "Not unless you're short on money, and the eggs have to last you till payday. Then you add milk to make them go farther. If you're really strapped, you can use powdered milk, but that tastes yucky. We haven't had to do that in a long time." Kayla added kindly, "I can eat it, though, if that's all there is."

"No, ma'am," said Clayt, keeping his voice expressionless. He hauled the gray egg carton out of the refrigerator. "You can have all the eggs and cheese you want, cooked to your specifications." He would give her the whole half dozen, and drive to the convenience store when it opened at six to restock the larder for the family's breakfast.

. . .

Frank Whitescarver's wife called his home office "the War Room" because it reminded her of Churchill's headquarters in World War II, which she had seen once on a five-day tour of London. The trip to Europe had been organized by a local travel agent, and she went with three retired schoolteachers and a couple of lawyers' wives, whose husbands couldn't take time off to go, either. When she got back, every dish in the house was dirty, and the bedroom was ankle-deep in newspapers, but Frank had sold four houses and a tract of timbered mountain land to some couple who wanted a nice site for a retirement home. "You spend it, Betty Lou, and I'll keep on making it," he would tell her, smiling.

"The War Room," Frank's pine-paneled den, had an old kitchen table for a desk, a black-and-white television for watching football games, and a fax machine so that he could be in touch with anybody, anywhere, right from home. One whole wall of the compact basement room was covered with maps of the northeast Tennessee counties. They were survey maps, drawn on a large scale, with circular lines for hills and markings indicating every creek and farm pond, and every single road, even dirt ones that were hardly more than cow paths. Betty Lou couldn't make much sense of them herself, and, truth to tell, she wasn't all that interested, but Frank was captivated by them. He could spend hours staring at the little push-pins and squiggles on those maps, just the way some people could look out of a picture window at a beautiful view and never tire of it.

"This is my territory, Squaw, and I have to keep watch over it," he would tell her. He called her "squaw" sometimes when he was in a teasing mood, on account of her brown eyes and her sharp, angled cheekbones that supposedly came from a Cherokee great-grandmother, somewhere back in the family history.

Frank had written all over those wall maps in his own special code. He claimed to know who owned every foot of land in Wake

County, and most of Carter and Unicoi, besides. He knew where the best views were, and how deep the wells were from one farm to the next, and who had the best soil for growing tomatoes. He didn't boast about knowing those things, though. He kept the information in reserve in case it should ever come in handy. The other part of his work, though it didn't occur to most people, was to be around: visible, accessible, and friendly to the community as a whole. He went to the Little League games, never missed a men's prayer breakfast, and had served a couple of terms on the board of county commissioners. Frank Whitescarver knew everybody.

"I can dial a wrong number and still talk," he would tell her, jutting his chin out, the way he always did when he bragged.

Betty Lou often wished that she had Frank's way with people, but that was past praying for, she reckoned. Oh, she was polite to all and sundry—never a harsh word from her lips to anybody—but she just never did seem to cotton to people as much as Frank did. He seemed to thrive on five straight nights of community meetings, topped by a Saturday morning trash pickup with the Ruritans. Just thinking about it made her tired. She didn't mind people every now and again, but she was never sorry when they went away, either. Fortunately, Frank didn't insist on her trying to be pup-friendly, like he was. Sometimes she even thought that's why he married her—so that he could have a rest at home from all the grins and chitchat.

She stood in the doorway, watching him poring over his maps. His bald head shone in the lamplight, and his glasses were slid clear down to his nostrils so that he could see the fine print next to the pushpins. "I'm going up to bed, Frank," she said. "Can I get you anything before I go?" She pointed to the pile of papers on the floor near his desk. "A garbage bag?" But her voice was teasing.

Frank looked up at the dark outline in the doorway and smiled back. "No, thank you, ma'am. I won't be long here. I just needed to come up with a few more land prospects before the city folks commence their spring migration. I was thinking about some of those places up on the ridge near the national forest. It's nice table land with good views. Good trees, too."

"Are any of those places for sale, Frank?"

He smiled at her. "Why, Squaw, there's not a foot of land in the entire world that's *not* for sale, if you go about it right. I just have to do a little investigating and see what it's going to take to shift those folks off some prime development land at a bargain price. I heard today that old man Stargill was taken to the hospital in Johnson City. I think I'll drive up there tomorrow, and see if I can be of any help at all to his family."

Betty Lou Whitescarver frowned. She couldn't remember if the Stargills were anyone she should know, or if any of them were in one of Frank's many organizations. She wondered how he had heard about the illness in the family, but then, Frank always seemed to know the most peculiar things, often as not before everybody else found out about it. "Will you need me to go with you, Frank? Or send a cake?" She could not keep the reluctance out of her voice. "I have to get my hair done tomorrow afternoon. It's my regular day. And then I thought I might go to the mall."

"Oh, don't you worry," said her husband, waving away her tentative offer. "You won't have to go. This condolence call is in the nature of business. Why, I might just be an answer to prayer for Randall Stargill's boys. Yes, sir. An answer to prayer."

Randall Stargill, earthbound by tubes and glowing machinery, dreamed on. A young nurse, making the rounds of the third floor in the darkest hours of the night, looked in on him, checking his vital signs, and recording the results on the chart at the foot of the bed. He seemed to be holding steady again. A few hours earlier, there had been rapid fluctuations in the old man's heartbeat, and a flock of white-coats gathered around his bedside, waiting to see if he would let go of life at last, and ready to drag him back if he tried.

But when the crisis passed without their assistance, and without the patient ever awakening, the staff members drifted away to more urgent and promising patients.

Word had got around among the nursing staff that this scraggly old man was the father of a famous country singer—not that such a thing would make any difference in his care, because in any case they would do the best they could for a patient, but more staffers than usual dropped by to have a look at him, and at the nurses station, they wondered aloud whether anybody famous from Nashville would turn up during visiting hours.

The young nurse wondered if the poor old man knew where he was; if he could feel all the tubes intruding into his body; and if he minded all the effort being made to keep him alive for another useless day.

He looked peaceful now, except for the occasional flutter of an eyelid, indicating whatever passes for dreams to the comatose. She stood looking down on him, feeling neither pity nor sorrow, and thought to herself that, for all intents and purposes, the two of them were each alone in this bright, sterile room.

In the cool darkness of his hospital room Randall Stargill stirred under clean sheets and took flight again. It was autumn this time, and Randall was walking with a young woman on Shawnee Ridge. She was nearly his own height, and slender, with hair as dark as any Indian's, but her eyes were a clear blue that looked right past you and into forever. He wasn't thinking about that, though, because her lips were red and sweet, and she was holding his hand as if she were afraid that the wind would blow her off into the valley.

She was pretty, graceful, and quiet, but the thing that Randall Stargill liked best about her was that he couldn't make her laugh. He was smaller than the other boys in the high school, and a little smarter than most, so to keep tempers on an even keel, Randall had got into the habit of clowning, laughing away an opponent's resentment, jesting his way past an A-plus. He was popular enough, but sometimes he wished his classmates would like him for himself, without his having to try so hard. She never laughed at him. She seemed to like him better when they would talk together about serious things.

"You ever wonder what the hawk sees when he's sailing up there?" he said, pointing to a brown speck among the clouds.

"The valley down there, same as we're seeing," she said, smiling.

"Yes, but we have to stay on this one ridge, while he gets to fly all around and look at things from every which way. You can do that from an airplane, you know."

"Guess you can, if you're not too scared to look."

"I wouldn't be scared! I want to go up in one of those planes. This summer when the fair comes back to Hamelin, I'm going to get one of the barnstormers to take me up in his biplane. And I don't want any old tame ride, either. I want to see the kind of stunt flying those fellows did in the Great War."

"I heard it was ten dollars to go up in one of those things."

"I know it, but I'm saving up. I can get ten cents a gallon for picking blackberries, and I can dig up some 'sang there in the woods and sell that to the root collectors for fifty cents an ounce. Then I can take me a ride and see this valley and all creation just like a hawk does."

"That would be a fine sight," she said. "Especially when the leaves have turned. But I'll stay here on the ground and watch."

"You're not scared, are you?" He squeezed her hand. "Afraid I'll crash?"

She shook her head. "No, Randall. You'll be all right in that airplane, and the ones to come."

She could have told him to save his money. He would see enough of the earth from the inside of a plane in seven years' time, as the turret gunner in a flying fortress over France. But if Nora Bonesteel knew what was in store for Randall in the years to come, she never said. Just as they never talked about what was past. About Fayre.

CHAPTER FIVE

It is Never to Late to Do good. [*sic*]

—DANIEL BOONE

Breakfast began with a platter of rubbery scrambled eggs, peppered with forced pleasantries from the women about the weather and duties of the day and consumed in a strained silence by the Stargill brothers. Kelley had decided to let her daughter sleep late, so that the adults could have an uninterrupted breakfast. Lilah, still in her turquoise caftan, bustled about the kitchen, fetching a salt shaker and napkins, and asking if anyone wanted seconds. Thirds? But no one seemed much in the mood to eat. Even a jar of homemade jelly, marked *Merry Christmas from the Jessups*, had failed to whet their appetites.

They drank coffee and stifled yawns. Clayt, who had driven to the convenience store down the mountain at six to restock the egg supply, was beginning to feel his lack of sleep; otherwise, he might have thought of something to say to these strangers with whom he shared breakfast—and bloodlines.

"Well, I guess we ought to plan today's schedule," said Lilah, as she poured the last of the new pot of coffee into Robert Lee's half-full cup. "Tell us what you guys will be doing, and when you want to be fed. Meals for eight people don't just happen in ten minutes, you know."

"First I thought we'd go out to the barn," said Clayt. "Garrett wanted us to take a look at some rosewood that Daddy's had stored out there in the barn loft."

"What about the hospital?" asked Robert Lee.

"Visiting hours are in the afternoon," said Clayt. "But they might let you in any time, seeing as Daddy's so ill."

"I called at five, when I got up," said Garrett, who was still in the T-shirt and sweatpants he had worn running. "They said he's in stable condition."

"But not conscious?" asked Charles Martin.

"No."

"If you all want to go to the hospital later on, I could stay with the little girl," said Debba.

Everyone turned to look at her. It was the first thing she had said all morning, besides "please" and "no thank you." She looked pale and tired.

"Or I could cook something while you were out." She twisted her hands in her lap. "It's just that I hate hospitals," she said.

"I don't think there's any need for all of us to go," said Kelley. She had felt as much relief as pity seeing Debba's stricken look, because she didn't think she had any business going to the hospital as if she were a member of the family. Why, she hadn't even met old Mr. Stargill. It was one thing to come along to give Charlie moral support, but quite another to overstep her bounds as a guest and a stranger. "I'll be glad to stay with you, Debba," she said. "Hospitals don't much care for crowds around the very ill. I'm sure there are things we could be doing here."

"Well," said Clayt. "There's something I've been meaning to ask all of you, since you didn't hear us talking about Daddy's list last night. This is as good a time as any. Do any of you know what a scripture cake is?"

He got only bewildered looks in reply. "I guess it's a custom from Daddy's childhood, or something. New to me. Well, some old lady from the church is bound to come by, and she'd be the likeliest person to know. Just remember to ask about it, will you? The next thing is more difficult. Do you do any sewing? Especially quilting?" He addressed the question to Lilah.

Kelley said, "I was taught when I was a little girl. My grandmother used to make quilts, but I never did one myself. Just sewed seams for Mamaw sometimes."

"What is it you want done?" asked Lilah. "My sewing is more of the mending variety. It was never something I cared to do."

"Debba does needlepoint," said Garrett. "She did us a cushion once."

His wife ducked her head. "Oh, it wasn't very good. My fingers get so numb."

"Are you thinking of the burying clothes?" asked Lilah. "I guess Daddy Stargill's suits are all too big for him now that he's taken so ill. If you've got a sewing machine, I guess I could take them in some. Passable enough for a viewing anyhow—not to wear on the street."

Clayt shook his head. "That coffin Daddy wants us to build—we're going to need a lining for it."

"I never did anything like that," said Kelley. "But it doesn't sound real hard. Is it like a blanket?'

"I expect so," Lilah said. "They could measure the inside of the box, and we could make a quilt big enough to cover the entire inside. The boys could tack it down around the edges so that it wouldn't slip or bunch up once it was in the casket."

"I think we could do that," said Kelley. "I'll be glad to help out all I can." She smiled over at Charles Martin. "Is there a piece goods shop around here?"

Charles Martin sighed. "That doesn't seem right, somehow. Buying new, fancy material to fit out a homemade coffin. I mean, if we're going to abide by Daddy's wishes, we may as well do it properly. Store-bought just doesn't fit the traditional burying he seems to want."

"I suppose next you'll be wanting a glass coach pulled by

black-plumed horses," snorted Robert Lee. "We have to be practical, folks."

"It might *be* practical," said Clayt. "I wonder if those old trunks are still up in the attic?"

"Scraps?" asked Kelley.

"All kinds of stuff. See, our family has lived here for nigh on two hundred years, and none of our people were big on throwing things away. They didn't waste much in the old days. So there's old trunks up there with old baby things, outgrown clothes, raggedy quilts. We used to root around up there when we were kids. No telling what you might find."

"Unless Daddy cleared it all out after Momma died," said Garrett. "Still, you could have a look."

"You want to line Daddy's coffin with rags?" Robert Lee stood up from the table, shaking his head. "That's not showing any kind of respect."

"No. Wait," said Charles Martin. "There's a lot of sense to this. Clayt didn't suggest using the family cast-offs to be stingy. If Daddy wants a traditional burial, it seems to be that he'd want as many family connections as he can get. What better way to finish a coffin made by his sons than to line it with a quilt made from the clothes of his loved ones? A piece of Mama's wedding dress, scraps from our baby clothes, or a square of his mother's shawl. Remember that black embroidered shawl, Clayt?"

"I think it's a beautiful idea," said Kelley. "Like that Dolly Parton song, 'The Coat of Many Colors.'"

Charles Martin frowned at her so fiercely that she wondered if she had just killed a new song idea for him. He was always trying to mine real life for things to put into his music, but he never seemed to be able to think up things out of the blue. He only knew a song idea when he heard it on somebody else's lips. Like the quilt discussion: he had probably been thinking up tunes while they were still talking about it. Even when it was his own father dying, Charles

Martin seemed to look at life through a plateglass window—like he didn't take it all *personally*, she thought. Part of him always stood back and watched. He had stopped looking at her now, so Kelley went back to pushing spongy egg fragments around her plate, and resolved to keep her mouth shut and stay out of his family business.

"Well," said Lilah, collecting plates from the table. "Sitting around here all morning isn't going to get any work done. You guys go out to the barn, and let us see what we can find in the attic, and get started on the quilt."

When Lilah started clearing plates away from the table, the men set off for the barn to see about fulfilling their father's last wish. It was a fine day, temperate for March between gusts of wind off the ridge, and Clayt cast a longing look at the field and the woods beyond as he led his brothers from one enclosure to another. A cabbage butterfly flickered past his line of sight, and he was tempted to follow it, but a glare from Robert Lee pulled him back.

The barn had been there as long as any of them could remember. It figured in sepia family snapshots dating back to the twenties. Even then it had been a weathered structure, mud brown, without a trace of paint, but the doors had been kept in good repair, then and now, and the patched tin roof kept out the rain. The barn looked none the worse for wear, although it had outlasted its usefulness. No livestock lived here, and no grain was stored in its corncribs.

"This place sure brings back memories," said Charles Martin. "I keep seeing a whole bunch of different scenes in my mind, all superimposed, like one of those music videos where things flash by almost too fast to register. I smell fresh hay, and I see Grandmaw out here in an apron feeding chickens, and that brindled calf Robert Lee took to raise one year. Oh, lord, and the hayloft. Why, that would be a whole video in itself. Remember the time Garrett jumped out, playing paratrooper, and got a tine of the pitchfork stuck in his leg?"

"I still have a hell of a scar from that," said Garrett. "But I count myself lucky. It was just a deep flesh wound. If I had landed just a little bit to the left, or a little bit harder, it would have killed me."

"You didn't cry much, though," said Charles Martin. "What were you, then, about eleven? The main thing I remember is seeing that big black point sticking through your thigh, and being surprised that you weren't screaming bloody murder."

"He was probably in shock," said Clayt.

"No," said Garrett. "I'm always like that. People tell me I have a high threshold of pain. But I always figured that hollering about being hurt didn't accomplish anything, except maybe throw your rescuers into a panic. And we were always around blood on the farm. Hog blood—people blood. What's the difference?"

Robert Lee said, "I don't remember that incident. It must have happened after I left home, which is just as well, because it sounds terrible. Surely, Garrett, you have better memories of the hayloft than that."

Garrett grinned. "None that I want Debba to hear about."

His older brother reddened. "I don't want to hear about them, either, thank you! Didn't we used to have a rope swing in the loft for playing Tarzan?"

"I remember that!" said Charles Martin. "Now that would make a good visual, I think, for a number built around barn memories. Milking cows . . . kissing girls . . . sitting on a bale of hay, practicing the guitar."

"Will you forget your goddamned singing career, Charlie? Remember what we're here for," said Robert Lee.

"Now you need to be quiet in here," said Clayt, yanking the barn door open with a rope slipped through the hasp. "There's at least one red bat living up in that loft now, and I don't want to disturb it any more than I can help."

"Bats?" said Robert Lee, even more exasperated than he had been with Charlie. "Well, damn it! Can't you just shoot them?"

"I can't, Robert. No. Because they do a lot of good. They eat a ton or so of insects a year, which is more than I can say for—" He shrugged, and turned away. "The light switch is over here."

The unspoken insult hung in the air, and Robert heard it as plainly as if it had been shouted. ". . . *More than I can say for car salesmen.*" He set his jaw, and walked on, without hazarding a glance at any of the others.

"Do any of you still do any carpentry?" asked Charles Martin.

"I've put up some bookshelves, and mended a fence or two. Nothing as fancy as what Daddy wants," said Clayt. "I'm willing to try, though, if the wood is any good."

"Should be, if it was stacked right," said Garrett. "Long as it stayed dry up there in the loft." He looked up at the vertical wooden ladder, nailed to the wall of the barn. "Looks like it'll hold us. Guess I'll go first," he said. "I can handle the trapdoor. Clayt, why don't you go last, in case Charlie gets a splinter in his manicured fingers, or you have to catch Robert Lee."

Ignoring their protests, Garrett lunged for the ladder and shinnied upward, disappearing into the loft above. "It's all right up here!" he called down. "The floor seems sound enough. And the wood has a tarp over it."

Charles Martin, who had turned the small bedroom in his house into a weight room, had no trouble with the ladder, but Robert Lee took a good five minutes of hard breathing and tentative footing before his head poked through the opening into the loft. "I don't see why we all had to come up here and look at a woodpile," he said, his sides heaving with the extra effort of speaking.

"Because if the wood is all right, Robert, we have to get it down out of here," Charles Martin told him.

Garrett, who had already removed the covering from the stack of wood, was studying the boards, running his fingers along them, and even sniffing at them. "It's stacked right," he said. "One board lengthwise, then one crosswise, so that there are spaces in between to let the air circulate."

Clayt emerged from the trapdoor and wandered over to look at the sleeping bat in the rafters, but he saw nothing except the tattered web of an orb weaver, strung from one beam to another and studded with dead flies encased in gossamer. On another beam, the papery white of an old wasps' nest stood out against the shadows, but he saw no insects hovering around it. Too early yet, and too cold for them. Clayt went to inspect the woodpile. "Rosewood," he said, tapping the end of a board. "You can't even get this stuff anymore."

"I've seen it advertised," said Charles Martin. "In Mexico, I got Kelley a little hand-carved jewelry box—"

"They call the new stuff rosewood," said Clayt. "But the wood products described by that name nowadays are actually made from the wood of the cocobolo tree."

"You mean it isn't wood from rose bushes?" As soon as he said it, Charles Martin grimaced. "No. I guess not. Look at the size of those boards. They can't be cheap. Why do they call it rosewood, then?"

"Color," said Garrett.

"Looks brown to me."

Clayt nodded. "Those boards are untreated. They'll turn a deep reddish color when they're sanded and finished, same as your Mexican jewelry box, but it isn't the same wood. The old rosewood—these boards here—was a rain forest tree. It is now an endangered species, and it is no longer harvested. Certainly it's illegal to bring it into the U.S., even if you could get hold of some."

Still short of breath, but interested, Robert Lee said, "So this stack of boards is valuable?"

"Maybe a couple of thousand dollars," Clayt told him. "Hardwoods grow slowly. An old walnut—say, twenty feet tall or so—can fetch as much as five thousand bucks. I've heard of people going off to church and coming back to find the old tree in their front yard chopped down and hauled away by timber rustlers."

"If it's so valuable," said Robert Lee, "why did Daddy let it sit here in the barn all these years? Anybody could have broken in and taken it."

"It's been here a good fifty years," said Clayt. "Maybe longer. I'm not sure when real rosewood started getting scarce. My guess is that Granddaddy Stargill bought it to make a wardrobe or a table for Grandmother, and he never got around to it."

"And it was too good to use for scrap," said Charles Martin.

"It wasn't cheap, even back in the old days," said Clayt. "You wouldn't waste it on fence boarding or patching jobs. This lumber was meant for a piece of fine woodwork."

Garrett tried to scrape off a sliver of wood with his fingernail. "Damn, this stuff is hard! We're going to have a hell of a time trying to work with it." To Clayt he said, "Have you been in the woodshop, lately? What kind of equipment are we talking about here?"

"Old hand tools, from what I remember," said Clayt. "I haven't looked at 'em in years."

"Hand tools." Garrett scowled. "You know how long it would take just to plane this stuff with hand tools?"

Charles Martin scratched at the top board and sighed. "'Bout as long as it took to grow it, I reckon, boys."

Reverend Will Bruce was making his late afternoon hospital rounds, visiting his ailing parishioners. He had left the call on Randall Stargill until last. Someone from the rescue squad had remembered to call him to report Randall Stargill's sudden illness, and, while he knew that the old man might be past knowing that someone had come by, he felt it his duty to come anyhow and say a prayer at the bedside. Besides, some of the family might be present, and he could express his sympathy and offer whatever comfort they felt in need of.

Will did not really feel like a pastor to old Mr. Stargill. His father—whom he sometimes still thought of as the *real* Reverend

Bruce—had been the minister of most of Randall Stargill's long life, and Mr. Stargill had plainly regarded the elder Bruce's successor as an unnecessary modernization, inadequate to his spiritual needs. Will Bruce was more than forty years younger than the old man, and, although he had known him all his life, he felt no closer to this parishioner than he did to any stranger he passed in the hall. Randall Stargill had always been polite, but never more than that. His few utterances were seldom about anything more personal than the weather. He sat in church like a man waiting for an overdue bus.

Will Bruce was not even sure what prayer the old man would want uttered in his behalf. Did he want to live? He had not seemed grief-stricken at the death of Clarsie a while back, but some widowers swallow their sorrow, and then die like abandoned dogs a few months after their bereavement. He had not thought Randall Stargill would be one of those. He seemed sufficient unto himself, and perfunctory in accepting the condolences of his neighbors. Was Randall Stargill a tired old man who had seen enough, and was ready to go?

He wondered if Randall Stargill's sons knew any more about his frame of mind than his pastor did. They had never seemed a close family. The boys always behaved—in church, in school, in the community; Randall saw to that. But they behaved without excelling, and their father never seemed to take any pride in their accomplishments. It was enough for him that they did not embarrass him by getting into trouble.

Some of the Stargill sons were close to Will Bruce in age, but Dwayne, who had been in the same grade with him, had died years back, and the others had left the community. Will Bruce and Dwayne Stargill had been, by common consent, acquaintances, but never friends. Dwayne, of course, had been the exception to the family rule. He had got into whatever trouble there was going, from smoking in the bathroom in the sixth grade to drag-racing on country roads in his high school years. He never finished school. Dropped out and was gone one day. Randall Stargill's countenance at church was unchanged. One by one the boys left, and he seemed unmoved by their absence. Then Clarsie died, and he sat through her funeral as impassively as ever, and went home to an empty house. He had been alone on the mountain for more than a year.

Will Bruce slipped into the hospital room, returning the smile of a passing nurse. He was a regular here. Most of the members of his church were elderly. The still form in the bed lay unmoving, eyes closed, and looking younger than he had in recent years, as if the long sleep had smoothed out the wrinkles from his life.

Will Bruce did not notice the still figure sitting in the straight chair in the corner until his name was called.

He turned from the dying man and struggled to sort names and faces in his memory. The stout, red-faced man in gray polyester pants and a shiny blue jacket stood up and extended his hand with a sad smile of welcome. "Good of you to come by, Pastor."

He had it now. The oldest son: a salesman somewhere in the Midwest. "Robert Lee! I'm glad to see you after all this time. I wish it could be under happier circumstances."

"Well, Daddy's close to eighty. He's worn out. We knew it had to come. Didn't think he'd outlive Mama, and worried about how he'd look after himself if he did."

"He may pull through yet," said Will, looking back at Randall Stargill's expressionless face. "He looks at peace, though, doesn't he?"

"I expect he is," said Robert Lee, sighing. "He hasn't solved his problems, though—he's just passed them along to us."

Will Bruce waited. He knew that most of grief counseling consists of listening. He pulled up the other chair, sat down next to Robert, and prepared to hear him out.

"We decided to come one at a time instead of all together to sort of space out the visits," Robert explained. "Clayt was here earlier. I don't know if Daddy hears us or not. Feels kind of funny talking to someone who just lays there with their eyes closed."

The minister nodded. "I know. I do a lot of visiting with the sick, you know, so I see this—well, quite a bit. I always assume that folks can hear me, though, even if they can't give any indication that they do."

"I can't get over seeing him like that," said Robert with a tinge of wonder in his voice. "Helpless. Look—I even put on a coat and tie to come see him." He laughed. "Guess I can't stop trying to impress him, even when he doesn't know I'm alive. At least he has a good excuse for it now."

After a moment of silence, Robert Lee leaned over and addressed his father. "It was hard to impress you, Daddy, since I never did know what it was you wanted me to do. 'Work hard,' you said. 'Get a good steady job with some security to it. Settle down.' That's what you told me. I remember it word for word. Guess you forgot it, though. Seems like all I ever heard from you was about how Charles Martin met some big-time person in show business or how many tanks Garrett blew up in Desert Storm. Why didn't I just become a bank robber and be done with it?"

Will Bruce knew that his presence had been forgotten. He wondered if the old man in the bed could hear his son. Knowing Randall Stargill, Will thought it was just as well that he could make no reply to his son's lament.

Randall's mother had forsythia beauty: a blond brilliance that blooms in earliest spring, lasts only a moment, and then fades, without a trace of its former glory. But when she looked at him, her eyes lost the opaqueness of fear, and she seemed to him as lovely as the moon. The small boy did not notice her dresses of flour-sack calico, and her work-roughened hands. He would sneak past his grandmother with a fistful of handpicked ditch lilies or white and yellow yarrow flowers, and hold them out to her, hoping for the rare tentative smile or the brush of her lips against his cheek.

She had not smiled for a long time now. Her eyes were as red as her hands, and she stared off at nothing while she worked. There had been a lot of people around at first, and they had brought cakes and homemade jams and had asked him a lot of questions in gruff voices, but finally they all went away, and the house was silent again. They did not speak of the matter. Grandmother had said that God's will had been done, and that it was a judgment on the sin of the mother for having had the child out of wedlock. She said God had taken away the evidence of sin, and that lamenting over what happened would be a blasphemy and an insult to the Lord.

Grandmother went about now with her lips pressed together so that not even a crack showed, and her eyes were narrowed, as if she dared anyone to cry. He did not cry. He was waiting for Fayre to come back, so that he could play outside again without making tears run down Mother's cheeks.

Mother had crept into his room that first night, touching his shoulder beneath the ragged quilt to waken him. He sat up, opening his mouth to cry out in the dark, but she whispered for him to be quiet. Her eyes were big in the dark, and she kept glancing toward the door, while her fingers plucked at the tatters in the quilt.

"Is it time to get up?" whispered Randall. The square of glass behind the curtain was still black, but perhaps the rain had darkened the day well past dawn.

"No, hon, it's still night," she said, stroking his hair. "I just couldn't sleep is all. I thought I'd come talk to you."

He nodded, trying to will his eyelids to stay open, straining to hear her voice over the sound of the rain.

"Stay awake, Randall!" she whispered. "It's raining outside. And it's cold for May. So cold on the mountain."

"Uh-huhh."

"Please, Randall, tell me what happened to Fayre."

"We went into the woods," murmured Randall. "I told already. Told and told."

"You didn't tell it all!" she hissed at him. "You left out part."

"We went looking for the Boone tree, I said. Looking for that tree with Dan'l Boone's name carved on it."

"Randall, did you see anybody else in those woods? Did somebody go with you?" She was holding him up by the shoulders now, not shaking him, but trying to keep him from burrowing back down into sleep.

"I don't know," he mumbled, nuzzling the pillow.

"Can you retrace your steps, Randy? Can you take me to where you left her?"

He shook his head. "Grandmother says I'm not to go in the woods anymore. The woods are bad."

"Randy, Fayre is your sister. You love her, don't you?"

"Grandmother says she'll buy me a whole sack of penny candy at the store if I'll be good."

He felt his mother's hand loosen her grip on his shoulder then. She sat there for a long moment, while he pretended to be asleep, and then she stood up and left the room as silently as she had come. He could not ever remember her touching him again.

CHAPTER SIX

The women could read the character of a man with invariable certainty. If he lacked courage, they seemed to be able to discover it, at a glance, and if a man was a coward, he stood a poor chance to get his washing, or mending, or anything done.

—a pioneer, recalling Boonsborough

The breakfast dishes had been left to dry on the drain board, and Lilah, who had changed out of her turquoise caftan and into a matching green sweatshirt and pants outfit, was leading the way to the attic. "There's no telling what we'll find up here," she said. "I haven't been up here more than half a dozen times in twenty years, and that was mostly to get Christmas decorations for Mama Stargill, or some extra blankets or some such. I never really investigated, if you know what I mean."

"Attics are so interesting," said Kelley. "It's like having a time machine, isn't it? You can see what people wore, and what furniture they had. Even old letters, sometimes."

Debba Stargill shuddered. "They give me the creeps. I heard a story once about a girl who was playing hide-and-seek, and she went up in the attic and got locked into a trunk, and when they found her she was a skeleton."

"I don't think this house has that kind of skeletons," said Lilah.

Debba said, "What kind do they have?"

"Oh, skeletons in the closet, as the saying goes. The usual family things, I reckon. Fights between married folks, and one child favored over the other, and squabbles about money. I don't think they ever had any convicts in the family or heavy drinkers—barring Dwayne—or even a divorce until, well . . ."

"Until this generation," said Kelley, glancing back toward the room where Kayla was still sleeping. She wondered what Randall Stargill would have thought of her, and if his opinion would have mattered to Charles Martin.

"I don't remember much about the family history," said Lilah. "Robert never cared much about ancestor research, and tales about the Stargill family, ancient or recent, are not something Mama Stargill seemed to know much about. Daddy Stargill may have known more, but he wasn't one to tell family stories. You could hardly get him to pass the time of day at the dinner table, much less air any dirty linen from years past. I heard somebody mention a tale once, I think, but I've forgotten all the details. Maybe Clayt knows. He's always poking into the history of one thing and another."

A small storage room at the end of the hall had been turned into an upstairs bath with old-fashioned porcelain fixtures and a black and white linoleum floor. In one corner next to the claw-footed tub, three steps led up to a small pine door. Lilah picked up a wet washcloth from the side of the tub and handed it to Kelley. "We'll need this."

She opened the door, revealing a steep flight of a dozen steps to the attic. "It shouldn't be dark up here," she told the others. "You may have noticed the little dormer windows from the front of the house. And there's a bare bulb on a cord up here at the top of the stairs, if it isn't burned out." She plunged ahead into the gloom, before Debba could demand a flashlight.

"Are you sure we'll be able to see well enough to pick out samples of material?" asked Kelley. "How will you recognize things in semi-darkness?"

"I thought we could take things over to the windows," said Lilah. "Daylight is best for judging color anyhow. We can clean the grime off them with that washcloth I got from the bathroom."

When she reached the top of the narrow steps, Debba Stargill ran straight for the dormer window, and leaned against it, taking deep breaths as if she could reach the fresh air outside. Kelley and Lilah looked at each other, and shrugged. "Least said the better," murmured Lilah. She clicked on the light that dangled on a black wire above their heads, but its feeble wattage did little to illuminate the area.

Kelley looked around. In the dim light from the far windows, she could make out a dusty wooden floor, littered with cardboard boxes, old chairs, and stacks of empty picture frames. She saw bits of old furniture, hatboxes, and a scattering of children's toys strewn haphazardly about the room, and in one corner, a blond doll with a china head and painted waves of hair sat in a child's rocking chair, fixing them with her painted smile. Kelley shivered and turned away.

Glancing again at Debba Stargill, Lilah said, "I think this big trunk will be the best place to start looking. You want us to scoot it over there to the window, Debba?"

"Yes . . . please," came the faint reply. "I don't much like little, dark places."

"A brass-bound trunk," said Kelley, fingering the ornate metalwork on top of the trunk. "I'll bet that would cost a lot in an antique shop." She grasped the leather handle at one end of the trunk, and Lilah took the other one. Together they dragged it into the square of light beneath the window. The trunk was too heavy for them to lift, but its contents made no sound as they slid it across the floor.

Debba Stargill did not turn around. She kept her nose pressed against the dusty window, still taking deep breaths. "You two go ahead and open it," she said.

Kelley thrust the wet washcloth into Debba's hand. "Fine. You scrub the window, then." She knelt and examined the brass fittings on the front of the trunk. "It's not locked."

Lilah lifted the lid. "Old clothes," she announced. "Just what you'd expect to find in an attic trunk." She took out the top garment, shook it out, and held it up against the light. "Mama Stargill's old winter coat. Last one she ever had. I don't know why they didn't get rid of it. It's just about worn out." She folded the brown coat, and set it down out of the way. "We might as well start a pile of things to get rid of, while we're about it. I'm sure these things would do more good keeping poor folks warm next winter than they would moldering in a trunk up here."

"Do you think the boys would mind if you gave their mother's things away?" asked Debba, who had consented to look into the trunk, since no rats or skeletons had been forthcoming.

Lilah favored her with a pitying smile. "Child, an old cloth coat from J.C. Penney is nobody's idea of a family heirloom. I'm sure we'll be able to tell what's worth keeping and what isn't."

"I wonder why Mr. Stargill didn't give these things away when his wife died," said Kelley.

"Well, I'll tell you," said Lilah. "The Stargills don't care much for hobnobbing with people at the best of times, and, aside from his grief, Daddy Stargill had just had to put up with a stream of neighbors and relatives, all coming in to keep him company and express their sympathy. I expect it was a lot easier for him to stuff Mama Stargill's things in this trunk than it would be for him to take the clothes to a bunch of strangers at a charity office. I don't know but what my Robert would do the same thing with my belongings if I were to pass first." She sighed and shook her head. "Robert would be worried that the charity people would look down on him because the clothes weren't up to their standards."

Kelley had continued to rummage in the oak trunk. "Look at this hat!" she said, putting the soft, homemade sun bonnet over her red curls, and tying the strings beneath her chin. "Don't I look like somebody on *Hee-Haw*?"

"Mama Stargill called that a poke bonnet," said Lilah. "She wore it when she worked in the garden. She sewed them herself. I think it's a very old design, though."

"We ought to keep that then," said Debba.

Kelley set the bonnet aside, and held up a fringed shawl of rusted black satin, embroidered with curling vines and flowers in red and blue. "Isn't this beautiful? Do you suppose she made that?"

Lilah shook her head. "Daddy Stargill sent her that from overseas." Seeing the blank look on the younger women's faces she added, "World War Two. He was stationed in England—navigator on a bomber, I think. He never talked much about that, either. He must have got to visit the Continent after the fighting was over. Looks Italian, doesn't it?"

"It seems a shame to cut it up," said Debba, fingering the delicate embroidery. "I wonder if his wife ever wore it."

"She never did," said Lilah. "My mother was the same way. My daddy sent her some embroidered linen pillowcases from France, and she put them away in the cedar chest in her bedroom. And there they stayed for forty years. I found them after she passed away, yellowed with age but otherwise brand-new. That generation believed in saving things for a rainy day. I guess they never got over the Depression."

"And now, fifty years after he gave it to her, the shawl becomes part of the lining of Mr. Stargill's coffin." Kelley sighed.

"At least it will be put to some use," said Lilah. "And maybe it carries sweet memories, which must be what he wanted when he asked for a homemade burying." She set the shawl aside. "That's the first bit for the lining, then."

"I wonder if we can find her wedding dress," said Debba. "That would have sentimental value, wouldn't it?"

"I expect so," said Lilah. "But it won't be the pretty scrap of lace and satin you're expecting to find. It was wartime. Clarsie Stargill was married in a wool suit with a gardenia corsage pinned to her breast pocket. The wedding snapshots are in the family album, her and Daddy Stargill posing on the front steps of this house, looking shy and ridiculously young. He was in his army uniform, and his ears are poking out underneath his hat."

"She wore a suit?" said Kelley. "Somehow I figured them for a traditional wedding—being country people and all."

"Well," said Lilah, "I think the war had a lot to do with it. They had clothes rationing back then, and he was probably home on leave, so there wouldn't have been time for a big to-do. And maybe Clarsie thought she ought to catch him while she could. There are pictures in the family album of young Randall with a pretty dark-haired girl, who just puts little Clarsie in the shade for looks. It's no use asking me what became of her, though, because nobody ever talks about it."

"We're not what you'd call a close family," Debba told Kelley.

"Well, at least Randall and Clarsie made a go of their marriage, even if they did it in a hurry and she wore a suit," said Kelley. "I eloped, but I still had a white dress. It wasn't floor length, but it had lace on the bodice." She blushed, and looked away. "We got divorced after ten months, though," she said. "Guess you need more than a white dress to make a marriage take."

"Keep looking for it," said Debba. "Even if it is just a wool suit, it's still her wedding outfit. That makes it a symbol of one of the most special days of their lives. Maybe we could use a little piece for the lining."

"I might recognize it if I saw it in here," said Lilah, piecing through the stacks of clothing. "It had shoulder pads and a straight skirt. I think it was dark green. What did you get married in, Debba?"

The silence stretched on for nearly a minute before Debba Stargill answered. "A long dress. Sort of champagne-colored with a big sash. And what they call a picture hat, like the wide straw bonnet Scarlett O'Hara wore at the garden party."

"That sounds nice," said Kelley.

"Well, I had wanted the long white dress and the veil, and all, but Garrett had been married before, and my minister didn't think it was right for us to have a big white wedding, with him being divorced and all."

"I didn't know Garrett had been married before," said Kelley. In fact, she knew very little about any of them, because Charles Martin hardly ever mentioned his family.

"I never met her," said Debba. "He got married real young, and it didn't work out." She scooted away from the trunk, and knelt before a stack of dusty cardboard boxes. "I think I'll look in here, while you two go through the trunk. Maybe I can find some things that belonged to Mr. Stargill's mother and father, or some family baby things we could use."

Kelley shrugged and turned back to the contents of the trunk. "So I guess Clayt is the only one who never married."

"There was another brother," said Lilah. "Dwayne."

"Oh, right, you mentioned him. The drinker. He got killed, didn't he?"

"Car wreck in Florida. None of us went, though, except his mother. Dwayne had been wild from the time he was fourteen. He was the next oldest after Robert Lee. Enlisted in the army after he got kicked out of high school—or flunked out, I forget which. Went to Vietnam, and got some medals for being wild. I don't think the family really expected him to come back alive from overseas, so when he burned himself up in a car wreck on I-95, it didn't seem to surprise any of them. Charlie and Clayt used to call him 'Audie'—you know, after Audie Murphy, the war hero. I guess Dwayne was kinda like him. Fearless. Roadhouses and fast cars were his natural habitat. You could tell by looking at him that he wasn't going to be around long enough to get old."

"Did he leave any family?" asked Kelley. "Wife and kids or anything?"

"Not that we ever heard about," said Lilah. "He may have had some cocktail waitress-type in Daytona, but if so, she never bothered to look us up. She must be long gone by now, if she ever existed at all. I'd be surprised if he ever made anything legal. Dwayne wasn't one for legal formalities—he jumped bail often enough."

"He was a convict?" said Debba faintly.

"Oh, no. Just a good old boy with more honor than sense. Barroom brawls was about the extent of it. He had a hair trigger when he was drinking. Robert Lee was mortified, of course. Called Dwayne the black sheep of the family. I think the other boys just laughed it off. They may have been sorry when he died, but they sure weren't surprised."

"Was Clayt ever married?"

"Not so far. I keep thinking he'll settle down one of these days," said Lilah. "He's just having a longer childhood than usual. Not that he can afford a wife and family on the little bit he makes doing jack-of-all-trades work. Clayt came close to tying the knot once that I know of, but then he took a notion to go walk the entire Appalachian Trail—all two thousand and some miles of it; takes about six months—and when he got back, his girl wasn't his girl anymore."

Debba, who had been shaking out a pile of dusty baby clothes, sneezed three times in quick succession.

Lilah turned to her and smiled. "They say when you sneeze like that, there's an angel passing by."

In the office of the Wake County courthouse registrar of deeds, there was a coffee mug with Frank Whitescarver's name on it, but he had to drink from it at the public counter, because not even an old regular like Frank was trusted with food or drinks near the precious deed books in Mrs. Oakley's care. Today, abstaining from coffee in dedication to his task, he sat hunched over the deed book in a trance of compass measurements and legal jargon, occasionally scribbling a note to himself on a legal pad. He had draped his gray suit coat across the back of the chair, and loosened his red tie.

"You looking for property again, Frank?" asked Dallas Stuart, a local attorney, who had come in to do a title search. "When are you going to buy a new house for Betty Lou? Seems to me with all those fancy homes you're putting up all over creation, you two ought to be living in style up on Boone's Mountain instead of in that same brick rancher you've had since Ford was in the White House."

A plaster smile was the best that Frank Whitescarver could manage. He took himself seriously—always had, even as a child—and affronts to his dignity stung him. It was one thing to have to be friendly to everybody on account of his work, but quite another to have to take guff from them. People didn't like Frank much, and beneath his amiability, he returned the sentiment, but he was always courteous, and, by god, he expected folks to return the favor.

"Oh, we're simple people, Dallas," he said, shrugging. "And we have no children, so a little house suits our needs. I keep telling Betty Lou I'll build her one of those French chalet things up on a hill somewhere, but she just shudders and says, 'The idea of having to pack up and move all your junk makes me want to crawl under the bed and never come out.'" He had the answer pat. It had served him well for many years, although Betty Lou could not remember ever having said it.

"Just looking for land for other folks to buy, is that it?"

"That's right, Mr. Stuart."

"Well, I can't say that I approve of all this new building going on around here. Taking perfectly good farmland and woods, and turning it into another set of bedrooms for Johnson City, but I guess people have to live somewhere. And there are some people around here who need the money, Lord knows. Land for development fetches a pretty price nowadays. Makes me wish J. Z. Stallard would sell that farm of his, before the county takes it for taxes."

Frank Whitescarver waited two beats, so as to seem unconcerned, and then he said, "Stallard. Up on the ridge next to the Stargill place?"

"That's right. Wasn't ever much of a farm anyhow, my daddy used to say. All the good land is bottomland, and the folks up on the mountain took the leftovers, and got 'em cheap. Used to be a joke, you know: 'The folks in the valley look down upon the folks up the mountain.'"

The realtor smiled politely. "Of course, these days the ridge runners may be having the last laugh on the valley people. Those with mountain land own the views now, and that's worth a good bit more than flat grazing land for Holstein cattle."

"Well, that's true," said Stuart. "The new people want fancy homes, and most of them couldn't grow a tomato in a tub of manure. They want a pretty view from the picture window and the wraparound cedar deck. How much do you reckon a place like Stallard's would be worth on today's market, Whitescarver?"

"It's hard to tell. I can't say that I'm all that familiar with the property, although I know exactly which farm you're talking about. I could take a ride out there, though, and talk to Mr. Stargill, if you think it would help."

"Wish I could say I thought so," said Dallas Stuart. "J. Z. can be the most pigheaded man alive when it comes to that farm of his. Never mind that he's no youngster any more, and all the help he's got is that daughter of his, Dovey. I don't say she's not willing, and capable enough, but I'm of the old school, Whitescarver, and I say running a farm is no job for a lone woman. Why, it would dry her out like a pippin. She'd be old at forty-five, with scraggly hair and skin like the cover of a Bible."

"And you say the Stallards are having tax problems?"

"Of course, they are! They lost their barn last year, and they've had livestock problems. They came to me to see if I could get some kind of waiver for them on taxes, on account of all the setbacks they'd had, but the best I could do for them was to get them a six-month extension, and to talk the bank into giving them a loan. They don't have the cash to pay high land taxes. None of the farmers around here do. All their money is in land and equipment, but the damned government wants to be paid in cash on the barrelhead. Every year."

"It's hard on farmers," said Whitescarver. "And I expect it's going to get worse. Now that folks are building fancy homes out in the rural areas, the land values are bound to go up for everybody. Which means even higher taxes, even for those folks still trying to farm."

"It's a damned shame," said Dallas Stuart.

"Better to sell the farm for a tidy sum than to see it auctioned out from under you for unpaid taxes," said Whitescarver.

"It's still a damned shame."

Kayla had awakened to a quiet house. She dressed herself in tiny jeans and a red sweatshirt from her canvas suitcase and went downstairs, calling out for her mother, but all was quiet. Kayla was not particularly disturbed by this. Until recently, her mother had worked changing shifts at a twenty-four-hour dry cleaners in Nashville, catering to people in the music business, who kept odd hours themselves. Since night shift child care was almost impossible to find, much less afford, Kelley had dispensed with it on the weeks she worked eleven to seven, reasoning that Kayla might as well sleep in her own bed, and that the money would be better spent on food and clothes for the child. Kayla was used to waking up alone. She rummaged through the refrigerator, and found orange juice and homemade jam. The bread was in a wooden box at the back of the kitchen counter, but by dragging the chair over to the counter, she found that she could reach it and the toaster beside it.

While the toast was browning, Kayla walked along the countertop, opening the hanging cupboards and taking down a small plate and a cartoon jelly glass for her orange juice. Toast and jam was about all she wanted for breakfast anyhow, and with the grown-ups gone, she could eat in the living room and watch *Mr. Rogers*, or whatever was on here at this hour. Kayla wasn't particular.

By the time she finished breakfast, there was nothing on the tube but boring talk shows, so she went out into the yard to play.

The cars were all there, which meant that the folks were around somewhere—maybe the barn, or up the hill for a walk—but she didn't feel like looking for them. Grown-ups never had time to play with you anyhow, and they had an annoying habit of thinking up things for you to do that weren't at all what you had in mind. Besides, Kayla's mother was always so grateful when she looked after herself. She would smile in relief, and say, "She's just a regular little lady." Kayla liked that.

First she explored the yard. There were some little purple flowers growing wild here and there in the grass. They looked sort of like hair curlers growing on a short stalk, no longer than her finger. There was a tree with white flowers, too, and along the side of the house a tall hedge blazed with tiny yellow star flowers. It would have been fun to crawl into the hedge to make a fort, but the branches were too thick together to let her in.

She wished she had brought some toys along. She had Sally, but her mother had been careful to explain that Sally came all the way from Germany, and that she had cost Charles Martin a lot of money, so she wasn't an outside toy. She had to stay clean and new looking.

Kayla wondered if there were any discarded toys stored in the old house, and if her mother would let her ask about them. Surely, with so many boys in the family, there would have been a wagon, or a toy train, or something. And none of them seemed to have any kids to pass the toys along to. Kayla didn't much like the toys little boys played with, but they were better than nothing.

She went into the barn, in search of yard cats or baby chickens, but the place was dark and musty smelling, and she heard voices from the loft. Charles Martin and his brothers, arguing about something. She slipped out again, half wishing that she could hang around with Clayt, who seemed pretty nice, but she was sure he wouldn't be any fun today, because he was busy acting old with the rest of them.

She peeked into all the outbuildings, but they were muddy and empty of all life, except spiders. Kayla knew better than to get dirty when they were off visiting. Her mama wouldn't want to have to do emergency laundry right now.

Kayla walked up to the top of the hill, but the wind up there made her shiver, despite the sunshine. She lingered among the gravestones, trying to read the weathered inscriptions, but the dates and the word *Stargill* were all she could manage. She recognized that from the record albums and concert posters Charles Martin had in his den. Kayla's mother had taught her the alphabet, and she could recognize some words by their shape—like *McDonald's* and *Coca-Cola*—but she couldn't really read yet.

Back in the yard, Kayla tried turning cartwheels, then walked a little way along the top rail of the fence, before she fell off into the damp grass, crushing purple flowers, and sending a bee droning off for a more peaceful feeding spot. She had been exploring the farm for half an hour, when the old woman appeared at the front gate.

She was standing on the flagstone walk, holding a wooden box with something in aluminum foil set on top of it, and she looked really sad—the way Kayla had expected Charlie to look with his father dying and all, only he hadn't. She was a tall woman, with a smooth big-boned face and her hair pinned up in a bun, strands of dark hair mixed in with silver. She wore a dark blue dress, which looked like an outfit for church, and a gray wool shawl to keep away the wind. Kayla wasn't afraid of her, exactly, but she felt that this was somebody that people were quiet around.

She came out from behind the big evergreen bush, and walked right up to the old woman. "Hello," she said. "My name is Kayla. May I help you?"

"I'm Nora Bonesteel," said the old woman. "I live over the ridge a ways. I am a friend of Randall Stargill. He wouldn't be your granddaddy, would he?"

"No, ma'am," said Kayla in her best company voice. "I'm just visiting. We are with Charles Martin Stargill." The child said this with the air of someone who has produced the magic word. Mentioning Charles Martin's name often did work wonders, in Kayla's experience. It had got her and her mother better seats at concerts, permission to go backstage, and rich-folks service in restaurants and Nashville stores. This time, though, the name had failed to conjure gasps or respectful glances.

"A visitor," said the old woman, nodding. "Yes. You don't have the look of a Stargill. But you're about six years old, aren't you?"

Kayla nodded. "Six and three-quarters."

"You're not here by yourself?"

The girl pointed to the four vehicles parked at various angles on the driveway and in the grass. "I reckon they're all around here somewhere, 'cause none of the cars is missing. I believe they were going to the hospital, though, later today." She looked out at the road, puzzled to see no visitor's car parked there. "Are you needing a ride?"

The old woman smiled. "Not just at present, thank you. I walk a fair bit. I have brought something for the family, you see. Do you think we could find someone bigger than you to give it to?"

Kayla was about to offer to lead the visitor to the barn where the menfolk were, when they heard a tapping on an upper window. They looked up at the dormer window of the attic, and saw Kelley's face, grimacing behind the newly cleaned glass. She was pointing downward.

"That's my mama," Kayla said. "Guess they're all upstairs. I didn't think to look there. Look like she's wanting us to go inside."

"All right."

Kayla was now at nose-level with the aluminum foil–covered plate atop the wooden box. She took a deep breath. "Did you bring cookies?"

Nora Bonesteel nodded. "I thought somebody might want some. Would you like to take one before we go in?"

Kayla hesitated. Not asking for food was one of her mama's cardinal rules of little girl etiquette, but she hadn't exactly *asked*, she told herself. She turned up a corner of the aluminum foil, and smelled warm chocolate from the fresh-baked cookies. "Can I have a couple?" she asked. "Not just for me," she added quickly. "I saw a little girl playing way off in the woods a little while ago, and I was thinking if I could find her, she might like to have some, too."

Nora Bonesteel stared at the child for a long moment. Finally she said, "I don't think that little girl will be wanting a cookie. Why don't you come inside with me?"

CHAPTER SEVEN

Next to the law . . . the best branch of business in America is that of adventuring in lands, and procuring inhabitants to settle them.

—SILAS DEANE, colonial attorney

Frank Whitescarver drove up the ridge through winter woods, still an undifferentiated blur of brown that would attract no one's attention. Impossible to tell yet which brown sticks would blaze with the purple flowers of redbud in early April, which twisted trees would light the hillsides with the cruciform petals of the dogwood. There was still time.

After his conversation with Lawyer Stuart in the courthouse, Frank had slipped into the tax office to have a few words with a clerk who had been accommodating in the past. Hadn't the Stallard tax problem been left unattended for quite a long time? Could something be done to speed up the foreclosure process? The wheels had been set in motion.

By the time the forest was gaudy with white and purple blossoms, and gilded with forsythia, he would have prospective buyers in his Jeep Cherokee, and newly acquired mountain land with which to tempt them. The riot of color lasted a few weeks at best, but his anticipation of the coming spring had nothing to do with his own pleasure at the sight of the returning greenery. He had long since ceased to appreciate the splendor of a mountain April. It seemed to

Frank that each flower had a secondhand, ticking away the opportunities for new transactions, better deals, a return on his investment. A year of planning could be blighted by one late frost. Oh, people still bought property throughout the late spring and even into the fall, when moist weather and a cold snap could give him rainbow ridges of autumn leaves, and a second chance at the impulse buyers. But at no other season were sales so easy as they were in those first glorious days of spring. He must prepare now, while the hillsides were still drab, before even the landowners themselves remembered what a treasure the mountains could become.

He had intended to pay a premature condolence call on the Stargills, but that could wait. By the road from Hamelin, he would reach the Stallard farm first, and his business there was more pressing.

The Stallard place was old: a two-story white frame house with a covered porch, and old maple trees shading the front yard. The house was set near the creek, at nearly the lowest point on the property, while on a distant treeless hill, the ruins of the burned barn dominated the landscape. "One thing I could never figure out," he would tell his clients, "is why the old-timers who built these farms always gave the cows the best view." It probably had to do with sheltering the main dwelling from the elements, and with the proximity of roads and a water supply, but it did look strange to modern eyes to see that the building with the commanding view was the cow barn, set up in solitary splendor, overlooking all creation.

The house looked as if it could last another century, although it could use a coat of paint and a new roof, but Frank Whitescarver was not concerned about that. The house would have to go. Perhaps three more modest-sized units could be fitted into its two-acre grounds. He might be able to save the maple trees.

He turned off the main road, and into the winding dirt track that ended at the Stallard homeplace. As the Jeep crested a small rise in the road, he saw a dark-haired woman kneeling in the grass near one of the unpainted outbuildings. Thinking at first that she was injured, Frank stopped in the middle of the dirt track, and ran to her side. "Miss Stallard, is it?" he said. "What's happened?"

Dovey Stallard, her jeans and flannel shirt streaked with blood, held up a handful of iridescent feathers. "The bastards!" she said, wiping her eyes against the sleeve of her shirt. Her hair was bunched into a knot at the nape of her neck, and rivulets of tear-streaked dirt creased each cheek. Frank thought she might clean up right pretty, but it was hard to tell in her current state of dishevelment. She held the bunch of feathers practically under his nose and shook them.

"Are you all right?" asked Frank, still unable to make sense of the scene.

She stood up, still holding the blood-stained clump of feathers. "That," she said, "is all that is left of a prize Majorca rooster."

Frank blinked. "Well . . . that is a pitiful shame," he said at last. "He must have been a beauty in life, with that colorful hank of plumage. Did somebody shoot him by mistake?"

"He wasn't shot. Look at him. There's nothing left but a few bones and feathers." Her voice was still shaky, but her cheeks were dry.

"A fox, then? Or a coyote? I've heard there's been some seen around these parts lately."

Dovey Stallard shrugged. "I don't know. Maybe. Or it could have been a hawk. I don't know. I ought to ask Clayt. He may not know much else, but he's an expert on wild things." She glanced back at the chicken run where chickens of all sizes and colors milled around, pecking desultorily in the dirt, oblivious to the death in their midst.

"It's a terrible shame, a pretty rooster like that," said Frank, shaking his head. He wondered who Clayt was. "Sometimes I think the job of farming would try the patience of Job. So many things can go wrong."

Dovey set the feathers down, and looked closely at the stranger in the business suit and tasseled loafers. Her eyes narrowed. "I'm sorry to be taking on so," she said. "Was there something you wanted?"

Frank Whitescarver tried his self-deprecating smile. "You'd be

J. Z.'s daughter, wouldn't you? Is it Miss Stallard, still?" She was thirty-five if she was a day, and not all that bad to look at. Stubborn streak, though. He could tell by the set of her jaw. Still, a young man besotted by a girl like her might overlook that telltale sign of temper, and marry her. He'd live to regret it, though.

"That's right," she said evenly. "I'm Dovey Stallard. And this is my dad's place. Just who are you?"

He reached into his coat pocket and fished out an embossed business card. "Frank Whitescarver. Realty and Construction. I know your daddy, of course. Fine member of the community." He probably did know J. Z. Stallard from somewhere: Ruritans, civic meetings, American Legion functions. Surely in a county as small as Wake their paths had crossed.

"Uh-huh." Dovey studied the card and offered to hand it back, leaving a thumbprint of dirt and rooster blood just over the word *Realty*, beneath Frank's name.

"No, you hang on to that one," said Frank, backing away. Nothing would induce him to put that gore-streaked card into his dry-clean–only pocket. "I was hoping I might see your dad. Is he around?"

"Somewheres," said Dovey indifferently. "If you've come about the barn, you're wasting your time, 'cause we're not taking bids on rebuilding that yet."

Frank bit back the words, "*I don't do barns.*" He was nettled that she had not heard of him, but years of experience in dealing with surly mountain folk kept him calm and smiling. "Why don't we go look for him?" he suggested. "Maybe he saw what killed your chicken there."

"Suit yourself," said Dovey. "I have to go get cleaned up, and make a phone call. You're wasting your time, though."

She hurried toward the back door without a backward glance, and Frank waved her away, still smiling, and went off in search of her father. In truth, he was in no hurry to discover the whereabouts of J. Z. Stallard, because looking for him was the perfect excuse to look over the land. He wished he hadn't worn his good clothes for a tramp through the pastures, but it couldn't be helped. Time was short.

Good trees. Nice slopes. Decent soil. With a practiced eye, Frank Whitescarver gauged the steepness of the hills in the pastures, the winter flood plain of the creek, and the views from each prospective home site. He liked what he saw. As a dirt farm in the Tennessee mountains, this place was a ticket to starvation, but as a retirement community for the Knoxville country club set, it was a gold mine.

He had climbed the hill to the charred remains of the barn, and was admiring the view across a band of blue misted hills, when a quiet voice from behind him said, "Was there something you wanted?"

Frank turned, knowing that he had a split second to figure out what tack to take with his opponent, and to assume the expression that best fit the part. He saw a lean, silver-haired man wearing khaki work pants and a canvas vest over a sweatshirt. The man wasn't armed, but he was watching Frank with a wary expression that was more fear than anger at a trespasser. Frank decided that the poor fellow needed an ally, someone to listen to his troubles.

"Frank Whitescarver," he said, sticking out his hand, and shaking Stallard's vigorously. "Beautiful place up here." He nodded toward the ruins of the barn, and said, "I hate to see a fine old building go like that. They just don't build them like that anymore."

"They probably could if you could afford to pay the price," said Stallard. "Which I can't, right now."

"No, farming sure isn't cheap, is it? No wonder we have all these fellows with day jobs in Johnson City farming on weekends. It's the only hedge against the bad luck that Mother Nature seems to dish out pretty regularly. If it's not a May frost or a forest fire, it's a spring flood or a cattle virus, isn't it?"

"Seems that way," said Stallard. "You do any farming yourself?"

Frank shook his head, hoping to imply regret rather than relief. "Me? No-oo. Never had the knack for it, I guess. A couple of rows of tomato plants is about all I run to, and I'm lucky to get my money back in tomatoes, even then. What about you? You ever want to do anything else?"

Stallard considered it. "Maybe when I was young," he said. "Used to think about being a pilot. All little boys are the same, I guess."

"What about now? Ever wish you could just walk away, and not have to worry about another flood or frost, a gypsy moth swarm. Long as you live?"

J. Z. Stallard studied the man carefully. "Why do you ask?" he said. "You working up to trying to buy this farm?"

"Well, the fact is that I am, Mr. Stallard. And I hope you'll take it in the spirit it's intended, as one neighbor trying to do a good turn to another." He rummaged in his coat pocket for another business card. "Frank Whitescarver. Realty and Construction."

Stallard stared at the card without commenting, so Frank went on talking. "*Realty*. The printers over in Johnson City made a mistake once and did me a thousand cards that said *Reality*. They replaced them at no charge, of course, but that error of theirs set me to thinking. Maybe *reality* is a good name for the land business. I try to find honest solutions for people needing a place to call home—and for people needing to get out from under a hundred or so acres that's burying them while they're still alive. Land can be a burden as well as a blessing, Mr. Stallard. That's reality."

"Stallards have always farmed this place."

Frank Whitescarver shook his head, smiling gently. "Oh, don't you believe it, J. Z. That's how you get a hundred acres on your back, weighing you down to where you can't stand up. Your family may have been here five, six generations, but before that they were in Ireland somewhere, likely as not, and probably thought their little piece of land back there was the center of the world, too. We're newcomers here by historical standards. The Indians had these mountains before we did, and they sold them to us, so don't feel that you owe your ancestors anything by staying on a dying farm that's taking you with it. Times change, J. Z."

"Times do. People don't, so easy." Stallard wasn't looking at him. He was looking out over the valley, toward the white house under the maples and the little cluster of tombstones on an adjoining hill.

"Let's be honest about this. You're not getting any younger, and farming is no life for your daughter—a single woman alone. You've had a run of bad luck, and the tax man is breathing down your neck. I'm only offering you a way out. Three hundred dollars an acre. Cash."

J. Z. Stallard didn't like strangers much, and because of his dislike, he was always careful to be absolutely courteous to them at all times, because quarrels are a form of intimacy. He waited a few moments, as if to consider Whitescarver's offer. Finally—with infinite courtesy—he said, "It's kind of you to make the offer, Mr. Whitescarver, but I just can't see my way clear to do it. I know I've had bad luck the past couple of years, but the county people have been right understanding about my difficulties, and I believe I can hang on until things get better."

To an outsider, the speech might have sounded tentative or even grateful, but Frank Whitescarver knew better. Trailer trash running him off their property with a shotgun would have been no less adamant than J. Z. Stallard with his quiet refusal of a rock-bottom offer. Frank had been prepared to dicker further; maybe to offer to throw in a little brick rancher in town to sweeten the deal, but he could see that such gambits would be useless. J. Z. Stallard had the same stubborn set of jaw as his daughter.

Frank would have to resort to other means now, and, Lord, he hated to do it. He didn't like bad feelings any more than Stallard did, but business was business.

The three Stargill women hurried down out of the attic, carrying piles of old clothes and baby things. They hadn't finished the sorting yet, but since they had to come down anyhow to meet the visitor, they decided to save themselves a trip later by bringing down the garments they had chosen for the quilted coffin lining.

Kayla had ushered the old woman into the parlor, and now she was sitting beside her on the sofa, talking about mountain lions, but the old woman didn't seem to be paying much attention. She sat expressionless, holding a wooden box in her lap, while Kayla prattled on and helped herself to cookies from the plate on the coffee table.

Lilah Rose Stargill set down the stack of clothes she was carrying, and advanced to meet the visitor. "Now don't get up," she said, smiling. "I'm Mr. Stargill's daughter-in-law Lilah, and this is Garrett's wife Debba—" She nodded toward the small, colorless woman in the brown print dress. "And this is Kelley. I see you've already met her daughter."

Nora Bonesteel nodded. "You keep an eye on her," she said to Kelley. "Farms can be dangerous places for little folks."

"I will. Would y'all excuse me?" Kelley, mindful of the lack of introduction, however gracefully covered, beckoned for Kayla to come with her into the kitchen. "Wouldn't you like some milk to go with that fistful of cookies?"

The old woman turned to the two Stargill wives, now seated in chairs facing her. "You won't remember me. We met years ago, in church one Christmas. I am Nora Bonesteel."

Lilah's smile wavered for a moment, an indication that she indeed had heard of Nora Bonesteel, but she hurried on. "It's a real kindness for you to come and call on us. Mr. Stargill lived here all his life, of course, but we're just complete strangers here. Hardly know a soul. And you brought cookies, too?"

"Mr. Stargill isn't dead yet," said Debba. She blushed as the other two turned to look at her. "I thought you might have heard he was," she muttered. She leaned back into the protective blinders of the wing chair, intending to contribute nothing else to the discussion.

"No," said Nora Bonesteel. "I know he's lingering in the hospital." She paused as if there had been more to say.

"We're hoping for the best," said Lilah. She thought of mentioning her angel, but something about the old woman's solemnity made her decide against bringing it up. "Meanwhile, he's got a nice private room, and we called for a bouquet of carnations to be delivered up there today."

"He's likely to go suddenly," Nora told her.

"Oh, we mustn't be pessimists. He's old, but—"

"He's likely to go suddenly," Nora Bonesteel said again. "And I wanted to see that the family had this before—before the burial arrangements were made." She ran her hands along the smooth surface of the box lid. The box was old: a dark, reddish wood about a foot high and eighteen inches wide. It looked homemade, but carefully crafted, with doweled joints, rounded corners, and filigreed brass fittings. The hand-rubbed linseed finish had been kept shiny with beeswax, polished over the years until the wood glowed with the mellow luster of age.

"The box?" asked Lilah. "It's real thoughtful of you to bring it back. I know the boys will be tickled to have it." Bewilderment colored her voice. This conversation was not going the way Lilah expected condolence calls to run, but she responded gamely, while she tried to think of a way to get the conversation back along conventional social lines. Debba was no help. The puny little thing just sat there looking like a stuffed goose, letting her do all the talking. Lilah wished Kelley would come back in. The girl might be living in sin with Charles Martin, but at least she made herself useful. "What fancy woodwork there is on that box. I never saw the like. Did Mr. Stargill make the box?"

"He did. A long time ago."

"Well, you're ever so thoughtful to return it." Lilah hoped the subject could be dismissed at that. By now she had realized that the old woman before her was the same dark-haired beauty featured in the family photo albums. Those cheekbones hadn't changed in half a century, and the eyes were as dark and clear as they had ever been.

This was the girl that Randall had loved before he married Clarsie. What in God's name could she be bringing the family now? Love letters? What would the boys think of that? She knew what Robert Lee would think, and she decided that nothing in creation could persuade her to let him know about it. There wasn't enough Maalox in Tennessee to get Robert Lee through such an ordeal.

She took the box from the old woman, surprised by the weight of it, and set it on the floor beside the sofa. "You know, we're just so glad you came by," she said brightly. "Because we had a question about something we're supposed to be doing for the wake—if, Lord forbid, it comes to that. Mr. Stargill has left us a whole list of written instructions about his burial—"

"He'll want this buried with him," said Nora Bonesteel.

Lilah's smile wavered. "This box?" The conversation always kept coming back to that damned box. She was beginning to think this old lady was not right in the head, but as a charitable woman with an angel as a personal adviser, Lilah felt that it was her duty to persevere. "You think Mr. Stargill would want this box of his laid to rest with him?"

"What's in it. The box unopened would be best." Nora Bonesteel stood up. "I have to get back now. But I had to bring you the box. Randall wanted it done."

"Wait!" Lilah called after her. "We need to ask you about a scripture cake. He wants one."

Nora Bonesteel turned to look at her. "That can wait," she said. "I have to go now."

"Nice to meet you," said Debba, as the woman walked away.

Lilah walked with Nora Bonesteel as far as the front door, thanking her in jumbled sentences for the cookies and the visit—pleasantries that went unanswered. She stood smiling on the door stoop, and waved the visitor away down the path. When Lilah closed the door, she leaned against it and let out a sigh. "Great crown I reckon," she said. "If that wasn't awkward!"

Debba frowned. "She was quiet, but she seemed okay to me. What was awkward about it?"

Kelley came back into the room and picked up the stack of baby clothes. "Kayla's gone back out to play. I expect we ought to wash these out before we use them. They have a musty smell. Ivory Snow or Woolite, do y'all think?"

"Of course, you two wouldn't know," said Lilah, ignoring the laundry question, and sinking back down on the sofa. "But *that* was Mr. Stargill's old girlfriend, from years ago. The one I told you about, that was in the snapshot album. I hardly knew what to say to her. And she kept harping on that wooden box until I thought I would scream. I mean, it's a little late for romantic gestures, I would have thought. They're over seventy, for heaven's sake. I'm surprised she even remembers who Randall is."

Kelley smiled. "I think you're making a big deal over nothing," she said. "Why, they broke up before World War II. I know people back home who invite ex-wives to parties—much less old sweethearts. In a small town, you can't afford to ignore all the people you've fallen out with, or they'll be nobody left to talk to."

"Still, don't you think it was odd that she showed up here with that box, about as full of the social graces as a frozen turtle, and asked that it be *buried* with him?"

"Is that what she came for?" Kelley shrugged. "Sentimental, maybe. Too bad more people don't take love that seriously these days."

"What's in the box?" asked Debba.

The woodshop was a small, unpainted room partitioned off at the back of the barn. It could be reached via an outside door that led into the barnyard, or through a makeshift door of hammered boards that led into the main interior of the barn. One dirt-encrusted pane of handblown glass let the light in, and an electric bulb dangling from a cord in the center of the room provided artificial light. The worktables were handmade from scrap pine, and the rows of shelves, laden with paint cans and jars of rusting nails, had been assembled with two-by-fours and plywood. An assortment of old hand tools hung from pegs on the wall next to the window.

Randall Stargill's four sons had managed to haul the rosewood lumber down from the barn loft one piece at a time, and, considerably dirtier than when they started, they had stacked it again near the door, and carried one board into the old woodshop in the back of the barn to test it with their father's old hand tools.

"Should have packed old clothes," said Robert Lee, whose gray polyester pants had a tear at the knees. "I always did ruin pants legs in this barn."

"I guess I can kiss these jeans good-bye," said Charles Martin, trying to brush caked dirt from the legs of his Levis with one grimy hand.

"I thought you rich country singers only wore a pair of jeans once anyhow," said Garrett.

"Naw, we're into recycling." He grinned at his older brother and gave him a mock salute. "It's the American way, Major."

"You two stop fighting," said Robert Lee, fanning dust motes away from his face. His eyes were watering, and he stifled a cough with his fist. "Look at the state of this place. It's ankle-deep in dust. We have enough work to do without having you two bickering with each other every five minutes. Maybe Daddy has some old clothes in his wardrobe that we could wear for working."

"It's like we're turning into kids again," said Clayt. "Us arguing, and you bossing us around, Robert Lee."

"All right," said Garrett. "Let's get to work, then. That'll keep us off each other's nerves." He picked up a hand planer and blew the dust off it. Its steel blade had darkened with age, but the oak handle with spiral hand grips was still a polished golden brown. Randall Stargill had taken care of his tools, almost to the end of his life. "I know we have to clean things up before we really get started, but I just wanted to try a test piece here," Garrett said. "Set that board up on the table over there." He tested the blade of the planer with his thumb, and, satisfied that it held an edge, he bent over the rosewood plank and raked the planer against the surface of the wood. Barely a scratch appeared in the wake of his blade.

"I was afraid of that," said Clayt, bending over to inspect the results. "This lumber is about the hardest wood you'd ever want to work with. Takes a long time to grow, ages to season, and good luck trying to plane it! No wonder Grandaddy gave up trying to build anything with it, and let it sit up there in the barn loft."

"Well, it's too good to let go to waste," said Robert Lee. "And it'll make a fine coffin, even if it takes a lot of work from all of us to get it done."

"Do we have enough wood for a coffin?" asked Charles Martin. "I'd hate to put a lot of work into this, and then come up short, and have to buy one from a funeral home anyhow."

Clayt took a retractable metal tape measure out of his pocket, and tossed it to his brother. "Here! Go find out how many board feet we've got to work with. I'll figure out how many feet we're going to need. Anybody got a pen?"

Garrett handed him a ballpoint and a deposit slip torn out of his checkbook. "You can write on that. We need to know what measurements we want for height and width of the shoulders." He looked at his brothers. "I'd say Charles Martin comes closest to Daddy in build, wouldn't you, Clayt? You're too tall and Robert is too fat."

Clayt smiled. "You want me to measure Charlie?"

"Sure. It'll be close enough. Unless you want to ride over to the hospital, and run the tape over Daddy."

Clayt walked away. "Come here, Charlie!" he called into the darkness of the barn. "I need you and the tape measure both."

"What do you want me to do?" asked Robert Lee, who had been poking around in drawers, looking for more tools.

Garrett shrugged. "Clean this place up, I guess. Wood dust will make you sick enough, without adding all the rest of the dirt in here. There's a broom over there in the corner."

"With my dust allergies?" Robert Lee shuddered. "I'd be sicker than Daddy if I tried to stir up dust in here. I'll have to get a mask before I can work on the coffin with you."

Clayt joined them, jotting down notes on the back of the deposit slip. "He can run errands, can't he, Garrett?"

"Suits me. What kind of errands?"

"More groceries, for one thing. You all still eat like teenagers. And we'll need hardware for the coffin. Maybe a brass nameplate from Things Remembered in Johnson City. You got another deposit slip? I'll make a list. Here are Charlie's measurements, by the way. He didn't care at all for being the model, either."

"Did you find any other planers while you were rummaging through here, Robert?" asked Garrett. "I don't guess it matters, though. We'd need an electric one to make any headway on this wood. We could buy one, I suppose."

"Are you sure this place is wired for power tools?" asked Clayt. "I wouldn't count on it."

Garrett shrugged. "We'd be better off paying to have it done."

"There's a cabinetmaker in Hamelin. Old Dalton Wheeler. He'd probably plane it for us. I could ask him."

"Good. See how long it will take, if we get it there by this afternoon. And how much he'll charge us."

"Has to be done, no matter what," said Robert Lee. "Deduct it from the estate."

"Hadn't we better find out if there is an estate first?" asked Clayt.

"This farm is worth a good bit," said Robert Lee.

"We're taking things one at a time here," said Garrett. "Clayt, tote up those numbers you got on Charlie's measurements."

"I already did. He's five feet-nine, and about twenty-four inches across the back, give or take a couple. He wouldn't hold still. So I'd say six feet in length, maybe two and a half feet wide."

"Shouldn't we allow more length?" asked Robert Lee. "There's usually a pillow under the head of the deceased, and a few inches of it sticks up beyond where his head lays."

"Maybe we ought to ask somebody to make sure," said Garrett. "We can't afford to get it wrong. Clayt, do you think Dalton Wheeler will know anything about this kind of job?"

"I can ask him for advice," said Clayt. "But I say we have to do the work ourselves."

"It isn't going to be easy," said Robert Lee. "Or quick."

"We can do it, though." Charles Martin came back into the woodshop. "We have sixty board feet of lumber. We can't waste much of it, but there's enough to build a man-sized box. And I think we ought to do it ourselves, because Daddy asked us to."

"I agree," said Clayt. "Two hundred years ago, when our people settled this valley, they tended to their own needs, without buying help for anything. They delivered their own babies, grew their own food, and buried their dead in homemade coffins. We were the West back then! We were the pioneers. Have we lost so much of our heritage that four grown men can't build one simple box without hiring professional help?"

"I can," said Garrett. "Thanks to the army, I'm as fit as any pioneer you'd care to name. It's the rest of you I'm worried about, with your time limits and your manicured hands."

"Don't fret over me," said Charles Martin. "Being a musician is no desk job, believe me. I can pull my own weight in this."

"I'm the only one of you who has done this before," said Robert Lee.

They heard the shouting then, and Debba Stargill jerked open the door to the barn and stood there screaming for her husband. Kelley, pale but calm, pushed past her and ran to the open door of the woodshop. "You all better come inside," she said. "There's something in there you need to see."

. . .

Jane Arrowood's white house on Elm Street reminded people of an English cottage, and its well-tended garden, bright now with early tulips and daffodils, was in keeping with that image. The house was larger than it looked, though. Much too big a place for an aging widow whose only living child was a grown man with a place of his own. She kept the place because it held the memories of her children and her moderately happy marriage. Her oldest son, Cal, had been killed in Vietnam in 1966. She felt that if she ever left this house, she would lose even the memory of her lost boy. She kept it, too, because she thought the place might be hard to sell, and there was nowhere else in town that she wanted to live. An apartment would be more convenient, but she would miss her garden and her neighbors.

Jane knew, though, that the main reason she kept the white house was because her son Spencer wanted his old homeplace to stay the same. He fretted at any little change she made: the upholstery on a sofa, or new kitchen curtains. He wanted things to stay exactly as they had been when he was growing up. It was exasperating, but endearing, too, Jane thought, that he would value so much his memories of the home she had made for him. She indulged him by remaining, the curator of the museum of Sheriff Spencer Arrowood's childhood. He did not want to live there himself anymore, but it gave him a feeling of groundedness to know that his old home was there, unchanged, and that at any time he could walk into it, and be "home." She understood that, but it worried her sometimes. "What will he do when I'm gone?" she would ask herself. Perhaps find another place that would be home to him, she supposed. He had tried that once, long ago, when he married his high school sweetheart, but the acrimony of that union seemed to have soured him on trying again. She hoped he would outlive the bitterness. Marriage wasn't perfect, she knew that firsthand, but it was a comfort when the world around you seemed to be growing younger and more alien with each passing day.

It was a warm afternoon, and Jane was outside in her khaki gardening pants and one of Spencer's old sweatshirts, tending the mint bed. It was a weed, really: early up in the spring, the better to take over the entire flower bed, if you didn't keep it in line. Sometimes, in a fit of exasperation at seeing another clump of pansies engulfed, she would be tempted to root out every stalk of mint in the garden, but Spencer liked it. He said there was nothing like fresh, homegrown mint to flavor iced tea in the summertime. Jane sighed at her martyrdom to mint, and kept on weeding.

"Good afternoon, Jane."

"Why, Nora Bonesteel! You scared the life out of me. I was humming, and didn't hear you come up. Can I get you some tea?" Jane tried to mask her surprise with offers of hospitality. Nora Bonesteel seldom came to town. She had no car, and it was a good seven miles down the mountain. Jane's first guess would have been illness, but the old woman looked fit enough. She was wearing her blue wool church dress, and a hand-woven shawl, and she looked more troubled than Jane had ever seen her. She ushered her visitor into the house, making small talk about gardening, because it wouldn't do to question a guest standing out in the front yard.

When Nora had been settled in the red Queen Anne chair next to the living room fireplace, and Jane had put the kettle on in the kitchen, she sat down on the loveseat, and said, "Now, I'm delighted to see you, but I can't help wondering if there is anything the matter, because you're not exactly a frequent visitor. How did you get here?"

"My neighbor down the hill was kind enough to give me a ride in his pickup."

"Thank goodness for that. I was afraid you had walked. Of course, I'll drive you home when you're ready."

Nora Bonesteel smiled. "That may not be necessary," she said.

"But I do wish you would call the hospital in Johnson City, and ask them how Randall Stargill is doing."

The hospital. Jane stared. She knew that her friend had no telephone in her house on Ashe Mountain, but it seemed strange for her to come all the way to Hamelin to make a phone call. She had never heard Nora mention Randall Stargill, either. Perhaps they were kinfolks. "Would you like me to take you to Johnson City to visit Mr. Stargill?" she asked.

Nora shook her head. "He's not up to seeing anyone. But I would like to hear how he is."

Jane heard the whistle of the teakettle in the kitchen. "I'll just fill the teapot," she said. "And while it's steeping, I'll make the call. Can I get you anything else?"

"A Bible."

"A *Bible*?"

Nora looked apologetic. "I know it well enough," she said, "But I haven't got it by heart. A large-print one, if you have such a thing. And a paper and pencil."

Jane nodded and went to her bedroom to fetch her King James leather Bible from the drawer of her nightstand and a pad and pen from beside her bedside telephone. She began to wonder if Nora had suffered a stroke. She was quite unlike herself today. But the old woman seemed alert and in good spirits when Jane returned and handed her the things she had asked for. As she hurried to the kitchen to make the tea, Nora Bonesteel began to leaf through the Old Testament, running her finger down a line of scripture with a practiced hand.

Jane made the call from the wall phone in the kitchen. "He's in critical condition, but stable," she announced, as she came back into the living room with the tea tray. "You were right about his not receiving visitors. He is in a coma." She paused to gauge her friend's reaction to this news, but Nora Bonesteel said nothing. She continued to consult the Bible, and to make notes on the pad.

Jane set the tray on the coffee table in front of Nora's chair, and glanced at what the old woman had written. *I Kings 4:22. Judges 5:25.* It seemed an odd time and place for Bible study, Jane thought, but she decided that Nora might be distraught over Mr. Stargill's grave illness.

"Was he a close friend of yours?" she asked. "Or a cousin?"

Nora Bonesteel closed her eyes. "A long time ago, I almost married him. Randall was a handsome man in his officer's uniform." She smiled. "He knew it, too."

"Were you afraid that he wasn't coming back from the war?"

"No. I was afraid he was. And that would mean leaving my house on the mountain to live on Stargill land. Randall loved that place, more than he loved me, even. He wasn't ever going to leave his farm, except feetfirst. It's a fine place, I reckon, except for such as I."

Jane considered it. "You mean, you—saw things—at the Stargills?"

Nora sighed. "It's best left alone," she said. "It will end soon. Now I'm keeping you from your work. You'll be wanting to make lunch for Spencer, won't you?"

"Spencer? He never comes home for lunch."

Nora Bonesteel settled back in the armchair, the Bible in her lap. "Well, Jane, when he calls, tell him I'm here."

CHAPTER EIGHT

If we give way to them now, it will ever be the case.

—DANIEL BOONE,
letter to Colonel Henderson, April 1, 1775

Robert Lee hurried into the house ahead of his brothers. Garrett was attempting to calm his shrieking wife, and Clayt and Charlie were talking to Kelley, who was at least making sense. Where was Lilah? Robert Lee didn't quite know what he had expected to find in the house. A medical emergency perhaps. Lilah had smoked in her youth, and, now that she was past the change of life, her weight made her a possible candidate for a heart attack. He wondered if anyone had called the rescue squad. He could feel his own heart pounding as he stumbled up the back steps, fearing the worst.

He found his wife in the living room, calm and not stricken by illness. She was holding a polished wooden box, lid closed, and staring at nothing with a solemn, frozen look that made him think of church. She looked up when she heard him come in, smiling gently in his direction.

"What's the matter?" he asked, heaving the words as he tried to catch his breath.

"Sit down, Robert," said Lilah. "The girls just had a fright is all. Young people lead such sheltered lives, don't they?"

"I suppose," he said. He wondered if the angelic Rudy was mixed up in this; in fact, he caught himself glancing around the room as if his wife's angel might be lounging in a corner watching the excitement with a bemused, seraphic smile. Lilah claimed that she never saw Rudy, but he was always afraid that *he* might. "What set them off, Lilah? I thought you'd had a stroke or something, the way they carried on."

Lilah shook her head. "An old friend of your father's dropped by," she said. "Nora Bonesteel, her name was."

Robert Lee swallowed hard. Everyone in these parts knew about Nora Bonesteel. Were scared of her, too, the way she knew things. She went out of her way not to bring bad tidings, but it made folks uneasy, anyhow, wondering what it was she knew about them. "Did she say anything about Dad?" he whispered.

"No. She knew that he had been taken ill. Well—let me take that back. She seemed to fear the worst. She brought us this box, and said that Daddy Stargill would want to be buried with it. Isn't that extraordinary, Robert?"

"I guess it is," he said. "But Miz Bonesteel is an unusual sort of woman." He was ashamed at the relief he felt. Far better for Daddy to die quickly now, without suffering, than to fight his way to a tenuous, helpless recovery, only to require constant nursing or to succumb weeks or months from now, forcing Robert to take off from work all over again.

"I recognized her, of course," said Lilah, with a complacent smile. "She was that dark-haired beauty that your father used to run around with before the War. There are pictures in the family album, though why Clarsie let them stay there is more than I can guess."

"That was a long time ago, honey," said Robert, patting her shoulder.

"Well, that's what Rudy said. I was working my way up to telling her that Daddy Stargill's illness was a family matter, and that she *wasn't* family, when Rudy said, just as plain in my head, he said:

'Lilah Rose, you got no call to go sticking your damned nose into what went on before you were born and doesn't concern you now.' "

Robert shifted uneasily. "*Damned?* He said that?"

"He did," said Lilah, nodding emphatically. "He's a dirty-talking angel, sometimes, when he's worked up."

"And Nora Bonesteel left this box to be buried with Daddy. That's strange, all right. I don't ever remember them so much as passing the time of day together at church even."

"No. Your father did his courting when he was young, and when that was over, he had nothing left to say to women in general," said Lilah. Her conversations with her father-in-law had been perfunctory and few.

Robert sat down beside his wife, and took the polished box out of her lap. "It's heavy enough. Good workmanship. What's in it? Love letters?"

"That's what *we* all thought," said Lilah. "Open it."

Robert started to lift the lid, but he was distracted by the rest of the family, who came trailing into the room. Debba was still making snuffling noises, and hanging on to Garrett's arm, and Kelley, still whey-faced, murmured that she had to check on Kayla, and fled.

"Get on with it!" said Garrett. He and Charles came behind the sofa so that they could look over their brother's shoulder as he opened the box. Robert Lee took a deep breath—*Nora Bonesteel!*—and flung back the lid.

His first irrational thought as he glimpsed the contents was that someone had packed away a collection of ivory carvings, but an instant later he realized that he was seeing bones. Small, delicate bones. They were yellowed with age, with a root growing through a crack in one long bone, and the tips of some of them were pocked with tooth marks, but the bones were as clean as if they had been newly washed before being set in the box. The eggshell skull rested beside them on a knitted blanket. Robert Lee heard Charles Martin gasp, and even Clayt had been shocked into silence.

"It's human," said Robert Lee, poking at the skull with his forefinger, and hoping that when he lifted it, he would find the elongated facial structure of a fawn, but no. It was a human skull, tiny and perfect, with fine seams crisscrossing the cranium, and it bore the small opening at the crown of the head that gradually closes as a child grows into adulthood. This one would never close.

Across the room, Debba swallowed a sob, and buried her face in the upholstery of the red chair. "Take it easy!" said Garrett, but he looked more exasperated than concerned. He leaned forward for a closer look.

"Isn't it sad?" said Lilah, as calmly as ever. "I suppose she wants the baby to be buried with its father."

"What are you talking about?" said Robert. "My father and Miz Bonesteel never—never married."

"No, Robert. But that wouldn't have prevented their having a child together. Perhaps the baby died at birth, and she has kept it all these years. She never married, did she?"

Garrett picked up the skull, and, holding it inches from his nose, he peered at it. "This is no baby," he said at last. "I mean, I'm no expert, but—without going into any details here—I've seen some skulls in my time, and this one is too big to be an infant. I'd say this is a young child—five or six, maybe."

Robert looked puzzled. "Nora Bonesteel never had a child. Certainly never one that lived to be five or six. That's a secret that you couldn't keep in a small community."

"Well, who is it then?" asked Lilah. "If it's not their child, why else would she want it buried with your daddy, Robert?"

"How do you reckon it died?" asked Clayt.

Robert looked down at the little pile of bones in the box on his lap. "I don't know. I think we ought to take them to the sheriff, and see what he can make of them. Miz Bonesteel didn't tell you what was in the box, or explain why she brought it?"

Lilah shook her head. "She didn't seem to want to talk about it."

In the kitchen the telephone rang. Clayt hurried out of the room, motioning for everyone else to stay put.

"If the woman offered no explanation, we should consult the sheriff, for sure," said Garrett. "This isn't something we need to be worrying about, what with everything else going on right now."

"Should we phone the sheriff?" asked Charles Martin. He had been staring at the bones in an abstracted way, and his fingers were making chords on the sofa.

"Clayt's still on the phone," Lilah pointed out.

Garrett shrugged. "Might as well take them to him. Save him a trip up here. It isn't as if this were a crime scene. And *we* don't know anything. I guess he'll have to talk to Nora Bonesteel."

"Who's going to take them in?" asked Robert Lee.

Clayt came back in time to hear his brother's question. "I'm dropping the wood off at the cabinet shop," said Clayt. "And then I'd better go to the Stallard's place. That was Dovey calling, upset, wouldn't say why. I was going to offer to take the young-un with me, if you think Kelley wouldn't mind."

Charles Martin shrugged. "Sure. Whatever. But you can't be hauling her around with a skeleton in the car. Kelley wouldn't care for that one bit."

Garrett looked over at his wife, and scowled. She was going to need an entire afternoon of tea and hand holding, and he didn't want to do it. Let Lilah cope with her. She looked like the motherly type. He straightened up. "I'll take the box into Hamelin. Sheriff's department still in the same place, Clayt?"

His brother nodded.

"Like everything else in Hamelin," said Garrett, grinning. "Nothing ever changes around here."

Charles Martin looked uneasy. "Listen, Garrett, could you tell the sheriff to keep quiet about this situation here? Ask him not to talk to reporters. I wouldn't want this to get splashed all over the supermarket tabloids. You know: *Country Singer Finds Skeleton in*

Family Closet. That kind of publicity would just make it tough on all of us."

Garrett's eyes narrowed. "I'll be sure and do that," he said:

Clayt looked at his watch. "Eleven o'clock. Guess I ought to get going. Come help me load the wood into the truck."

Garrett picked up the box. "I'll head out, too, then. Let's go."

When they had left the room, Debba raised her tear-stained face, and looked at Lilah. "He's mad at me again."

"Who? Garrett? Well, patience is not a virtue the army sets much store by, Debba." She paused, and then decided to say it straight out. "Courage is."

Debba's mouth tightened. "Garrett Stargill may not understand, but he *knows*."

Lilah shrugged. She knew by now not to meddle in other people's troubles. She bent over a box of baby clothes, and began sorting tiny embroidered garments as thin and yellow as parchment. "That poor child in the box," she murmured. "I wonder did she ever have nice things to wear." She listened for Rudy's rejoinder, but the only sound in the room was Debba Stargill's sniffling.

Garrett stopped for a moment to look at his brothers' vehicles, parked in a row beside his own '95 Chevy Blazer. "What are you driving?" he said aloud. It was a standard greeting among the old men of east Tennessee. They said it when you turned up after a long absence. Not "How are you?" but "What are you driving?" Maybe it was the same question, he thought, looking from Charles Martin's Lexus to Clayt's battered seventies four-wheel drive. He supposed that his Blazer answered the question about himself truthfully enough: he had a good job, and he didn't care for the pretense of fancy cars.

He backed out of the driveway, and headed down the hill toward town. The carved box rattled on the floor of the passenger side, and Garrett glanced down at it, hoping it wouldn't tip over. He had seen enough dead bodies, one way and another, not to be panicked by them, but the sight of a child's bones saddened him. He wondered if it was an Indian baby, plundered from an ancient burial ground. He knew his father had been a digger of arrowheads in his youth. Perhaps he had stumbled upon this find somewhere in his rambling. No other explanation made sense. They were the Stargills, not the outlaw Sorleys or the white trash Harkryders. There was no violence in the family as far back as anybody could remember. Only Dwayne's drunken escapades had ever cost the family a legal fee.

Garrett tried to concentrate on the road, remembering other trips down the mountain, riding like a hound in the back of Daddy's old pickup with Charles Martin and Dwayne, or racing his first car down the mountain, taking care not to ride the brakes, because he couldn't afford new ones. He was a cautious driver now. He was older; he and death were better acquainted; and Debba had cried until all the joy of bravado had left him, even when she wasn't in the passenger seat to reproach him for his recklessness.

He thought he would go to the hospital after he finished his business at the sheriff's office. He'd like some time alone with the old man. The thought of a deathbed crowd scene made him squirm. He wished he had put aside some time for his father while they still could have talked. They had never compared war stories, for one thing.

Randall Stargill had two funny stories about World War II, one involving a pet bulldog he'd had on base in England, and one about the time the people in the pub thought that his buddy Schlintz was a German agent, because he talked so funny. Schlintz was from Alabama. If heroic things, or tragic things, had happened to Lieutenant Stargill during the war, he had kept it to himself for the next half century. Garrett was the same way. He preferred not to talk about his missions, but if somebody outside the unit pressed him for details, he would trot out a carefully edited story, just dull enough to discourage further questions about his work.

Garrett wished he had talked to his father about his own battles, frankly and without censoring out the fear and the intensity of combat. *Did you have a hard-on when you when into battle, too, Dad?* He could not imagine saying such a thing to the laconic old man. But no matter how drunk he'd have had to get, he would have told it all, and insisted on a response in kind. They could have met on common ground then, and accepted each other as men, as fellow soldiers. As it was, Garrett knew that to his father he was still a wet-eared adolescent, and to him, Randall Stargill was a man he barely knew. The opportunity to change that was lost. He wished that it could be otherwise.

Randall Stargill lay alone in his hospital room, undisturbed by staff or visitors, oblivious to his surroundings, drifting. Still and silent in sweat-soaked sheets, he was trying to reach the coast of England, straining for a glimpse of green fields beyond the ragged gray of the cliffs in mist. It was the spring of 1944, on his eighth and last bombing mission in the B-17 nicknamed "The Pistol-Packing Mama" by the mountain boys who flew her. The Judy Canova hit tune about a gun-toting hellion had been a great favorite with the pilot, a West Virginian who fancied himself a tenor. They had decorated the side of the cockpit with a Varga-style portrait of a bosomy cowgirl with a six-gun in each hand, an American Valkyrie leading honky-tonk warriors into battle. Randall could remember each line of that painted lady's face, better than most of those he had seen since.

The raid had been uneventful until they were flying back through Holland. As they passed too near a German E-boat base at Ymuiden, the German ground troops opened fire with a battery of 20mm guns. The *Mama* took a hit in its number two engine, but they flew on over a green and gray patchwork of sea and clouds, counting themselves lucky that no real damage had been done to the plane. They sang "On Top of Old Smokey" on the flight back to

England, and Randall called everyone over to look down at the wreath of clouds below them, saying how it put him in mind of looking down at the valley from the cemetery ridge on the Stargill farm back in Tennessee. "I was up there with my girl oncet," he was saying, "and telling her how I was saving up for a plane ride—"

They were laughing so hard at this that it took a moment for Thompson's shouts to be heard. The second engine was on fire. The oil pressure had dropped to zero. They had been hit. The pilot feathered the propeller. They activated the fire extinguisher, but the blaze stayed strong, making clouds of its own in the mist.

Randall felt the plane lose altitude. The engines stopped, and his throat closed on bile as he waited for the crash, but just then the props began to turn again, and the landing gear dropped. *He's trying to blow out the flames*, Randall thought.

It didn't work. Now the other crew members were running past him, scrambling for their parachutes, heading for the open bomb bay. *"Bail out! She's going to explode!"* It was the last thing he'd heard the captain say.

They were six hundred feet above the waves when Randall and—was it Schlintz?—dropped through the forward escape hatch. Six hundred feet—just enough distance for the static line chutes to open. The ones who left by the bomb bay only seconds later weren't so lucky. Randall had just pawed his way out from under the floating parachute when he saw the wing explode as the pilot tried for a water landing. The B-17 spun to the right, cartwheeled, and plunged into the sea. Randall never saw the captain again.

A PBY Catalina seaplane fished three of them out of the water alive. Randall had some broken bones, but he would make it. The other guy was unconscious, but they managed to hold him up until help came. Thompson died in the rescue plane, and the bodies of the others were recovered later from the Channel, or from an English beach.

Randall never told his sons about that day. He never told anyone how, when he was floating in that water, he kept seeing Nora Bonesteel's face that morning up on the ridge above the farm, remembering the sad look she got when he told her how much he wanted to fly. He wrote her a letter from the hospital, breaking off their engagement, and not long after that he got some leave, went home, and married plain, serious, little Clarsie Hollister. He made sure his cane wouldn't show in the wedding pictures. He didn't see Nora Bonesteel then or later, but sometimes he dreamed about her. He'd see her standing beside that open bomb bay, tears streaming down her face, and he'd scream at her, "Why didn't you warn them?" Then he would wake up, cold and shaking, and lie there dry-eyed until morning.

Clayt Stargill had taken the rosewood planks to Hamelin's cabinetmaker to be planed. They would be ready late tomorrow, Dalton Wheeler promised him. "H'its hard wood to work," the old man said. "Right nice when you finish, but you'uns will want to be careful how you nail it, because it would as soon split as look at you. So don't go trying to rush the job now."

Clayt promised to pass along the warning to his brothers. Kayla had come with him on the drive to Hamelin, saying little along the way, and standing well back from the machinery in Wheeler's workshop, a blond shadow who watched everything, without attracting any attention to herself. She was a child who knew how to make grown-ups forget she was there, he thought, and he wondered if behaving that way was her idea or a lesson she had learned in the course of her short, hard life.

"You want some ice cream?" he asked her, as they headed back toward the highway.

Kayla shrugged. "Sure. If it's no trouble. I like chocolate."

Clayt smiled at her. "Women mostly do," he said. He swung into the parking lot of the Dairy Queen, and took her in for a large dip-cone and a fistful of napkins to protect the seat covers.

"I don't usually spill stuff," she told him. "Not that I eat in cars all that much."

"I'll bet you don't," said Clayt, thinking of his brother's silver Lexus. "So what do you like to do, besides watch television?"

Kayla shrugged. "Coloring books. Swim. I can't read much yet."

"Do you like animals?"

"Mama says I can't have a dog. They're too messy."

"You don't have to own something to like it," said Clayt. "Look at that bird on the telephone pole over there. See him? The gray one?" Kayla leaned in the direction he pointed, and nodded. "That's a mockingbird. State bird of Tennessee. They put his picture on road signs."

"What are the little fat ones that just flew over the car?"

"Snowbirds," said Clayt without looking. He had noted them as they went past, as methodically as he catalogued every facet of nature in his mind, but he hadn't thought them interesting enough to mention.

"Nah. They can't be *snowbirds*. They're not white."

"They're not supposed to be. People call them snowbirds because you see them in the winter, especially around the bird feeders. The proper name for them is junco. Ours have bluer bills than the flatland juncos. Don't ask me how come."

"What's your favorite bird?"

"Well," said Clayt, "I'll tell you, but I can guarantee we won't see one. It's called a Bewick's wren. It's a little fellow with a brown body, with white underneath, and white outer tailfeathers."

"How come we won't see one?"

"Well, because there may not be any more of them. They used to live in these mountains on the farmsteads. They liked open fields, and the kind of cleared land that the settlers made. They like to nest in abandoned buildings, junked cars, tin cans . . ." He sighed. "They're gone now. I think the last sighting was ten years ago. Never seen one myself. Not for want of trying, either. I've about worn out my binoculars looking for one."

"What happened to them?"

"Well, the land changed, for one thing. A lot of those farms went back to National Forest, and for another thing, newer, tougher bird species moved in and ran them off."

"You sure do know a lot about nature and stuff."

"Uh-huh. It's my job. I go to schools and talk to kids like you. Tell them about the environment."

"Can we go out for a walk and talk about nature and stuff when we get back?"

Clayt hesitated. "Maybe late this afternoon, if there's time. After we get you some ice cream, I'm going to take you back home, and then I have to stop by a farm up on the ridge to see a young lady of my acquaintance."

"Dressed like that?" asked Kayla, nodding at Clayt's dirtstreaked jeans and rumpled shirt.

"She won't mind. She needs help, it sounds like. Besides, even after working in the barn all morning, I bet I'm cleaner now than Daniel Boone was for most of his life."

Kayla blinked. "How come?"

"No central heating back then, and no hot water coming out of a tap just for the asking. If you wanted hot water, you had to light a wood fire, and boil it yourself, so baths were an awful lot of trouble. It was hard to keep clothes clean, too, so head lice were pretty much a fact of life."

Kayla wrinkled her nose until it almost disappeared into her forehead. "Bugs in their *hair*?"

"Oh, sure. One time Boone's daughter Jemima got kidnapped by some Indians, and she knew her father and his men were tracking the war party, trying to get her back. So when the Indians stopped to rest, Jemima started picking lice out of the chief's hair, so that he'd relax, and not be in such a hurry to leave."

"I wouldn't pick no bugs out of anybody's hair," Kayla declared.

"You would if it would get you rescued," said Clayt. "It worked, too. That Indian was so pleased to have Jemima taking the bugs out of his scalp that he clean forgot to watch for the approaching settlers. By and by, Boone and his men burst in and rescued the captives, and Jemima was home by nightfall."

"What happened to the Indian?"

"Uh—" Clayt looked at her, wondering what he should say to a little girl.

"They killed him, of course," said Kayla, after a moment's thought.

"Yeah. Daddies can be pretty fierce when they're protecting their little girls."

"I wouldn't know," said Kayla, looking away.

Clayt searched the landscape for a new topic of conversation. "Look over in that maple tree on your side of the road. There's a kestrel perched up there near the top. He's a hunter. Those snowbirds we saw better watch out."

The girl peered out the window, her interest in nature revived. "What are those black birds in the field over there?"

Clayt frowned. "Starlings. Whole flock of them, too. Hope the kestrel gets a few of them for his supper."

Kayla studied him carefully for a few moments while she tidied the sides of her ice cream cone with her tongue. Then she said, "Starlings. They're nice and shiny. How come you don't like them?"

"Lots of reasons. First of all they don't belong here." Seeing her puzzled look, he said, "Starlings are not native to North America. They were imported relatively recently. They've only been here a hundred years or so. Daniel Boone never saw one."

Kayla smiled. "That's why you don't like them. Well, how did the starlings get here?"

"Some fool named Scheifflin, a manufacturing tycoon with more money than sense, imported them in 1892. He got it into his head that America ought to have every kind of bird that is mentioned in the works of William Shakespeare, so he brought a bunch of species over from Europe and let them loose in Central Park in New York City. A lot of the newcomers died, but not the starlings. No, siree. They just loved it here. Within a few years they had spread out all over the continent, making a complete nuisance of themselves."

"How can little old birds be any trouble?" asked Kayla. "They don't look big enough to hurt anybody."

"They hurt other birds, though. They're loud, and mean, and pushy. Before long, they had begun to drive our nice native songbirds out of their homes. They'd beat them up, and steal all the food. They travel together in huge flocks, and they crap all over everything. They're noisy, too."

"Can you do bird calls? What do they sound like?"

"Well, that's the other thing I don't like about starlings," said Clayt. "They don't even have their own songs. They sing everybody else's songs. You'll hear them imitating other songbirds: robins, cardinals, whatever. They just take everything that used to belong to somebody else: the land, the food, even the songs of the birds that belong here."

Kayla thought about this for a moment. "They're the ones that ran off your Buick wrens, aren't they?"

"Bewick's wren," murmured Clayt. "Yep. They sure are. They just shoved their way in here and took over."

After a half mile of silence, Kayla tapped his arm. "You know what?" she said. "I betcha that Indian chief with the head lice would have said the same thing about the pioneers. I bet he thought Daniel Boone was just a walking starling, taking the land, and the deer, and everything that used to belong to the Indians and kicking them out."

"I guess he did." Clayt drove in silence for half a mile or so, wondering if a world without starlings would also lack pioneers.

Dovey Stallard found her father sitting on a rock in the sheep pasture, looking out at the folds of mountains. He looked bleached and brittle in the afternoon sun, as if the land were leeching its sustenance out of his body. She forgot, sometimes, that he had grown old. In her mind, he had stayed a lean and silver fifty-one, but sometimes, especially when he was worried, she could see the years carving a landscape on his face.

She put her hand on his shoulder. "Did you see the lamb?" she asked.

He nodded. "What was left of it. I'll take it off and bury it directly."

Directly didn't mean "at once," Dovey knew. It meant "in a little while," or "when the spirit moves me to do it." She sat down on the ground beside him, and patted his hand. "Let me do it. You have enough chores. Besides I thought I'd bury my Majorca rooster—what's left of him. I found a pile of blood and feathers in the chicken run. I've called Clayt Stargill to see what he says about this. There might be something we can do to stop the killings."

J. Z. Stallard shook his head. "Maybe it's a sign, Dovey. We sure have had our share of troubles here lately. Maybe the Lord wants us to quit the land, and find another life."

"I don't want another life," said Dovey. "I can go out and get a job. You know I wouldn't mind doing it if we need the money. I could get on the night shift somewhere—a factory, maybe—and still do my work around here in the daytime. I should have done that when we lost the barn, but you were too stubborn to let me. I don't know why I let you talk me out of it then."

"Your mother never worked, Dovey."

She sighed. "That was a long time ago, Daddy. Different world.

Besides, Mama had a husband and two kids to raise, and her share of the farm to run. Nobody worked harder than Mama did. Compared to her, I don't do much. I don't bake bread very often, and we have an automatic washer now. Cooking for two people is no chore, and there's hardly enough farm work for the both of us, now that we've sold off the Holsteins . . ." She saw him stiffen at the mention of his dairy herd, and he fixed his eyes on the blue mountains, as if he'd forgotten that she was there. She shouldn't have reminded him.

"I'm getting too old," said J. Z. Stallard. "It might have been different if Tate had come back, and taken over the running of the farm. He could have kept things going."

Dovey's lips tightened, but she said nothing. Her older brother, Tate, had joined the Marines after flunking out of Milligan College. He hadn't made it back from Vietnam, and she was sorry about that. She mourned and missed him still, and she thought their mother might not have given in to her cancer so easily if Tate had been around—but if he had come back alive and well, she didn't think Tate would have been the answer her father was searching for. He never cared for farming, or for working either, as far as she could tell. As likely as not, he would have come back long enough to have another fight with Daddy, and then lit out for the first big city he could think of, with whatever money he could coax his father into parting with. No point in saying any of that to her father, though. Bickering about Tate wouldn't change the here and now.

"Did you see that fellow in a suit that came by this morning?"

Dovey nodded. "What was he selling?"

"Nothing. He was looking to buy. He's a real estate fellow from Hamelin. Whitescarver Realty. Gave me his card. Said he wanted to make us an offer on the farm. Three hundred an acre."

Dovey snorted. "Did you take after him with the pitchfork?"

"No. I told him I wasn't of a mind to sell. But I've been thinking about it ever since. Maybe it would be the best thing, after all." He pulled a crumpled letter out of the pocket of his work pants. "I didn't tell you about this. Guess I should have."

Dovey unfolded the tattered letter and scanned the typed lines. "Notice of foreclosure . . . Tax sale! Daddy, how long have you known about this?"

He shrugged. He would not look at her. "Couple of weeks, I guess. I tried to put it out of my mind. Kept thinking I'd go see a lawyer about it, but I never got around to it."

"But we could lose the farm, Daddy!"

"I suppose so. I've prayed over it, though."

Dovey sighed. "Why didn't you tell me? I could have hired a lawyer, maybe talked to somebody down at the courthouse. We could have done something."

"I think this is meant to be," said J. Z. Stallard. He wouldn't look at his daughter.

Dovey's eyes narrowed. "Oh, do you? Meant to be. Well, I don't intend to give up Stallard land without a fight, just because a bunch of city people want privacy and a view. This is our land. It always has been."

"Well, Daughter, I just don't see any way out of this, unless your mother up in heaven can persuade the Lord to grant us a miracle."

"Oh, crap, Daddy! Faith isn't going to get those tax wolves off our doorstep. We have to fight to keep what's ours. We've always had to fight to keep going."

"Lord, Honey." J. Z. Stallard gave his daughter a pat on the arm and a sad smile. "You can't fight the government."

"You see if I can't," said Dovey.

CHAPTER NINE

I can't say I was ever lost, but I was bewildered once for three days.

—DANIEL BOONE

Garrett Stargill had no trouble finding the sheriff's office. The business district of Hamelin was one street that widened after a few blocks into a state road that snaked its way up Buffalo Mountain to a series of farms and communities in higher valleys, among steeper mountains. The sheriff's office stood behind the courthouse, an old two-story brick house on a side street. It had a small porch with newly painted gingerbread trim, and a planter of geraniums on either side of the steps. Garrett looked at the geraniums, and wondered if he had seen more of death than these lawmen had. He'd bet on it.

He parked his truck in the gravel lot and crossed the street, cradling the box in his arms. Its heaviness was the wood of the box itself; the small bones within added little to the burden.

Garrett stopped at the steps to the brick house, studied the wooden sign that said "Sheriff's Office," and wished he had worn his uniform. He would have felt more credible dressed as a soldier—one uniform to another, instead of a civilian facing a uniformed lawman. He resolved to mention his rank in his first breath.

He balanced the box, turned the knob, and went in. "I'm Warrant Officer Garrett—" A blond girl—she couldn't have been much more than twenty—with long straight hair and mascara too dark for her coloring, blinked up at him. She must be the receptionist, he thought. A name plate on her desk said "Jennaleigh." Garrett decided that he needn't explain his errand to her. "Is the sheriff in?" he asked, careful not to smile.

The young woman looked at Garrett's stern face, then at the box. She seemed to think better of questioning him herself. "Wait here. I'll get Sheriff Arrowood." She tapped on a door at the back of the reception room, and disappeared inside.

Garrett set the box down on a straight-backed chair, but he felt no inclination to be seated. He paced the pine floor, and studied the notices posted on the bulletin board. There were a couple of federal wanted posters, some legal notices headed "State of Tennessee," and a typewritten document entitled "Tax Auction," which he had been about to read when the sheriff appeared.

"Spencer Arrowood. What can I do for you?"

Garrett turned, speechless for a moment, at the sight of a blond man of about medium height, about his own age. He was wearing a badge on his khaki uniform, and a 9mm Glock holstered on his hip. It was several seconds before Garrett remembered to extend his hand. "Sorry to act so startled," he said. "I'm Garrett Stargill, Warrant Officer, U.S. Army. Pleased to meet you, Sheriff. You kind of caught me off guard there for an instant. It's stupid, I know, but—I was expecting Nelse Miller."

The sheriff nodded. "Nelse passed away quite a few years back, Mr. Stargill. He's still missed, though. Not least by me. He was sheriff a good many years here. I take it you're from around here originally?"

"Randall Stargill is my daddy. You probably know our farm."

"I believe I know your brother, too," said Spencer Arrowood. "Charles Martin Stargill, the country singer? I went to school with him. How is he these days?"

Garrett grunted. "He drives a silver Lexus."

"I hear him on the radio every now and then." Spencer Arrowood studied his visitor carefully. His glance took in the wooden box resting on the chair by the door. He waited politely.

A few seconds of silence passed before Garrett realized that the sheriff was waiting for an explanation. He picked up the box. "This is what I came about. Can we go into your office?"

The box sat in the middle of the sheriff's desk. Spencer Arrowood heard him out, without any sign of impatience, while he explained about the visit from Nora Bonesteel and her instruction that the box and its contents be laid to rest with Randall Stargill. "My daddy's dying, you see," said Garrett. "At least we think he is. He's in a coma, anyhow, over in the hospital in Johnson City, so we can't ask him about this. She just ups and brings it. As if we didn't have enough on our minds, worrying about him, and the expense and all the rest of it. Anyhow, we thought this had best be brought to you."

"All right." Spencer Arrowood pulled the box toward him. "I know Miz Bonesteel, and she is a rare individual, I'll grant you that. Let's see what she has brought you." He undid the latch, and opened the box. Garrett thought he saw a flicker of surprise on the sheriff's face, but it vanished quickly. "A skeleton. Young child. Old bones, from the look of them. That root has been there for years. And you say she brought this to you with no explanation?"

"That's right," said Garrett. "It's no use asking any of us about this, Sheriff, because we don't know what's going on or who that is. We didn't have any brothers or sisters who died as children."

"You did right to bring this to me," the sheriff told him. "I'll see what Miz Bonesteel can tell me about this."

"This doesn't have to be made public, does it?" asked Garrett. "The family doesn't want any kind of scandal. And it doesn't seem fair, with Dad in a coma, unable to tell his side of it. Whatever happened, I mean."

Spencer Arrowood was still examining the bones, fingering them carefully for signs of breaks, or other abnormalities. "Public?"

he said. "I don't think so. At this time we have no evidence of foul play, and no answers about who this is, and why the bones were brought to you. If that changes, I'll be in touch."

"We appreciate that. Charles Martin was concerned. You know how the tabloids like to hound people in the entertainment business."

"So I'm told. But your family honestly has no idea who these bones belong to, or why you were given them?"

Garrett shook his head. "My sister-in-law thinks it's my father's child by that Bonesteel woman. Claims they used to be lovers before Dad married my mother. I think she's just speculating, though. I never heard anything about any such incident."

Spencer closed the lid of the box. "Neither have I, Mr. Stargill," he said. "And I think I might have heard before you did."

Frank Whitescarver counted the vehicles as he pulled in to the driveway of the Stargill farm. He was a little later in arriving than he had planned on, and some of the brothers were obviously elsewhere, but at least there wasn't a passel of visiting neighbors to contend with. In the old days, there would have been. People came and sat with the about-to-be-bereaved, brought food, helped sew the grave clothes—did whatever needed doing—but Frank doubted that many people would be visiting the Stargills. The boys had left long ago to pursue careers in the big cities. They were strangers now. Seems like most of the younger generation ended up leaving these days—college or the army or just the need to get a job that paid enough to support a family. When the old people died off—as Mr. Stargill was in the process of doing now—the strangers came in. No use wishing for the old days to come back, though, Frank thought. That way of life was as dead as the passenger pigeons, and perhaps it was a good thing: not much money in real estate when the land stayed in the family.

He parked his Jeep Cherokee, noting the old truck and the other late-model car, and hoping the latter wasn't paid for. He helloed the house. He probably didn't need to, with a younger generation of town boys in residence, but it was a habit worth keeping in the wilder parts of the mountains. People didn't like you to sneak up on them. A holdover from who knew what terrible times in the past. Revenue men, armed for a raid, perhaps, in the early part of the century. Or Civil War guerrillas who turned the war in the southern mountains into a house-to-house feud, stealing livestock and ambushing the householders. You might even trace their wariness of strangers back to Scotland, the Rising of 1745, when the Duke of Cumberland sent his soldiers into the Highlands to kill the Jacobites—that is, anyone they could find. Many of the ones who hid—who distrusted strangers, and therefore survived—ended up here. The lessons of the past would not desert them easily. They distrusted trespassers instinctively. Frank didn't blame them. Even today, a trespasser might be a hunter who would shoot your cow by mistake, or a tourist who figured that the whole state was a theme park, open to the public. He had learned to smile broadly, and to use the front path.

Still, he thought the Stargills would be glad enough to see him when they heard what he'd come for. He went back to the Jeep, and reached into his glove compartment for a handful of Whitescarver Realty key chains and ballpoint pens. It always helped if you gave folks something at the outset. They seemed to feel obliged to be polite to you, if they took your trinkets.

A heavyset man appeared on the front porch, squinting out at the visitor with a look of apprehension. Frank waved and grinned. This Stargill was fiftyish, with polyester trousers and a seersucker sport shirt. Frank loosened his tie, and hurried forward, assuming the look of neighborly concern.

"Mr. Stargill," he said in hushed, but cordial, tones. "I came to pay my respects. How is your father doing?"

"Well, we think we're going to lose him." Robert Lee contrived to look appropriately solemn. He sensed that this was not a social call, but he extended his hand in a cautious welcome.

"Would you mind telling me which Stargill boy you are?" said the stranger. "I'm Frank Whitescarver, by the way." He deposited a keychain and a refrigerator magnet in his host's outstretched hand.

"Robert Lee. I'm the oldest."

"Knew you weren't the singer. I'm glad to know you, Mr. Stargill. Reckon you're the head of the family now."

Robert Lee was pleased at this assumption of his importance, although he was by no means sure that he could exert any authority over his brothers. They were a stubborn lot, reckless with their lives and their money, and none of them had ever listened to good advice.

Frank Whitescarver looked admiringly at the white house and plantings of daffodils in the flowerbeds, Clarsie's legacy to the land. "This is a real nice place you've got, Mr. Stargill," he said, smiling. "We'll be right glad to welcome you back to the community."

"Welcome me back?"

"Why, sure. With your dad's passing, you'll be coming home to take over the farm, surely? I hear good things about sheep raising in these hills—good pastures, lots of clean water. Of course, wool prices are down, and we've got coyotes coming into the area. But maybe you know more about the farm business than I do."

Robert shook his head. "I have a life in Cincinnati," he said. "I couldn't afford to leave it, and take on a farm. It takes capital to get a livestock business going, and it's backbreaking work, even for a young man, which I'm not."

"Backbreaking work. It is that," said Frank, strolling around the yard, admiring the forsythia and the redbud. "Makes you respect those pioneers who carved these farms out of the wilderness, doesn't it?"

"Reckon they were young men, too," said Robert Lee.

Frank nodded. "Right nice flowers there. I'm partial to daffodils myself. Bet your mother was a gardener."

"She was that." Robert Lee was inspecting the Whitescarver Realty trinkets that Frank had given him.

"Well," said Frank. "Flowers don't get you through the winter, do they? I can see how a man might be loath to give up Cincinnati for a lonesome farm in the middle of nowhere. Don't suppose your famous brother would want to keep this place as a summer home away from Nashville?"

"Charles Martin couldn't get away from here fast enough," said Robert Lee.

"Guess it's just a case of the grass being greener," said the realtor, smiling. "Seems like all the young folks from around here can't wait to hightail it out of here, and all the people from somewhere's else are standing in line, trying to buy a place up here in the mountains, because it's so beautiful. Seems downright peculiar, when you think about it."

"I suppose so."

"Makes my job easier," said Frank, wandering into the backyard. He wanted to continue the uphill work of this conversation without going inside the house, if he could manage it. He had seen a curtain twitch at the front window, and he was afraid that the interview would not go quite so smoothly if Robert Lee Stargill's relatives were allowed to participate. "Yessir, I sure do have a pleasant job sometimes. Almost like being a fairy godfather, you might say."

Robert Lee glanced again at the refrigerator magnet business card. "Real estate?"

"That's right. Land is dreams, Mr. Stargill. Every day I get to grant wishes. Folks come to me, and say, 'Mr. Whitescarver, please find us a little piece of land with a view so we can retire to these beautiful mountains, and call them home.' And other folks call me up, and say, 'Frank, you know Mama has passed away, and left us the farm, but we have good jobs in the big city. We can't come home and pour our savings down the drain, trying to keep up an unmechanized dirt farm. And they're wanting the taxes paid. What can we do?'—

And I can help. It makes me happy to be helping folks in their hour of need."

Robert Lee nodded. "You buy farms, and sell the land to rich people for vacation homes."

"Everybody's happy, Mr. Stargill. People who want to move here get their dream home, and folks who left for the big city, and want to stay there, don't have to be dragged home by family circumstances. They get some extra money to pay off their bills, or maybe get a new car. And both sets of folks are grateful to me, buyer and seller." He tapped his chest. "Isn't that better than driving an ice cream truck? I ask you."

"What kind of money are we talking here, Mr. Whitescarver?"

The magic words. Frank Whitescarver suppressed a grin. "Well, we'd have to sit down and talk about it. I thought I'd broach the subject with you first—in case your brothers needed some advice from the new head of the family."

Robert Lee shook his head. "I'm not sure that I could persuade the rest of them to sell. They're every one contrary."

"Have you talked about it at all? This is a big place, you know. You couldn't just let it fall to ruin while you all went back to your lives outside."

"I know. It's so hard, with Daddy taken so sudden—"

Frank saw his exit cue. Now was the time to leave the owner with the thought of money dancing in his head. "And Lord knows I'm not pressuring you," he said, patting Robert Lee's arm. "But I wouldn't feel that I had been a good neighbor to you if I didn't warn you that the taxes on this place are likely to go up."

"They generally do," said Robert Lee.

"More than you think, though. By the time the next tax bill comes due, they'll probably double. And that assessment will probably cost you a bundle in inheritance tax for Uncle Sam."

"Why?"

"Because the tax assessors will value this land at an outlandish rate. More than you could sell it for. You see, this mountain is fixing to be rezoned—residential instead of agricultural. So they'll figure its worth as if you had two houses per acre, which you don't—and won't, because some of your acreage here is pretty near vertical. Doesn't seem fair, but that's the government for you." Frank endeavored to look sympathetic. Robert Lee Stargill was of the generation that believed you can't fight city hall; they even felt it was mildly unpatriotic to try.

Robert Lee blinked. "But that doesn't seem right. Why would they—"

"I can tell you in confidence," said Frank, dropping his voice to a church murmur. "The Stallards farm is about to be sold—not for much money, I'm afraid—but it's going to a developer. Now those fellas are looking to put a whole community of fancy new houses on that property—paved streets, water and sewer—the works. When they do that, it will up the tax value of your place here, because the government will say you could be making a lot of money off your land. Never mind that you aren't."

"But why would they do that to a family who has been here nigh on forever?"

Frank Whitescarver shook his head and sighed. "I gave up asking why when the government has a hand in things," he said sadly. "I'm just trying to help you folks out of a mess here. But you sit down and talk it over with the family, then give me a call. I'll work with you any way I can. That's a promise."

Spencer Arrowood had called his mother to see if she needed anything. If he had to go out on a non-urgent errand, he generally stopped by the market on his way back, and took her a loaf of bread or a quart of milk, in order to save her a trip. This time, though, instead of reciting a grocery order, Jane Arrowood had said, "Nora Bonesteel said to tell you she's here."

Spencer swore under his breath. He had the box on the desk in front of him, and he was getting ready to drive up Ashe Mountain to ask the old woman about it—and now, here she was, visiting his mother, and sending word to him about where he could find her, as if she'd been expecting him. "Tell her I'm on my way over," he said.

Jane Arrowood replied, "Yes, dear. I'm fixing you some lunch. Got it on the stove."

Spencer hung up the phone, and swore again—out loud this time.

"Something wrong?" asked Jennaleigh. She was new as a dispatcher, and she seemed to think that anytime anybody got angry, it was her fault.

Spencer managed to smile. "Just my mama, Jennaleigh," he said. "You know how mothers are. And I was wishing Martha Ayers was back from Morristown, so I could stick her with the task of finding out about this box. You hire a female deputy to handle the sticky emotional situations, and where is she when you need her?"

"Getting trained at Walters State Community College," said Jennaleigh, as if it had been a quiz. "You sent her there yourself."

"I know. I just didn't figure on needing her quite so soon."

"Well, she can't come back, can she? I think Deputy LeDonne said that if people who take the course miss any days of the course, they have to start all over again."

"It's all right. I want her to finish the training. I'm just grousing, that's all." Spencer Arrowood tucked the box under his arm. "I can handle this," he told the dispatcher. "All I have to do is question an old lady I've known all my life. It's not like the O.K. Corral, for god's sake!"

"Bet you wish it was," said Jennaleigh, but she took care to be out of earshot when she said it.

Charles Martin Stargill stood beside his father's hospital bed, feeling an awkwardness that never came to him when he faced a thousand people from a dark stage. He had set the Martin guitar in a corner of the room, and he glanced at it now, as if it could tell him what to say. "Hello, Daddy," he said softly.

The old man lay there, frowning slightly in his oblivion. Charles Martin wondered if pain could reach down into a coma and make itself felt, even through all the medication, or if bad dreams troubled even the deepest sleepers.

"Well, Daddy, I'm back," said Charles Martin. "I swore I wouldn't be, didn't I? I guess I never did fit in around here, and I couldn't wait to get gone. I was the big nobody at the high school—didn't play sports, didn't run with the popular kids, so-so grades. When I left, I sure as hell didn't look back, but it always nagged me that nobody thought I'd amount to anything, and they cared less. Guess I thought that when I made it big in country music, folks around here would sit up and take notice. But you know what? It didn't work like that. They just got to ignore me on a grander scale. Daddy, I've given interviews to the *New York Times*, the *Nashville Banner, Parade* magazine—hell, even the *Manchester Guardian* in England, one time—but you know who never asked me for an interview? *The Hamelin Record.* Didn't even run my press release when I played Johnson City. My publicist marked it "local interest"—as if they gave a damn. Bet they looked at it and said, 'Old Charlie Stargill is at ETSU this Friday, so what?'

"Daddy, I got a CMA nomination for hit single of the year last year. I'm on the charts in *Cashbox* and *Billboard.* But the radio station here doesn't even play me. How do I know? Believe me, I know. Kathy Mattea asked me to do a duet with her on her next album—and I don't reckon they'll ever play that, either."

He looked down at the still form, shrunken under bright lights and crisp sheets. "Did you ever ask them to, Daddy? Did you ever call the bastards up and say, 'My boy is somebody! Now play his goddamn record.' Or did you agree with them? Did you think that I must be exaggerating my own importance because I boasted about it. Hell, Daddy, I was driven to bragging. People just pretended I didn't exist. I might as well be managing a Burger King in Nashville, it seemed like. Y'all don't know how hard I worked, Daddy. How many nights I slept on the tour bus, and ate Rolaids for dessert. How many times my fingers bled from the Martin's steel strings after eight-hour sessions. I worked harder than any dairy farmer, Daddy, and all the while I knew that my very best might not be enough. Wanting it isn't enough. It'll get you to Nashville, all right, but it isn't enough to make the magic happen. Who the hell knows why people pick some ordinary folks to be stars, and leave the rest in the dust?

"I wouldn't take no for an answer, though. I just kept showing up. Writing songs. Hanging out. Talking to the men in suits. And I made it happen. By god, I did, Daddy. I *willed* myself right onto the charts, and I've never looked back." His voice quavered. "I wish to god somebody besides me gave a damn that I made it."

Charles Martin sat down in the straight chair beside the bed. He could feel his teeth clenching and his hands had curled into fists. He took a couple of deep breaths, letting the last one out in a long sigh. "Seems like I've been talking a lot about me, and forgetting what bad shape you're in," he told the sleeping man. "I hope you pull out of this, Daddy. Of course, we both know I wouldn't be talking to you like this if you were awake."

He waited, but there was no sign from Randall Stargill, not even the flicker of an eyelid to tell him anyone was listening.

"Wish I knew if you could hear me, Daddy. So you'd know I came to see you. I did care. I came, didn't I? There's a girl I'd kinda like you to meet. Her name is Kelley. I've been seeing her for a couple of months now, hoping I could make it work this time. Make it stick. She's had it rough before me, Daddy, and she has a smart little girl. Hell, I'd hate to let her down, but it's so hard for a celebrity to walk that line. I just—"

He ran out of words then, reddening with the effort of talking about anything more personal than his public life on a stage. He retrieved his guitar from the corner by the window. "Maybe you don't even know I'm here, Daddy," he said. "But in case you do, I thought I'd help you pass the time. We used to do a lot of singing on the back porch in the long twilights with this old guitar—before it got to be worth a New York fortune. This might bring back some happy memories for you."

He strummed the guitar and leaned his head down until it almost touched the neck of the instrument, and he began to sing "Will the Circle Be Unbroken?" in a clear baritone that wavered with unshed tears.

Deputy Joe LeDonne spent his lunch break in the patrol car, trying to write to Martha Ayers. There wasn't much to talk about, except to say that he missed her, and that he cared about her, but LeDonne wasn't much for putting feelings on paper. Surely she would realize that he wouldn't write to her unless he cared.

They had been together for several years now, first a tentative alliance between two lonely, wary people, and then with more resolve, as a troubled couple trying to make this last chance work.

She had been the office dispatcher when they first began seeing each other. It was only recently that she had been given the job of deputy. That change in their relationship had been harder on his ego than he cared to admit, and he had almost screwed up the relationship by getting involved with another woman. He had been trying to hurt Martha, and he had succeeded much too well.

They were still together, but there was a look in her eyes sometimes that made him ashamed. She looked like a whipped hound who is taking care never to get beaten again. He wondered how long it would take to make her trust him again, and if she ever would completely.

But he could say none of that in a letter to a fellow officer. He could say none of that, ever. LeDonne straightened the piece of paper, and began: *Dear Martha, Hope all is well with you in the training program. I'll try to call you soon. Things are as slow as ever around here. The only in-*

teresting thing is that spring seems to be on the way, which is good news to me because the heater in my patrol car is on the fritz. Of course, good weather will mean more tourists to contend with. Oh, well . . .

I miss you. Speeders are getting an easy time of it in Wake County with only two of us doing the patrols . . .

He thought he might sign the letter "Love, Joe," though he wondered what would be harder: his saying it or her believing it.

Spencer Arrowood parked his patrol car in his mother's driveway, and sat for a moment looking up at the white house, trying to decide how to handle the coming interview. He supposed that his mother would be hovering in the background, ready to side with her old friend against the prying questions of the law, and he had to admit to himself that he didn't want to ask the questions any more than she might want to answer them. If the bones had belonged to an infant, he might have assumed a stillbirth, and then he would have done his best to forget that he ever saw them. But this child had lived. And no matter how long ago it had stopped living, he had to try to find out what happened to it. Justice, he supposed. Even if the execution of justice disrupted the living and gave no comfort to the one he was trying to avenge, it was still his duty.

He walked toward the house, wondering if Nora Bonesteel had a better idea than he did about how the interview would go.

As he started up the front steps, his mother came out on the porch to meet him. "I'm glad you've come, Spencer," she said quietly. "Miz Bonesteel is sitting in there leafing through the Bible, and she's looking troubled. Has she had a vision about something?"

The sheriff shook his head. "I don't know yet. I'll have to talk to her. And I have to take the position that the state of Tennessee does not believe in visions, whatever you ladies here in the mountains aver to be true." He smiled at her, and edged past. "Now can I do this interview without having you for a deputy, please, ma'am?"

"You could tell me what it's about!" Jane Arrowood whispered as he opened the door.

Spencer glanced toward the living room, and then back at his mother. He signaled her not to follow him. "She may not want you to know."

Nora Bonesteel did not look up from the scripture when he came in and sat on the sofa next to the Queen Anne chair. Spencer watched her turn the pages of the Bible with a practiced touch that knew the verses as they came to hand. It seemed to him that she had hardly changed since he was a boy. He had thought her old even then, as he had most grown-ups, but there was a timeless quality about her that still held. Her hair was still dark, though streaked with silver, and her face was calm and smooth, with none of the helplessness he often saw in the faces of the elderly. He hoped that he could account as well for himself three decades hence.

"Miz Bonesteel," he said, gently touching her arm. "I believe you were expecting me."

She let the page fall back into place. "Good afternoon, Sheriff Arrowood," she said. She said "Arwood," giving his name the traditional mountain pronunciation. Only outlanders used all three syllables ar-row-wood, but he was used to it, and he answered to that, too. At least they knew how to spell it, he figured.

"I hear you've been having an eventful day," he remarked, keeping his voice genial. He didn't think it was in his power to frighten this old woman, but all the same he didn't want to risk it. Badges do funny things to people's perceptions of old acquaintances. He thought he stood a better chance of learning something if he kept the conversation friendly.

"I thought you might want to see me," said Nora Bonesteel. She looked at him steadily, solemnly. He could see no trace of uneasiness in her. Spencer relaxed a bit. Guilty people tensed up; looked away.

He said, "One of the Stargills from up the mountain came in to see me a little while ago. Said you'd visited their farm this morning, asking about Mr. Randall Stargill, and that you left them a carved wooden box. He said you asked that it be buried with Mr. Stargill, if he passes on from this illness."

Nora Bonesteel nodded. "It's his time, rest him. I don't believe he's sorry to go."

Spencer let that pass. He didn't want to get into what she knew before anybody ought to be able to know it. She scared some folks. He'd always found it easier not to believe such things and to tune out when his mother tried to discuss it with him. He leaned forward now, serious, but not angry, and said softly, "Now, ma'am, about that carved box that you took to the Stargills this morning. Did you know what was in it?"

"Bones."

"That's right." Spencer felt his chest tighten. "They were human bones. Not an infant, either. Looks to be a young child, though I reckon the lab will have to say for sure. Now where did you get that box?"

She sighed. "Randall made it himself, a long time ago."

"He gave it to you—with these bones in it?"

"No. Empty. It was to be a little hope chest, for fine needlework, jewelry, and such." She looked away. "We were fond of one another many years back."

There seemed to be a lot unsaid beneath her simple statement, but Spencer figured that lost loves were none of his business. He returned to the matter at hand. "But when you brought the box back to the Stargills today, it didn't contain needlework and jewelry, Miz Bonesteel," the sheriff said. He kept his voice quiet and soothing, hoping to coax the truth out of her while she was lost in the past. "Did you put those bones in there?"

She nodded, still looking away. She sat very still, but her clasped hands twisted in her lap. Spencer waited a moment for her to go on. In his years as a peace officer, he had learned that silence works better than questions with some folks. The guilty ones, who are anxious anyway, rush into speech to justify themselves, and invariably say too much. Nora Bonesteel did not seem to mind the silence.

Finally he said, "I need to know who these bones belonged to, and where you got them."

"I can't tell you that," she said.

He managed to smile. "I know this must be a scary conversation to be having with a lawman, Miz Bonesteel, but we've known each other a long time. Let me see if I can put your mind at ease. Now I know these bones have been—wherever they've been—for a long time. We've had no missing children in this county in my lifetime. I checked our case records before I came. Didn't need to, but I looked anyhow, just to make sure. Whatever happened to this child took place a long time ago, and it's more than likely too late to do anything about it."

Nora Bonesteel was listening passively.

When she did not reply he went on. "Now, I'll tell you something that I hope never becomes public knowledge. It's not the kind of thing a sheriff enjoys admitting, but it's the truth. I think you can tell I'm being honest with you, ma'am. The fact is, I've looked at those bones, and there's no obvious cause of death. No smashed skull, no bullet hole, no nicks from a knife blade. No way of knowing the cause of death. And there sure aren't any witnesses. So, what I'm trying to tell you is that I need some testimony to close out this case, and whatever you say, I'm going to believe it. Maybe this child wandered off in the woods and froze to death, or he ate poison berries and died alone on the mountain, and you came upon the remains. Just tell me something, Miz Bonesteel, and I'll write it down, and then I'll leave you alone."

The old woman's eyes were dark with sorrow. "Those things would not be true, Sheriff," she said.

"Tell me the truth, then," said Spencer, not sure he wanted to hear it.

"No."

CHAPTER TEN

A man needs only three things to be happy: a good gun, a good horse, and a good wife.

—DANIEL BOONE

The bare oak that stood alone on the top of the ridge looked as if it had borne black fruit, so thick were its branches clustered with dark, bulbous shapes. Now and then one black form would detach itself from a limb and drift out on the wind, inscribing a lazy circle of the hill before floating back to its perch. Sometimes one would disappear into the forest, and two others would spiral in to jostle for space on the sagging branches. All of them faced the two people who watched them from the pasture fence, staring back with two hundred pitiless eyes.

"There they are," said Dovey Stallard. She shivered and pulled her sheepskin coat more tightly around her. "They make my skin crawl."

Clayt nodded, keeping his eye on the tree, some fifty yards in the distance. "That's a feeling you probably share with most of creation. Those old boys are death with a capital D. When you said you were worried about birds attacking your stock, I was expecting turkey buzzards, which these are not, and maybe a dozen strong—not this grisly air force. Must be a hundred of them."

"The feathers on their necks look like monks' cowls." She clutched at his arm. "Is that one coming at us?"

"Just doing a little reconnaissance. Checking us out. Guess we look healthy enough. See, he's gone back to the tree now. Keep your voice down, Dovey. You'll scare them."

"Scare them! I wish I knew what it would take to scare them. When I found the lamb, I ran screaming at them, flapping my arms like a wild woman, and they just drifted a few yards away, and sat down staring at me, as if to say, *You're next, Lady*."

Clayt looked from the tree to the pasture below, where the Stallards' speckle-faced sheep grazed. It was a small flock of Kerry Hills, but they were a rare breed imported from Britain, and given the year the Stallards had had, they could ill afford to lose one. Clayt thought, though, that Dovey was more horrified by what had happened to the lamb than upset by the financial loss. Insurance wouldn't cover the lamb. He wondered if she knew that yet.

Clayt squatted down against the fencepost, ducking the wind, and motioned for Dovey to follow. "They're *coragyps atratus*, black vultures," he said. "Turkey buzzards have red heads and uniformly dark wings. These boys are gray-headed, and they have little white patches on their wings. See that one flapping? Did you see that flash of white?"

"I don't care," said Dovey. "This isn't a bird walk. I hate them."

"Well, they are more aggressive than turkey vultures, but you have to give them their due: they get rid of a lot of messy roadkill, and all those other bodies that Nature leaves strewn around all over creation. Would you rather wait for the maggots?"

She took a deep breath. "What a hell of a day this had been. First I found my Majorca rooster dead in the coop—nothing but blood and feathers—and then some creep from a real estate office came out here nosing around. I guess I'll have to worry about him pretty soon, too."

Something in her tone made him uneasy. "Is anything the matter, Dovey?"

Dovey shook her head. "Nothing you can help with, Clayt, unless you win the lottery. That realtor was a two-legged vulture, if I ever saw one though. Anyhow, while Daddy was getting rid of him, I came out here to check on the ewes, and I found a newborn lamb, off by itself in the pasture, surrounded by black vultures. They were taking turns pulling at it. Its eyes were gone. But it wasn't dead yet." She turned away so that he wouldn't see her tears. "Yesterday when I was driving home, I saw a swarm of them go after a calf in a field up the road. I thought vultures ate dead things. What's happening here?"

From force of habit, Clayt looked out across the distant valley, to make sure that no smoke was rising from the valley to mingle with the wreath of clouds that gave these mountains their name: the Smokies. He saw no sign of fire. It was still early days yet for campers along the trails. The trees were not yet leafed out, and he could see the red-tipped branches of budding maples and the silver limbs of birches, as insubstantial as cobwebs against the far hills. He scanned the sky, but the golden eagles and the lesser hawks he sought were not to be found.

At last he said, "I've heard stories from the old-timers of attacks by black vultures. Never saw it myself, though. They're migrating, and they're starving. I guess they ran out of carrion to feed on." He looked back at the bare oak, their roost. "That's a big flock. At least a hundred, I'd say. They weigh about four pounds apiece. They'd need a lot of meat to sustain themselves."

"What can I do about them, Clayt? I can't post a twenty-four-hour guard on my lambs." One of the black shapes swooped low over the pasture, and Dovey threw a rock at it. She missed, and the vulture drifted away, unconcerned by the futile attack. "I never thought I'd hear myself say this, but I want those birds dead. I don't think I could bring myself to shoot them, but I could put out some poisoned meat."

"You can't do it, Dovey." He held up his hand to stem her protests. "I'm not going to give you the naturalist's lecture about not interfering with environmental processes, because I know you're in no mood to listen to it. And it's not as if you were one of these people who builds a house in a woodland habitat and then wants to shoot the deer for spoiling the garden, and poison the raccoons for getting in the garbage. I know that."

"So why can't I kill these damned vultures, Clayt? They're a nuisance, and they're on our land."

"Because they're federally protected. Vultures may be mean and ugly, according to our lights, but they are also migratory birds, and the Migratory Bird Treaty Act of 1936 protects them just as surely as it protects a pretty red cardinal on your bird feeder. If you kill them, the feds can get you for $5,000 and six months in jail per bird. Now, with upwards of a hundred vultures roosting in that old tree, I'd say that was a pretty expensive act of revenge, even in exchange for an imported Kerry Hill lamb."

"What can I do? Daddy and I can't afford to lose any more of our stock. We're bad off as it is. Can we contact the department of agriculture or whoever decides these things, and get special permission? Or will the government come and trap them and take them away?"

Clayt shook his head. "You'd probably get back a form letter. The only thing I can suggest is that you might make yourself more of a nuisance to them than they are to you."

"In what way?"

"Well, they're not big on noise," said Clayt. "If it was me, I'd tell your dad to get his chain saw and spend a couple of hours a day cutting firewood and brush within a close proximity of their roosting tree. Be sure you do it in the early mornings or at twilight. They stay gone most of the day—on carrion patrol. If that doesn't work, then a transistor radio with a sufficiently loud volume, tuned to the right rock radio station ought to spoil the ambiance for them."

"Our sheep won't like it, either," said Dovey.

"Well, it's still pretty early in the season, and they are migrants. Maybe they'll head on north when the weather warms up."

"I hope so. They're evil. Look, they're staring at us now, like they're waiting for something."

Clayt Stargill smiled. "You haven't heard bells when they fly over, have you?" he said.

She turned to stare at him. "Bells? No. Why?"

"Why, it's an old mountain legend. In the old days folks said that when somebody important was fixing to die up in these hills, a big old buzzard would fly over the area, with a bell tolling in his wake, to warn of the coming bereavement."

Momentarily distracted, she smiled. "You're making that up, Clayt. That's just more of the moonshine you try to pass off on unsuspecting outlanders, like the story about the catfish monster in Watauga Lake."

"There's people that believe that one, too," said Clayt solemnly. "But I'm not making up the story about the death buzzard. It's an authentic legend from frontier America. When *we* were the frontier, that is. Maybe he's an inelegant variation of Mr. Poe's raven, or a folk memory of the Irish banshee transported to the Colonies. I don't know. He only comes for prominent folks, though, and so I'm not surprised he hasn't been seen around these parts lately."

Dovey Stallard stared at the tree, dark with silent, watching vultures, and shivered. "Nothing special about this bunch," she whispered. "They just signify common, everyday death. Ugly, ignoble, and quite ordinary—death."

Spencer Arrowood was back at his desk, scowling at the scattering of bones across his desk, while an iridescent film formed over the untasted coffee in his mug. His deputy, Joe LeDonne, had pulled the other chair up to the desk, and he looked from the evidence to the sheriff, without comment.

"You know Nora Bonesteel," the sheriff said at last. It wasn't a question, and LeDonne didn't answer it. He had not grown up in the county as Spencer had, but after nearly ten years in Wake County he had at least heard of almost everyone. Law officers tend to see the same folks over and over, as detainees for a series of petty crimes or domestic disputes. Good citizens make the law's acquaintance when they become victims. LeDonne had not encountered Nora Bonesteel in either capacity, but people talked about her every now and then, usually in hushed voices, or with a little laugh that prefaced a remark like, "Of course, I don't believe in such things as a rule, but . . ."

"She's over seventy," the sheriff was saying. "Friend of my mother. Taught me in Sunday school. My lord, I can still do the sword drill in record time." He laughed. "Fastest draw in the pulpit!"

"Sword drill?" said LeDonne. "In Sunday school?"

"It's a colorful Baptist expression. No weapons involved, except the Good Book. It's a competition to locate Bible verses faster than your opponents. Your teacher calls out, 'Galatians I:12,' and you—"

"I get it," said LeDonne. "Sweet old lady."

"Tougher than a Marine drill sergeant. Little boys don't come willingly to Bible study, you know. Come to think of it, she was going through her Bible when I talked to her today. You see, she showed up at Randall Stargill's farm with this box of bones." He explained Garrett Stargill's visit to the office, his version of the events on the farm that morning, and his own attempt to question Nora Bonesteel.

"So you want me to take the evidence to the crime lab to see if they can determine cause of death."

Spencer Arrowood frowned. "No, I don't *want* you to. I don't see that we have any choice in the matter, though. I wish to God that Nora Bonesteel had just left those bones where they were, if she's going to be so secretive about it. It's one thing to give this child a decent burial, but I don't need to be dragging old folks into court for things that most likely happened way before we were born."

LeDonne shrugged. "No statute of limitations on murder."

"You just don't see shades of gray, do you, LeDonne?" sighed Spencer Arrowood. "I am not letting a child killer get off. I went ahead with the Harkryder case, didn't I? And I sure felt sorry for that little girl. But this child"—he indicated the yellowed heap of bones—"is probably older than we are."

LeDonne was unmoved. "That's an S-W-A-G," he said.

"A scientific wild-ass guess? Sure, it is. I'll bet I'm not far off the mark, though. Still, there's no point in arguing with you, because we have to investigate this matter, like it or not, and the bones have to be sent for analysis."

"You're not detaining Miss Bonesteel, then?"

"You mean pay board for her to go sit in a jail in Erwin? I think she's more in solitary in that house of hers on Ashe Mountain. A lot of folks wonder how she stands it alone up there. Besides, we don't even have a cause of death for this individual, much less evidence of a crime. Being in possession of old bones, and asking that they receive a decent burial, is not against the law. I will agree with you that it is odd as hell, but that's not illegal either. So, I'd say that detaining Nora Bonesteel is not an option, even if I were inclined to do it, which, Lord knows, I'm not."

LeDonne shrugged. "Okay, your call. I'll deliver the package. You want a rush job?"

"Not particularly. So we'll probably know in two days. If I wanted an answer in a hurry, they'd take weeks. I wish we could wait until Martha got back from Walters State. Maybe she could get some kind of an answer out of an old woman."

LeDonne came as close as he ever got to a smile. "Deputize your mother."

"No," said Spencer. "I think there's somebody else I might try asking first."

. . .

Nora Bonesteel had not said a word since Jane Arrowood put her in the car. Spencer had said that it was all right for her to take the old woman home, but he wouldn't say what he'd talked to her about.

"I was thinking about Randall Stargill," Nora Bonesteel said at last. "We've been apart for a long time now, but it still seems strange to think of waking up in a world that he's not in any more."

"Yes," said Jane. "I felt that way when Hank died. I did miss him at first—more than I thought I would, perhaps—but above all there was that eerie feeling that part of me had gone, too. Of course, we had been married a long time, Hank and I. I'd have thought that you'd have got used to being without Randall."

"Oh, yes, I learned that lesson a good while back. Cried buckets about it, too, but I knew that's how it was meant to be. It troubled him that I—saw things. And Clarsie was a sweet, quiet girl, who would give him a peaceful life. At least I hope he found peace. He wasn't a happy young man.

"We'd known each other since grammar school, you know. It was a one-room school—one teacher for all the grades—and they promoted you if you could do the work of the next grade, so pretty soon I got put up with Randall." Nora Bonesteel smiled a little. "I lasted a day in second grade. When Teacher caught me reading Zane Grey behind my spelling book, she moved me on up to third. Randall was small for his age, and I was younger, so I guess we were just drawn together."

Jane Arrowood slowed the car down to take a curve of the two-lane Ashe Mountain Road. On the left, the trees parted for a few yards, giving travelers a glimpse of the brown vista below, just tinged with the first green of spring. "And the two of you became sweethearts when you got older?"

"Yes. It just seemed natural for us to be together. We had been—most always. And I think Randall was lonely. He still missed—someone."

"Were your families close?"

Nora Bonesteel considered it. "Neighbors," she said at last. "Stargills kept to themselves. Old Mrs. Stargill didn't much care for visitors. She could be a cold woman, although she liked Randall well enough—him being her grandson and all. Don't think she cared for his mother much, though. My grandma used to speak about it now and again—not to me, of course, but children don't miss much, do they?"

"No. Not much." Jane Arrowood had lived most of her life in Wake County, but she couldn't remember anything about the Stargills. Not that far back. Seventy years ago. Odd to be gossiping about bad blood in families that had long since returned to dust. She searched her memory for details about the family, but she remembered nothing. "Who was Randall Stargill's mother, anyway?"

"Her name was Luray. She was a wisp of a blonde, chocolate box pretty, but she wasn't the class of the Stargills. Father was a laborer in the town, I think. No land, no name, no money. Harsh things were said about her among the neighbors."

Jane Arrowood smiled. "It would seem funny to outsiders to think of poor farmers giving themselves airs above town folks who weren't very much worse off. I guess the land made them gentry. I know what you mean, though."

"Of course you do," said Nora Bonesteel. "You're a Miller, married to an Arrowood. You're blood kin to the Honeycutts, the McCourys, and the Barnetts. Your people settled these mountains before the Cherokee left for Oklahoma. That makes you one of the old ones—by marriage, at least. You belong."

"But Randall's mother didn't belong."

Nora Bonesteel nodded. "Never would. Takes more than a wedding ring to bring you in. I remember thinking how faded she looked, young as she was. Looking back on it, I think she may have been afraid of Old Miz Stargill. Randall's daddy wasn't around. I do remember that. It must have been hard for her, left on that lonesome farm where she wasn't wanted."

"It's a wonder she stayed."

"Where else could she go?"

They were midway up the mountain now. Oak branches formed an arch over the winding road. Only a few miles more to Nora Bonesteel's house in the meadow near the summit. Jane decided that she had to change the subject now, before the chance eluded her altogether.

"Now, you know I'm not one to pry," she began. She and Nora looked at each other and laughed. "Well, not more than usual for an old woman in a small town," she admitted. "And I don't know what my Spencer was talking to you about today, but I do know you were more than upset about it. I kept hoping you'd bring the subject up on the drive up here, but since you haven't, I'll just come right out and say that if there's anything troubling you, I'll do whatever I can to help. I've known you a long time, Nora Bonesteel, and you always have a reason for doing things—even if it takes the rest of us a while to figure out what it is."

The old woman sighed. "It's for Randall—for old times' sake. Something that had to be done. I keep forgetting how folks always want an explanation for every single thing, but it's not mine to give."

"If you need anything, you let me know," said Jane. "We're old friends. I'll talk to Spencer for you, if that would help."

"No, Jane. Just tell him—tell him to be careful—of old friends."

Clayt Stargill lay on his back, and looked up at the blue sky, streaked only with wisps of clouds far in the distance. Beside him, Kayla squinted up at the brightness. "What are we looking for?" she asked.

"Commuters," said Clayt. "Look! Here comes one."

"It's a big brown bird," said Kayla, after watching a speck in the sky loom larger above her, until she could make out brown wings and a splash of white about the tail. "Hawk?"

"Right. A mountaintop is a good place to see one. See, this

chain of mountains—the Appalachians—is a celestial interstate. The mountains run north to southwest all the way from Canada down to northern Alabama. Easy to see from the air. In the spring and the fall birds use the unbroken line of ridges as a navigation path when they migrate. Migrating means they go someplace warm for the winter." He pointed up at the hawk, drifting above them in a lazy circle. "The big boys—like that fellow right above us—ride the thermals between the peaks and the valleys, using the changing air temperature to move them along."

After Clayt returned from his visit to the Stallards, he'd found Kayla sitting on the front porch in her blue windbreaker and her faded sneakers, waiting for him to take her on the promised nature hike. He got permission from Kelley, who seem relieved to have her daughter out from underfoot, and Kayla climbed back into the truck, ready to see the wilderness. Clayt took her up a logging road to a mountain meadow with a view of all creation. It was one of his favorite spots for thinking about the mountains, past and present, his and Daniel's, and how they diverged, and when.

The wind was brisk, as it always was on a mountaintop in March, but Kayla claimed she wasn't cold, so they trooped out into the meadow, examining a coltsfoot plant in bloom and deer tracks as they went along.

Kayla got to her feet, and looked out at the folds of mountains that stretched away into the distant haze, like so many colored headbands piled in a drawer. "No houses," she said. "Can't see any traffic, either. So, you come here a lot?"

"Right often."

"Why? Is this what Daniel Boone saw?"

"Not even close," said Clayt. "But it's the best we can do nowadays."

Kayla looked around her—long brown meadow grass, evergreens and just leafed hardwoods, and here and there a splash of a golden forsythia. "Everything looks okay to me. How is it different?"

Clayt pointed to the clouded peaks on the horizon. "It's a brisk spring day. Not much pollution, compared to the summertime haze. I'd say you're seeing mountains that are about twelve miles away," he told her. "In 1761—Daniel Boone's time—you could have seen into the distance for ninety miles."

"How far is that?"

"All the way from here to Knoxville. To the Virginia Blue Ridge. I can't even imagine it myself."

"So how come we can't do that today?"

"Pollution."

Kayla peered up at the blue sky. "Looks okay to me."

"You've never seen a clear sky," Clayt told her. "When I was a kid, visibility was maybe twenty miles—a far cry from Daniel's time, but better than now."

"So can we fix it?"

"I doubt it. Too many cars, factories, furnaces. Even burning wood in a log cabin messed up the air quality, so it was starting to go, even back in Daniel's lifetime. We'll never get back to 1761. You asked how it was different. Look around you. See the trees? They're different now. Small, for one thing. There was a lot of virgin timber up here then. Full grown trees that had never been cut, hundreds of feet tall. These woods of today would look mighty puny compared to them."

"There's still deer around, isn't there?" She said *idn't,* not isn't; Clayt wondered if that nugget of regional speech could be traced back across the water to the Hebrides or the glens of Antrim.

"Yes," he said. "Don't expect to see them in broad daylight, though. They don't like to be easy to spot out in the open. Look for them at the edge of the woods at twilight. The old Celtic word for deer meant the children of the mist."

"Celtic?"

"Like Ireland," Clayt explained. "St. Patrick. Leprechauns."

"Johnny Cash," said Kayla. "He's got a song called 'Forty Shades of Green' that he wrote about Ireland. He's really nice, and we have all his albums."

"You must enjoy living in Nashville, and getting to meet all those famous people," smiled Clayt.

"I wish we could live up here," said Kayla.

"It's not to everybody's taste. Charles Martin never cared for it. You can't make much money up in these hills. The Irish had another saying: *the Green Martyrdom.* Martyrdom means that you are put to death for what you believe, like ancient Christians getting thrown to the lions in the arena. And green martyrdom was when the missionaries had to go to some backwater place like Ireland—like this—to convert the local heathens. They must have thought that being stuck out here in the wilderness was like being dead. So sometimes I tell people that staying up here in the Smokies is my green martyrdom."

"It's not, though," said Kayla. "Those old fellas in Ireland thought it was punishment to have to live in the country, but you think it's heaven up here."

Clayt smiled at her. "I guess sainthood is a state of mind."

Charles Martin Stargill had been sent down the mountain for provisions. His sister-in-law Lilah had checked the larder and found it wanting, so the women had conferred, weighed the merits of several possible menus, and after due consideration, they had drawn up a list. Charles Martin, who had the misfortune of being the first male to walk into the kitchen after the list had been made, was sent off to the Hamelin Mick or Mack to purchase supplies.

He had parked the Lexus in the gravel lot as far as he could get from the rusting Chevys and battered pickups. Now, squinting at the penciled list, he pushed the shopping buggy down the canned goods aisle, searching for the brand names Lilah had specified. He wondered if he could make substitutions.

"Hello, Charlie," said a familiar voice behind him.

He turned, with his celebrity smile plastered on, and ready to make small talk until he could figure out the identity of this well-wisher from his past, but the delaying tactics proved unnecessary, and the smile sagged. He would have known Dovey Stallard anywhere. She had that same dark hair, and the freckled nose, shiny from lack of face powder, and she looked just the same as he remembered her, Levi's and all. She wasn't holding any groceries.

"Well, hello, Dovey," he said, giving her the quick kiss on the cheek that passes for a cordial nod among show business folk. She did not return the embrace. "I was hoping I'd get to see you," he lied. "I wish we could go somewhere and catch up on old times, but I have to get this shopping done, or Robert's wife will have my hide." He waved the list with a helpless smile.

Dovey looked at him. "Charlie, you can't read that fine print worth a damn without your reading glasses, can you?"

His smile froze. "How did you—I mean—"

"I was watching you. You were holding the paper about a mile from your face, and squinting at it like it was Greek. You couldn't even read the labels on the cans. Why don't you wear reading glasses?"

"Left 'em at home," he said.

Her look said that she knew exactly why he wouldn't wear them, but she only smiled and reached for the list. "Why don't I walk along with you and read out the items?"

"It's mighty nice of you to offer, Dovey, but don't you have shopping to do?"

She shrugged. "Not much. With just Dad and me, there's not much cooking to be done. He's been off his feed lately anyhow, what with all this farm trouble. I wanted to talk to you about that."

"Clayt told us about you two finding Daddy, and getting help, and all. I sure do want to thank you for that, Dovey."

"We did what we could," she said. "Don't get that mayonnaise,

Charlie. You know y'all won't eat anything but Duke's. Your sister-in-law is from Ohio, so she doesn't know any better." She put a black-labeled jar into the buggy, and motioned for him to replace the one he had chosen. "Take a left at the end of this aisle."

"How have you been?" Charles Martin asked, wondering as he said it if it was a safe question.

"I've been better," she said. "We've had a run of bad luck on the farm. Barn burned down last year, and now they're after us about the taxes. I guess you were right, Charlie."

"How's that?"

"I guess I should have married you."

Right in the middle of the aisle at the Mick or Mack, he thought. Dovey Stallard never did have a lick of tact or timing. And that admission could hardly be called a triumph on his part, because she still wasn't saying she loved him. Just that she'd missed out on a good investment. He patted her arm, and put on his aw-shucks grin. "Shoot fire, Dovey," he said. "You had a narrow escape. Show business is a hard enough life for the performer, but for the person who's married to one, it must be like doing life in Leavenworth."

She was stacking packages of spaghetti on top of the canned goods in the cart. "I probably wouldn't have been any good at it," she said. "All I ever wanted to do was stay up here, and after Tate died, I had to help Daddy keep the farm going. People always said I should marry one of you Stargills so that we could join the two farms. Didn't work out, though."

"No," said Charles Martin. Talking about it still hurt after all these years, and that surprised him. All the Stargill boys had been sweet on Dovey Stallard at one time or another—except Robert Lee, but he was so much older that he had hardly figured in the childhoods of any of them. Charles Martin remembered a fistfight with Garrett over which of them would take Dovey home from a basketball game; it hadn't mattered to either of them that they were going home in the same car. He had lost that battle, but he knew he was going places, so he always assumed that he would win the war. It hadn't turned out that way, though.

"Well," he said, "Dwayne, now. Dwayne never was much on farming. I don't reckon any of the rest of us would have been any better, but he wasn't exactly the pick of the litter, Dovey."

For an instant he was gratified to see the look of pain mirrored on Dovey's face, and then the wrinkle between her eyes smoothed out, and her thoughts were closed to him. She shrugged, not bothering to deny it. "I didn't think anybody knew about it," she said. "I never told your folks—or mine, for that matter."

"I don't reckon they ever did know," said Charles Martin. "I never told. I had a letter from Dwayne after he went to Florida, telling me that you all had eloped one Saturday night when he was home visiting. Said he was going to send for you when he got settled down there. The wreck wasn't long after that. I figured there wasn't any point in bringing it up after that." He shrugged. "I didn't want to talk about it anyhow. I guess after all these years, I'd kind of like to know why you did it."

Dovey sighed. "Dwayne Stargill. You know, I can't even remember his face clearly anymore. All I have is a couple of grainy snapshots taken at the lake. Not as clear as your album covers—or as flattering."

Charles Martin stood there, with his knuckles white on the handle of the shopping cart. He had waited years for the answer to his question, and he could wait a while longer. Until the store closed, if he had to.

After a moment of silence, Dovey said, "We can't keep standing here in the bread aisle of the Mick or Mack, Charlie. If you're going to cross-examine me, we better go someplace else."

He left the cart where it stood. Dovey protested that the store would be closing soon, and that he'd better get the groceries while he had a chance, but he walked out of the market as if he didn't even see that store full of people, with Dovey following at his heels, nagging him to slow down.

He had started the Lexus before she even closed the door, and he roared off along the old road to Johnson City without a word.

"Well," said Dovey. "There's a Kroger in Johnson City. They stay open till all hours. You didn't forget the list, did you?"

"Why Dwayne?" said Charles Martin. His eyes were fixed on the road ahead. Dovey watched the speedometer numbers jump ahead.

"Slow down and I'll tell you," she said.

The car eased back down toward fifty-five, just in time for a sharp curve. "Go on," he said.

Dovey let out a long breath. "We're too old for this, boy," she said. "But all right. Why Dwayne Stargill. With four-fifths of the Stargill boys courting me at one time or another, why did I choose Dwayne, who was going nowhere from the day he was born. The star-crossed Stargill. It seems strange even to me now, but back then . . . Dwayne was fun. He was handsome enough with those wild blue eyes, and he had charm—great charm. He made me laugh. The rest of you were all so serious."

"We were not! How about the time I—"

"I'm not talking about your tomfool pranks, Charlie. I mean, you took yourselves so seriously. You were hellbent on becoming famous, and Garrett wanted to become a general and conquer the world, and Clayt was turning into Johnny Appleseed, always wandering off into the woods, mooning over some rare bird, or some threat to his precious wilderness. None of you much needed me. I would have been a nice accessory, but I didn't come first with any of you."

"Don't tell me you did with Dwayne. He never had a cause in his life except getting enough to drink and not having to work for it."

"I didn't care," said Dovey. "I guess I wanted to run away from serious matters. We were struggling on the farm. Hell, we've been struggling ever since I can remember, and Mama and Daddy never did get over losing Tate. Even when we were having fun, there was a hint of sadness about them, an expectation of something that wasn't ever going to happen. You know, Mama set one too many places at the table until the day she died. Dwayne." She closed her eyes. "That summer, I was twenty, and you had all gone off to make names for yourselves. There was Dwayne, with his fast car, and a smile like a barn on fire, and he was going to Florida. 'Come with me,' he says to me. 'I'll love you till winter.' Then he laughed. 'And in Florida, Dovey,' he says, 'there ain't no winter!' "

"Just hurricanes," said Charles Martin, easing past a slow-moving sedan.

"And car wrecks," whispered Dovey.

"But you agreed to go?"

"I married him," said Dovey. "Told Mama I was going to Myrtle Beach with Mary Louise, who really was going, and she covered for me. Dwayne and I eloped that weekend to Dillon, South Carolina, and got married before a justice of the peace. I was wearing a strapless yellow sundress, and Dwayne had on a Gatlinburg T-shirt. Afterward we ate Kentucky Fried Chicken at the motel, and—and the next morning we came on home. I had him drop me off at the mailbox, so my folks wouldn't see his car. Three days later Dwayne left for Florida. I kept living at home with Daddy and Mama, 'cause Dwayne wasn't ready to have me come join him yet. It would have about killed Mama to know I'd eloped instead of having a church wedding, but I never got pregnant, so she didn't have to know. I kept the secret and I waited. And then one day your mama told mine about the wreck. Said she was going down there to see to his ashes. I could have told everybody then. Could have gone with her. But I didn't want to."

"Do you really think he would have sent for you?" asked Charles Martin. "Dwayne?"

"The question I keep asking myself, Charlie, is: would I have gone?"

"And you never married again. After all this time . . ."

Dovey shook her head. "That wasn't Dwayne's doing. My heart's not in the grave or anything. Folks tried to fix me up with dates every now and again, but all I ever seemed to get were fat farmers who were divorced, or boys like Dwayne, but without his charm. Losers, basically, who stayed up here because they didn't have the brains or the ambition to go anywhere else. Oh, there are some nice guys around, but they're all married, and I never wanted a husband bad enough to steal one. I figured I was better off alone." She took a deep breath. "I hear you finally found somebody, Charlie."

It took him a few seconds to remember Kelley. Then he said, "Oh, yeah. We're not married, or anything. She's a redhead—really pretty. Met her in Nashville. She's from a small town in Kentucky, but she had the sense to get out."

"And look where it got her," said Dovey softly.

Charles narrowed his eyes, but she was not smiling, and there was no sarcasm in her voice. "Well," he said. "She seems happy enough." He had intended to add, "I know I am," but he heard himself asking, "How come you wanted to see me tonight, Dovey?"

CHAPTER ELEVEN

Boys, we have to fight! Sell your lives as dear as possible.
—DANIEL BOONE

Charles Martin Stargill ran his hand along the newly planed board. The heavy musk of rosewood weighted the air, and made his eyes tear. "I guess we might as well get started," he told his brothers. "This is taking longer than I figured on."

"It'll take even longer if we screw it up," said Garrett.

They had been working on the coffin for two days now. Clayt had retrieved the planed boards from the cabinet maker three mornings earlier, and they had spent most of that first afternoon making sketches on the back of a grocery bag, and arguing about the design of the coffin. Robert Lee favored making a straight-sided wooden box, which he said they could assemble easily in a few hours, using power tools. Charles Martin countered with remarks about "indecent haste," insisting that a proper coffin had to be triangular at the head and taper down to straight sides. After much discussion the brothers agreed to make a traditional coffin, using hand tools, but they agreed that if they met with time constraints or other difficulties, they would take short cuts.

They had finished the bottom of the coffin on the previous afternoon.

"We're not really going to use hand tools for sanding, are we?" asked Robert Lee, dabbing at his nose with a crumpled tissue. "That stuff was clogging me up before we even started working with it. If we keep fooling around with handsaws, and then try to use panes of glass for scrapers, I'll be dead before Daddy."

Garrett sighed. "Let's just take it as it goes, all right? Robert, get you some pills or something. And a box of tissues from the house. I don't want to listen to you sniffling for another twelve hours. Yesterday was bad enough."

"I'll measure, and you cut," Clayt told Charles Martin. From the pocket of his plaid jacket, he took out a metal tape measure and the stub of a pencil. He nodded toward the handsaw. "Let's give that a try. We can always switch to something fancier if it gives us trouble."

"Can we have a radio in here?" asked Robert Lee.

"Oh, god, no!" said Charles Martin. "I can't listen to radio anymore. It gives me heartburn. I don't want to know who these yahoo deejays think are the stars of country music. I'd rather listen to Robert Lee sniffle, and that's saying a lot."

Breakfast that morning had been cold cereal and skim milk, because—as Lilah had explained—no one had slept well enough to want to get up at five a.m. and start cooking.

Clayt, who had got up at five a.m. for his morning walk, finished eating before the others, and made the call to the hospital to check on his father's condition. Randall Stargill remained unchanged.

The women had been inclined to drink coffee and linger at the table, but none of the Stargills could ever sit still for long, so when Garrett muttered an excuse about the hours of carpentry work that lay ahead of them, the others gulped the last swallows of their coffee, and were at his heels before the back door could close behind him.

Now they were congregated in the small, cold woodshop at the back of the barn, picking up where they left off at twilight the night before. Some of the planed boards had been measured and cut.

"There's something we need to talk about, boys," said Robert

Lee. He had been waiting for an opportune moment to bring up the subject, and this was not the time, what with Charles Martin humming and Garrett swearing at Clayt over the last measurement, but the suspense was giving him heartburn, and so he blurted it out to ease his anxiety.

"Now what?" said Garrett, who did not look up from his task.

Robert Lee licked his lips. "What are we going to do about the farm?"

"That again?" Charles Martin groaned. "Haven't we already told you to wait until Daddy's cold, before you start divvying up—"

"We need to decide sooner than that," said Robert Lee. "Unless you boys want to sit around here for another couple of weeks after the funeral settling the estate. We've had an offer."

Clayt looked up. "What do you mean, an offer?"

"Couple of days ago, a real estate fellow stopped by to say he was interested in the farm. I didn't say anything about it because I figured Daddy was due to pass on any time now, and then we could discuss it, but he's lingering, and we need to start making some decisions. I mean, even if he doesn't die, he can't come back here and live by himself, can he?"

"Well . . . that's a point," said Charles Martin.

"Of course it is. He's old and frail. If he lives, we'll want him to have the best care, and that takes money."

Clayt scowled. "A real estate man—they're as good as the buzzards at smelling death coming. What kind of offer did this man make to you, Robert? Does he want to farm up here?"

"Well, no, Clayt. Nobody in his right mind would want to farm up here these days. The money is in selling luxury homes with a view. This Whitescarver is a developer. He wants to buy the farm and put one of those planned communities in here."

"Out of the question," said Clayt. "It would spoil the whole ridge. Ruin the habitats of scores of species. And it makes me want to vomit just thinking about it."

"Well, we ought to think about it," said Garrett. "I'm not saying we should accept right off, but Robert Lee has a point about Daddy not being able to live here anymore. And we have to do *something* with the land."

"Why?" said Clayt. "We've done without it all these years. We don't really need the money—wouldn't be all that much, divided four ways. Why don't we just deed it to the National Park Service, on the condition that it be kept a wilderness area?"

"Maybe you can sneer at money, Mr. Hippie, but some of the rest of us have Daddy's medical bills to worry about, and positions in the community to maintain." Robert Lee's face was red with indignation. He hated people who pretended that there was something indecent about practicality. It wasn't as if he wanted a bunch of money to buy sports cars and take Caribbean cruises. If there was anything reprehensible about wanting to pay down a mortgage, settle some bills, and build up some savings in case he became disabled when he got older, he'd like to hear it. The very people who liked to pretend that money didn't matter were always the first to step over you when you no longer had any.

"Well, I see Clayt's point," said Charles Martin. "It would be a shame to mess up such a pretty stretch of mountain with a bunch of brick houses. And I'd kind of hate to think of our family home disappearing."

"I know," said Garrett. "It's a funny thing about family land. None of us would ever want to come live here again—we couldn't, even if we did want to—but we just want the place *to be* here, never changing, to remind us of who we are. I like knowing that the farm is here on the mountain, just the same from one year to the next. It kind of makes me free to go out and try other places, other jobs—because I know I have roots somewhere, and I could always come back."

"This farm has been Stargill land for close on two hundred years now," said Charles Martin. "It wouldn't be right to let it go."

"Well, it's going to go anyhow!" said Robert Lee. "I never heard such hogwash in my entire life. What do you think this is, a lost episode of *Bonanza*? This farm isn't some storybook spread that takes care of itself while you're gone away living your lives. You don't just turn off the television when you leave here, and have time stop until you tune in again. The farm goes on without you, and it sure as hell changes. The paint peels, the roof starts leaking, the pastures go to seed, the fences rot. Somebody has to be here to feed it sweat and money, or the mountain will just creep in and turn it right back into wilderness.

"When Daddy's gone, who do you think's going to keep the home fires burning up here? Do you want to see this place fall in from termites or vandals or dry rot, just because none of you has the time to take care of it, or the guts to turn loose of it? Grow up, why don't you!"

"We're just trying to do the right thing, Robert," said Garrett. "No need to get all het up about it. We just hate to see this land spoiled, that's all. Maybe we can find somebody who does want to own a farm up here. Lots of city people don't know any better."

"If a landowner had a second income, like a job at the university, this farm probably wouldn't be so hard to keep going," said Clayt. "You could farm for the exercise instead of for an income. Still, I wouldn't want to make the commute in winter. Has your developer thought of that, when he's talking about putting houses up here?"

"He'd fix up the road," said Robert Lee.

"That would cost a fortune, and it wouldn't be good for the environment up here, either," said Clayt. "It would change the drainage, maybe cause erosion. Why, we've got endangered wildflowers—"

"It's going to happen anyway, Clayt, so stop whining about it! Now either we cash in or we throw away a chance to profit from all this, but you can't stop it."

"Speaking of profit," said Garrett. "We'd timber the land before we sold it, wouldn't we? I was remembering what Clayt said about those walnut trees being worth five thousand dollars apiece."

"No way," said Clayt. "Timbering those trees would be an obscenity. Now hush! I want to hear what Robert Lee was saying. What do you mean, it's going to happen anyway?"

Robert Lee's features seemed to shrink to a point in the middle of his red face. "I don't know that I'm allowed to divulge that information," he said primly.

"He means the Stallard place," said Charles Martin. "I ran into Dovey a couple of nights ago, and she told me about it."

Clayt scowled. "What do you mean, she told you?"

Charles Martin looked away. "I saw her in the grocery store, and we got to talking about old times. She mentioned that some developer is after their land, and they're about to lose the place for taxes. She wanted me to help them save the farm. Lend them some money."

"Did you?" asked Garrett.

Robert Lee's laugh was bitter. "Charles Martin isn't that forgiving," he said.

"It wasn't that," said Charles Martin, scowling. "If you ask me, Clayt is the one whose nose is still open over Dovey Stallard."

"But you didn't lend her any money," said Garrett.

"I don't keep a lot of money sitting around in the bank, for god's sake! I tried to explain it to her. I have expenses, investments. I have a tour bus, and a back-up group, and costumes to buy every whipstitch. Everybody thinks country singers are rich, but, believe me, the money goes out just as fast as it comes in."

"Yeah, you're driving a good chunk of it," said Robert Lee.

"I can't believe she asked you for help," said Clayt.

"Well, little brother, who else was she going to ask?" Charles Martin's smile was bitter. "You? If locomotives were selling for a dime apiece, all you could do would be to run up and down the track, yelling, *Ain't that cheap?*"

"So she went crawling to you, and look where it got her," said Clayt.

"It's definite then?" said Garrett. "The Stallards' farm is going to a developer?"

"Looks that way," said Charles Martin. "The Stallards can't afford to fight it. And that means we have to decide what to do about this place, because if the mountain gets zoned residential, the taxes will eat us alive. Maybe we should talk to this developer."

"Maybe we should try to help the Stallards," said Clayt.

"Write them a check," said Robert Lee. His eyes sparkled with malice. "That ought to buy them a doorknob, or two. And I know she'd be grateful to you. Don't expect the rest of us to pitch in, though. We have a monster hospital bill coming at us. You'd better think about those medical expenses, too, before you get on your high horse about preserving the farm."

"I'm not against money, you guys," said Clayt with a weary sigh. "You're right: I don't have two nickels to rub together. You think I wouldn't like to have a place outside town, and a truck that wasn't disintegrating in the driveway? Or that I wouldn't like to buy some free time to do some volunteer work for local conservation groups, instead of having to hustle every waking moment for enough money to live from one month to the next? Yeah, I could use money, maybe more than most of you. But I believe I'd rather starve than to sell out the family land to some developer, who'll put in a hundred houses on lots the size of postage stamps. Do you know how many habitats would be displaced if we let this happen?"

Garrett Stargill put his hand on his brother's shoulder. "You can't appoint yourself guardian of the planet, Clayt," he said. "You can't save it all. Now think about what Daddy would want us to do."

Robert Lee laughed. "No mystery about that," he said. "Daddy didn't give a damn about nature, far as I could tell, unless you could shoot it and eat it. He'd have sold the farm to strip miners if they had made him a halfway decent offer."

"He stayed here, didn't he?" said Clayt.

"Maybe he didn't care much for the rest of the world," said Charles Martin. "The only time he ever saw it was in a war. And he got shot down in the English Channel, remember? That would drive anybody back up the mountain. I never could talk him into going back to Italy, even when I played Rome."

"He wouldn't go anywhere around here, either," said Clayt. "Remember, he always used to tell us how he'd take us camping sometime, or on a long canoe trip down the Nolichucky? But we never did anything with him. He'd work all day, and then he'd lay on the couch and watch television with a paperback western in his lap."

"Farming is hard work," said Robert Lee.

"Not that hard. Not all the time," said Garrett. "And when we were kids, he wasn't any older than I am now, so don't tell me he was too old and tired to manage."

"He didn't want to be bothered," said Charles Martin. "Remember how he'd start looking around when you tried to talk to him, and then he'd say something like, 'How about that?' so that you weren't sure if he heard you or not."

"Fathers weren't supposed to be nurturing in those days," said Robert Lee, making the word into a sneer. "You ought to be glad he didn't beat the tar out of you, and stay drunk all the time. We had friends with fathers like that."

"Well, if he cared about us or this farm, he sure managed to keep from showing it," said Charles Martin.

"Well, I care about the farm," said Clayt. "Besides, this land issue isn't about Daddy. We're Stargills, and this is Stargill land. It's our turn to say what becomes of it."

"Okay," said Charles Martin. "Let's hear your say, Clayt. What should we do? Hang on to the land, and lose it to taxes, or watch it get hemmed in by crackerbox houses? Or should we try to find a buyer we approve of? Or do you just want to give it to the government for free, and have nothing to show for two hundred years of Stargills' work?"

Clayt went to the window, and began to rub the dust away with his palm. "The land has the look of winter yet," he said, peering out. "That's why you can talk so easy about giving up this land. Three weeks from now those words would stick in your throats. You've forgotten, haven't you, what it's like here in late spring? So beautiful it takes your breath away. The lilac bushes reach almost to the second-floor windows by now, and they'll be covered with flowers, making the breeze smell like perfume. The maples will be leafed out on the hills. You can see ridge after ridge from here—all the way to North Carolina. The stream will be ready for trout fishing, and the blackberries will be gearing up for summer. And at twilight fawns come out to play under the trees in the meadow. You couldn't give it up if you remembered."

"Well, we did give it up," said Robert Lee. "Remember? I've been living in Cincinnati for more than thirty years, and Garrett and Charlie are in the flats of west Tennessee and Kentucky, so don't give us a song and dance about the beautiful mountains, because we've already lost the land, cold turkey. We couldn't afford to live here."

"Maybe we ought to talk to this developer," said Garrett. "At least we could hear him out. Maybe he can address some of our concerns, and we can find a solution that we can all live with."

"I can't live with any solution that includes a developer," said Clayt.

Spencer Arrowood was not especially pleased to see Frank Whitescarver on the threshold of his office the first thing in the morning. The pudgy man in the polyester suit had a look of urgency on his face, which Spencer figured meant bad news for somebody.

Dabbling in local politics was a necessary evil that went along with the job of sheriff, and Spencer managed it well enough, but he did not enjoy it. He had seen too many elderly good old boys get elected because a shiny suit and a down-home accent made the working folks feel that the candidate was one of them. They would not learn until too late—if ever—that their possum-faced country boy had traded their interests for his own gain. They would find their road requests indefinitely tabled, the landfill slated for their section of the county, or the trailer park approved for their community, while the more affluent county residents were represented by officials who would tolerate none of this. Meanwhile, the genial poor folks' representative sold his land to the state for a new elementary school, or managed to purchase new acreage at just the right location to capitalize on some future venture. Frank Whitescarver was just such a local politician. He was forever serving on one board or the other, to no one's benefit but his own, as far as Spencer could discern.

Still, it wasn't the sheriff's business to judge the unindicted, or to make gratuitous enemies, so he stood up and extended his hand. "What can I do for you, Mr. Whitescarver?" His expression was one of polite concern. He'd be damned if he'd smile.

Whitescarver's jowled face looked solemn, and his hand was sweaty. "Well, Sheriff," he said, "the fact is that I need you to act in your official capacity to enforce a county ruling." He reached into his pocket and took out a sheaf of typed papers.

Spencer scanned the first few lines, and looked up, his eyes narrowed. "An eviction notice?"

The realtor nodded. "I'm just as sorry about it as I can be, but I have to think it's the kindest thing sometimes to save these poor old farmers from their own stubbornness, before they starve to death and ruin their families along with them."

The sheriff had been reading the document. When Frank stopped talking, he said, "You bought J. Z. Stallard's land for unpaid taxes?"

"Oh, I made him an offer first," said Frank, shaking his head sadly. "I drove out there special, early this week, ready to buy the farm from J. Z.—and I'd still have have had to pay the taxes, you know—but he wouldn't hear of it. I guess people just can't face facts, sometimes. But he's getting old, too, and it's hard for some of these old-timers to let go."

"So there was a tax sale?" said Spencer, keeping his voice neutral.

Whitescarver pointed to the bulletin board in the outer office. "You've got the notice posted right out there, Sheriff."

"And you bought J. Z. Stallard's farm?" He felt as if he were spitting out the words, but Frank Whitescarver's expression did not change.

"That's right."

"And you want me to go kick them off their land?"

"I believe the state of Tennessee considers that your sworn duty, yes, sir." Frank Whitescarver had stuck his chin out, and his eyes had gone piggy, as if at last he had become a bit embarrassed at the situation, but he was determined to brazen it out. He had a signed legal document, after all.

Spencer Arrowood sighed. He still had inquiries to make about the box of bones that Nora Bonesteel had saddled him with. The words *See Rattler* were penciled on his desk calendar for this morning. Besides, there was more work of every kind, now that he and LeDonne were splitting all the duties again. He would never admit to Martha Ayers how much they had missed her work. "Well, I'm kind of busy right now," he said, "But I'll try to get around to it. How long are you going to give them? Six months?"

"A week."

"A *week?*"

"They've had years to pay their taxes, haven't they?" Frank Whitescarver shrugged. "They knew this was coming. No use postponing the inevitable. They need to get on with their lives. It might be easier to get it over with quick, like pulling out a splinter, don't you think?"

"All right," muttered the sheriff. "I guess it has to be done."

"I thought I'd ride out with your deputy when he serves the eviction notice—"

Spencer Arrowood shook his head. "I'm going to do it myself. I owe them that at least."

. . .

Lilah Rose Stargill pushed herself away from the breakfast table with a contented sigh. "Well, ladies," she said, "as soon as I fix my face, we can get started on our sewing again." She smiled as she patted one wrinkled cheek. "I always say that the best makeup would be some plaster of Paris mixed with spackling, and a little color thrown in. That would cover the damage, wouldn't it?"

Kelley yawned. "I don't see why you should get dressed up just for us."

"I never bother with it at all," said Debba.

Lilah looked at her. The girl looked like a peeled grape with her lank hair, her lashless eyes, and her bloodless lips. "Well, you're young yet," she said kindly, because Rudy disapproved of needless unpleasantry. "I'm always afraid that the world would just rise up and throw me overboard like Jonah himself if I didn't make an effort to look presentable." She smiled at the others and hurried out of the room, before the debate on cosmetics could continue.

Kelley looked at Debba Stargill and shrugged. "Who are we to argue with her? She's been married for thirty years at least. I think I'll go put on some lipstick."

Debba Stargill stayed at the breakfast table, because she didn't really feel like primping. She was finishing the last of the coffee when the little girl appeared, rubbing sleep from her eyes. She was already dressed in tiny blue jeans and an Opryland sweatshirt. "Where's my momma?" she asked. She did not ask to be fed. Debba Stargill was not the sort of person children imposed on.

"In her bedroom, I think," said Debba. As an afterthought she added grudgingly, "Can I get you anything?"

Kayla had already opened the refrigerator, and was helping herself to strawberry jam and a bowl of grapes. "This'll do," she said, reaching for the plastic wrapper containing the bread. "I'm used to getting my own breakfast." She dipped the butter knife into the jam jar, and began to smear a slice of bread. "You all gonna be sewing again today?"

"Yes. We're just getting ready to begin. Would you like to watch television? I guess we could work somewhere else." Debba didn't sound happy about the prospect. She didn't have any children, and she wasn't sure how to talk to them, so she treated them with careful politeness as if they were tuxedoed waiters in a restaurant she could barely afford.

"That's okay," said Kayla with bread-stuffed cheeks. "I'm going outside to play. It's kinda neat up here. I saw a rabbit yesterday. And Clayt's been telling me a lot about birds."

"Well, that's nice," said Debba, "but you need to be careful out there. A little girl could get hurt in those woods. And if you see any strangers out there, you run right back, you hear?"

Kayla nodded. "Sure," she said, as she stuffed a sprig of grapes into the pocket of her jeans. "Tell Momma I'm gone."

Frank Whitescarver had lapsed into silence. Now he was looking out the window of the patrol car, studying the blur of landscape with a practiced eye. Spencer Arrowood had answered all his attempts at small talk with monosyllables, and finally with silence, as he pretended to concentrate on the road. Frank could tell that the sheriff didn't want to be on this errand, and he especially didn't want company, but that was too bad. Maybe it wasn't pleasant to put people off their land, but it had to be done, and there was no point in the sheriff sulking about it, because it was his sworn duty to uphold all the laws, not just the ones he approved of. Frank gave up trying to talk to him though. He concentrated on the scenery—you never know what you might find, even on a road you've driven a hundred times.

The road climbed, and circled the ridges, offering glimpses of the valley, and an occasional clump of early wildflowers brightening the road ahead. Not far now. Frank straightened up. "The turnoff is a dirt road up here to the right," he said. "Do you know it, Sheriff?"

"Yeah." Spencer Arrowood's lips tightened. "I played basketball in high school with Tate Stallard. I used to take him home after games sometimes. He was a good friend."

"I remember him," Frank nodded. "He didn't come back from Southeast Asia, did he? We lost a lot of good fellas over there. Yep. Might have been different if he'd lived."

Spencer swung the patrol car into the gravel turnoff by the mailbox marked "Stallard." Up the steep drive, he could see clabbered clouds in blue haze, wreathed by maple trees as old as the century. As they reached the crest of the hill, the white frame house came into view, in need of a coat of paint, but proud and sturdy against the hills.

"It's a likely spot, isn't it?" said Frank.

"It is now," said Spencer.

"They're home. I see J. Z. Stallard's truck parked there beside the barn. Do you want me to stay in the car while you serve the papers?"

Spencer took a long, hard look at his passenger. "You do that," he said.

"Of course, if you need me to do any explaining, you just give me the high sign, and I'll be right there to help you out."

The sheriff stopped the car next to the house, collected the papers, and got out, slamming the door as hard as he ever had. He helloed the house. "Are you there, J. Z.? I need to have a word with you." A sudden movement beside the barn made him turn. He saw two figures emerge from the building, and stand in shadow. He waved, but they stood where they were.

Spencer's fingers touched the leather of his holster—a habit with him when the situation got touchy, but he managed a tight smile and began to walk toward the Stallards. He had known them all his life.

. . .

Lilah Stargill settled down on the living room sofa with the squares of the quilted coffin lining in her lap. "I guess we can get started now," she said. "Shall we keep doing like we have been? Kelley cut, while Debba and I sew?"

"Fine with me," said Kelley. "But we're down to just a couple more squares from Mrs. Stargill's wedding suit. We need to pick something else to cut up."

"Have we used something from each one of the boys?" Lilah ran her fingers along the length of cloth. "Baby blanket, wedding outfit, Eye-talian shawl . . ."

"What else can we use?" asked Debba. "Something from the boys now? Did all of 'em bring a necktie? That would work."

"I don't know," said Kelley. "I only packed one tie for Charles Martin, and it's a real silk one from Italy. I don't know about cutting it up."

Debba nodded. "Garrett's is a special one, too. I mean, it doesn't look fancy. It's just a regular army issue necktie, but he's real superstitious about it. He thinks it brings him luck."

"I wonder if Clayt even owns a tie," Lilah mused.

"Neckties are all well and good," said Kelley, "but the boys might need them for the funeral, and, besides, ties don't contain a lot of material. We've got more than half this liner to sew yet, and we're running out of things to put in it."

"I guess we could go through the old trunks again. See if we can figure out which pieces belonged to Mr. Stargill's parents." Debba shrugged. "Maybe we should just choose pretty fabrics. We're pushed for time, aren't we?"

"What about a piece of cloth from Nora Bonesteel?" asked Kelley.

"Oh, honey, they weren't married," said Lilah. "That wouldn't be right."

"Well, what of that?" said Kelley. "Charles Martin and I aren't married, either, but I think—I'd like to think—"

"Well, hon. You never know how a man feels about you unless he's willing to make it legal."

Kelley's eyes narrowed. "Judging from the number of married men that have hit on me, I'd say being legally joined is no guarantee, either. At least I know Charles Martin stays with me voluntarily."

Lilah gave the younger woman a pitying smile, but she did not reply. No point in telling her that even with the best will in the world, men need a little enforcing of the "voluntary" as the years roll on. If Kelley and Charlie stayed together long enough, she would learn.

"What about part of Mr. Stargill's military uniform?" Debba suggested. "I know Garrett would want part of it used, if it was him. Well, of course, Garrett wants to be buried in uniform, but you know what I mean. Men set a store by it."

"It's their equivalent of a wedding dress," said Lilah, nodding. "We'll have a look for it. Anything else? The bedspread? Tablecloth?"

"The doily from on top of the television," said Debba. The others stared at her, and she said, "*Well*—I mean, you know—he must have stared at that thing sixteen hours a day. He hardly ever looked away from it when we came to see him. I guess he loved that television as much as he did his kinfolk."

"He wasn't much on showing affection," Lilah admitted. "I remember when Dwayne died. Why, I've seen people take on more about losing a dog than he did with his own son lying dead down in Florida. But that doesn't mean he didn't care. He just wasn't one to carry on about his feelings."

"Is that what your angel says?" Kelley's feelings still rankled from the marriage discussion.

"No. Rudy hasn't expressed any opinion about Daddy Stargill or the coffin lining. He's not one to gossip about other folks. He makes me walk chalk, and that's all he seems to care about. I haven't heard from him today."

Kelley and Debba exchanged glances. Kelley shrugged. "Well, this isn't getting the work done. I guess I'll go to the attic, and see what else we can use. I'm bringing down anything pretty I find. We're running out of time for symbolism, ladies."

Spencer Arrowood was walking up the hill toward the Stallards' barn. He wished he could talk reassuringly to the shadowed figures, but he was too far away to make them hear. He had some Social Services numbers on a card in his wallet, and he'd mention them if he thought the Stallards would listen, but he was betting they wouldn't hear of taking charity. Maybe he should have come prepared with some alternatives—a place to stay, or an offer of help from the church—but Whitescarver had sprung this thing on him before he had a chance to think it through. Well, they had a week to pack up and get out. Maybe by then he could come up with something that their pride would allow them to accept.

He glanced back once when he heard a car door slam. Frank Whitescarver had climbed out of the patrol car, and was trailing him, his red face glistening in the mild sunshine. Spencer quickened his pace. The unpleasant task that lay before him would only be made more difficult by the presence of the developer. He didn't want the Stallards shamed by having the eviction papers served in front of the man who was taking their land.

It seemed to take him forever to walk up that hill to the burned-out barn, but although he was sorting through soothing phrases in his mind, he was unable to think of anything that might comfort the Stallards. This task was as unfamiliar as it was unpleasant. As sheriff he had now and again been called upon to evict indigent ne'er-do-wells from the trailer park, but never one of the old families from land they'd held longer than anybody could remember. He'd rather evict the most cantankerous knife-wielding drunk from a rusty trailer than to politely ask a man like J. Z. Stallard to leave. Spencer knew that both his deputies, LeDonne and Martha Ayers, would feel otherwise about it, and perhaps that was why he had to do this himself.

He was close enough now. He could see J. Z. Stallard in his faded gray work clothes, looking as solemn and dignified as ever a deacon had looked in church. He did not smile or hold out his hand, but his expression was not one of anger. Spencer thought he looked hurt, or perhaps ashamed. Well, that made two of them.

"Hello, Mr. Stallard," he said gently. He stopped a couple of feet from the older man. He didn't want this to feel like an arrest for either of them. "I guess you know what I've come about. I have some papers to serve."

J. Z. Stallard hung his head. "It's my fault, I reckon," he said. "I never did like asking anybody for help. There might have been some kind of government farm aid we'd have qualified for, or an extension we could have got, but I never could beg. I never could."

"It's not begging," said Spencer, with more conviction than he felt. "It's your tax money. If they give it out to other people in need, why shouldn't they hand some of it back to you?"

J. Z. Stallard shook his head—at the offer of help or at the whole idea of the government? Spencer didn't know. He said, "Mr. Whitescarver down there has bought your farm in a tax sale. It's all legal, and he has the documentation, if you'd like to see it. You might want an attorney to look it over. I can recommend one, if you'd like."

The old man shook his head, and Spencer hurried on, "Anyhow, he's the new owner, and he says he'd like to take possession of the property in one week. Now, I know that's real short notice, Mr. Stallard, and there may be steps that you can take to delay the actual transfer, but right now, my sad duty is to notify you—"

"We're not moving." Dovey Stallard came out of the shadows of the barn, and stood a few feet behind her father, watching the sheriff with the wary look of a cornered felon. She was bundled up in a shabby coat of imitation sheepskin, scowling. She was ten feet from him, but she didn't appear much older than Spencer remembered. There were circles under her eyes, though, and she looked as if she hadn't slept much lately. He wanted to tell her that he had been a friend of her brother Tate, but she glared at him, eyes narrowed, as if it were his fault that this thing had happened. It would do no good, he knew, to remind her that he only enforced the laws; he did not make them. People in pain needed to hate somebody, and the sheriff was that somebody often enough, but he never got used to it.

"Miss Stallard," he said. "You must have heard what I told your father. I'm awful sorry it has to be this way."

"It's not fair!" said Dovey with tears in her voice. "This is our farm! It isn't right that some greedy old toad should put us off our land so he can get rich carving it into lots to make playhouses for city people."

"I don't disagree with you," said Spencer, "but there's not a lot either one of us can do about it."

"You gonna throw us out of here yourself, are you? Put our furniture out by the mailbox?"

"You won't make me do that," he said. He couldn't look at her.

J. Z. Stallard was silent now. It was Dovey who fought for the land.

"If you're not willing to throw us bodily into the road, then you'd better leave," she said. Her jaw was set, and her lips had tightened to a thin, bloodless line. "And you can take that bastard with you."

Spencer turned and saw that Frank Whitescarver was puffing up the hill, still about sixty feet away, but smiling at the three of them, and motioning for them to come forward. Spencer didn't want to referee a shouting match between the realtor and a distraught young woman. "Excuse me," he said to the Stallards. "Let me go and speak to Mr. Whitescarver." He hurried down the hill, and blocked the man's path. "What do you think you're doing?"

"Why, I thought I'd just come and have a word with these folks." He paused, gulping for breath. "See if I could help them out at all. I have a little trailer on a lot in Hamelin that's vacant right now. The hot water heater's broken, but—"

Spencer swallowed the urge to shout at the red-faced man. "No, sir," he said. "The best way for you to help all of us is to go back to the patrol car, and sit down. Please."

Frank Whitescarver was determined to be bountiful. He waved past the sheriff at the Stallards. "Hello, folks! No hard feelings, hear? I've got me a little trailer in town—oh Lord, Sheriff, she's got a gun!"

Spencer Arrowood did not have time to turn around. He lunged at Frank Whitescarver and bore him to the ground just as he heard the roar of the rifle.

CHAPTER TWELVE

I now began to mediate an escape.

—DANIEL BOONE

Officer down. The words gave Millie Fortnum chills. The Wake County Rescue Squad had never responded to such a call before, but they knew the procedure well enough: they were to wait for other law enforcement personnel to secure the area before they approached the injured man. At any crime scene, their orders were to wait until it was declared safe for them to go in. But this wasn't just any crime scene. This was one of their own.

Please let the lawmen be there already, thought Millie. It was one thing to gamble with the life of a drunken good old boy or an abusive husband—but she did not think that she could listen to the seconds tick by in the safety of the ambulance while Spencer Arrowood bled to death on the ground outside.

She decided that if the shooter was not actually standing over the sheriff brandishing the gun, then she would get out and do what she could for him, whether LeDonne had arrived on the scene or not.

"I can't believe that somebody shot Spencer Arrowood," said Carlton Scott, Millie's partner for the run.

Millie shrugged. She didn't want to talk now. She kept hoping that more information would come over the radio, but all was silent.

She wondered if the ice water in the pit of her stomach was from fear or from the fact that Carl was taking the roads as if there weren't any curves in them. He was new to the rescue squad, and inexperienced in handling emergency situations. He had no medical training beyond the brief course work offered to county volunteers. Millie had been patching people up for years, but she wasn't even a paramedic—just a housewife who had once dreamed of being a nurse. Suddenly it seemed too much responsibility to bear. Spencer Arrowood was her friend. He deserved better than her well-meaning efforts. *Please let it be a flesh wound*, she thought.

It wasn't.

There was no sign of the second patrol car when the ambulance pulled up in front of the Stallard house, but there was no sign of the gunman, either. Millie was out of the vehicle, and running up the hill toward the body before Carl had time to put the emergency brake on. She and Carl could argue about her decision later, she decided.

J. Z. Stallard was kneeling beside the body, holding a green woolen army blanket in his lap, as if he were unable to decide whether to cover up the wounded man or not. He kept pulling at the corners of the blanket and staring down at the victim. He didn't even look up when Millie knelt beside him. *He's in shock*, she told herself, but there wasn't time to tend to him.

"Did you move him at all?" asked Millie.

J. Z. Stallard shook his head. "I waited. Thought somebody ought to stay with him."

She nodded. "You did right."

Spencer Arrowood was unconscious. He lay on his stomach. Millie could see a spreading red stain on his khaki shirt. The bullet had entered the sheriff's left side a few inches above the waist—at least it had missed the heart, she thought. She knelt down, and began to check his vital signs, forcing herself to concentrate on Spencer as simply another body to be evaluated. She couldn't afford to lose precious seconds in shock or grief over a friend.

His pulse was rapid, but his blood pressure was low. Internal bleeding, of course. She wondered what organs had been hit, and how fast he was losing blood. His breathing was shallow. She put her head against his chest and listened for a moment. No rales. And no air bubbles appeared in the blood at the wound site. His diaphragm hadn't been hit. But then, he wouldn't have lived this long if the bullet had pierced his diaphragm: once the seal is broken on the chest cavity the lungs stop working. He would have died before J. Z. Stallard had time to run to the house and call for help. She had to get him out of the cold.

"Where is the assailant?" Millie asked the old man who stood over her, still twisting his hands in the blanket. She kept working as she talked, getting Spencer ready to be moved into the ambulance.

After a moment's hesitation, J. Z. Stallard said, "She took off."

She? The shooter was a woman? Millie glanced up at the man's ravaged face, and decided not to ask any more questions. The hows and whys didn't matter to her, anyhow; it would be enough if she could patch up Spencer Arrowood so that he could make it to the medical center. She tried not to think of all the times that they had been together at scenes of tragedy: wrecks, fires, and now and then a shooting. She mustn't think about it now. Every second mattered.

Carl was beside her now with the stretcher. "Millie, we were supposed to wait in the ambulance—" She looked at him, and his voice trailed off. "Oh, hell," he said. "We couldn't just let him lay here, could we? The sheriff."

Together they lifted him onto the stretcher and wheeled it back down the hill to the ambulance. Millie wished they could race away, as medics did in television dramas, but real life wasn't nearly so neat. It would be several more precious, frantic minutes before they could leave. Carl had to radio the hospital with information on the patient's condition.

Millie was putting the I.V. in Spencer's arm. "Tell them *left lateral abdominal gunshot wounds, no rales,*" she said to Carl. "*Probable circulatory shock due to blood volume loss.* Tell them I'm doing an art line on the subclavian artery. The vital signs are . . ."

"Patrol car just pulled up," Carl announced. "Wake County Sheriff's Department."

"LeDonne. Fine. If he yells at you for entering an unsecured crime scene, yell back. Just keep him away from here." She adjusted the oxygen mask on Spencer's face. "Radio JCMC. I'm about ready to go."

Deputy Joe LeDonne was in charge now, but that fact gave him no pleasure. He had never felt so alone.

When the call came in from Stallard's farm, notifying him of the shooting of Spencer Arrowood, he had double-checked to make sure that the rescue squad had been dispatched to the scene, and then he had attempted to beat them there, taking the curves of the Hamelin back roads at a speed just short of suicidal. They were closer to Ashe Mountain than he was. He hoped they'd had the sense not to wait. He didn't think that this particular assailant would pose a threat to ambulance personnel. If he was wrong, he'd deal with it when the time came.

The incoming message had been garbled. J. Z. Stallard spoke clearly but did not elaborate. He had sounded, strangely calm as if he himself did not believe a word he was saying. LeDonne's own sense of shock and rage, coupled with shrieks in the background from the uninjured Frank Whitescarver made the conversation disjointed and nearly unintelligible.

Spencer was alive but unconscious: that much he knew.

Damn Martha, he thought, as he drove. If she were still dispatcher, instead of off taking cop lessons at Walters State, the investigation would be proceeding like a military exercise, and he would be able to linger at the hospital until he knew for certain that the sheriff was out of danger. Martha would have known what to do, whom to call. Jennaleigh, whose tenure as dispatcher could still be measured in weeks, needed explicit instructions, and he would have to return to the office and instruct her. No one had covered this contingency in her hasty training session. As it was, LeDonne would have to swallow his rage—grief was still a long way off—until he had the assailant in custody. He kept his hands from shaking on the steering wheel by picturing himself shouting at a recuperating Spencer Arrowood. "Didn't I tell you not to trust anybody!" he would say. "Old friends, my ass! A woman with a gun is like a chimp with a hand grenade." He prayed that he would have the luxury of that anger.

Later—much later—he would have to call Martha to tell her that things were under control and that she needn't come back to help. He would promise to keep her informed of the sheriff's condition. When she blamed herself for not being here, he would choke back words to keep from agreeing with her. He decided that he might even wait a day or so to call her. Let her know about the crisis after the urgency was past, and he could truthfully say that the suspect was in custody and the sheriff recovering from his wounds. She mustn't abandon her training out of guilt or sympathy, and she mustn't be allowed to think that LeDonne couldn't handle an emergency on his own. It occurred to him that the shooting of a county sheriff would make headlines all over Tennessee, and that Martha would know sooner than he planned to tell her. He must call her as soon as he could spare a moment. She mustn't hear this news from someone else. And Spencer's mother. She had to be told. But there wasn't time. Could Jennaleigh handle so delicate and tragic a message? Jane Arrowood had already lost one son in a firefight. Please let her not lose another.

LeDonne tried to think of six things at once—anything except the possibility that his brother officer was going to die.

He did not hit the siren until a quarter of a mile from the turnoff. He would say that he didn't want to draw attention to his presence in case the suspect was nearby, but the truth was that with everything else crowding in on his thoughts, he had simply forgotten to hit the switch. There was noise enough in his head—so much that he did not even notice the absence of the siren. He swung the patrol car into the dirt road beside the mailbox marked Stallard. The ambulance was still there, its motor idling, and the lights on. There was no sign of the squad themselves, though, and no sign of a body. He pulled up next to the driver's side.

Don't waste time parking and walking over there, he thought. There may not be any more time.

Carlton Scott's face appeared at the driver's window. He rolled down the glass and peered out. "We've got him," he said. "We're stabilizing for the run."

"JCMC?" The Johnson City Medical Center was the best and closest facility. They had sent people there often enough: people from car wrecks, mostly, and an occasional wounded hunter.

"Right. We're almost ready."

"Where's he hit?" asked LeDonne, willing his voice to stay steady.

"Upper abdominal. He's losing a lot of blood, but he's lasted over twenty minutes now. That's a good sign."

"Let's go!" LeDonne recognized Millie Fortnum's voice, shrill with urgency. If there was anything to be glad about on this awful day, it was that she had been on duty when the call came in.

"Is he conscious?" asked LeDonne.

"No. We have to get him out of here fast. We're sending another crew in to check on the old man and the real estate fellow," said the ambulance driver. "The old man isn't injured, but he's had a bad shock. Go easy on him."

LeDonne nodded to Millie and her partner, and held his breath as they pulled away.

J. Z. Stallard was waiting for him in the yard. The old man looked on the verge of collapse, as pale and tottery as he was, but LeDonne had no concern to spare for a possible accessory. He slammed the car door, and without preamble said, "Where is she?"

"Gone. The real estate man is in the parlor. He's not hurt, just shaken up from being thrown hard to the ground." His voice quavered as he added, "She didn't mean to do it."

"No?" said LeDonne, who didn't much care what the suspect's intentions had been.

"She was upset about us losing the farm, and she was angry at Frank Whitescarver, who did us out of the land. He bought it at a tax sale, you know, and we reckoned that he's the one who made them have the tax sale to begin with. There's lots of other folks owes taxes, and nobody's putting them out of their homes. Dovey said it wasn't right, and that she wasn't leaving. I think she meant to scare him off with the gun."

"It's attempted murder," said LeDonne. "Where is your daughter now?"

J. Z. Stallard's eyes were wet. "I told you she's gone," he whispered. "As soon as she saw what she'd done—the sheriff jumped in front of Whitescarver, you know. He went down protecting that awful little man—Well, as soon as Dovey saw that, she lit out."

"On foot?"

"Yes. Into the woods."

"Where is the weapon?" asked LeDonne.

"She dropped it at the barn. But she took a pistol with her."

Kayla knew the ridge beyond the Stargills' fences well enough by now. In the forest the tangle of tree limbs and the occasional rustling noise just out of her line of sight no longer frightened her as it had when she arrived. Clayt had explained what the noises might be, and he had told her stories about wonderful plants and animals that lived in the woods. It seemed a friendly place to her now, not an endless closet full of monsters. When she tired of exploring the front garden and the barn, she glanced toward the house to see if anyone was keeping an eye on her, and, satisfied that she was unobserved, she slipped away up the hill toward the Stargill burying ground, and to the woods beyond.

Clayt had told her stories about playing pioneer in those woods when he and his brothers were children. Kayla couldn't picture Charles Martin Stargill doing anything as un-grown-up as playacting with a popgun. To hear him tell it, he had spent every minute of his youth practicing his guitar and writing songs. Kayla hadn't been able to find any toys in the attic, but she decided that she could play in the woods without them. Back in Nashville her mother had taken her to see the *Pocahontas* movie, and Kayla thought she might pretend that she could find a talking tree or a friendly raccoon in the forest as the cartoon Indian princess had done.

She wasn't worried about finding her way back. The tombstones on the hillside were her landmark. The pines were thick and dark on the fringes of the wood, but the other trees were just beginning to leaf out. She should be able to see the burying ground from a good ways off, she thought.

She looked around her as she walked, hoping to find a wildflower or a bird's feather or some other curiosity to take back to Clayt, so that he could spin her a tale about her discovery, but all she saw was pine needles and dead branches—nothing worth taking back to show Clayt.

Suddenly in the shadows farther on, one of the trees seemed to move, and Kayla felt her heart make a fist. She stood still for a moment, staring at the shape until her eyes could make out legs and an arm propped against a tree trunk.

"Hello!" Kayla called out. "Don't shoot me if you're hunting! I'm a little girl."

The figure came toward her, and Kayla could see that it was a lady. She had dark hair and blue eyes that were red-rimmed as if she had been crying. "What are you doing out here by yourself?" the lady asked her.

"Playing Pocahontas," said Kayla promptly.

The lady smiled as if Kayla had told a joke. "Pocahontas," she said softly. "Pleased to meet you. Then I guess I'll be Nancy Ward—again."

"Who's Nancy Ward?"

"She was a Cherokee lady who lived in these parts a long time ago. She tried to help the Indians keep this land. She was friendly to the whites—like Pocahontas."

The little girl considered this for a moment. The lady's eyes were very bright, and she sounded funny. Finally she said, "If you're so friendly, how come you got a gun?"

Charles Martin Stargill inspected his fingers for blisters. "This carpentry work is playing hell with my hands," he said. "I'll be lucky if I can play an A chord by the time we're finished." He brushed the sawdust off his black-fringed western shirt. "I should have been wearing gloves."

"You say that at least once a day," said Clayt. "Why don't you take your charge card to Kmart and buy some gloves?"

"We're almost finished now. No point in taking care of myself now." He grinned. "Anyhow, it'll make a hell of an excuse if I flub a note at the next concert. *I tore up my hands building my daddy's coffin.*"

"You care so much about what other people think that you never have time to worry about what you actually want, Charlie. Anyhow, if you'll put lotion on your hands, they ought to be better in a week or so," said Clayt. He was sanding the coffin lid by hand, sending showers of fine dust into the air.

"Well, Daddy would like it. He always loved it when I mentioned him onstage. A vicarious fame, I guess. 'Course the farther away I was, the better he liked me anyhow."

It was a cold day. The workshop window was fogged with moisture, and the portable heater was turned as high as it would go. Over Charles Martin's objections, the radio had been turned on, tuned to the AM station in Hamelin. The coffin was nearly finished.

Robert Lee was pressing a handkerchief to his nose, snuffling. "I wish I'd borrowed a surgical mask last time I visited Daddy in the hospital," he said. "This dust is killing me."

"It will be worth it," said Clayt, stepping back to admire the smooth strip of rosewood that he had just sanded. "Isn't this a beautiful thing?"

Robert Lee looked up with allergy-reddened eyes. "I guess so. If you don't think about the almighty waste of it all. Taking valuable wood and spending time and money to build it, and then slinging it in the ground to let it rot. People will think we're crazy."

Garrett Stargill smiled. "You want it for a coffee table, Robert Lee?"

"No. I just hope the old man appreciates it, that's all. It wouldn't be like him, though. You ever notice that every time you gave Daddy a gift he'd smile in that funny way."

"What way?" asked Garrett.

"You know—as if he were amused that you could ever have thought he'd want such an outlandish thing as whatever you were giving him. But he'd thank you solemnly, and set it aside, and you'd never see it again."

"Well, he'd be grateful for this," said Clayt. "It's what he wanted. And, besides, we're not doing this solely for Daddy. At least, I'm not. It's like a ritual to me. The last Stargill ever to live on this farm should be laid to rest with great ceremony in the family burial ground. It's the end of something fine, this is. From here on out, we're going to be rootless. In two generations, maybe our descendants will have forgotten all of it."

"It's just an old farm, Clayt," said Robert Lee. "It's not Monticello."

"Hush up!" said Garrett, leaning close to the radio. "I caught a word just now." He turned up the volume. "Something about a shooting . . . They said Wake County . . ."

They crowded around the black boom box, a Christmas gift from Charles Martin to his father a few years back. In a shaken voice, the announcer was giving sketchy details of a morning shooting incident on a farm in rural Wake County. Sheriff Spencer Arrowood was hospitalized in critical condition. . . . The suspect was not in custody. . . . No further details available at this time.

When the announcement ended, replaced by the blast of a local commercial, Garrett Stargill looked up at his brothers. "The sheriff of Wake County. I met him," he said. "He seemed all right."

Robert Lee shook his head. "It's as bad as Cincinnati. Seems like no place is safe anymore."

"It's safe enough," said Clayt. "Five percent of the people cause ninety-five percent of the trouble. Wonder who it was this time? One of the Harkryders?"

"Kayla! Are you in there?" They heard Kelley's voice echoing through the barn. "Kayla!" A moment later she appeared in the doorway, shivering in her sweatshirt. "I can't find that kid anywhere. Is she in here with you, Charlie?"

"No. Haven't seen hide nor hair of her all day. When did you see her last?"

Kelley frowned. "I don't know. She's always in and out. Independent as a hog on ice. Half the time she slips in and makes herself a jelly sandwich, and then goes back outside with it. Only way I know she's been in is the dirty knife on the drainboard."

Clayt laid aside his sanding tool. "She's probably roaming around the woods, Kelley. Why don't I go out and look for her?"

Kelley smiled. "I hate to put you out, but it's starting to get colder out here, and I don't want her getting sick on top of everything else."

"Of course not." Clayt smiled down at her. "She can't have gone far. You go on back to the house, and let me look."

He walked back through the barn with her, and out into the backyard. The wind had started to pick up now, and the afternoon sun did little to warm the day. Clayt glanced around the yard, and up into the old maple tree, in case Kayla was hiding out to play a joke on the grown-ups, but there was no sign of the child.

He was about to send Kelley into the kitchen to make cocoa for her wandering daughter, when he saw the uniformed trooper coming up the drive from the front of the house. Highway patrol. Nobody that Clayt knew. He saw Kelley stiffen beside him, and raise the back of her hand to her mouth, as if to stifle a scream. "It's Kayla!" she cried. "She's been hit!"

The trooper hurried toward them, his calm expression unchanged. Clayt wondered what it would be like to have a job that made people dread the sight of you. "What is it, Officer?" he said. "We're looking for a little girl who may have wandered off. Have you found her?"

The uniformed man hesitated. "A *little* girl?"

"She's nearly seven," whispered Kelley. "She knows not to play near the road. I've told her a million times."

The trooper shook his head. "Well, ma'am," he said. "I haven't seen her. I was taken aback for a moment there, because the fact is that I'm looking for a girl, too. A young woman, that is to say. She's a lot older than six, though."

They stared at him, still preoccupied with their thoughts of Kayla.

"There's a search party going on in this section of the county, and I'm doing a house-to-house to warn folks that the suspect is armed and considered dangerous."

"This has to do with the sheriff getting shot, doesn't it?" asked Clayt. Seeing the officer's look of suspicion, Clayt added, "We heard it on the radio. How is he?"

"He made it to the hospital, sir. That's all we know so far."

"And you're looking for a *woman*?" asked Kelley.

"Dovey Stallard. She's in her late thirties, dark-haired—"

"We know," said Clayt. "We're the next farm from theirs. But she wouldn't shoot anybody."

"She did. It was an eviction." The officer looked uncomfortable. He wasn't supposed to be gossiping about the case, and he knew it, but their disbelief had galled him. "Anyhow, according to my information, she is still armed, so if you see her, do not approach her on your own, no matter how well acquainted you are with her. Just call the sheriff's department and report her whereabouts."

Kelley looked stricken. "Dangerous." She clutched Clayt's arm. "We have to find Kayla. She might be off in the woods somewhere. And there'll be people out there with guns . . ."

Clayt nodded, but his thoughts were elsewhere. "I'll go," he whispered.

Joe LeDonne felt as if he were back in the war. It would be dark soon—days didn't last long in March—and the suspect had not been apprehended. He had thought she would be. Women, in his experience, were not violent lawbreakers, and if they had managed to shoot the boyfriend or otherwise run afoul of the law, they usually stayed put, sobbing as often as not, while they waited to be taken into custody. They usually spent the ride to jail trying to explain what they'd done. Women always tried to talk their way out of trouble. LeDonne had not expected this one to run. She had a clean record. She ought to have been waiting for him on the porch, with a box of tissues in her lap, and her lawyer at her elbow.

This was better.

He didn't want to have to be polite to the person who had gunned down Spencer Arrowood. She was an animal; now he could track her like one.

He had set up headquarters in J. Z. Stallard's front room, partly because it was close, and partly to keep Dovey Stallard from sneaking back home while they searched the woods for her. After an interview punctuated with gasps and choked sobs, Frank Whitescarver had phoned his wife, and was on his way to be examined at the Erwin hospital. The old man had been treated for shock, and taken to Reverend Bruce's house to be looked after—and to be out of the way while the searchers gathered.

It was going to get down to freezing out on the mountain tonight, but it wouldn't be peaceful out there. So many officers from half a dozen jurisdictions would be combing the area with so many spotlights and walkie-talkies that she'd think she was in a football stadium. LeDonne was coordinating the effort, but he didn't intend to stay in the Stallards' living room, giving interviews to the local news media and sticking pins in a map. He had put out a call for help from all the law enforcement agencies in the area, and then he had telephoned an acquaintance, a Carter County deputy named Stansberry, who had a reputation as an efficient officer. LeDonne had asked him to get leave from duty in Johnson City, and come to the Stallards' farm to coordinate the search teams. LeDonne could not keep pacing the living room if so, waiting for backup, and feeling like he was going to explode.

He was going out there to see if he could pick up her trail in the fading light. Later he would lead the searchers himself. He wanted to find her. And he wanted her to fight back.

Nora Bonesteel was playing hide-and-seek with the little girl in the woods. She was always "it," but she didn't mind, because there wasn't anyone else around to play with. Her mother had wanted her to stay in the yard because she was only five, and might get lost out on the mountain, but Nora was tired of feeding the chickens and chasing the wild barn kittens. The grown-ups were busy baking today, and they made it plain that they didn't want her underfoot near the hot stove. She must find her own amusement today. She wandered across the pasture and down into the deep woods, looking for May wildflowers to take back to Grandma Flossie.

She hadn't been very far from the edge of the meadow when she caught a glimpse of a small white face, peering at her from behind an oak tree. Nora had smiled and waved at the little girl, but she hadn't waved back. She was about Nora's age, with big dark eyes, hair so blond it was almost white, and a dress that looked dark and raggedy. She was barefoot, as all mountain children were as soon as it was warm enough. Nora had never seen the little girl before, but she was delighted to meet another child in such a solitary place. She waved again at the stranger. As an only child, she didn't get many chances to play with other children.

The little blond child looked startled, as if she hadn't expected to be noticed. Nora dropped the wild violets she had collected, and ran toward the girl, but she slipped into the laurels and headed deeper into the forest.

"Come back!" called Nora. "I won't hurt you!"

She ran as hard as she could for a hundred yards or so, but the stones and fallen branches hurt her feet, still tender in May from a winter spent in shoes. Nora sat down in a clump of pine needles, and began to speak to the child who had vanished. "I wish you'd come back here. I sure am lonesome. It's no fun playing by yourself all the time."

The pale face peered out at her from behind a locust tree, a dozen feet away.

Nora saw that she was listening, but she seemed frightened. "I'll just talk," said Nora. "I won't try to chase you. I can be your friend."

The girl was still staring at her, unmoving, but her expression softened.

Nora went on talking, soothing the frightened stranger with the sound of her voice. She talked about Grandma Flossie, and the barn cats, and about the garden patch that she had been allowed to tend all by herself. She sang all that she could remember of her favorite hymn, hoping that the girl would join in, but she only watched silently from a safe distance.

"You want me to sing some more?" asked Nora. "Grandma Flossie's favorite hymn is 'Abide with Me,' but I can never get the tune quite straight. Do you know that one?"

The pale child was looking past Nora, and her expression changed to one of alarm. Nora turned to see what had frightened her, and then she heard voices calling her name. "That's mama," she said. "I got to go now. Do you want to come home with—"

But when she turned around, the other child was gone.

CHAPTER THIRTEEN

Heaven is a Kentucky of a place.
—from a sermon, *The Christian Traveler,*
1828

Wake County Deputy Sheriff Martha Ayers had finished high school more than twenty years ago, but now that she was a student again, it felt more like two hundred. It would help if she didn't have to hold the book at arm's length to read some of the fine print while she studied. And she was too old for spartan dorm rooms, with a toilet down the hall and no microwave or refrigerator. If her stomach managed to survive the heavy meat-and-potatoes institutional food, or her muscles didn't give in from the constant strain of training, she would graduate in a few weeks' time, and then she would be a fully-qualified deputy sheriff in the state of Tennessee. She missed Hamelin, and she often wondered how Spencer Arrowood and Joe LeDonne were managing on their own. The hastily scribbled postcard from Spencer, and LeDonne's taciturn phone calls, were not much help on this point. Still, she knew that they would be glad to cut back on hours when their new deputy returned. Spencer might even take a vacation, which, Lord knows, was long overdue. She would encourage him to take some time off, maybe in June, after rhododendron season, when the tourist traffic had slacked off until Leaf Time in the fall.

Martha tried to keep her thoughts of home concentrated on the business side of her life. She didn't want to think too much yet about her personal relationship with Joe LeDonne. "We'll take it as it goes," she had said. She could see that he was trying to make things work, but she didn't know if she could accept his unspoken attempt at making amends. Forgiveness wasn't something she was good at.

"Ayers! Phone call!"

Martha looked up, and then down at her watch. It was far too early for LeDonne to check on her. He usually waited until eleven at night, when the rates went down. Besides, he had called day before yesterday, which meant that it was Martha's turn to phone him. She couldn't think who else it could be.

"Martha! It's Jennaleigh."

Martha felt her throat tighten. This wasn't a social call. The new dispatcher was not a close friend of her predecessor; they would have nothing to say in a long-distance chat. "What is it, Jennaleigh?" Martha's voice was brisk. Her mind had fast-forwarded through half a dozen tragedies in the moments it took her to ask the question.

"Is everything okay with you in the training program?" asked Jennaleigh. "We got your postcard. Listen, LeDonne would skin me if he knew I was calling you, but I figured you'd want to know. Men just don't understand about that, do they?"

No, thought Martha, but they get to the point quicker. "What is it?" She closed her eyes, and took a deep breath.

"The sheriff has been hurt. He's in the hospital in Johnson City. LeDonne is in a state about it, and he had me calling all over creation today, but he said you weren't to be disturbed."

"What's the matter with Spencer?"

"—On account of your training and all," said Jennaleigh, as if she had not been interrupted. "If you miss any days of classes or whatever, you have to start right back at the beginning, and that will take another six weeks, so—"

"I know about the course requirements," said Martha. "What I don't know is what happened to Sheriff Arrowood. Now are you going to tell me, or do I have to call Joe?"

At the mention of LeDonne, Jennaleigh gave a little gasp. "You can't let on I told you."

Martha waited.

"He got shot."

"Spencer? How?" *He was cleaning his gun, and he got himself in the foot,* Martha thought. Surely in a place as calm as Hamelin, nothing menacing had happened. And not to Spencer, for God's sake. LeDonne bristled most of the time, spoiling for a fight, to feed the combat high he missed so much from his Vietnam days. To hear that LeDonne had been wounded would be logical; Martha had long been afraid that someday somebody would take him up on the tacit invitation to fight that was in his every look and gesture—but Spencer? He'd lock up a drunk, and then buy him breakfast the next morning. What enemies could he have? None, of course. The badge did, though. She could imagine a lot of young toughs who would shoot at a khaki uniform without knowing or caring about the man who wore it. "Tell me how it happened, Jennaleigh."

"You know the Stallards? Live up the mountain a ways?"

"Yes." She remembered Tate from high school. But there hadn't been any other sons, and surely Mr. Stallard was past seventy now. "Go on."

"Well, they lost their farm to back taxes. There was an auction, and Mr. Whitescarver from the realty bought the place, but I guess the Stallards wouldn't leave, so he made Sheriff Arrowood go up there and kick them out."

Martha winced. He'd rather shoot himself in the foot than have to do that, she thought. "When was this?"

"This morning. Seems like weeks ago, though, with all that's happened. Anyhow, we got a call from Mr. Stallard saying that Spencer had been shot. By Dovey Stallard. A white female, age—"

"I know her," said Martha. She said nothing about Jennaleigh's lapse into jargon. At least the girl wasn't hysterical. She might make a dispatcher yet, Martha thought. "How bad is he?" she asked.

"Well, the doctors say critical, but they always say that to cover their butts in case somebody kicks off unexpectedly. The sheriff got hit side-on, as he was trying to throw Mr. Whitescarver to the ground, so he's hit in the side, and he's got internal injuries. He's still unconscious, last I heard. . . . Listen, I can't talk long. LeDonne is turning this place into a command center. He's got all kinds of people coming in to help."

"Help with what?"

"The search. Didn't I tell you? Dovey Stallard fled from the scene. She's armed, and she hasn't been apprehended. There's a big search going on, with officers from Unicoi and Carter coming in to help, and some city police from Erwin and Johnson City. LeDonne even had me call the ATF to ask them to send in their heat-seeking plane in case we have a night search."

"I'll come back," said Martha.

"No! That's just what LeDonne was afraid of. Why he wouldn't call you. Listen, it's more important than ever for you to finish that course now. Don't you see? Even if Sheriff Arrowood does recover—I'm sure he will, Martha. Honest!—he'll need time to recuperate. That means we'll need another deputy, because we can't run this department with only one officer. You have to stay and get qualified."

The fact that Jennaleigh was right made Martha even angrier. Of course she needed to get qualified, but she also needed to be searching those hills for Dovey Stallard before LeDonne went and got himself killed by an armed suspect. He would be spoiling for a confrontation now. This foolish frightened young woman had shot Spencer Arrowood. Joe LeDonne wouldn't want to take her alive.

"I have to go now, Martha," said Jennaleigh in a hoarse whisper.

"I need to talk to LeDonne."

"He's not here right now, but some of the other officers are beginning to arrive."

"Okay. I'll try to reach him later." Martha hung up the phone and leaned against the wall. She had to stay here at Walters State, and try to keep her mind on her work. Spencer would order her to stay, if he could. She would have to trust Joe LeDonne—something she had got out of the habit of doing.

No time. No time. The operating room team knew the drill, without anyone having to spell it out. The surgeon was scrubbing now; prep had to be done in minutes and seconds. The circulating nurse dumped the betadine straight from the bottle over the patient's chest and abdomen. No time to scrub him, or to remove the body hair from the area to be operated on. The drape was placed over the body, covering all but the skin of the belly.

"He's having some difficulty breathing."

Peter O'Neill nodded to the resident who had spoken. "All that blood in his abdominal cavity is impeding the movement of the diaphragm. Let's see where it's coming from." He made a midline incision from the tip of the sternum to the pubic symphysis. As the abdominal cavity opened, the surgeon stepped back a pace as the anticipated gush of blood spurted out. O'Neill waited while the staff cleared it away with sucker tips—tubing connected to suction bottles in the wall. He probed the left kidney, the renal arteries and renal vein. "So far so good," he muttered. "Bullet missed the kidney. Ah, found the gusher. Lacerated spleen. Kelly clamp."

The surgeon explored the cavity, tossing palm-sized blood clots on the floor, finally exposing the injured organ. Now that the pressure of the accumulated blood had been removed, the spleen began to spew more blood.

"This is the Wake County sheriff," the resident remarked as he watched the surgeon work. "And the shooter is still at large. If we lose this patient, they'll be turning east Tennessee upside down in the manhunt. Roadblocks everywhere."

O'Neill grunted. "He should consider a less hazardous line of work."

It would only take four minutes to remove the spleen, but they seemed long enough when the patient was in shock from a gunshot wound. Working with methodical haste, Peter O'Neill clamped off the spleen's attached vein and artery, and severed them. Then it was a few moments' work to remove the injured organ. It landed with an inelegant plop, ignored by all those present. They went on with their tasks, while O'Neill continued to suction and tie and sew.

The bleeding had stopped. Now they could see if there was anything else to worry about. O'Neill paused and took a deep breath, before probing for other injuries. Liver, pancreas, diaphragm, aorta, left kidney again. It checked out. "He's lucky," he told the staff. "Bullet nicked a rib on the way in, and missed most of the good stuff. Found it!" He fished the reddened bullet out of the abdominal cavity, and held it up. The nurse held out a shallow metal pan, and the surgeon tossed the bullet into it with the flourish of a free-throw shot. When it landed with a resonating clang, there was a brief silence. This ballistic tympany was a tradition with Peter O'Neill, picked up from westerns, perhaps, or old medical movies.

He was about to tell the chief resident to close.

"He's in v-fib!" There wasn't time for the anesthesiologist to say "ventricular fibrillation." No time. No time.

Somebody called for a crash cart.

"Want me to stand back?" asked O'Neill.

They swarmed around him. "Packs! Packs!"

"Right." He put wet laps—rectangular gauze pads—where the spleen used to be, and removed all retractors from the wound. "Want me to crack the chest?"

The anesthesiologist was injecting drugs into the art line. He waited a moment, and then checked his machine. He nodded to the surgeon. "Flat line. Get in there."

We're losing him. . . .

No time. No time.

Spencer Arrowood felt as if he were drifting. Sometimes on summer afternoons when he was a kid, Spencer and his brother Cal had gone to the river with huge black inner tubes from truck tires. On still summer afternoons when the heat blurred the air over the valley, they had gone tubing down the river to cool off. A long stretch of the Nolichucky was smooth and deep, and you could lay back in the inner tube and float slowly and soundlessly along, dangling your feet in the water, lulled to sleep by the cool serenity of the shady river.

He felt that way now. As if he were on an inner tube, being pulled along on a steady current to nowhere in particular.

"Hello," said the old man.

It seemed odd to be able to see the old man, and yet not any of the surroundings, the river or whatever it was. Spencer's mind seemed to be moving as slowly as the inner tube. He tried to think of something companionable to say to this elderly stranger, who seemed far too old to be floating on the river. He wondered where his brother Cal was.

"He's up ahead," said the old man, so Spencer thought that perhaps he had spoken aloud.

"Peaceful out here, isn't it?" said Spencer. He wondered if he knew the old fellow. He looked like somebody from these parts: short and wiry, with sparse white hair, and blue eyes with squint lines at the corners. Some farmer from back up the hollows, surely.

"Peaceful. Yes. It's supposed to be." The old man smiled at him. "I've been out here a while, to where I'm used to it."

Part of Spencer's mind was trying to remind him that Cal had died in Vietnam, and that he was the sheriff of Wake County, not a skinny teenager who should be tubing on the river. He couldn't feel the water on his legs, somehow. And it was March, wasn't it? Somewhere . . . it was definitely March.

"Rapids up ahead," the old man remarked. "Picking up speed. Feel it?"

He did feel something, an urgency about the current beneath him, and at the same time a feeling that he should fight it, make his way back upstream.

"You're meant to go back," said the old man.

"What about you?"

"Got some people waiting for me on the shore down there. Waiting to pick me up. My sister. She may be angry with me. I need to tell her I'm sorry about some things. But I don't think there's anybody meeting you. Not yet."

"Maybe you could give me a lift home," said Spencer. Had he left dry clothes somewhere on the riverbank? Had he ridden his bike?

The old man smiled and shook his head. "Your people are waiting upstream."

The conversation was broken abruptly by noise and lights, and a feeling that people were poking him. Spencer felt as naked now as a boy in the river, but the wetness was in his chest and shoulders, not his legs. Before he had time to puzzle out what that meant, he dropped back into a dreamless state of oblivion.

Jane Arrowood wondered if people always stood up when a doctor came out into the hall to tell them the news. It wasn't respect or awe for the physician, she thought, but some sense of the enormity of the message—that it should be received standing, with as much stoicism as one could muster. Prisoners stood in the courtroom when sentence was passed on them. It was something like that.

She had been waiting a long time in the waiting area reserved for loved ones of those in surgery. She had crumpled her good winter coat into a pillow, and there were coffee stains on the skirt of her gray wool dress, but she was not concerned now with her appearance. Surely doctors saw nothing but the eyes of their patient's family: the staring, pleading eyes that waited to hear what sentence would be pronounced on their loved one.

"Mrs. Arrowood?" He was a youngish man, and he looked tired, too. He could have done with a bath and a shave. The name tag on his white coat said: *Peter O'Neill, M.D.* "Sit down, please." He waved her to a plastic chair and took the one next to her.

"How is he?" Jane felt as if most of her were still standing.

"Spencer is out of danger now, I think. The bullet missed a lot of chances to really mess him up. All he lost was his spleen."

Jane felt tears spill onto her cheeks. "Is that bad?"

"He can live without it. The spleen is like a big sponge. It holds an extra amount of blood in case your body happens to need it for emergencies. So he's lost that, and maybe he'll be more susceptible to colds and things. Nothing major. If that bullet had hit him on the right side, it would have been a different story. Then it would have taken out the liver, and we'd have lost him."

"But he's all right?" Jane kept asking it. She could not hear the answer often enough.

"He is. He'll be on a ventilator for a while, so he won't be able to talk even if he comes to, but it's only for support. We'll remove it when he regains consciousness, which should be sometime after midnight, if all goes well. He's had a rough day." The surgeon let out a deep sigh, and patted Jane Arrowood's shoulder. "We all have."

Something in the doctor's voice made her wary. "Is there something else?"

He sighed, and ran a hand over his unkempt hair. "I'll tell you, Mrs. Arrowood, we almost lost him in there." He nodded toward the operating room. "He had been in shock a long time before they got him off the mountain and into the operating room, and it was almost too much for his system. We got a flat line for close to a minute, and we had to work to bring him around. But he's young and fit. He came back strong, and we got the bullet out. Removed the spleen. He'll have a good long scar for the rest of his life, but that's about the worst of it. He's in recovery now, still unconscious, of course." He looked at her worn face and reddened eyes. "I don't suppose you'd consider going home?"

Jane shook her head. She had been dreading this night for a long time—ever since her son was first elected sheriff. She had nightmares about it sometimes, and the memories were always mixed up with those of her older son, Cal. She hadn't been able to keep a vigil over his dying. Two uniformed army officers had come to her door one spring night in 1966 to tell her that, half a world away, her boy was dead. Bad enough to have to go on living after that. Then Spencer had gone into police work. He must find a job that risked his life every single day. She wondered sometimes if he were still competing with his older brother—if getting shot at were the whole point of it for him. And now it had come.

She had lived through this vigil many times in her imaginings, and she would not abandon it now that it had come. "It's safe for me to leave for a while. You're certain?"

"He's going to have to take it easy for a while, but I think he'll make it through this without any permanent damage. Try to see that he's not a damned fool about going back before he's ready."

Jane bowed her head. There were no words for the magnitude of her relief.

Dr. O'Neill glanced around the waiting room. "I should let the sheriff's department know that he's out of danger, shouldn't I? I'm told that they have been calling regularly"—he permitted himself a wry smile—"almost constantly, in fact, to ask about your son's condition. Will you call them, or shall I?"

Jane felt suddenly tired. She had been in the hospital since early afternoon, and she couldn't remember whether she had eaten or not.

"You call them, please," she said. "You may have to leave a message, though. I think they're out searching for the person who did this."

Dr. O'Neill frowned. "I hope they're not drumming up more business for me."

"I hope not, either," said Jane Arrowood. She meant, but did not say, that when it was over, she hoped that the officers in the search party would come out unscathed, and that the person they were looking for would be past needing the services of Peter O'Neill, M.D.

Kayla pulled her coat more tightly around her. It was getting dark now, and an occasional gust of wind would find them in the trees, making her shiver. They had been walking uphill for a long time. Kayla wasn't sure which way home was now or how far they had come, but she was tired. She was hungry, too, but she could tell that it wouldn't do any good to ask for food. There plainly wasn't any. Kayla had some jelly beans in her pocket, but she hadn't bothered to eat any. She might need them worse later.

The lady with the gun had let her sit down on a rock for a few minutes to catch her breath. Then they would walk some more. "I don't reckon we can build a fire?" Kayla said softly.

Dovey Stallard shook her head. "No. We shouldn't talk, either. Somebody might be close enough to hear us."

"Nah," said Kayla. "Posses are pretty noisy. They got dogs and flashlights, and walkie-talkies, and they yell all the time. If they were coming up on us, we'd know it."

"Posse," Dovey almost smiled. "You been watching cowboy movies?"

"Sometimes. Charles Martin likes them. He has a whole bookcase full of videos. All of Clint Eastwood. Some John Wayne. It's the right word, isn't it? When cops are chasing somebody, doesn't that make them a posse?"

"I guess." Her captor sighed. "We used to play games like this when we were kids, me and Charles Martin and his brothers. Never thought it would really happen to me, though."

"What did you do?" asked Kayla with interest. The lady hadn't hit her or anything, and she hadn't even pointed the gun at her lately, so Kayla wasn't particularly afraid of this new grown-up. She was sober, anyhow. Some of Kayla's mama's boyfriends had been a whole lot worse, even when they were *trying* to be nice. Besides, this lady was a friend of Charles Martin Stargill's, she'd said so herself. So she must be all right. And she seemed pretty scared. Kayla wished she could help.

Dovey shrugged. "Some bad men were trying to take my land," she said. "I shot at them to make them go away."

"You didn't kill one, did you?" Kayla's eyes widened.

"I—I hope not." She stood up. "No sense talking about it. We'd better get moving."

"Is that how come you took me? To keep them from shooting at you?"

"I don't know," said Dovey. "Mostly that, I guess. A hostage was better than nothing. And maybe I did it to hurt Charlie Stargill, too. He could have stopped all this, and he wouldn't."

"How could Charles Martin have stopped it?"

"He's rich. I asked him to give me the money to save the farm, and he wouldn't do it. So—whatever happens to us—let him live with it." Dovey pointed the barrel of the pistol at the ground, and helped the child up with her free hand. "Let's get going."

Kayla's eyes had adjusted to the darkness now, but she had to move slowly. She couldn't see the rocks or branches in deep shadows, and now and then she stumbled. "It's pretty dark," she said, dusting off the knees of her jeans after a fall. "You didn't bring a flashlight?"

"I didn't bring anything. I just—I ran."

"You know where we're headed?"

"Sort of. If I can find it again. Look out for this mountain laurel. It's pretty thick, and the branches can scratch you up good."

Kayla stood still and listened. Far off she could hear the baying of tracking dogs, and she thought she heard an occasional shout from one of the searchers. She wondered if her mother had missed her yet, and whether anybody had figured out where she was. Clayt would probably come looking for her. He was her friend. Charles Martin was nice enough, but Kayla couldn't imagine him ruining his custom-made Lucchese boots traipsing through the woods in the dark. Clayt wouldn't care, though; his clothes were beat up already. And he talked to her like she was a real person. Besides, trailing her through the wilderness was something Daniel Boone might have done, and Clayt would love it on account of that.

That thought stirred something in her memory. Daniel Boone had tracked a girl through the wilderness. Clayt had told her the story the day she'd gone with him to take the coffin wood to the shop. The Indians had kidnapped Daniel Boone's daughter, and he'd had to follow their tracks to get her back. Boone's daughter had helped him find her by stalling the Shawnees at their rest stops. She picked lice out of the old chief's hair. Well, that wouldn't work. The lady with the gun looked clean enough, just sweaty and scared. She wondered if she ought to make it easy for him to track her. She didn't want to get the lady in trouble, but she figured it would be okay if Clayt found them. He'd never shoot anybody.

Kayla fished a jelly bean out of the pocket of her jeans, and dropped it on the ground. "Want to play like we're Indians?" she asked the lady.

Dovey sighed. "I reckon that's what we're doing, child. Playing Indian."

"How come?"

"We're being hunted through the woods by men with rifles who have taken our land. You can't get much more Indian than that."

"I had me a Pocahontas dress for Halloween. They only let me go to four houses, though. What was the name of your Indian?"

"Nancy Ward. She was a great chief. Cherokee."

Kelley Johnson kept blinking the tears away from her eyelashes so that she could see the seam she was sewing for Randall Stargill's coffin lining. They had cut up some of Randall's old neckties and bits of old clothes they had found in the trunk, and Lilah had used almost all of the Italian shawl, scattered piecemeal throughout the design. Its silky sheen and the fine embroidery work brightened the quilt until it was almost too festive for a burial.

It was nearly finished now: seven feet long, five feet wide—soon she and Lilah and Debba would sew their three portions together, and lay it aside to wait for Randall Stargill to die and have need of it.

Around her in the parlor, all the Stargills—except Clayt—were sitting stiffly in little pools of light from the table lamps. The television was on as always, but the sound had been cut off, so that the people on the screen moved and gestured in helpless silence. Kelley felt as if she were one of them: screaming without uttering a sound.

The Stargills were making desultory conversation, and trying to seem natural. Kelley wanted to put down her sewing and throw her coffee cup against the wall. Anything to make them stop pretending. Her baby was out there somewhere in the night, and they were all acting like nothing was wrong. They had said how sorry they were, and they'd assured her that Kayla would be home safe by midnight—all, that is, except Debba, who stared at her with round, frightened eyes, anticipating tragedy, and transfixed by it. The others had seemed callous in their optimism. Kelley sewed in silence and hated them.

Lilah had tried to be helpful. She kept bringing Kelley cups of tea, and she'd wanted to call Dr. Banner to come and administer a sedative to the distraught mother, but Kelley refused. She didn't want to be numbed; she wanted to wait, and she wanted to be awake enough to pray as hard as she could that Kayla would be all right.

"I just can't believe Dovey Stallard would have shot anybody," said Charles Martin, for maybe the tenth time.

"That's the trouble with guns," said Lilah, peering through her reading glasses at the eye of the needle she was trying to thread. "You can do something in a split second, and regret it forever after. I'm sure she's very sorry about it now."

"It's the culture up here," said Robert Lee. "It's violent. Always was. We're well out of it, all of us."

Kelley looked over her needlework at Charles Martin. He had been avoiding her eyes for the last half hour. He sat in the wingback chair, cradling the Martin guitar in his arms, and picking a dozen notes of first one melody and then another. Kelley recognized the tune to "Footprints in the Snow," an old Flatt and Scruggs number about a fellow who finds a lost girl in the woods by tracking her steps in the snow. Charles could sing about it, but he couldn't do it.

He looked up suddenly and met her gaze. He looked away first. "Kayla will be all right," he mumbled. "Dovey wouldn't hurt a kid. She's hot-tempered, but she doesn't mean any harm."

"She shot somebody this morning," said Kelley.

"Well, that was over the land, honey. She was desperate to keep that farm. Don't ask me why. She's the last of the Stallards, so it'll go to strangers sooner or later anyhow, but—" He shook his head. "Dovey Stallard. I can't believe it."

"I can," said Robert Lee. "People around here are not sane on the subject of land. I get the feeling that Clayt would do the same thing, if it came to that."

"Well, at least it has drawn attention away from that box of bones you took to the law," said Lilah. "Maybe they can just gather dust in the sheriff's office, and we can bury your daddy in peace. Perhaps that's the silver lining in this terrible cloud."

"I think Dovey and Kayla are a damned sight more than

distractions from an old family scandal," said Charles Martin. "That skeleton won't matter to anybody except the tabloids. Tabloids! I can't believe I used to worry about them—and now I . . . I guess when you've got real trouble, it doesn't matter what anybody else thinks. I just can't believe that Dovey would do such a thing."

Kelley's stare told Charles Martin that he had been talking too much about Dovey Stallard. "I hope Kayla's all right," he said a little too loudly. His strumming pattern changed. He looked down at the Martin for a moment, and he began to pick out the melody to a different song. Kelley recognized "The Bounty Hunter" by North Carolina folksinger Mike Cross. "And Clayt, too, if it comes to that. Imagine him hightailing out of here to track down the fugitive! He's been playing Daniel Boone too-oo long, boys. Reckon he'll be back soon, though. Last thing those police officers want is some damn fool loose on the mountain when they're trying to find somebody. He'll be lucky not to get himself shot out there in the dark."

"I should have gone with him," said Kelley.

"No, I should have." Garrett Stargill stood up. "I'm the one with commando experience. I've probably done more night tracking in a combat situation than all those men out there put together. I should offer to help."

Debba Stargill grabbed at her husband's wrist. "You can't go, Garrett! It's dangerous."

"Oh, I don't think so," said Lilah. "Surely that young woman is more frightened now than anything. She doesn't want to harm anyone else."

Garrett laughed. "Frightened people are the most dangerous folks on earth. Isn't that so, Debba?"

She hung her head. "I guess so," she whispered.

"Debba ought to know," said Garrett, twisting his arm to make her let go. "Debba's an expert on the hazards of fear."

"Stop it." Her voice was expressionless. She stared at the floor.

Lilah looked nervously at them, then at Kelley, who was taking shallow deep breaths, and looking about an inch away from hysteria. "Maybe we should call the hospital," she said. "We could check on Daddy Stargill, and see how the poor sheriff is faring, as well."

"I expect he's gut-shot," said Garrett. "When a frightened woman shoots, she usually aims for the belly. Or maybe she aims for the heart and misses, because she's such a lousy shot. What would you say it was, Debba, intent or bad aim?"

She shivered. "I didn't mean to."

"I'm sure that's a lot of consolation for the corporal's family, Debba." He turned to the others. "Debba here gets nervous when I'm away. She thinks the whole of west Tennessee is conspiring to abduct her in my absence. She keeps a baseball bat by the front door, and a can of Mace on the nightstand. A regular suburban terrorist is little old Debba Stargill."

Garrett stopped talking, but no one interrupted him. His stare said that he wasn't finished.

"So two years ago when I was gone . . . Haiti? Somalia?" He shrugged. "Somewhere. I was supposed to be in peril, and the people back at Fort Campbell were supposed to be safe and sound, but Debba Stargill *never* feels safe. So one afternoon she heard a noise. One *afternoon*. Not three o'clock in the morning. Not a dark and stormy night. One sunny, peaceful, goddamned afternoon. So she goes outside to see what monsters of depravity have come to ravish her. And there's a kid in the yard. He's maybe twenty. He's looking for one of our neighbors. About the kitten ad. About the goddamned kitten ad in the newspaper. Which house. So he starts walking toward pretty, tiny Mrs. Stargill to see if she can give him directions, and that's when she puts a .44 slug into him, all the while screaming that he's trying to rape her."

Debba buried her face in her hands. "He shouldn't have come to our back door. He—"

"He was gut-shot, and he died before the ambulance could get there. Debba didn't call 911; she just stood there and screamed until the neighbors found her. So maybe we deserve each other, Debba and me. I get paid to kill people for Uncle Sam, and Debba works for free."

"I hate you," said Debba Stargill from behind the palisade of her fingers.

"I'm going now," said Garrett. "I'm going to try to get Kelley's little girl back. The rest of you stay with my lovely wife here. Keep her away from the kitchen knives and from Daddy's shotgun. I don't want her mistaking one of the policemen for a hundred-pound woman, and killing him in 'self-defense.' Of course, she'd probably get off. The Tennessee legal system seems to be awfully sympathetic toward delicate women who cry a lot at the inquest. She didn't even go to trial. Maybe Dovey Stallard can try that tack when they catch her. It might work. I doubt it, though."

He turned and walked out of the room, and no one spoke.

The hills were dark, but the search continued.

Joe LeDonne had begun alone at dusk, looking for the trail up at the barn, where Dovey Stallard had last been seen by the eyewitnesses. He was trying to locate a recognizable shoe print, or signs of bent grass and broken twigs that would lead him in the direction she had fled. The trail could still be followed at night, but it would be slower, and much more difficult to discern. The trackers would use high-powered flashlights. Crouching close to the ground, they would search for blades of grass bent at odd angles, crushed out of symmetry by a running foot. It could take hours to go a few yards. To speed up the process, the members of the search team were stationed great distances apart, each looking for the same thing: signs of disturbed earth, showing that someone had passed that way not too long ago. The first tracker began his search a mile from the starting point. The others were spread out behind him, slowly, painstakingly looking for the slightest hint of a trail. When one of the searchers found that trail, he would signal to the others, and those behind him would move ahead from their old positions and fan out from this new starting point.

It was slow going in the darkness. Sometimes the trail that had been carefully followed for an hour would halt in a patch of soft bare earth—at the hoofprint of a deer. Then the searchers had to backtrack to the last known position, and begin again.

Joe LeDonne was farthest out in front, praying for daybreak. The tedium of following a trail an inch at a time made his jaw ache from clenched teeth, and his legs were sore from hours of unaccustomed stooping to see faint signs in the frosted grass. He had not eaten since breakfast, but he was damned if he was going to stop now.

The trail had to be located tonight, because when another eight hours had passed there would be no trail. Bent blades of grass would spring back into place, and night-roaming animals might dislodge twigs or obscure footprints with their own tracks. When the trail became cold, there would be nothing to do but wait for the fugitive to make a mistake: break into an empty cabin or steal a car. Then the search could begin again from that new location.

One of the state troopers approached LeDonne, careful to stay behind the light, away from any possible trail. "They sent me to give you an update," he said. "The dog's about ready to quit."

LeDonne straightened up, scowling. A cold wind bit into him, and he wished he'd remembered his gloves. "The dog's quitting. Already?"

"Those tracking hounds are only good for about an hour. Apparently it takes a lot of effort to read a trail with your nose, and they just burn out on it real quick."

"So we can bring in another dog."

"If one's available. Your people are on the horn now trying to locate a K-9 squad that can be brought in to help. No luck so far. And the ATF plane is on its way, but there's a storm system between them and us, and they may not make it until morning."

"Fat lot of good they'll be then." He sighed. The trail was getting colder than the night wind. There were a couple of thousand square miles of Cherokee National Forest for Dovey Stallard to disappear into. If she were allowed to slip past the trackers on this mountain, the hunt could take weeks, not hours. Then there might be nothing for them to do but wait until the fugitive herself felt like quitting the chase. If she didn't get help from unsuspecting hikers, if she didn't rob somebody or steal a car, then she might get tired of being cold and hungry and hunted, and she'd give herself up. But if she managed to hitch a ride to Knoxville, say, or Charlotte, then she could disappear forever. LeDonne thought it was worth forgoing food and sleep for a couple of days to prevent that from happening. Because if Dovey Stallard did get away clean, he thought he might never sleep again.

CHAPTER FOURTEEN

Many dark and sleepless nights have I been a companion for owls, separated from the cheerful society of men, scorched by the Summer's sun, and pinched by the Winter's cold.

—DANIEL BOONE

Clayt was walking along an old logging road bordered by a marshy thicket of alders. Beyond it a hayfield lay in darkness. He wondered if the dew was heavy enough to show footprints in the dry grass. If he shined his flashlight close to the ground, he thought he might be able to see the traces of indentations worn across the wet field by someone walking. But could he tell deer tracks from human ones in the darkness? Probably not. And turning on the flashlight might be dangerous. The woods were full of gunmen tonight. They might mistake him for their quarry and open fire. He wondered if he should risk it. He had to find Dovey before they did. He stood still for a moment, waiting and listening, as he always did in the wild. A full moon was low on the horizon, and the air was beginning to take on the chill of night. He held his breath, listening.

The sound of the searchers did not carry to his ears; they were too far away. For a few moments, all was silent.

March was a quiet time in the hills. No crickets were serenading. Only a few night moths fluttered around in the moonlight. From the shadows of the hayfield, he heard a bird's cry, a *peeb* that always made him think of a telephone busy signal. If it were daylight, and later in the spring—say, April—he'd have said the call was that of a nighthawk, but he had never seen one return to the mountains this early in the year. A woodcock, then. The old-timers called them *snipe,* much to the annoyance of local ornithologists, who reserved the term for a similar looking long-billed bird of an entirely different species. Snipe hunt: another term for a wild goose chase. Was he on a snipe hunt tonight?

He heard the *peeb* again, followed by a whistling sound that meant the bird had taken flight. It was courting time for the woodcocks: high spiraling dances above the fields, loud cries and whistling wings, all to impress the hens, watching below.

Clayt crouched near the alder thicket, cupped his hands to his mouth and made the whooo-ing sound of the great-horned owl. That would stop the revels. Nothing ought to be merrymaking tonight, he thought. Before the sound had died away, a dark shape rose up before him with a raucous cry. Its wings brushed his cheek as it soared upward, and he staggered back, gasping from the shock of that sudden encounter. It was a woodcock, of course, fleeing from his owl noise. He stood there for several moments, bent over, his heart pounding, while he waited for the feeling of panic to subside. "Only a woodcock," he whispered, over and over. The mountain was a menacing place tonight, but he had to go on.

Clayt looked ahead to the darkness of the woods, and wondered whether it was more dangerous to use his flashlight, or to go on without it.

Kelley Johnson tapped on the bedroom door. Lilah was alone, she knew. After Garrett left, Debba had fled sobbing to her room, and no one followed her. Robert Lee found a basketball game on television, and he had turned the sound up to a deafening level. Charlie stayed in the room, looking at the screen sometimes, but mostly picking out chords on the Martin. Kelley slipped away, and left them happily watching the game, as if all the turmoil and anxiety had been confined to the previous cable channel, instead of there in the room with them. Kelley wanted to talk.

Lilah, in her turquoise caftan, opened the door and ushered her in. "Is there any news?"

Kelley shook her head. "I just came to see you," she said.

Lilah indicated the little chair beside the mirrored dressing table. "You need company," she agreed. "It's best not to try to bear these things alone." Lilah had brought a piece of the coffin quilt upstairs with her. She picked it up now, and began to make measured stitches like grains of rice against a background of green velvet.

"I feel alone," said Kelley. "Charles Martin isn't any help. He refuses to believe that anybody would harm Kayla, and he thinks that the police will catch that woman any minute now. He says Kayla will be home in an hour or two as if nothing had happened."

"I hope he's right."

"So do I, but I can't just sit back and watch basketball. That's my baby out there." Tears coursed down her cheeks, and she pushed them away with the back of her fist. "Charlie acts like he doesn't care a damn."

Lilah nodded with a sad smile. "That's Stargills for you, honey. I think they learned early on not to show their wounds. When something pains Robert Lee—a rude remark by a customer, perhaps, or something going wrong with the house that's going to cost money—you'd never know from looking at him that anything bothered him at all. Just for a second he gets a frozen look, and then he sets his jaw, and goes on like nothing happened. I've been with him thirty years now, and I can tell when he's just aching inside from something that's been said or done to him, but he holds it right in, and never lets on to anybody."

Kelley looked puzzled. "But then they stay angry. They never get rid of it. Never stop hurting."

"I think the old man taught them to be like that," said Lilah. "I expect he called it courage. It isn't easy on the rest of us, though, is it? It's probably hardest on them, though, holding all that pain inside."

"I had made up my mind to leave him," said Kelley.

"Well, you need to make up your own mind about that," said Lilah. "Ask yourself whether he'd be a good father to that little girl of yours, when she comes back safe. Don't think he doesn't care just because he didn't go traipsing off into the woods and risk getting shot at. Charles Martin isn't much on heroics, but would he be all right day to day? That's what matters. That's mostly the kind of bravery you need in this life."

"If he loved her—"

"Honey, there's a dozen policemen out there looking for the child. Do they love her? Or do they love the danger? Garrett went. Ask yourself why they're out there."

"I'm so afraid," whispered Kelley.

Lilah nodded. "I was going to pray about it, but I really do feel that Kayla will be kept safe."

"Why? Remember that box of bones the strange old woman brought here? Those belonged to a child. Maybe her folks prayed, too. Maybe they felt that she was going to be all right."

"Times were harder then," said Lilah. "Many a child sickened and died. We don't know what happened to the owner of those little bones. A disease, perhaps."

"Then why wouldn't the old woman tell us anything about the bones?"

Lilah smiled. "Old people are a bit peculiar at times," she said.

Kelley wasn't convinced, but she hadn't come to argue. "Do you really have a guardian angel?" A week ago she wouldn't have believed that she could ask such a question, but now any consolation seemed worth having.

Lilah sighed. "I have an angel, dear. At least, that's what Rudy says he is. And I can't see him, except as a fuzzy image in my mind, so I can't be sure that he has those feathery white wings that you see on the Christmas cards, but, yes, I believe that someone is with me. Not right now. No use you looking around for him, not that you could see him anyhow. Even I've never caught a glimpse of him. But . . . someone speaks to me."

"Why to you?"

"That is a bewilderment, isn't it?" Lilah was not in the least offended by the question. "I've often wondered myself why I should have an angel, when there's people who are more pious than I am, and people worse off, too, who could sure use one. I haven't got any answers to give you. He's just there."

"Could you ask him to help Kayla?"

"I could ask him. Of course I will, dear, but you mustn't pin your hopes on Rudy. He doesn't look at things quite the way we do. He very seldom interferes in worldly happenings. I have tried to ask him about it, but he says he's not here to debate theology. Those were his very words. He doesn't grant wishes like a fairy godmother, I'm afraid. Mainly he just lectures me about being a righteous person. He says miracles are pretentious."

Kelley shrugged. "What good is he then?"

Joe LeDonne was taking a break, sitting with his back against a tree. He was drinking coffee, mostly to warm his fingers, and listening to reports from the coordinating officer. The last likely trail had come to a dead end in some fox scat. Mistaking an animal's tracks across wet grass for the path of the suspect had cost the search team an hour, perhaps more. Now they must go back a quarter of a mile or so to the last definite point of reference, and begin again. And all the while Dovey Stallard could be putting more distance between herself and her pursuers.

LeDonne swallowed his rage. "Any word on the sheriff?" he asked the Carter County deputy.

"He's in intensive care, last we heard. He came through the operation all right, though. That's a good sign."

LeDonne nodded. He'd rather be here in the woods than pacing the floor at the Johnson City Medical Center. At least here his anger could be directed to some purpose. "Anything else?"

The deputy hesitated. "Did they tell you about the little girl?"

"What little girl?"

"A trooper was notifying all the people in the area late this afternoon, and he says there's a six-year-old missing from the Stargill farm up the ridge. Maybe the suspect took the child as a hostage."

LeDonne took a deep breath and blew it out slowly. That changed the equation. On the one hand, the woman would find it harder to travel with a small child in tow; on the other hand, a direct confrontation was now something to be dreaded. He didn't want any innocent people caught in the crossfire, least of all a child.

Now, though, it increased the urgency of the hunt. They must find Dovey Stallard soon, before she could harm the hostage, or before the girl died of exposure. If only it weren't such a long time until daylight. The tedious pace of night tracking made him want to ram his fist into a tree. He wished he knew where she was going. He wondered if Martha could have second-guessed her—another woman, and all.

"Maybe we ought to get the suspect's father out here," said LeDonne. "If there's a hostage involved, we may need to talk her out when we find her." He wouldn't think about the possibility of her getting away. "We've got roadblocks set up, don't we?"

"On most of the main roads, yes. There may be dirt roads out of here that aren't covered. No reports of stolen vehicles, though."

LeDonne nodded. That was something to be thankful for. "I should get back to it," he said. "Anything else?"

"We got a new volunteer who wants to help with the search," said the deputy. "Fellow from the next farm, the one the kid is lost from.

His name is Garrett Stargill. Says he has commando training in the army."

"When? I don't want some doddering gung-ho World War Two vet—"

"No. He's still with his unit. He's a warrant officer stationed at Fort Campbell. He's just here visiting."

LeDonne shrugged. "Put him out there. See if he can find a trail."

"Well, he says he's acquainted with the suspect. Says he might know where she's headed."

"How?" LeDonne stood up, and poured his coffee on the ground. "Where is this guy? I want to see him."

"He's back a ways with the others. Says Dovey Stallard used to play in the woods with him and his brothers when they were children. They had favorite places to hide, seems like."

"And he can find these places again now? In the dark?"

"He's willing to try."

Clayt Stargill stood for a moment on the crest of the ridge, looking at the full moon through the bare branches of a sycamore. Some things had not changed since Daniel Boone's time, but that fact gave him no pleasure. The moon was the same—maybe people were the same, too. A man had been shot and a little girl stolen away—Daniel would have felt right at home here today. But Clayt Stargill did not.

He was unarmed, still numbed with shock from the jumble of events—*Dovey!*—and he was frightened, too. He knew that the woods would be swarming with law enforcement people, and that if they mistook him for their quarry, he might be killed. Being out here on the mountain tonight was no less dangerous than it had been when Daniel Boone had tracked his daughter through the wilderness two hundred years before. At least Boone had the luxury of unalloyed anger: he wanted his daughter back, and he would kill without remorse to save her. Clayt wished it were that simple now. Dovey and Kayla . . . and the valley was full of strangers, hunting them both.

He kept walking along the ridge, wondering where Dovey would go. What would he do if half the cops in Tennessee were hunting him on Ashe Mountain? The question didn't arise, of course. If he had done this thing—he could not picture it happening, but say he had—he would have stood his ground, given himself up peaceably, and hoped that some conservation-conscious lawyer would take his case as an environmental cause. Clayt liked to talk his way out of trouble, and he had never met a cop who was a sympathetic listener. No way would he make himself the rabbit in their hunt. In their anger at having almost lost one of their own, it would be all too easy for them to forget the humanity of the hunted one.

Dovey wasn't much on talking, though. Sometimes in school she could have got out of trouble by making a show of being really sorry, if she had gushed contrition, the way other children did to save their hide or their grades, but Dovey never would. She'd get a sullen look on her face and a mulish glint in her eye, and as likely as not she'd get punished twice as much for half the mischief. Dovey never begged for mercy, so folks gave her precious little of it. Clayt guessed she still hadn't learned to play it the way the world wanted it played.

Daniel Boone was like that, too. In his memoirs he wrote of his father's method of punishing his unruly sons. Squire Boone would whip the boys until they pleaded with him to stop. Then he'd stop. It worked with all his other sons, but not with young Daniel. Daniel would grit his teeth, and take the beating and take it. "Why don't you beg?" Squire Boone would ask, when the whipping had gone on too long. "Why don't you *beg*?" Daniel couldn't and wouldn't. Not then, or ever. Maybe that's why he lit out for the wilderness—there's too much begging required in civilization.

"Dovey, maybe you should have played Daniel Boone," Clayt

whispered. "Nancy Ward sure didn't teach you much. She would have learned society's rules real quick, and she'd have done what had to be done to save her land. Why couldn't you have sweet-talked that sheriff, Dovey? Cry for the real estate man. Oh, Dovey, why couldn't you beg?"

Nancy Ward. Look where it got her, said a voice in his head.

Nancy Ward. . . . Something stirred in his memory.

The moon was full, but he still couldn't see well enough to follow a trail, assuming there was one. Clayt wasn't sure he could have done it in broad daylight. It wasn't something he practiced. As a naturalist he looked at tracks to identify the wildlife present, or he looked for signs of feeding: nibbled leaves or discarded seed husks, evidence that an animal had passed by, but as he wasn't a hunter, he never tried to stalk the animals whose presence he detected. He talked about tracking when he lectured school children on Daniel Boone, that was all. Knowing something from books was one thing; being able to do it when it counted was another.

As soon as Kelley had left the room, Robert Lee turned down the sound on the basketball game, and leaned toward his brother to talk.

"Do you really think the little girl will be all right? Dovey wouldn't hurt a child, would she?"

Charles Martin was picking out the notes to "Maid of Constant Sorrow." "I don't know," he said. "She was an awful hothead as a kid. I think she's still got a temper, but I can't see her being deliberately cruel to an innocent little girl. She knows that none of this is Kayla's fault."

"Maybe she's going to hold her for ransom—make you give her the money for the farm."

"That would be like stealing," said Charles Martin. "I think Dovey would rather die than steal. I wish I'd had the money to give her."

"Did they mention whether the real estate man got hurt?" asked Frank.

Charles Martin shook his head. "Not that I recall. I think the radio said just the sheriff."

"Don't look at me that steely kind of way." Robert Lee blushed. "All right! I was thinking about our land deal. That doesn't make me a monster. I'm just as concerned about Kelley's little girl as the next person, but somebody has to be practical in this family. Daddy raised me to economize, save my money, and be prepared for the unforeseen. I can't pretend I'm not worried about the farm just because a child is missing. I hope we get her back, too, but that doesn't change our financial predicament, does it?"

"I guess not, Robert," said Charles Martin. "Take it easy."

"I wish I could afford to be high-minded, like you and Clayt, but I'm not made that way. You can afford to be noble, and Clayt hasn't got any better sense, but I have to worry about my old age—and Lilah's, too. And Garrett had better be worrying about money, because from the looks of things, he'll have to be paying alimony by and by."

"I'm not blaming you, Robert. I guess I've got to know you better these past few days, and I can see how worried you are about the future and all. I guess I can't blame you. Hell, you may have more security than I do, after thirty years at the car dealership. Country music fans aren't that faithful. Someday they may stop buying my records, and then where will I be? Playing honky-tonks in Nashville or signing autographs at car shows for the old folks who remember me?" He gave his brother a sad smile. "I might even be selling used cars someplace. Anyhow, you turned out all right, Robert Lee. You're the only one of us with a good marriage, and you have a steady, respectable job. I think Daddy was proud of you. Maybe he worried least about you."

"How come?"

"There was always a chance that I'd go broke or Garrett would crash that helicopter of his someday or Clayt would run out of hippie jobs and wind up on welfare. Maybe he counted on you to keep us in line."

Robert blinked at him. Then he smiled. The telephone rang. "I'll get it, little brother," he said, padding off to the kitchen.

Charles bent his head over the strings of the Martin, and began to pick out "Worried Man Blues." Kelley hadn't figured out yet that she didn't have to read his mind. The guitar broadcast every mood he had.

"I was wondering if I could have a ride into town."

Charles Martin looked up. His sister-in-law was standing in the doorway, holding her suitcase, as awkward as a teenage runaway. He saw that she had been crying, and he wished he could like her. "Where are you planning to go, Debba?"

She shrugged. "Home, I guess. I could take the bus. Garrett doesn't need me around right now."

He set the guitar aside and stood up. "I guess I can take you. I could use a break from sitting here worrying."

Debba frowned. "I told her not to run off into the woods. I *told* her."

Robert Lee appeared in the doorway, tears coursing down his red cheeks. "He's gone!" His chest heaved, and he gasped for the words. "Daddy's gone."

They stood there for a moment in silence. Debba whispered, "I'll go get Lilah."

Robert Lee shook his head. "I'm going out to the barn," he said. "If I put another coat of varnish on the coffin, it'll be dry by morning."

Charles Martin hesitated. "Do they want one of us to come in?" he asked. "I'm on my way to Johnson City."

"I don't know," whispered Robert Lee. "I don't know."

"Well, I'll go anyhow. Come on, Debba. There's probably paperwork to be filled out. There always is in hospitals. And I need to tell them to call a funeral home, and ask them to pick up the body and deliver it here. If you see Kelley, tell her where I've gone."

Robert Lee nodded, and stumbled back toward the kitchen. They heard the back door slam, and then a loud wordless cry, as if

Robert Lee could not hold back his grief any longer. They stood there in dry-eyed silence for a moment, and then Charles Martin started for the front door. He picked up Debba's suitcase. "If anyone had told me that Robert Lee would be that torn up over Daddy's death, I'd have called them a liar."

"It's hard to know what people are really like," said Debba.

They walked out to the Lexus, and he held open the passenger door for her, before stowing her suitcase in the trunk. "Things are just kind of upset around here right now," he said to her as he eased down the gravel driveway. "Maybe you and Garrett can work things out in a few days." He didn't believe it, but he had to say something.

Debba had slid over against the door, as far away from him as she could get. She said, "We'll be all right, me and Garrett. Tell him I'll be home when he's ready to come. It'll be after the funeral, I expect. He's usually back after three days."

Charles Martin tried to keep the note of surprise out of his voice. "He's done this before?"

"Oh, yes. Every so often, especially when he's feeling guilty about something. And he always felt guilty about your father. I don't know why."

Charles Martin sighed. "Nothing was ever enough for Daddy. Whatever you did, he'd say something else would have been better. I guess we never got over trying to please him, and feeling guilty when we failed—which was always."

Debba nodded, and began to rummage in her purse for her gloves.

After a few moments of silence, Charles Martin could stand it no longer. "Why does Garrett keep doing this?" he asked. "You said he felt guilty."

"Yes. For leaving me alone. He was away on a mission, you see. And that fellow who came over, he was a friend of Garrett's. That's why he doesn't want to believe what happened that day."

"What did happen?"

"He tried to rape me. They made it sound like I lost my head and shot him by accident, so his family wouldn't be hurt. He had been in Somalia, you see, and he'd seen some of his buddies killed, so they thought he wasn't quite right in the head. Shell-shocked, or something. He was really young, and everyone felt sorry for him afterward. Even me. But I wasn't sorry enough to lie about it. Army wives suffer, too."

"Then why does Garrett blame you?"

Debba Stargill sighed. "He doesn't. He blames himself for not being there. Well, I guess he does blame me some. Men always wonder if you asked for it. And when the scars are healed, or enough time has passed, they wonder why you're not as good as new. I cry sometimes for no reason. And I stiffen a little every time he touches me. I'm afraid all the time, and it angers him, because it makes us both remember. He pretends that I was always this afraid, that I shot that boy because of my fear, but that's not true. The fear came afterward, and it swallowed me whole."

Charles Martin shivered. "You're sure he'll be back, though?"

She nodded. "I'd just as soon have him stay gone, but he'll be back. He feels guilty about me, you see. And I haven't the courage to leave him."

"Are we almost to where we're going?" asked Kayla. Her legs ached from walking. She felt tears sting her eyes, but she knew that the lady with the gun would only get angry with her if she cried. Though sometimes she would hear a sort of sniffling sound that made her think that the lady was crying, too. After a long silence, she asked, "Is there food there?"

"No," said Dovey. "I'm sorry about that. But we need to get someplace safe so those men with guns down there won't find us."

"Can you find it in the dark?"

"I think so. By moonlight, anyhow. I used to play in these woods when I was little. I knew them pretty well."

Kayla was picking her way carefully among the fallen branches, going a little more slowly than she needed to. She thought that talking would make that fact less obvious. "What did you play?"

Dovey Stallard sighed at the foolishness of it. "The Stargill boys and I used to pretend we were pioneers. They were always Daniel Boone, Davy Crockett, and John Sevier. Crockett wasn't from the right time period, but none of us could convince Dwayne of that. He was bound and determined to be Davy Crockett, so we gave up, and let him. Hurry up. We're taking too long."

"My feet are sore. So, who were you in the game?"

"Clayt always wanted me to be Daniel's wife. I had to go down to the library to find somebody more fun to be than old Rebecca Boone, who mostly stayed home raising babies. I decided to be a Cherokee chief called Nancy Ward."

Kayla nodded. "The Indian lady. You told me. You said she was a good person, though. Friendly to the whites."

"She was. But she could fight when she had to. Once when the Cherokees were at war with the Creeks, Nancy Ward won the battle. She picked up her dead husband's rifle and led the charge against the enemy."

Kayla considered it. "She sounds a lot neater than old Pocahontas. Are there any movies about her?"

"No. There's no happy ending. She died of old age not far from here, but a few years after that her people were put off the land. Most of them had to move out to Oklahoma."

"Reba McIntyre," said Kayla.

"What?"

"That's where she's from. Oklahoma."

"Oh, the country singer," said Dovey, shaking her head. "Do you have all your states memorized by musicians?"

"Nah. They're mostly from the same places. Mama's trying to learn me my state names, and when Charlie helps me that's how we do it. Loretta Lynn–Kentucky; Statler Brothers–Virginia; Randy Travis–North Carolina—and like that."

"Charles Martin Stargill sure has left his mark on you."

"Uh-huh. I listen a lot. He's okay. So, who took this land from the Indians?"

Dovey Stallard shrugged. "Daniel Boone, for one."

They were in a clearing now. The moonlight outlined the contours of a rocky hillside, making man-shapes of sapling sumacs and silvering the path of a small stony creek.

Dovey Stallard heaved a long sigh. Her breath made a little cloud in the clear night air. "We're here," she said. "We need to get across that branch without getting our feet wet."

Kayla looked around her. She blew into her cupped hands to warm her fingers. She had to pee, but she didn't want to pull her pants down in the cold night air. She had hoped that they would reach a cabin, or at least a car, but all she saw in the moonlight was rocks, and trees. And the mountain rising steeply in front of them. Her voice quavered. "I don't see nothing," she said.

"It's here, though. At least, it was when I was a kid." Dovey started across the brook, stretching to reach from rock to rock. At the midpoint, she leaned back and grabbed Kayla's outstretched hand. "You could almost jump across," she said, "but it's too cold to risk falling short."

"Mama doesn't like me playing in the water," said Kayla, drawing back.

"Come on! She wouldn't want you out here by yourself either."

When they were safely on the other side, Dovey led the girl to a thicket of rhododendron—mountain laurel, she called it. "It's grown over a lot since we used to play here," she said, more to herself than to the child. "I might have missed it if it weren't for these broken branches. Looks like something came through here." She stood still for a moment and listened. "Hope it wasn't a bear."

Kayla followed her into the thicket. It was too cold and dark for her to try to run away. She was no longer sure in which direction the farm lay. She crouched down and tried to scoot under the prickly branches. It was much darker now beneath the cover of laurel leaves, but just ahead she could make out the dark shape of Dovey Stallard, on her hands and knees at the base of the hill. She was breathing hard and grunting as she lifted pumpkin-sized rocks, or pushed them out of her way.

"Here it is!" She leaned back and caught hold of Kayla's jacket. "Come on. We made it."

With a cry of surprise Kayla stumbled forward, expecting to hit the rocks, but instead she lurched forward into complete darkness. She felt cold drops of water hit the back of her neck, and as she scooted forward, she could feel wet patches forming on the knees of her jeans. "It's a cave," she said, and her voice echoed softly in the darkness. She sniffled a little. They'd never find her in here.

Dovey's hand touched her shoulder again. Kayla straightened up, and crawled over to the wall of the cavern, huddling close to Dovey. It wasn't as cold in here, but it was damp, and she was frightened, because she couldn't see. "Are there snakes in here?"

"Didn't used to be. Anyhow, it's cold yet, so they shouldn't be awake tonight. We'll be all right here."

"We're not gonna stay here?"

There was a short silence, broken only by the plop of water pellets falling into a pool near the back of the cave. "Until morning maybe," said Dovey. "Then we can see to go on. Trackers can't find us here. Do you think you can get to sleep?"

Kayla was looking toward the entrance of the cave. Now that her eyes had grown accustomed to the dark, she could see a faint sliver of gray where the narrow entrance must be. She was crying now. "I want to go home. I'm cold. And I'm dirty. Mama doesn't like it when I get dirty."

"We have to stay here. It's too dangerous out there tonight.

There's some kind of goggles now that even let trackers see in the dark. They could shoot at us, and we'd never even know they were there."

"It's da-ark!" Kayla's voice rose to a wail.

Yellow light flooded the chamber. Kayla screamed and clutched at Dovey's arm, but Dovey shook her away, and thrust the pistol forward, its barrel wobbling as her hand shook. "Who's there?" she cried,

"Hello, Dovey."

"Clayt!" Kayla's weeping stopped abruptly. She scrambled across the muddy floor to reach him. "You found me!"

She flung herself at him, and he wrapped his arms around her, and bundled her close inside his parka. "Shh! Kayla, I'm here now. It's all right. You're fine."

"I didn't hurt her," said Dovey. "I had started off for your farm before I thought better of it. I found her out wandering around in the woods." She waited, but Clayt said nothing. "Are you part of the posse, Clayt?"

He set the flashlight on top of a flat rock so that it cast a soft glow around most of the small chamber. Dovey couldn't make out his expression in the dim light. "I'm not armed," he said at last. "I wanted to find you before they did."

"And you figured I'd come here?"

"Not really. We hated this place as kids, remember?" She nodded. "It gave us the creeps for some reason, but I knew it was about the only place out here on the mountain to be hidden from the search party. Besides, it was the only hope I had."

"I might not have found it if you hadn't broken those branches getting in."

He shook his head. "I found it like that. Something has been here recently." He heard Kayla whimper, and he hugged her again. "It's not a bear. I checked around with the flashlight. There's more to the cave than we thought, Dovey. I found a narrow opening far at the back. It had been blocked up with rocks before, but they've been pushed aside now. I didn't go in, but I called out in case you were back there. Then I decided to wait, because if you didn't show up here, I figured I'd never find you. I couldn't track you by night." He nodded toward the cave entrance. "I'll bet they can, though."

Dovey shrugged and jiggled the gun. "I'm ready for them."

"Why did you take Kayla? Why bring her into it?"

"I don't know. Maybe I thought I could use her for bargaining. Give her back if they'd let me go. It just made them more determined to get me, though, I guess."

"We could say that Kayla went willingly. You didn't harm her. She'd swear she went with you, Dovey. Then it wouldn't be kidnapping. And the sheriff isn't dead—at least he wasn't when I left the house. We can get a good lawyer for the trial, and maybe they can plead provocation, and get you off with probation. I bet Dallas Stuart would defend you for nothing. We could ask him."

Dovey shook her head. "I've had enough of the law, Clayt. The government sent my brother to some foreign country to die in a war they didn't even try to win. The government passed laws protecting those vultures that were killing our lambs—yes, and that vulture Frank Whitescarver, too. Then they took our land away from us with some legal hocus pocus. I'm done with them now."

"Dovey, you can't stay here. You can't fight them."

"Thank you, Daniel Boone. He did become a politician later in life, didn't he?"

Clayt sighed. "Not a very good one. I think he tried to be honest, but he wasn't sophisticated enough for that crowd. Not like Nancy Ward. Now she wouldn't hole up here with a gun. We can live in peace—remember? Share the land? She would have learned the rules and tried to win the politicians' game."

"Look where it got her. Frank Whitescarver wants to share the land, all right. He wants to put us in a trailer park in town. A modern version of the Trail of Tears. Well, I'd like to give him exactly six feet of Stallard land—enough to bury him! I wish I'd got him, Clayt. I wish to God I'd blown his head off."

"Dovey, listen! You don't have to go where Whitescarver says. Daddy's dying. We've been trying to figure out ways to keep the farm, only none of us can afford to stay on and run it. Maybe we could lease it to you and your dad."

She shook her head. "That's the trouble with the story of Nancy Ward. The ending. She died with a whimper, knowing she'd lost it all, and she didn't fight back." She brandished the pistol. "This time it's going to be different."

"It's a rundown hill farm, Dovey. It's not worth dying for."

"Then what is?"

He could hear the tremor in her voice, and he eased Kayla out of his arms and started across the cavern. "Dovey . . ."

She leveled the gun at him. "Get back. I didn't ask you for anything."

"Don't do this."

"It's done, Clayt. But you're right about Kayla here. Nancy Ward wouldn't have brought her into it. She saved Mrs. Bean from being burned at the stake. She wouldn't take a child down with her. Leave me the flashlight, if you're so determined to be my friend. Now you take her and get out."

"Keep the flashlight," said Clayt. "But we're not leaving you, Dovey."

Dovey's eyes glittered in the dim light. "If you want her to live, Clayt, you'll take her and go. Right now."

The sun was low against the flank of the mountain, and the old woman was sitting on the porch in the cool of the evening, waiting for the child. She appeared, finally, with muddy feet and berry stains on her dress, looking tired and a little wary that someone was watching for her. She took one backward glance at the woods, then climbed over the stile and headed for home.

"Where did you get to all day, Nora?" asked Grandma Flossie. "We were about to set out looking for you."

"I was playing in the woods." Nora's voice had the ring of innocence, but she was looking at the ground, scuffing up ridges of dirt with her bare brown toes. It was suppertime. The heat of July had eased off to the windless glow of evening, and Nora's mother was already setting bowls of beans and mashed potatoes on the red-checked tablecloth. Nora looked up at the screen door, and wrinkled her nose. "Can I go in now?"

"Directly," her grandmother replied. "You played out in the woods all day? All by yourself?"

"Uh-huh."

"Come out to the garden with me a minute, Nora."

"But it's dinnertime."

"We'll pick a few more tomatoes. Won't take long." The old woman walked out to the garden, keeping her steps slow, and waiting for the reluctant child to catch up with her. She knelt by the tomato plants and began to examine the fruit, choosing the ripest ones. Nora stood up straight, holding out the skirt of her calico dress for her grandmother to fill with ripe tomatoes. They did not speak.

After a silence that seemed to stretch on forever, Grandma Flossie said, "You've seen the little girl out in the woods."

It was not a question, just a statement of fact, made without any emotion, except perhaps a touch of disappointment. Nora hung her head, blushing at having been caught in a lie.

"And you've been playing with her out there all day? And other days, too?"

"Yes'm. We don't do nothing bad or go near no snakes. We just hide'n seek, mostly." She looked down at her dirt-streaked dress. "I try not to get dirty."

Grandma Flossie put her hand on Nora's shoulder. "Your clothes are not what troubles me, child," she said. "It's you I'm worried about. Yes, and that poor lost child out there on the mountain, too. You know she's dead, don't you, Nora?"

Nora's jaw tightened, and she looked away. "She's my friend."

"I know that, child. I know she is. And I wish she had come to know you in—in better times, but things didn't work out that way. Poor thing. It's too late for her to have you for a friend, because—well, she's lost right now, and bewildered. She's wandering, looking for a haven. She doesn't know it, Nora, but she has someplace to go, and you're holding her back."

"She's not wandering," said Nora. "She's always out there in the woods. She just wants somebody to play with, 'cause she's all by herself."

"She needs to let go of this world, Nora, and go on to where she's going, but she can't do that if you keep her tied to this world with your love."

"She's very sad, Grandma. Bad things happened to her. She needs a friend."

"No, Nora. She needs to go on." The old woman put her hands on the child's frail shoulders. "It's dangerous for you to be with her. Now promise me you won't go back to see her again."

Nora's mother called just then from the porch, shouting that supper was getting cold on the table. Nora flashed a grateful look at her and ran toward the house, the promise left unmade.

Perhaps it had been too late, though, even then.

CHAPTER FIFTEEN

My footsteps have often been marked with blood.
—DANIEL BOONE

Joe LeDonne was crouching behind an oak tree at the edge of the clearing, out of the line of fire. He was willing himself to be calm. Hours of shock, stress, and the intensity of the hunt had made his breathing shallow and his muscles tense. Now, when overdrive was beginning to feel like a normal pace to him, he had to force himself to slow down.

Dovey Stallard was in the cave. Garrett Stargill had been right on his third guess about where his old playmate might go. Once the searchers knew where to look, they located broken twigs, and finally footprints near the bank of a small stream. The forces were now concentrated around the cave, quiet, out of sight, but ready, in case anyone or anything moved at the opening.

Now the game was to wait. To do that, he must not be in a hurry. Time was on their side. As much as Joe LeDonne had wanted a firefight, and although his nerves sang with rage, he knew that he must avoid a violent confrontation if he possibly could. That poor young woman in there didn't need killing just because she was trying to defend her land, and he couldn't risk the lives of the officers with him just to satisfy his own need for revenge. Spencer would want this incident concluded peacefully. Even if the sheriff died as the result of the wounds she had given him, he wouldn't want her to die to avenge him.

LeDonne knew that the best chance of coming out of this confrontation without fatalities lay in doing nothing for as long as possible. When the crime was committed, the suspect was angry, acting on adrenaline and outrage, but that was hours ago. Now she would be tired, cold, and hungry. She was trapped in a dark cave with a gun, probably not many bullets, and unlimited silence in which to reflect over her actions.

LeDonne wanted her to have lots of time to think. He wanted her to ponder the possible outcomes of a firefight: her own death, a murder charge if she succeeded in killing a police officer. The more time Dovey Stallard was given to think, the less likely a gun battle became. He hoped she knew how many guns there were trained on the entrance to the cave. There was a sniper on the hill above the opening, too. He had told them not to shoot, but he knew that if Dovey Stallard fired first, nothing could stop these men from returning fire. He wished he had requested the SWAT team—the Special Operation Squad, they called them now—from Knoxville. But he hadn't wanted to lose control of the situation. The SOS takes over, and you do it their way, or else they go home. LeDonne wanted the decisions to be his. Spencer Arrowood would hold him accountable for whatever happened on the mountain, and he wanted to be able to say that he had done all he could.

He motioned for one of the deputies to come forward. "Did you check on the possibility of getting the father up here?" he asked.

"We sent Stansberry to the minister's house to ask. The word is that he's in a bad way—sedated—his only daughter and all. The local doctor forbids him to come out here."

"It might save that woman's life," said LeDonne. "Somebody needs to talk to her now. Somebody who won't make her feel threatened."

The deputy thought it over. "What about Stargill? The neighbor who led us here."

"I'm going to try to talk to her first. If she starts shooting, it might as well be me she's aiming at. Then I guess we could try Mr. Stargill, but in case that doesn't work, has anybody got a percussion grenade?"

"There's a kid in there, though, right?"

"I'll try to defuse this situation without hurting either of them, but if it doesn't work, we're going to use the grenade. The kid might lose an eardrum, but at least she'll be alive. Understood?"

The officer shrugged. "It's your show, Mr. LeDonne."

"Right. Anybody got a can of soda? I'll take a canteen of water if I have to, but Coke is friendlier." LeDonne figured he needed all the help he could get. People just naturally trusted Spencer Arrowood, but there was a distance, a coolness in Joe LeDonne that made people wary of him. He waited while the other deputy went off in search of a soft drink, turning over the phrases in his mind. He must be reassuring, but not so upbeat that she'd think he was lying. And he must be careful, because when he approached her to negotiate, she could blow him away in a heartbeat.

The deputy returned, holding out a warm, dented can of Mountain Dew. "This is all I could find," he said. "It'll probably explode when she opens it, fizz all over the place."

"Doesn't matter," said LeDonne. "It's a peace offering. If she takes it I'll warn her that it's going to bubble over when she opens it. That might help, too." He took the soft drink can, and began to edge toward the base of the hillside. "Cover me. Don't shoot unless you have to."

LeDonne took a deep breath, and stepped forward. "Dovey!" he called out. *Use her first name. Try to make her forget that you're The Law.* LeDonne had taken a course in SWAT team negotiation, but even the instructor agreed that he didn't have the knack for it. He had to try now, though. "We know where you are, Dovey. You're hiding out in the cave, and I need to talk to you. It's not a trick. I'm not coming after you. I just want to talk. To see if you and I between us can stop this thing."

He waited, shivering in the wind that seemed to blow colder now that he was out of the trees. Or perhaps it was the ice water in the pit of his stomach that chilled him. He was looking into darkness. He could be dead in seconds. All was silent.

"Dovey, are you all right? I know you've been in these woods all day, and you're probably hungry and thirsty." A pause. "I know I am. Anyhow, I brought you a can of Mountain Dew. It's kind of shaken up from being hauled around half the night, but I'm going to send it in there to you anyhow. I'm going to roll it. See? I'm putting it on the ground and I'm going to roll it toward the entrance. I don't know how good my aim is in the dark."

"You throw anything this way, and I'll blow your head off." Her voice was quiet and even, not shrill. Maybe that was good. She wasn't going to get hysterical and shoot him in a panic, but she didn't sound like someone who could be easily persuaded, either. And at least he had her talking. That was a start.

He held up his hands, palms out. "Okay," he said. "Okay. It really is a Mountain Dew, Dovey, and if you don't want to drink it, maybe the little girl wants some. Can I talk to her?"

Another long silence. Finally she said, "I let her go. And I don't want your damned soda."

LeDonne tried to sound cheerful. "Then I sure do," he said. He held the can away from his body, and popped the metal tab on the lid. A jet of yellow liquid shot into the air, and froth ran down the sides of the can. "Hardly worth it, was it?" he said loudly, taking a swig. "Not enough left to wet my whistle."

He hoped that she would laugh at his discomfort, but there was no response. *You had her*, he told himself. *Get her back*.

"Listen," he said. "I'll talk seriously to you now. You've let the little girl"—*Don't say hostage*—"little Kayla go. That's good. That's very much in your favor." Something else occurred to him. "Where is she, Dovey? I've got people all over the place out here, and we haven't seen her. Is she wandering around the woods all by herself?"

"Why don't you send your people out looking for her while we talk?" She sounded amused.

He clenched his teeth. *Stay calm for now. The child may still be inside the cave.* He took a deep breath, and tried to sound encouraging. "I sure am glad you let her go, Dovey. Now there's somebody else you need to think about. Your daddy is worried about you. He's about collapsed and needing a doctor, fretting about all that happened today. Don't make it any worse on him, Dovey. He's an old man. If you were to get yourself hurt, I reckon it would just about kill him."

"He's used to it. He lost his son. That was the government's fault, too."

Her brother had been killed in Vietnam. He remembered hearing that somewhere. *Use it.* "I was in Vietnam, too, Dovey," LeDonne called out. "And I didn't like it when I came home, and people called me a bad guy. I'll bet your brother wouldn't have liked it, either. Don't make me a bad guy tonight, Dovey. I'm trying my level best to help you."

A sound. Perhaps a snort of disbelief. *Keep talking.*

"The sheriff is going to be all right, Dovey. They got him to the hospital in time, and he made it through surgery. So listen up: you haven't done anything yet that we can't put right. Believe me. I know about the eviction business. I know you were upset. I can't say I blame you for it, either. And you reacted in anger—not premeditated. We're talking simple assault here, Dovey. And no permanent injury inflicted. The sheriff isn't paralyzed. He didn't lose a kidney, or anything. He just took a hit in the side. No big deal." He hoped he sounded convincing, and that none of the listening officers would chime in. One snicker could stop the dialogue forever.

"Dovey, you say the word, and I'll get a bail bondsman out here right now. Let you talk to him. And I will personally talk the judge into giving you an affordable bail. You can be out tonight. Go see your daddy."

"You're going to let me go home, huh?" He heard the mockery in her voice. "Except that I haven't got a home, remember?"

He lost his patience then. He could hear the edge in his voice. "I can't fix everything, dammit!" he said. "I can keep you from getting killed out here. And I can arrange for your punishment for shooting a peace officer to be less severe, if you'll cooperate and quit this grandstanding. Give yourself up. Then maybe you can address your grievances. You can't do it from the penitentiary, and you damn sure can't do it *dead*."

After nearly a minute of silence, broken only by the rustle of leaves as his men angled for position, LeDonne called out, "Come on, Dovey! What's it going to be? You have no food or water. You aren't going anywhere. Make it easy on us, and come out now. These good people out here want to go home."

He waited again: three, four, five of the longest minutes in his life. He heard no sounds from the cave, and nothing moved. LeDonne turned back toward the trees, wondering if his failure was a personal one, or if nobody could have talked her out of there, not even Spencer Arrowood.

Clayt was carrying Kayla on his shoulders. She was so tired from her ordeal that she was out on her feet. He wanted to run, but she wasn't up to it. He had got Kayla safely away from the cave. His plan now was to get her back to the farm and to her mother as quickly as possible and then to come back. He had to get Dovey out of that cave before the trackers found her. If it hadn't been for Kayla, he would have stayed. He would have tried his best to help her escape, if that's what she wanted. He didn't think he could stand to lose the land and Dovey, too.

The moon was high now, and he could pick his way along an

overgrown trail. He had left the flashlight with Dovey. Maybe it was safer to travel without it. He knew this path by heart; as children, the Stargills and the Stallards had used it when they went to play in the woods. He remembered it well, but still he had to go slowly. Fallen tree limbs from last winter's ice storms might block the path in some places.

He hoped for Kayla's sake that if anyone saw him, they wouldn't mistake him for Dovey. He had to get the child home safely.

He thought she must have fallen asleep. She had been groggy from exhaustion when he found her, and she had not spoken now for several minutes. Her body lolled against his neck, warm and nearly weightless. He was glad that she'd gone to sleep. The sound of their voices might attract the attention of the searchers. Silence was better. He wished he could make less noise when he walked, but the burden of Kayla made it difficult for him to tread carefully through the leaves.

"Hold it right there."

Clayt froze, willing himself not even to look in the direction of the sound. "I've got a little girl here!" he shouted. "The hostage you were looking for. Dovey Stallard let her go."

"Is she all right?" The voice was nearer now, but moving quietly. Clayt couldn't hear any footsteps or the rustle of grass. He could feel cold sweat on his temples.

"She's fine. I'm taking her home."

A uniformed officer approached. Clayt couldn't see well enough to tell what outfit the man belonged to. "You shouldn't be out here wandering around by yourself," the officer said. He had a deep-south drawl foreign to the Tennessee mountains. FBI? "This bunch of trigger-happy good old boys might shoot anything that moves. Might end up shooting each other before the night is out."

In the moonlight Clayt could see a young black man with a pencil mustache. The black officer seemed calm, even a bit bemused to see them. His weapon was holstered, and he was smiling. Clayt relaxed a little. "Could you radio them our position? So they don't shoot us by accident?"

"I'll do that, sir," said the officer. "But if you keep following this old trail along the back of the mountain, you'll get to the farm all right. There's nobody searching between you and home."

Clayt looked doubtful. "How do you know?"

"Sir, it's my job to know. Go on now. Get the child in out of the cold, and, when you get back, let your womenfolk feed her some cocoa. The rest of us can worry about what happens out here. My chief concern was making sure that you and the youngun made it safely off the mountain." He turned and walked off into the darkness.

Clayt called after him, "Can I borrow your flashlight, officer?"

The answer sounded a good ways off now. "Never use one, myself!"

Garrett Stargill was calmer than most of the lawmen. He was in Special Forces; LeDonne thought he might have been in firefights more often. He squatted down beside LeDonne, watching the cave even while he talked. "So what's your plan?" he asked. "Rush the entrance?"

A cowboy. LeDonne looked at him, expressionless. "No," he said evenly. "We're going to make one more try at talking her out. That's where you come in. She's alone in there."

"What about Kayla Johnson?"

"I don't know. Miss Stallard claims that she released the child, but we haven't seen her. We have to assume they're both in there. So for now we talk. I don't want a firefight when there's a hostage. A kid. No way."

"Okay. What do you want me to say?"

LeDonne scowled. "Sir, I struck out with her. Now you're supposed to be an old friend of hers. I was hoping you could tell us."

"If you want me to try, I will," said Garrett, shrugging. "I don't think she'll shoot me, but I really just came to help you locate her. I'm good at tracking, at night patrols. If you want somebody to soft soap her, you'd be better off getting my little brother Clayt. I think he's carrying a torch for her. Maybe true love could bring her out."

"Why don't you try, sir? I don't want to risk any more civilians than I have to. At least you have experience in an adversarial situation like this."

"Yeah, I've been shot at on three continents. I'll give it a whirl."

"Good. Get about twenty feet from the cave. Stay as close to the trees as you can. And try to be upbeat when you talk to her. We don't want her to panic, and we don't want her to kill herself in there. Just play down the legal issues, and tell her we can fix anything if she'll come out."

"Can you?" asked Garrett.

"Who knows? Pretty woman. Rotten luck with the farm. A judge might let her off with probation. *I* wouldn't. But it won't be my call."

Garrett Stargill sighed and stood up. "A pretty woman with a gun. God help us." He walked out into the clearing. "Dovey! It's Garrett Stargill. Long time, no see. I came to get you, Dovey. You know me. I'm not a badge with a gun. I'm one of the Stargill boys. I joined up with your brother Tate, and I've been in the army ever since, so you can trust me when I tell you that these boys out here are armed and serious. They mean business, Dovey. And I owe it to Tate and to your dad to see that no harm comes to you. Come on out."

Nothing.

"I'm here for you, and I'll stay right here with you the whole time until your lawyer arrives. And I'll see that nobody roughs you up or gives you a hard time. I know you didn't mean to hurt anybody, especially not the sheriff. Come on out now. You're safe."

As he spoke, he began to walk toward the entrance to the cave. Within it, all was silent. Garrett Stargill's hands were down, palms out, away from his sides, so that she could see he was unarmed.

"What is that damned fool doing now?" muttered LeDonne. He stayed where he was though. If he ran after Stargill, or even shouted at him, he might frighten her into shooting. LeDonne leaned forward with his own weapon trained on the dark hole in the rock. Around the clearing a score of weapons were pointed at the same spot. "Stay out of the line of fire," he whispered, as if Garrett Stargill, twenty feet away, could hear him.

But Garrett Stargill had eased into the mountain laurel bushes now, and his body blocked their view of the narrow adit in the rock. He was speaking more softly now. LeDonne couldn't make out the words. There seemed to be no response from within.

Suddenly Garrett ducked out of sight.

LeDonne started forward, weapon in hand. "What the hell—" He began to run, clenching his jaw as he waited for the sound of a gunshot.

Garrett Stargill reappeared, hands high, in case any trigger-happy volunteers mistook him for their quarry. "She not there!" he called out. "She's gone."

Lilah Stargill had put on Randall's old plaid car coat over her caftan, and an old scarf over her pink foam hair curlers. She stood in the entrance to the barn workshop, making little clouds with her breath, and watching her husband polish the rosewood casket. He had not seen her yet. His back was to the door. She could hear his ragged breathing, ending now and then in a sob, as he made circles on the coffin lid with the rag. He kept rubbing the same spot over and over, and looking away at nothing, as if his polishing arm belonged to somebody else.

Lilah went over and stood behind him. She put her arms around his waist. "I should have known you'd take it the hardest," she said. "He loved you the least."

He turned to face her, with tears coursing down his plump red cheeks. "Well, I tried to make him proud of the man I became. I wasn't a war hero like Garrett, or a Grand Ol' Opry star, or a college boy, but I have responsibility at the dealership. A new car every year. The house will be paid for in five years, and we have savings. I guess it isn't much, but there's a lot that have less."

"He knew that, Robert," whispered Lilah, hugging him. "And now that he's in heaven maybe he knows more—that you are really and truly loved. The only one of the Stargills that has roots instead of wings. He could depend on you, Robert. More than he deserved, I often thought." She took the rag out of his hand and laid it on the table. "That's enough for tonight. There'll be things to see to in the morning. The Stargill family is more than the land. It's the people in the family staying together, and you're the only one who can keep it together. Those other three are too wrapped up in their own problems to see above them, but you're the head of the family now, and you'll pull them together."

"Do you think so?"

"Of course I do." She patted his arm. "Now come in the house, Robert Lee. It's too cold out here in the barn. I'm making some cocoa for Kayla, and you'd better have some, too."

Robert Lee swallowed the last of his grief. "Kayla? Is she back then?"

"She's on her way," said Lilah, steering him through the door of the workshop and toward the barn's open door. "Rudy told me."

"Rudy?"

"Yes, Robert. Now hurry. If I burn that cocoa, he'll just give me hell."

"What do you mean she's not there?" LeDonne pushed past Garrett Stargill, and stooped down beside the mouth of the cave, a little to the left, though, out of a direct line of fire. He clicked on his three-cell mag flashlight, and peered over it. No shots. No sound of scuffling feet against the rocks inside.

Where the hell was she?

He turned to Garrett Stargill. "Do you know this cave?"

"Thirty years ago. It's only that one chamber there, just big enough to hold four or five kids. We didn't go in it much. My brother Clayt thought snakes might live there."

"There's no back way in?"

"Not that I ever heard of. That's something you should ask Clayt, though. I enlisted at eighteen, and I haven't been back much since. Clayt's been roaming around in these woods all his life."

"All right," said LeDonne. "I'll send somebody to ask him. You go on home now, Mr. Stargill. And thank you for your help. We'll take it from here."

Garrett started to protest, but this deputy was clearly in charge. Arguing wasn't going to do any good. He took a deep breath, mumbled, "Glad I could help," and walked away. It wasn't the heroic finish he had envisioned, but at least he had made the effort. If Dovey Stallard wanted to get herself shot, that was her problem, he thought. He had to get back to Debba. She'd be afraid with all the searchers crawling all over the mountain. He shouldn't have left her alone. She never felt safe without him, and his first duty now was to protect her always, to make up for that one terrible time when he had not been there to save her. He didn't know what hurt worse, the betrayal of a fellow soldier, or the unspoken reproach he had lived with ever since. Blaming her was the only way he could live with it.

Joe LeDonne walked back to the trees, where the rest of his men were waiting, weapons drawn. "I'm going in there," he said. "She's not in the part of the cave that I can see from the entrance. Anybody willing to go in with me?"

He waited through an uneasy silence, knowing that these men weren't going to be anxious to volunteer for what could be a fatal ambush. Even an empty cave was dangerous; add an outlaw with a gun and it became a death trap. But with or without backup, LeDonne was going in.

"I'll go, sir." The voice sounded like a kid's.

A young man in a leather jacket and camo trousers stepped forward. "I'll go. What the hey."

"Are you a police officer?" asked LeDonne.

"Yes, sir. Off duty when the call came in. Thought I'd come give you a hand. I live over here, work in the next county over. Figured I knew these woods well enough to help out from all the hunting trips I've been on up here."

LeDonne looked at the kid, idly wondering if he even wanted to know his name. What the hell, in combat he had entrusted his life to kids younger than this, but that had been a long time ago. And he hadn't known some of their names, either. Some of their faces, though, he would never forget. He had spent twenty years trying.

"Right," he told the young policeman. "You're with me."

They walked away from the others. "I'm going in first," said LeDonne. "I'll have the light. You'll go as backup, low to the ground, with your weapon drawn." He looked again at the kid. "Don't point it in my direction," he added.

"No, sir."

"Go slow and easy in there. The floor is uneven. Don't trip on an outcrop of rock and shoot yourself, either."

He knelt at the entrance to the cave. "I don't know how far back she is in there, and I don't know what the rest of the cavern is like. It may be narrower. It may be flooded. We may not be able to stand up in it." He started to add that it was a perfect place for an ambush, but he thought better of saying it. Either the kid was smart enough to know that, or else he'd be spooked by it, which might make him more likely to do something stupid.

"I'm with you, sir."

"If anything happens to me—a rockfall, for instance—you get out and go for help. You are not to try to carry on single-handed. Is that understood?"

The young officer nodded. "Got it, sir."

There was nothing else he could say to postpone the inevitable Much as he dreaded it, it was time. LeDonne took a deep breath and plunged into darkness. He hated caves—any dark, closed, starless place made the back of his neck tingle, and tightened his throat muscles. In Vietnam there had been tunnels. They were used for hoarding weapons, for ambush and traveling by stealth, and finally, they were used as a last-ditch refuge by Vietcong. LeDonne had to go in such a tunnel once. Just once. Twenty-odd years ago now, but he was still fighting his way out of it in sleep. He knew that if he got out of this cave tonight, he would sleep with a light on for weeks, waiting for the worse darkness to come back for him in dreams.

He flipped on the three-cell mag light to get his bearings, and to make sure that the anterior chamber was empty. It was. He kept the light on, and turned to his backup man. "Okay," he whispered. "We're going through that opening in the back. Don't make any noise as you advance."

He threaded his way around a pile of small rocks scattered around the narrow opening. It looked as if the passage had been blocked at one time. He wondered if Dovey Stallard had uncovered it. The rocks had not been moved by tremors or ground water. He pressed his body against the damp rock on one side of the opening, and reached out to illuminate the interior cavern, holding the big light in the center of the opening, well away from his body.

He waited to a count of ten, listening to the kid breathing a few feet behind him. No shots. No sounds of scurrying in the darkness ahead. LeDonne edged forward and peered into the next chamber. He could see boulders near the wall of the cave. They blocked his light, leaving shadowy recesses at the far end of the passage. In the center of the chamber a wide section of floor had given way, leaving a jagged pit more than six feet across. He was too far from the edge to see into the crater, but he could see something sticking up on one side of the hole—a stick, perhaps. Nothing alive. He wondered if Dovey Stallard, rushing into this second chamber to escape her pursuers, had fallen into the pit. She might now be lying unconscious or dead on the rocks below. But in order to find out, he would have to leave the safety of the narrow opening, and venture into plain sight in the center of the cavern. Oh, this was bringing back memories. It was like having two nightmares at once.

He lowered the light and sat back against the wall for a moment, trying to decide what to do next. Maybe he should have let Knoxville send the Special Operation Squad, but he didn't think they'd have had any better luck getting her to surrender. It was up to him now, and he had to find out if she was in the back cavern—and if she was still alive.

He motioned for the young cop to come forward. "I'm going in there. There's a pit in the center of the chamber, and she may have fallen down there. Keep your light in readiness, but don't turn it on unless you have to. And cover me."

"You're going into that hole?"

"Not unless I have to. I have to check it out, though."

He edged forward. Still keeping the light to one side, but he thought that was a futile gesture. In the confined space of the cave, the three-cell light gave off enough of a glow to reveal his position. He might as well shine it on his face. Why pretend that he had the advantage of surprise. "Are you in here, Dovey?" he asked in a conversational tone. "You've got a lot of heart if you are. 'Cause I sure as hell hate this place."

"We always did, too."

Her voice was calm, as casual as his. There was a slight echo in the cavern, but he could tell that the sound came from behind the rocks at the far end of the chamber. She sounded weary. "We found this cave when we were kids. We played pioneer out in these woods, looking for the Boone tree, and we came in here a time or two, but there was always something about the place that made us uneasy. We never saw any snakes, but it felt like . . . like a snake crawling across your foot, just being here."

"Tell me about it," muttered LeDonne. He had reached the edge of the pit, braced himself against a rock, and directed the light down into the darkness below. He saw an old wooden ladder propped up against the side of the hole, which looked no more than eight or nine feet deep. There was no shine of water reflected in the beam of light: dry, then. He saw what looked like a clump of rags near some rocks in the pit, and a scattering of small bones, too small to be human. The remains of a bear's dinner, perhaps? An old Indian campsite? He called out to Dovey, "Where'd you get the ladder?"

"It was here. We never went in this part of the cave when we were kids. It was blocked up. I didn't go down there. Looks like a snake pit to me."

"Too deep for that." LeDonne marveled that they were talking like two hikers meeting on a trail. Dovey Stallard was hidden by darkness and by the boulders at the far end of the cavern, but he was conversing with her in something approaching a normal tone of voice. They were talking about childhood memories—not the phony dialogue of negotiator and fugitive, but real talk. He tried not to think about the fact that she probably had a gun aimed at his head.

"There's something down in this hole," he said, peering over the side of the pit. "I'd like to check it out sometime. But right now what I'd really like is to get out of here. I don't care for small dark places. You want to come out now so we can leave?"

"You're scared?" She sounded amused.

"Caves bring back bad memories for me," he said. "And futility makes me antsy. Look, there's no back way out of this place, is there? No—'cause you're still here. So why are we postponing the inevitable, Dovey? Why can't we just walk out of here?"

"Because if I walk out of here, we lose. My father and I. We lose the land. And we don't deserve to have that happen. My father has worked hard all his life on that farm. We never took charity from anybody. It shouldn't end like this."

"Maybe this isn't the end. Maybe you should come out so that you can keep fighting."

There was a long pause before she said, "I'm tired."

"So am I," said LeDonne. "Let's go home. Please."

"Two against one?" She was wary now.

It's supposed to be a lot more than that, LeDonne thought, but he could sense her weakening. She wanted to trust him, to let it be over. The two of them were communicating. They could work it out. Perhaps one more small show of faith was all it would take. "You can go, Officer," he said to his backup, loudly, so that she could hear him.

In the darkness he heard the kid gasp. "Sir, we're not supposed to—"

"On my authority. Go out now. Tell them everything is all right."

Another long pause. Then the young officer muttered, "Whatever you say, sir." He scrambled for the opening that led to the outer chamber, dislodging rocks, and cursing softly as he went.

When his footsteps had died away, LeDonne said, "All right. Now it's you and me."

Dovey Stallard said, "Dwayne Stargill was a lot like you. He didn't play by the rules either."

"Dwayne?"

"The wild one. Younger than Robert and Charlie, older than Garrett and Clayt. I married him—a long time ago. He's dead now." She sounded weary. "I never did have a lick of sense. Clayt was worth ten of him."

"It's not too late," said LeDonne. "Come out, and we'll go find Clayt. He's worried about you."

"I think you're more my type." There was bitter amusement in her voice. "I think you understand me better than Clayt ever would."

"I've done some fool things in my time," said LeDonne. "I try to put them right, though. It's all we can do, isn't it?"

Silence.

"I could help you put things right again, Dovey."

He heard a slow, deep sigh.

"All right. I'm coming out." She stood up then, a long shadow against the wall of the cave. LeDonne was still kneeling at the edge of the pit, holding the flashlight at his side, careful not to shine it in her face. He watched her emerge from the darkness, hands at her sides, and in that split second he saw the pistol in her hand, as she leveled it at him. He froze, caught in the light, knowing that he did not have time to fire first.

Two snapping sounds, like firecrackers. LeDonne threw the flashlight away from him, and rolled sideways on the dirt floor, feeling sharp bits of rock cutting into his flesh. He waited for the searing pain to tell him where he was hit, but there was no sensation except coldness and the spurt of fear. Then the adrenaline kicked in, and his body went into the old familiar combat high, with no sensation of danger to himself.

The light had fallen into the pit, but in its glow he could see her outline against the rocks.

It was happening in slow motion for him, the way a firefight always had—in the seconds that it had taken for him to drop the light and fall, to pull his pistol from his holster and point it in her direction. No time to aim—just squeeze off round after round until the shadow falls.

All in slow motion.

He felt that he had all the time in the world—to tell her that he was sorry, that if it had been his farm, maybe he would have done just what she did. He thought about the shots ricocheting off the rock and coming back at him. He wished he could see Dovey Stallard's face, but then maybe it was better that he hadn't. He wondered how you could hate somebody and love them at the same time. *You understand me better than Clayt ever would.* Hell, yes, he understood her. And if she hadn't shot Spencer, he would have let her get away. Whatever that was worth. For an instant he could even see himself taking off with her. If only she hadn't shot Spencer. . . . All these thoughts in a jumble of seconds between the snapping sounds from his pistol. Maybe five heartbeats.

It took five heartbeats more for him to realize that the only sound in the cavern was the discharge of his weapon, and the echoes.

Dovey Stallard was falling forward, the gun tumbling from her hand.

He lay there, motionless and staring, with his weapon pointed at the bare rock. He waited for some sound, some movement. But all was still.

Finally he struggled upright, and edged along the floor toward Dovey Stallard's body. He couldn't see plainly enough to tell where she was hit, but he touched her neck for a pulse and found none.

LeDonne holstered his weapon and sat there for what seemed like a long time, absently stroking her hair. But he didn't say he was sorry.

After what seemed like minutes in slow motion, LeDonne felt a hand on his shoulder. "Are you all right, sir?"

The kid. LeDonne had forgotten all about him. He must have come back in after he heard the shots. Now he skirted the edge of the pit, and kicked the gun away from Dovey Stallard's outstretched hand.

LeDonne stood up, taking stock of himself. "I'm okay," he muttered. "Just bruised some. We need an ambulance. I think she's dead, though."

"You got her." The young officer was kneeling beside the body, checking for vital signs. He shrugged. "Suicide by cop. I guess she wanted it this way." He sounded shaken. "You okay with this, sir?"

"Yeah." LeDonne didn't seem particularly upset by the chain of events. Philosophical, perhaps; detached—as if the past few minutes had happened on a television show he was watching. Or perhaps it hadn't sunk in yet, and his emotions would catch up with him later.

"Well," the young officer said. "At least it's over."

LeDonne was silent. *Had* she wanted it this way? Or had she intended to kill him and try to escape outside? Perhaps in her weariness she had even forgotten when she came toward him that the pistol was in her hand, and he had killed her for nothing. He would never know.

LeDonne stood up, and stumbled toward the opening of the passage. He had to get out of here now. He could feel his throat tighten, and his stomach begin to heave. It wasn't over. He knew that it would be happening again often enough. Every time he closed his eyes for a long, long time.

Clayt Stargill's arms ached, and the cold mountain air chilled his lungs, but he had made it. He could see the lights of the farmhouse in the distance. He straightened his shoulders. Kayla was still sleeping, mostly from exhaustion, he'd decided. He could feel her warm breath on his neck, and every now and again she'd give a little moan that might have meant a bad dream. "It's over now, honey," he murmured, trudging on toward the lights. "I got you home."

Kelley Johnson opened the door herself. He wondered if she had been staring out the kitchen window, waiting for some sign of her daughter's fate. Her cheeks glistened with tears, and she held out her arms without a word.

"She's heavy," whispered Clayt. "I'll take her up to bed."

"No. Not yet. Can you put her on the sofa. I—I want to look at her."

He smiled. "Sure."

She followed him, taking a lap rug from the armchair, and spreading it over the sleeping child. "Should we call a doctor?"

"Nothing wrong with her that a bath won't fix, but it can wait.

I'd let her sleep now." He looked around. The house was quieter than it had been in days. "Where is everybody?"

"Gone," she told him. "Lilah came in and made some cocoa—it's on the stove if you want some—and then she went back out in the barn with Robert Lee. Charles Martin took Debba to the bus station. She's going home, and then he was going to—oh!" Her eyes widened, and she looked up at him with fresh tears. "You don't know."

"Tell me."

"He was going to the hospital. Your father passed away."

Clayt sat down on the sofa beside the sleeping child. He took a deep breath, and straightened the comforter around Kayla's shoulders with exaggerated care. At last he said, "Well, I guess he's at peace now."

Without replying, Kelley went into the kitchen and poured him a cup of cocoa. She handed it to him, and sat in the armchair beside the sofa. "What happened out there?"

He shrugged. "It isn't over yet. Or it wasn't, when I started back. She's hiding in a cave where we used to play as kids. I found her, and she sent Kayla back with me. Maybe she can get away when it's morning."

She could tell from the way he said it that it wasn't going to happen that way. "You didn't tell them where she was?"

"No. I kept thinking I'd bring Kayla back and then go out again and try to talk her into coming out, but it wouldn't be any use. I said all there was to say, and she wouldn't listen. She never would."

Kelley nodded. "At least you tried."

"Yes. I tried for a long time."

"I know how that is," said Kelley. The silence went on for a while. "Thank you for getting my baby back, Clayt."

He smiled and touched the child's tangled hair. "She's a great kid. Smart as all get-out."

"She likes you, too."

"Yeah, she's got a real feel for the woods, you know. Like she belongs here. She's learning her bird species faster than I did. I wish—"

Kelley waited for him to finish the sentence, but he never did. Just sat there looking down at the sleeping Kayla, as if he had forgotten she was there.

Nora Bonesteel had not been five years old in more than seventy years.

Tonight she was alone in her house on the mountain. It was past midnight, and she had been awakened by the familiar sound that she had grown to dread. The knocking. She stood still in the dim light of the front hall, with her hands pressed against the lock of the front door.

The knocking began again.

"You can't come in, Fayre," she said softly. "I know you're lonesome out there, but—it won't be long now." She sighed, picturing the tiny fair-haired girl she had once befriended, and said, as she had said so often over the years, "I can't play with you anymore."

Grandma Flossie had told her that if she left Fayre alone, the dead child might find the way to wherever she was meant to go, but it had not happened. Every now and again—Nora could never find a pattern in it—the child would come back, wanting little Nora to come out and play.

"I did the best I could for you," Nora whispered. "When I knew that Randall was dying, I even took a ladder and went to the cave to get you, so that you and Randall could rest together."

The knocking came again. "Nora! Are you there? It's Jane Arrowood. Can you hear me? Are you all right?"

"Well," said Nora Bonesteel. She opened the door and saw her friend standing on the porch, shivering in her rumpled black coat. "Jane! What are you doing on the mountain at this time of an evening?"

"I didn't want to go home to an empty house," said Jane. "I've just come from the hospital. Spencer has been shot."

Nothing in Nora Bonesteel's expression indicated whether or not the news came as a surprise to her. Finally she said, "I'm so sorry, Jane. Come inside. I'll make us some tea while you tell me."

"He's going to be all right," Jane said, following her into the kitchen. "I waited at the hospital until he was out of danger. He lost his spleen, but the doctor says you can live just fine without one."

Nora nodded, filling the kettle as she listened. "He's in Johnson City then? Tell me how it happened."

Jane explained about the eviction, and the searchers who were combing the valley for Dovey Stallard. "Oh, and something else, Jane. When I was leaving the hospital, I saw Charles Martin Stargill, the singer, going in. Somebody said that his father had just died."

"I'm glad it's over for him," said Nora. "He had a good life, I think, after his sorrows early on. And Spencer is recovering well, you say?"

Jane Arrowood's voice was filled with relief for her son, her only living child. Despite her exhaustion, she talked on happily, explaining the circumstances of the shooting, and the operation that followed.

Nora Bonesteel nodded encouragingly to keep her talking, but her thoughts were elsewhere—outside, on the dark mountain, where tonight there was only silence. She wondered if a little girl had at last gone home.

CHAPTER SIXTEEN

We must submit to Providence, and provide for the Living,
and talk of our Lands.

—DANIEL BOONE

Spencer Arrowood was squinting at a copy of *Sports Illustrated*, still indecipherable at arm's length. He must remember to ask his mother to bring his reading glasses to the hospital. He was still a bit weak from surgery, but the recovery had been uneventful. After two days he was feeling well enough to be bored. He had a view of the mountains, though, from the window of his room, and he found it pleasant to stare at those green shapes in the distant haze. It would be full spring when he got out into the world again.

"Are you receiving visitors?"

Nora Bonesteel stood in the doorway of the hospital room, holding a mason jar full of yellow jonquils. In her gray dress and her handwoven crimson shawl she made him think of maples on the hill, with their slender, silvery trunks and their red-tipped branches.

The sheriff smiled and motioned for her to come in. "I'm glad to see you," he said, laying aside the magazine. "You look like springtime, and I'm weary of my own company. I haven't had this much idleness in years."

"Time isn't always a blessing, is it?" said Nora. She put the flowers on the bedside table, and sat down in the plastic chair beside the bed.

"I feel guilty lying here doing nothing, when LeDonne has to police the whole county by himself. Martha will be back next week, though, and that will help some." He was watching her as he spoke Her solemn expression told him that this was not entirely a social call. He waited a moment to see if more small talk was needed before they got to the point. When she said nothing, Spencer said, "Was there something you wanted to see me about?"

"Randall Stargill passed away," she said.

She said it as if he had been acquainted with the old man, but Spencer couldn't place him. "I'm sorry to hear it," he said. Then he remembered. "That's who you wanted the bones buried with, isn't it?"

"Yes. If you're willing to release them now, I'd be grateful."

"LeDonne came by yesterday. Told me that the medical examiner's report had come back. No discernible cause of death. And he figures the bones have been out there a long time."

She bowed her head. "That's so."

"He told me something else, too. When he went into the cave on Ashe Mountain after Dovey Stallard, he found a ladder in a pit in one of the chambers. They checked it out later when they were retrieving a flashlight, and found the remnants of a little girl's dress, so old that it tore like paper. Beside it were some scattered seeds and chicken bones. I thought there might be a connection."

"I can tell you now," said Nora. "Randall is dead. The little girl was his sister Fayre."

"Go on."

"His half-sister, really. She was born on the wrong side of the blanket, before Randall's mother married Ashe Stargill—Randall's daddy. After a couple of lean years on the farm, Ashe went off to the city to find work and left his wife and the two younguns with his mother. She was a hard woman. I remember her, though I wasn't much more than six myself. She had dark dead eyes and a mouth like a drawstring purse."

Nora Bonesteel was staring out the window at the green haze of mountains. He thought she had forgotten him entirely. She was far away from him now—more than seventy years in the past. Spencer waited for her to continue, knowing better than to remind her of his presence by prompting her.

"My mother used to talk about old Mrs. Stargill. Said she didn't like having a stray child about the place, an extra mouth to feed. And times were hard. So—" The old woman took a deep breath, and her voice quavered. "So one day she took the two children for a walk in the woods, and she came back with only one."

"Wasn't the child reported missing?"

"They searched. My daddy and my uncle Roy took the hunting dogs and combed that mountain. . . . Randall just said that he and Fayre had gone to play in the woods, and that she'd wandered away from him. I want to think he lied because he was afraid of that old woman. But I don't know. I don't *know.* He was so little. If she'd offered him a bag of candy to keep the secret . . ."

"Mrs. Stargill put the little girl in the cave?"

Nora nodded. "In the pit, where she couldn't climb out. I think she'd hurt herself falling in, but she didn't die—not right away."

"And they left food for her?" asked Spencer, remembering the seeds and chicken bones.

"No," whispered Nora. She twisted her hands in her lap. "No. The old woman just left her there. It was Randall who took her the food. He used to save some of his dinner, steal food from the kitchen, and take it to her, but he was little. He couldn't get her out. And it was cold and damp in that cave. She took sick, of course. He could hear her coughing and crying for her mother. And after three or four days he went in, and he didn't hear anything at all."

The sheriff tried to put the image out of his mind—a little girl in a dark cave, eating table scraps, and waiting on a cold, slow death. Alone in the dark. He gritted his teeth. "Did Randall tell you this?"

Nora Bonesteel turned to look at him. "I was told," she said. "But it was too late then." It was not Randall who had told her. It was

Fayre. But Spencer Arrowood wouldn't understand such things. It didn't fit into the world as he knew it. She would not tell him of meeting the little girl in the woods, of befriending her, before she understood.

"Why didn't you tell anybody?"

"I was a child," said Nora. "Not even school age. Who would have listened?"

You won't tell on Randy, will you? the blond child had asked her. Her eyes were dark and sad, and they held such a look of sorrow that Nora wanted to cry just looking at her. They'll whip him for sure if they know what he did. And she will hurt him, too. You won't tell?

I promise, Nora told her. I promise I won't tell. Cross my heart and hope to—

"It all happened before I was even born," said Spencer. "Surely when you brought the bones in, you could have explained."

"It wasn't over. Not while Randall was alive. He might have recovered, and then there would have been questions. I didn't want to put him through that. He had suffered enough for it, I reckon. But he loved her—more than anybody else ever, I think. And they need to be together again."

Spencer nodded. "All right. I'll have LeDonne take the remains to the funeral home."

"They'll be having the burial at the homeplace."

"All right. I'll tell him. Are you going to the funeral?"

"I have said my good-byes."

"But what are we going to tell the family about the bones? The truth?"

Nora shook her head. "Not all of it. They need to remember their father in a better light than this. No need to sully his memory. Say that the bones have been identified as Fayre Stargill. That she got lost in the woods, and now she needs to be buried in consecrated ground. It's true enough."

"The truth but not the whole truth," said Spencer.

The old woman sighed. "The whole truth is something very few of us want to hear."

Randall Stargill's funeral took place on a sunny morning in late March. Clarsie Stargill's flower beds were a glorious riot of color, with early tulips, crocus, and daffodils all trying to outshine each other.

Randall looked waxen and gaunt in his black Sunday suit, hands folded on his chest. He was wrapped in the grave quilt fashioned by his daughters-in-law and lying in the gleaming rosewood casket built by his sons. Tucked into a corner of the coffin, beneath the squares of the quilt, lay a smaller wooden box, containing a collection of tiny brittle bones. It would be a double funeral, really, but the Stargills had decided not to mention that fact to those assembled. Robert Lee declared that it was nobody's business.

The simple parlor had been scrubbed and polished with beeswax so that the scarred old furniture shone like the coffin itself, and an assortment of food was spread out on the dining room table.

Robert Lee Stargill stood at the door, receiving the visitors, and Lilah hovered nearby, ready to take the meatloaf or the homemade pound cake into the kitchen to join the other offerings of food brought by church members and neighbors. Garrett was there in his dress uniform; Charles Martin wore an Armani suit; and Clayt had on a navy blue blazer and gray pants, which was the extent of formality allowed by his wardrobe.

Reverend Will Bruce arrived just as Lilah sailed off into the kitchen bearing aloft a macaroni and cheese casserole.

"Good of you to come, Parson," said Robert Lee, looking mournful. "We're about ready to start the services. Charles Martin wants to sing 'Peace in the Valley' to start off, if that's all right."

"Certainly," said Will. He was unable to stop himself from glancing about to see if any country music stars had come to the funeral, but the occupants of the room were all familiar to him, mostly residents of Ashe Mountain. He wondered why Nora Bonesteel was not among them.

Before he could say anything consoling to Robert Lee, more people appeared at the door, and Will found himself handed over to a pretty redhead who introduced herself as Kelley Johnson, explaining that she was a "friend of the family." "Ex-fiancée," she said, with a little smile.

Will Bruce wondered whose ex she was, but he didn't think this was the time to ask. She seemed cheerful about it, though.

Kelley led him into the parlor to view the deceased. "He looks peaceful, doesn't he?" she said softly, looking down at the face of the man she'd never met.

"Yes. Yes, he does," said Will.

"He had a good life here on the farm," said Kelley. "He was lucky in that way. I love it up here. I don't see why any of them ever left."

"Well—jobs. Nobody can really afford to be a small-time farmer anymore."

"Clayt says he'd like to try," said Kelley.

"You're not selling the farm? I thought—"

"Well, they are and they aren't," said Kelley. She lowered her voice to a conspiratorial whisper, and steered Reverend Bruce to the relative privacy of the dining room. "Robert and Lilah needed the money for their old age, and Garrett may be getting a divorce, so he wants to sell, but Charles Martin and Clayt were all for holding onto the land, on account of it having been in the family for so long. So they just decided to split it—like Solomon did with the baby. You know."

"I do know," nodded Will Bruce. He decided not to correct her on the Bible story, but he wondered if the farm would fare as well as the baby had.

"The real estate man bought the land nearest the road for his new development, and Clayt kept the woods and steep part of the mountain. He wants to build a house there—or maybe a double-wide, at first—and run some cattle. Of course, he'll still keep his regular jobs."

Will almost smiled at hearing Clayt Stargill's various attempts at wage-earning referred to as a "regular job." It was anything but that. Instead he said, "What about Charles Martin? Surely he can't devote much time to farming with his music career going strong in Nashville?"

"No. But he doesn't need the money too awful bad, so he's going to hire somebody to look after his part for him." She glanced around, and then whispered in his ear. "It's Mr. Stallard. He lost his own place, you know."

Will nodded, thinking of the sad funeral he had performed the day before. Clayt Stargill had been present at that simple ceremony, but his tight lips and red-rimmed eyes had warned the minister not to engage him in conversation. Suddenly he realized that this young woman must be the mother of the child who had been kidnapped. Later, perhaps, he would ask her how the little girl was doing.

"Charlie can't wait to get back to Nashville, but I just don't want to go. I'm tired of it. . . . I wish . . ."

"Kelley! That girl of yours is in the kitchen, eating chocolate cake with both hands, and Clayt Stargill is egging her on. You'd better see to her—hello, Reverend Bruce, just the man I wanted to see." Lilah Stargill, formidable in a shiny black dress with shoulder pads and an empire waist, thrust a piece of paper at him. "What do you make of this?"

Will Bruce read the list of Bible verses, wondering exactly what the question was. "A selection of readings for bereavement?" he said. The collection of verses, mostly Old Testament, was unfamiliar to him. He wondered if she would be disillusioned if he admitted that he would have to look them up. "Where did you get them?" he asked.

Lilah smiled. "I wondered if you'd recognize them. Before your time, I expect. Nora Bonesteel brought them yesterday. She came to the door, handed Robert Lee a cake and this list, and went away."

Will Bruce looked at the paper again. It was the spidery handwriting of an elderly woman, but the notations were plain enough:

1st Kings 4:22. Four and a half C.
Judges 5:25. One C.
Jeremiah 6:20. Two C.
1st Samuel 30:12. Two C.
Nahum 3:12. Two C.
Numbers 17:08. Two C.
1st Samuel 14:25. Two TBSP
Leviticus 2:13. One-fourth TSP
Judges 4:19. One-half C.
Amos 4:5. Two TBSP
Jeremiah 17:11. Six, medium

Tsp? Tbsp?

He had it.

"I haven't seen this recipe in years," he said, smiling, and handing it back to Lilah. "My mother used to make it for church social. She called it a scripture cake. You have to look up each verse to find out which ingredients to use. I should get a copy of this recipe for Laura. Have you tried it yet?"

"Not to bake," said Lilah. "I tasted a smidgeon of the one Miz Bonesteel brought. Nice of her to remember that we asked about it. It's a kind of fruitcake, seems like. Dates, figs, almonds."

Will Bruce smiled. "I don't think you'll find chocolate mentioned in the Bible."

"Rudy says it ought to be."

Before Will could ask who Rudy was, someone touched him on the shoulder. "We're ready to begin, Reverend."

He nodded. "I'm coming right now." He set his face into an expression of solemnity, and went back into the parlor. It was time to pay the final respects to the dead, so that they all could get on with the business of living.

"Hello. My name is Daniel Boone."

It was early summer now. From the stage in the auditorium, Clayt Stargill faced an audience of adults, who had come to the Storytelling Festival in Jonesborough in search of quaintness, or perhaps looking for their Appalachian origins in the faces of the mountain people or in the patterns of the old stories. And now they were seeing Daniel Boone, or a reasonable facsimile thereof, in leather breeches and a fringed deerskin shirt. They wondered why he wasn't wearing his coonskin cap. Some of them wondered why he had been at the Alamo, because an actor named Fess Parker had played both Daniel Boone and Davy Crockett on television, thus confusing an entire generation of Americans about the two Appalachian pioneers.

In the front row, Kayla Johnson sat with her arms wrapped around her knees, watching Clayt with shining eyes. "He's gonna be my daddy," she whispered to the tourist beside her, a blond young man wearing a white linen jacket over a black T-shirt. The man looked startled to be receiving confidences from a strange child, but Kayla smiled up at him, placed her finger on her lips, and turned back to hear the storytelling.

"Daniel Boone . . . You may have heard of me. I passed through here many a time on my way to and from Kentucky. The Boone trail goes right through here, you know, and Jonesborough was a place of consequence in those days, and the scenery has an even more pleasing and rapturous appearance than the plains of Kentucky. But there were already too many people here. Why, from the front door of your cabin, you could oftentimes see your neighbor's chimney smoke, so I lit out for wilder country.

"We bought the land in Kentucky from the Cherokee at Sycamore Shoals in 1778, and there's some that have said it wasn't theirs to sell. That the deal was tainted by chicanery, and that there was a curse on those who took it from the Indians. I can almost believe that, my friends. The fact is that most of us settlers lost the land just as surely as the Shawnees did. And we ended up moving west right along with them.

"Didn't you think that in the old days, when this was a young, mostly empty country, that you could just claim a piece of land by homesteading it? Get in a covered wagon, go someplace where nobody had lived before, build you a cabin, plant your crops and the land was yours. Didn't you think that? It sure looks that way in the movies, doesn't it?"

Some of the audience nodded, and no one seemed put off by the fact that "Daniel Boone" was talking about movies. Clayt said, "We'd like to think that the world was once that uncomplicated, but the fact is it plain flat never was. Daniel Boone is living proof of that.

"I led the first settlers through the Cumberland Gap and into Kentucky. I surveyed the land, built a fort at Boonesborough, and claimed three hundred thousand acres of Kentucky for myself. Excepting the Shawnee, who had more right to it?"

He sighed. "Claimed three hundred thousand acres. Ended up with less than three hundred acres. And lost that.

"How did that come about, you ask me?" He grinned and shook his head. "I'd give worlds to know, neighbors. What I learned after the fact was: the way to get hold of land in a new territory is *not* to go there in a wagon and tame the wilderness. No. A lot of the people who ended up owning Kentucky in the 1700s were fellows who never left Richmond, Virginia. Kentucky was part of Virginia in those days, you see. So these speculators made friends with someone in the state legislature, and in return they were given land grants of thousands of acres in the new territory.

"Imagine that. You go to the wilderness, fight Indians, go hungry, freeze in the winter, and work yourself to death carving a farm out of an endless forest—and then you discover you have a landlord. And you owe him rent on your land. And that's not the worst of it. The fact is, the Virginia legislature handed out a whole raft of land grants to all their city friends, and the amount given amounted to more land than there was in all of Kentucky.

"Now when people have more land grants than there is land, you know you are in for trouble, and the one fellow certain to lose out is the honest man without any political strings to pull. That pretty much sums me up. The surveyors didn't help any, either. Most of them weren't very good at measuring land, and they added to the confusion. I ought to know: I was one of them. Never did have much of a head for figures.

"So the land was claimed half a dozen times over, and then the lawyers got into it, and that's when it's time to quit.

"The only help for it is to keep moving west, and try to outrun civilization, before the bureaucrats and the tax collectors can run over you.

"That's how come I ended up in Missouri in 1800 without an acre of land to my name. I was sixty-six years old. World famous, on account of a fellow called Filson writing a book about me, but I was broke and rootless.

"Well, I guess they felt sorry for me, friends. First the Spanish government gave me some land, and when they reneged I went to the United States Congress, and I asked them to give a little land to the fellow that had opened the wilderness. I was careful not to call those politicians crooks, mind you. I just said it was a shame for an old man, a hero of the Revolution, to be so bereft in his final years.

"And they gave me some land down there in the county of Femme Osage, Missouri. Even made me a magistrate of sorts. So I settled there, hunting and fishing, and enjoying the land. Sometimes, a few Shawnee would ride in, old adversaries of mine from the settling days in Kentucky. We were all old men now, and we had more in common with each other than we did with the young people of our respective tribes. We'd hunt together and talk about the old days. About Kentucky. The land that we both lost.

"Land. I used to say I explored from the love of Nature. *'I've opened the way for others to make fortunes, but a fortune for myself was not what I was after.'* When you're old you have to stop grieving over what might have been, I guess. But I would have liked to have been a fine Kentucky gentleman, with blood horses, and a big house for Rebecca, and fields as far as the eye can see.

"There's something about the human spirit that makes us love the land, and makes us want to own it, as if being master of all we survey will give us life everlasting, or perfect happiness. We know it isn't so, but we can't help ourselves. The Bible says the Lord made Adam from a lump of earth, and we've been trying to make the land turn us into Somebodies ever since.

"Land. The only thing worth dying for.

"I finally got me some land in Kentucky, you know. In the year 1845. Oh, yes, I was dead by then. Gone some twenty-five years, when the state of Kentucky declared me a hero and dug up my remains and shipped me back to Kentucky to be buried on a hill in the state capital. Got my land at last. Free and clear forever.

"Six feet of land. All a man needs."

ACKNOWLEDGMENTS

My thanks to all the generous and knowledgeable people who assisted me with technical information in the preparation of this book. I am especially grateful to Appalachian poet and naturalist Clyde Kessler, who advised me on ornithology and took me on field trips so that Clayt Stargill could speak about the wilderness with an informed voice. I am also grateful to Warren May, dulcimer maker from Berea, Kentucky, for his advice on woodworking with rosewood; to Marge Quinlan Hundley for the scripture cake; to Garry Barker and the Berea College Crafts program for their advice on building a coffin; to author and Knox County, Tennessee, sheriff's deputy emeritus David Hunter and to Police Sergeant J. A. Niehaus for their advice in police procedure; and to the following people for help with detail and for their enthusiasm for this project: Bill and Susan Wittig Albert; Major Sue Tiller, USA; Kathryn Kennison; Jeffrey Marks; T. Campbell Welsh; Dr. Clarence Taylor; Brad Stansberry; Martha G. Whaley; Charlotte Ross; Jack Pyle; Taylor Reese; and Skeeter Davis.

The following works were most helpful to me in preparing this novel. If you read only one of these books, let it be *Mountains of the Heart*, a truly lyrical guide to the natural history of Appalachia.

Mountains of the Heart by Scott Weidensaul, Fulcrum Publishing, Golden, CO, 1994.

Daniel Boone by John Mack Faragher, Henry Holt and Company, 1992.

Tales from the Cherokee Hills by Jean Starr, John F. Blair Publisher, Winston-Salem, NC, 1988.

Old Frontiers by John P. Brown, Southern Publishers, Kingsport, TN, 1938.

History of the Lost State of Franklin by Samuel Cole Williams, Overmountain Press, Johnson City, TN, 1933, rpt. 1993.

Nancy Ward: Cherokee Chieftainess by Pat Alderman, Overmountain Press, Johnson City, TN, 1978, rpt. 1990.

Where Legends Live: A Pictorial Guide to Cherokee Mythic Places by Douglas A. Rossman, Cherokee Publications, Cherokee, NC, 1988.

Belled Buzzards, Hucksters and Grieving Specters/Appalachian Tales: Strange, True and Legendary by Gary Carden and Nina Anderson, Down Home Press, Asheboro, NC, 1994.

Seasonal Guide to the Natural Year: Mid-Atlantic by Scott Weidensaul, Fulcrum Publishing, Golden, CO, 1992.

Death and Dying in Central Appalachia by James K. Crissman, University of Illinois Press, 1994.

Dancing at Big Vein by Clyde Kessler, Pocahontas Press, Blacksburg, VA, 1987.

The Moon Is Always Full by David Hunter, Pocket Books, 1991.

THEMES AND DISCUSSION QUESTIONS FOR *THE ROSEWOOD CASKET*

In *The Rosewood Casket,* I wanted to talk about the passing of the land from one group to another, as a preface to the modern story of farm families losing their land to the developers in today's Appalachia. The voice of Daniel Boone is central to the novel's message, a reminder that the land inherited by the farm families was once taken from the Cherokee and the Shawnee. The novel begins with Cherokee wisewoman Nancy Ward, in the last spring of her life, as she realizes that her people are about to lose the land that she tried so hard to preserve for them. As a reminder of that transience of ownership, in a passage in chapter one of *The Rosewood Casket,* I trace the passing of the land even further back, to a time at the end of the last Ice Age, twelve thousand years ago.

Appalachia was a very different place at the end of the Ice Age, when the first humans are believed to have arrived in the mountains. The climate of that far-off time was that of central Canada today, too cold to support the oaks and hickories of our modern forests. Appalachia then was a frozen land of spruce and fir tree, but it was home to a wonderful collection of creatures: mastodons, saber-tooth tigers, camels, horses, sloths the size of pickup trucks, and birds of prey with wingspans of twenty-five feet. The kingdom of ice that was Appalachia in 10,000 B.C. was their world, and they lost it to the first human settlers of the region, who hunted the beasts to extinction in only a few hundred years. Losing the land is an eternal process, I wanted to say. It seemed fitting to start with these early residents, as a reminder that even the Indians were once interlopers.

Although the title came from a nineteenth-century Tin Pan Alley tune ("The Rosewood Casket"), for me the theme song of the book is "Will the Circle Be Unbroken?"

The supernatural aspect of the book is actually magic realism—the blurring of the line between the real and the supernatural with the equal acceptance of both. I put this in the book because I find it in the culture itself as an echo of the traditions brought to the region by the settlers from Celtic Britain. You will find the same patterns of second sight and revenants on both sides of the Atlantic.

The family relationships in the book are a microcosm of the dilemma faced by families whose children must leave home to have careers.

QUESTIONS

1. You will be better prepared for this discussion if you do a little googling first. Find out about the Cherokee *Ghigau* Nancy Ward, the biography of Daniel Boone, the literary convention of magic realism, and the introduction of the starling songbird into this country. Also, read my essay on the land connections between Appalachia and Celtic Britain.

2. This book contains many examples of people and things losing their land. I can think of five off the top of my head. How many can you find?

3. Nora Bonesteel's gift of the Sight is not uncommon among people of Scots-Irish descent. What examples of it have you seen in people you know?

4. What effect does luxury land development have on the original residents of an area? If this were happening in your community, how would you deal with it?

5. Robert Lee Stargill's wife believes that she has a guardian angel named Rudy. Rudy actually (physically) appears to another character during the course of the novel. When and where does he show up, and how is this an example of magic realism rather than fantasy?

6. Try making Nora Bonesteel's scripture cake.

7. Describe the landscape of east Tennessee in 10,500 B.C. (the end of the last Ice Age). Climate, air quality, inhabitants? What plants and animals would you see?

8. *I believe the future is simply the past, entered through another gate.* How do modern characters in the book echo historical figures (e.g., Dovey Stallard and Nancy Ward, Clayt Stargill and Daniel Boone)?

9. One of the problems of Appalachian stereotyping is that people assume that Appalachia is synonymous with poor people. But the differences between people are more a question of economics and social class rather than regional affiliation. It is important to stress this. Cities are judged by their richest inhabitants, and rural areas are judged by their poorest. How does your own region or ethnic group suffer from stereotyping?

10. How are the conflicts between the songbirds—the starlings and the Bewick's wrens—a metaphor for the plight of the people in the novel?